"The interrelationships between the people in the town are almost as intriguing as the mystery itself and the author lets readers piece together images of Dawson's Clough in bits and snatches. The setting gave the story a brooding mood which matched Dylan Scott's character well indeed."
—*All About Books* on *Presumed Dead*

"*Dead Silent* is an engrossing and spellbinding mystery that is full of surprises. With a wide variety of startling twist and turns, Shirley Wells brings *Dead Silent* to a stunning and unanticipated conclusion that is guaranteed to shock her readers."
—*The Readers Roundtable* on *Dead Silent*

"Each book in Ms. Wells's highly addictive series brings an exciting new tale that is uniquely its own story while carrying on the same characters from book to book. The emotional/human component of the story is well-written and enriches the book immensely. I'll be stalking the author until I have the next story in my hands!"
—*Twimom* on *Deadly Shadows*, 4 stars

Deadly Shadows

SHIRLEY WELLS

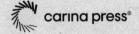

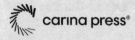
carina press®

ISBN-13: 978-0-373-00267-2

Deadly Shadows

Copyright © 2013 by Shirley Wells

Recycling programs
for this product may
not exist in your area.

www.CarinaPress.com

Printed in U.S.A.

Dear Reader,

I have very fond memories of watching TV mystery shows with my late mother. Here in the UK, we had *Z-Cars* and *Softly, Softly*, and then the American shows arrived, including *Kojak*, *McCloud* and my all-time favorite, *Columbo*. (Yes, I'm showing my age.) My mother and I were addicted, and we eagerly tried to outwit the sleuths and uncover the truth before they did. If the puzzle was too easily solved, we were bitterly disappointed.

We loved stories where nothing was ever as it seemed, and one of the reasons I enjoyed writing *Deadly Shadows* so much is because nothing or no one is quite what they appear to be. I also enjoyed sending Dylan undercover in this story, especially to a place where he was in constant danger of being recognized.

The story is set, as many of my Dylan Scott books are, in Lancashire, and I hope you enjoy visiting this corner of the UK, where I live with my husband and our dogs. I especially hope you enjoy reading *Deadly Shadows* as much as I enjoyed writing it.

I love hearing from readers, so if you want to let me know, or want to talk about anything else, you can contact me through my website, www.shirleywells.com.

Happy sleuthing!

Shirley Wells

Dedication

For my big sister, Linda

Acknowledgments

As always, I'm indebted to my amazing editor, Deb Nemeth, who made this story so much stronger with her insight, expertise and sound advice. Thank you, Deb. And thank you for being such a joy to work with.

I'm also truly grateful to everyone else at Carina Press for their hard work, dedication and professionalism. And to Nick, who keeps the faith. Thank you.

Chapter One

"WHAT THE—? WHAT are you doing?"

"What do you think?" He smacked the heavy chunk of wood across his hand. "No one, especially a little shit like you, goes asking questions about me. You shouldn't have poked your nose into matters that don't concern you. Your brothers told you, I told you, but no, you wouldn't listen, would you?"

"And what are you going to do about it? Kill me too?"

His answer was to bring the wood down hard. Blood fountained into the cold night air. Bone cracked against the stone wall.

Droplets of warm, sticky blood landed on his face, but that was okay. He'd soon wash it off.

He clenched the wood tighter in his hand and brought it down again. There was more blood and another satisfying crack as the skull splintered. Blood oozed from a motionless mouth. He was probably dead, but there was no point taking chances.

He used the wood and his boots to great advantage for a full five minutes. When he finally stopped, he was pleased to note that he hadn't even broken into a sweat.

He stood for a moment, drawing in deep calming breaths. Then, after one final kick at the lifeless body, he took a couple of handkerchiefs from his pocket and wiped his boots clean. Confident he wouldn't leave bloody footprints, he turned and walked briskly down the dark alley until he emerged onto Cromwell Street. It was dimly lit, which suited him perfectly.

He walked on to the railway bridge that spanned the narrow river. Underneath that bridge, he paused long enough to take off his gloves and his long black overcoat and wrap them around the murder weapon. With his bundle under his arm, he walked on until he came to the gated entrance of Meredith's Joinery Business. In the yard, a couple of skips overflowed with scrap wood waiting to be hauled away.

He squeezed through the gap between gate and hedge, and tossed his unwanted clothes and his trusty weapon into the nearest skip. The photos went in too. There was plenty of litter blowing in the wind and he grabbed a handful of flyers, mostly for local fast-food outlets, and threw those in the skip. He took his Zippo lighter from his pocket, lit the paper and moved back to the shadows of the building.

The smile of a job well done curved his lips as he watched the wood catch.

He let himself out of the yard by the same way he'd entered and walked casually along the street, turning only once to see flames reaching up to the sky.

Meredith's wouldn't be too worried. They'd put it down to an act of vandalism by bored kids and would be secretly pleased they didn't have to pay to have the wood taken away. The police were so used to such incidents that they wouldn't even bother to investigate.

The evening's work was done.

He walked on to the brightly lit town centre. Youngsters with hoods pulled over their heads to ward off the cold January frost ambled around, looking for mischief. Half a dozen young men came out of a pub and

stopped to light up cigarettes. Two girls emerged giggling from the Chinese takeaway. One clutched a white
bag heavy with food and the other girl was in charge of
a bottle of wine.

It was a normal Thursday night in the northern town
of Dawson's Clough.

Chapter Two

Joe thought there was something familiar about the man sitting on the barstool next to him. Something unusual too. Instead of eyeing up the tempting array of flesh on display, this man chose to stare morosely at the drinks.

Saluka, a tall Moroccan girl, walked onto the stage and was soon wooing the men in the crowded room. All she wore was a white G-string that existed merely to hold crisp notes close to her body. Dark skin gleamed beneath the pulsating lights as she gyrated to the thumping music. Her eyes, as black as the devil's soul, missed nothing.

Tempo was proud of its reputation for being the loudest nightclub in the northwest of England. It wasn't the noise that had brought in the customers though. It was a combination of the floor show and the promise of cheap drinks until ten o'clock.

Joe knew better than to mess with the dancers and he could take or leave the cheap drinks, but he presumed the latter had brought this man to the club. As he was balanced on a barstool it was difficult to tell, but Joe would put him at five-ten or maybe six feet tall. He looked to be in fairly good shape too. He was about forty, his blond hair was in need of a cut, and a few weeks' worth of untrimmed beard hugged his face. He wore round glasses that looked a little ridiculous. But perhaps he'd been a fan of John Lennon. His leather jacket had been quality but was battered through years of wear. An equally well-worn pair of denims plus grubby running shoes completed the outfit.

"Whisky, please." The man banged down his glass on the bar. "You'd better make it a double."

The barman considered this. "One more," he said, "and then you're on your way, mate. Okay? You've had more than enough already."

"Sure."

Joe watched him pay for his drink, paying particular attention to where he put his wallet. The idiot put it in the back pocket of his jeans, the easiest place in the world to lose it.

Joe had picked pockets since he was ten years old, and almost forty years later he was still an expert. He soon had the leather wallet, worn thin from years of use, in his hand. Its owner was too busy staring into the bottom of his glass to notice.

He held it out of sight, behind the man's back, to open it. Inside he found a train ticket stub, a betting slip, a driver's license and a tatty five-pound note. Regardless of the barman's views, this man was too short of cash to get any more drunk than he already was.

Joe checked out the driver's license. *Well, well, well.*

He closed the wallet and tapped its owner on the shoulder. "You dropped this." He had to shout to make himself heard above the booming dance music. "Hey, I'm sure I know you."

"I shouldn't think so. I'm not from these parts." The man took his wallet from him and shoved it in the same pocket, ready for a less honest pickpocket to come along. "Thanks."

"Me neither," Joe said, "but I never forget a face.

Here, let me get you another drink. The prices will double in a couple of minutes."

"I can't afford to be proud so I'll take a drink from anyone, but you're confusing me with someone else. I guarantee we've never met."

Joe won the barman's attention. "One more for us both. They're on me. Oh, and don't worry about my friend here. He won't cause trouble. I'll make sure of that."

"This is definitely his last," the barman warned, but he filled two clean glasses with whisky and put them on the bar. Profit came a long way above the law in this place.

"Well, I never." Joe tapped his new friend on the shoulder. "I've got you now. I told you I never forget a face."

"Yeah, yeah." He lifted his glass. "Cheers."

"You're welcome, my friend. So what brings you north, Dave?"

"Eh? How do you know my name?" He leaned so far back on his barstool, he was in danger of falling off.

"Down in the Smoke. We're going back about five years. No, it's closer to eight. It's Joe. Joe Child. You must remember me. We met when we were both working for McCoy. You can't have forgotten."

Dave Young narrowed bloodshot eyes to peer more closely at him. "I remember McCoy."

"Then you must remember me." Joe laughed. "How many whiskies have you had?"

"Joe. Joe Child. I vaguely remember—oh, yeah. Bloody hell. It's Joey. Right?"

"That's it." Joe slapped him on the back. "We had some times, didn't we?"

"I remember. You fleeced me for a load of cash at

poker. Christ, that's going back a bit. You were McCoy's right-hand man."

Child shrugged. "We got along okay."

"I was only doing some driving for him."

"Yeah," Joe said. "I remember."

"McCoy's dead, you know. A couple of months ago. Well, you'll know that. Can't say I'm too upset about it. It's thanks to that bastard I got sent down."

"Oh? I didn't hear about that." Joe had made a run for it before the shit hit the fan. He'd been too busy waiting for someone to grass him up to worry about Young.

"Remember the night he got busted?" Young said. "I was doing a delivery for him. One fucking delivery and I ended up doing eight months." He took a big swallow of his drink. "You were on holiday in Ireland, I remember. Convenient, that. Still, it's forgotten. We're best out of it. The money was good, but I can do without getting banged up again." He swayed on his barstool and leaned in close. "So what brings you up here, Joey?"

"Me and the wife felt like—you remember Doll, don't you?"

"Doll? 'Course I do. You're still together then?"

"Till death do us part, Davey boy. Well, we felt like getting away from London. I've changed, you see. I've put those dark days behind me. Look—" He took a card from his shirt pocket and handed it over. "You can find me here now. There will always be a welcome for you."

Young squinted at the card. "A home for the soul? What the fuck's that about?"

"I've seen the light." Smiling, Joe tapped the side of his nose.

"Eh?"

"God's shown me the way. He's taken care of me over

the years so now I'm giving back. I'm trying to show others the light."

"You're a fucking Bible basher?"

Joe shook that off with a smile. He'd been called worse, much worse. "I'm teaching God's Word to those who need to hear it."

"Fuck me."

"Perhaps you need to hear it. What did you say you were doing up here?"

"I'm doing nothing. Sweet fuck all. The girlfriend buggered off and—" His voice was becoming increasingly slurred. Once again, he leaned in close to Joe's ear. "Me and a mate did a job, only a small one, but the heat was on so I legged it. I took a train north, but I fell asleep on the fucking thing and instead of getting off in Manchester, I ended up in this shit hole. What's the name of it again? Dawson's Clough? What a bloody place. I only got here this morning but I'll be gone tomorrow."

"Gone where?"

"Fuck knows. Anywhere. Manchester, if I can hitch a lift."

"This place isn't so bad." Joe tapped the card. "Call in at the refuge before you leave. It's a couple of miles out of town. You can't miss it. Come and say hello to Doll. She'd like to see you again. And if you need somewhere to sleep, we can fix you up. Work, too."

"What sort of work?" For a moment, Young looked interested.

"The honest sort. A bit of building work at the refuge. Or serving hot food to the homeless in town. We all pitch in and do what needs to be done."

"Thanks, but that doesn't sound like my sort of thing, if you get my drift. I like to keep myself to myself."

"You can do that," Joe said. "There's plenty of time for privacy, reflection and talking with God."

"What the hell would I have to say to God? I can't see him listening to me, can you?" He laughed at the idea.

"Why not? He's listened to me, Davey. I did some bad things—"

"So? Christ, we've all done bad things. You served your time, didn't you?"

"Oh, I've been banged up a few times, but some things—well, let's just say I've done things I didn't get locked up for, things I'm not proud of. I've seen the light, and now I'm helping others find the right path."

"You won't catch me talking to—" Young broke off when he saw that two uniformed coppers had entered the building. "I thought I could smell fucking bacon, Joey. Can you? What are those pigs doing here?"

Joe put a restraining hand on his arm. "Leave it. We don't want any trouble, do we?"

"Hey, you!"

"Leave it," Joe said again. "They're not here to bother anyone."

"What? That's all they fucking do. Eight months I did, thanks to those fuckers. Oi, over here!"

"You did eight months for moving Class A drugs around." Joe knew he was wasting his breath because Young was too drunk to care, but he had to try. "You earned a lot of cash while you were doing it too. Come on, forget it. You don't want to spend the night in a cell, do you?"

His words were pointless. The police officers were heading straight for them.

"David Young?" the taller officer asked, and Joe groaned.

"Who wants to know?" Young asked, flexing his muscles.

"Are you David Young?"

"I might be David Young and I might be the king of Siam. What's it to you?"

"David Young, I'm arresting you—"

"Oh, no you're not, sunshine. I've done nothing wrong. You can fuck right off."

"There's been no trouble, officer," Joe said. "He's with me. I'll see he gets home quietly."

"Fuck 'em, Joey." Young grabbed an empty bottle from the bar and smashed the neck against the metal stool. He brandished the lethal weapon in the copper's face. "Come any closer and you'll get this, you bastard. Come on, then. What are you waiting for? Come and get me."

Joe tugged on his sleeve and tried to grab the bottle from him. "Put it down, Davey. See sense, man. You're drunk."

"Fuck 'em." Davey continued to wave the jagged glass at the coppers, daring them to get close enough to cuff him.

It took both coppers, Joe and a furious barman a good five minutes to disarm and cuff him. Young staggered against Joe. "I know what this is about, but if I hadn't fallen asleep on that fucking train, I wouldn't have got in an argument with the inspector, would I? I tried to explain, but he wouldn't listen. Of course I didn't have a ticket further than Manchester because I hadn't wanted to go past fucking Manchester, had I? He was—" The coppers dragged him away. "See you, Joey."

"You know where I am," Joe called back.

Young wasn't listening. The idiot was too busy hurling abuse and kicking out at the coppers.

Men like Young never learned. They did small jobs here and there, spent half their lives in jail, and continued to dream of the big job that would set them up for life. They weren't bright enough to realise that the only way to beat the law was to outwit it. That was what Joe did. He always stayed one step ahead of the law.

He drained his glass, said good-night to the barman and headed down to the viaduct. There she was—pulling on a cigarette, shivering inside a tight black leather jacket, legs clad in knee-length white boots. Long, curly black hair was flicked into her face by the stiff breeze.

When she spotted him, she tossed her cigarette into the gutter.

Joe didn't speak. There was no point because her English was worse than useless. He neither knew nor cared where she came from. The Ukraine, possibly, but he wasn't sure. He didn't know how old she was either. Fifteen or sixteen probably. That didn't matter either.

He grabbed her wrist and pulled her behind some corrugated tin sheeting erected to keep squatters out of the old mill. He pushed her up against the tin, pulled up her skirt, pressed himself hard against her as he fumbled with his zipper and then rammed himself inside her.

Less than five minutes later, he adjusted his clothing, pushed a ten-pound note at her and strolled toward the taxi rank.

Chapter Three

"DAVID YOUNG?"

"At last." He pushed himself away from the wall, eager to escape. He'd had enough of police cells to last him a lifetime. He'd had enough of this sodding beard too. People seeing him scratch probably thought he had fleas. Perhaps he had. For all he knew, all sorts of exotic creatures could be breeding in it.

A copper frog-marched him away from the cells, up to the second floor and along the corridor to interview room 3, where a couple of detectives waited. They'd been deep in conversation until he arrived.

"Thank you, thank you." The older detective shooed the young officer away and, when the door had closed, he put out his hand. "Good to meet you at last, Dylan. Keith Rhodes. And this is Craig Miller. Miller, meet Dylan Scott, aka David Young. Ex-copper—but we won't go into that."

He spoke with a smile, as if Dylan's expulsion from the police force was something of a joke. It bloody well wasn't. Dylan doubted he'd ever stop feeling bitter about it. He'd arrested a well-known piece of scum, a habitual criminal, and had ended up in hospital for his trouble. Said piece of scum had then claimed that he, Dylan, had used unreasonable force. It would have been laughable if the good old British police force hadn't been brushing up on politics at the time and deemed it necessary to show Joe Public that complaints about its officers were taken very seriously indeed. Instead of getting a bloody medal, Dylan had ended up in a cell before being kicked off the force.

Still. No use dwelling on it. Water under the bridge and all that.

"Sorry it's taken a while to get you here," Rhodes said, "but it took longer than anticipated to reactivate your identity."

"That's okay. It gave me time to grow this." Dylan fingered his beard.

A smirk almost crossed Miller's face, but he soon had it under control and continued to scowl his disapproval. Detective Sergeant Miller was late thirties maybe. Shaven-headed. Bull-headed.

His boss, Detective Inspector Rhodes, was taller, slimmer and far more conservative in appearance. His suit was well cut, his silk tie was a muted blue and his shoes looked handmade. Clothes like his didn't come cheap and a copper's salary rarely ran to such style. Dylan wished it wasn't so, but he couldn't help weighing up every copper he met and wondering if he was on the take.

"There was an incident earlier too. An as-yet-unidentified body was found in an alley. It was a particularly vicious killing." Rhodes sighed at the inconvenience the murdered man had caused. "It never rains, eh?"

It was the first time Dylan had been in an interview room since his dismissal from the force, but it seemed that nothing had changed. This one was cold and windowless. A wide table and three chairs sat in the centre. In one corner was a small table with a laptop perched on top. Décor was a kicked-and-scuffed white.

"Please, sit down," Rhodes said.

Dylan sat opposite the two detectives.

"So how did it go, Dylan?" Rhodes asked.

"It was surprisingly easy." He forgot the room, and how the building gave him the creeps, and dragged his mind to the more important matter of Joe Child. He'd been taken aback at how quickly Child had remembered him. True, Child had needed to pick his pocket to confirm his suspicions, but he'd been more than eager to take up their old "friendship." "Your bods pitched up earlier than I expected, but yeah, it was fine."

"Was there a need to brandish a broken bottle in their faces?" Miller asked.

"I thought so, yes," Dylan said. "As I'm planning to tell Child that I've been forced to stay in the area until my court case comes up, I wanted it to be convincing."

He'd enjoyed hurling abuse at those coppers though, even if it had been only playacting. The fact that they hadn't known it was all for show had merely added to the fun.

Dylan wasn't stupid. He knew his perceived crime hadn't been forgiven or forgotten. No way would his being brought in have been sanctioned if the force hadn't been desperate. Communities panicked when young girls vanished. People started complaining about police forces being quick enough to dish out speeding tickets but being unable to catch real criminals. Faith in the country's forces dipped. Worse, the public started taking the law into their own hands. Dylan knew CID would much prefer to have one of their own going undercover, but time was against them. He'd worked undercover and been close to Child before, so he could walk straight into the bloke's life and save them months of hard work.

"A coffee would be good," he said. "And a bacon butty, if there's one going."

Miller's lips thinned to a straight line. His eyebrows beetled together. Oh, yes, Dylan would enjoy winding him up.

He was hungry though. And tired. He hadn't been able to sleep in the cell and had spent most of the night pacing and reminding himself that he only had to endure it for a few hours.

"Of course, Dylan. Sorry," Rhodes said. "We'll get something organised." He nodded at his sidekick. "Get me a coffee while you're at it, will you? And a Mars bar."

Miller didn't bother to reply. He didn't bother to close the door quietly behind him either.

"Do you want to fill me in?" Dylan asked. "Or shall we wait for Detective Sergeant Miller to come back?"

He found it impossible to say the words *Detective Sergeant* without a sneer curling his lip. He'd once been proud to call himself that, but now, if they offered him a million pounds, he'd tell them where they could stick it. Well, perhaps for a million he'd have a rethink. He was broke. He was always broke. A mortgage, a wife and two kids was the fast road to bankruptcy. He hadn't had a well-paying job for months either. He certainly hadn't had an interesting one. People didn't realise that private investigators spent the majority of their time staring at computer screens.

"I can give you a brief recap." Rhodes opened a thick folder but didn't consult it. He knew its contents by heart. "A year ago, Caroline Aldridge left home and went to live at Child's—" he broke off as if uncertain what to call Child's premises, "—commune," he settled on, his nose wrinkling with distaste. "Three months later, she vanished. The last confirmed sighting of her was at the bus station in town. Ten minutes before that, she'd called her parents. Her stepfather insists she was simply calling to tell them not to worry and that she was safe. Who knows? He was brought in for questioning, and for a while we were convinced he was involved in her disappearance." Rhodes nodded at the laptop in the corner of the room. "We'll show you the interviews we had with him."

"That was when?"

Rhodes consulted the folder. "April the fourteenth last year. Then, a couple of months ago—" He checked the contents of his folder again. "November the twentieth, to be precise, another girl, Farrah Brindle, went missing. She'd been living at home with her parents for the last month, but before that, she too had spent a few weeks at Child's commune. She left her parents' home on the night in question and a taxi driver dropped her off at a local service station. We have her on CCTV and she looked as if she was waiting for someone. We didn't see her meet anyone and we've checked every frame of the CCTV, so we can only assume she was picked up in a car away from the cameras. Probably close to the roundabout."

"So she wasn't living at Child's when she disappeared? Hadn't been there for a month?"

"That's right. As I say though, Child's place is our only link between the two girls."

Miller returned with a tray that bore a bacon roll on a plate, three coffees in polystyrene cups and a Mars bar. *Ask and thou shalt receive.*

"Thanks." Dylan grabbed the roll and bit into it. It didn't taste as good as it looked, but it was okay.

Rhodes blew on his coffee. "I was just telling Dylan that the only link we can find between Caroline Aldridge and Farrah Brindle is that place of Child's."

Miller nodded. "We believe it's a front for some scam or other."

"No doubt. Joe Child finding God is on a par with Mother Teresa snorting crack cocaine while pole dancing with polar bears." Dylan washed down his mouthful of bacon with hot coffee. "Any ideas what he might be up to?"

"Not really, no," Miller said. "That's why you've been dragged in."

He made it clear that if it had been up to him, there was no way a disgraced copper would be allowed within half a mile of the building.

"We thought drugs when he first set up that commune," Rhodes said, "but with the girls going missing, we're wondering if he's branched out and is embracing the sex trade. We've got nothing on him. Not a thing."

"How old are the girls?" Dylan asked. "Both seventeen?"

"Yes." Rhodes flicked through his papers and pulled out two ten-by-eight photos that he placed on the table in front of Dylan.

Both girls were slim with blond hair. Both were smiling for the camera.

"Caroline—" Rhodes tapped the photo on the left, "—left home after a row with her parents. She's always been a bit of a rebel, apparently, so a place like Child's would have appealed to her. I can't say I blame her for leaving home. Her mother's a fat, idle waste of space and her stepfather's a violent drunk. Caroline has three older brothers and they're all regulars at the courts for minor offences."

He nodded at the other photo. "Farrah, by all accounts, was a bright, happy young girl looking forward to university when she suddenly changed. She comes from a good family. Her father's a teacher and her mother's a doctor. One brother and one sister, both older, both doing well. Her parents say Farrah became moody, argumentative and lost all interest in school and a future at university. They believe something happened or she met someone before she ended up at Child's. She lived at Child's place for a month or so, and when she returned home, she was—" he shuffled through papers to quote, "—'a little better. Quiet and secretive, but not unhappy.'"

"So they're both local girls?" Dylan asked.

"Yes. And that's about all they have in common," Rhodes said.

"They're both local, both young, slim and blonde," Dylan said.

"Yes." Rhodes drummed his fingers on the table. "You got to know Child well, Dylan. What do you think he's up to?"

"Anything that makes money." That was an easy one. "Drugs. Sex trade. Organ trade. Who knows? What he won't be doing is having a nice cosy chat with his maker."

"We'll show you the recordings of interviews with John Taylor, Caroline's stepfather," Rhodes said, nodding at Miller.

Miller messed around with the laptop, sighed, hit a few more keys, sighed again, and finally said, "Ready."

The three of them clustered around the laptop. Dylan

angled the screen so that he could see something other than a reflection of the ceiling light.

John Taylor, a tall, wiry man with thin dark hair, gave monosyllabic responses to most questions. He didn't look particularly nervous. Nor did he seem too concerned that his stepdaughter was missing.

"She can be a right bitch at times, like her mother," he said, "but I never done nothing to her. I never laid a finger on her."

"That's not what we heard. Someone said you knocked her about."

"Like hell I did. Well, I might have slapped her once or twice, but kids need to know who's boss, don't they?"

"Where do you think she is?" he was asked.

"How would I know? She's not mine so she can do as she likes, so long as she behaves herself under my roof."

"So you've no idea where she was going after she phoned you?"

"No."

"She didn't mention anyone she might be meeting?"

"No."

"She rang you to let you know she was safe?"

"Yes."

"Why would she do that? You said yourself she was free to do as she pleased. Why would she bother phoning you?"

"Money, I expect. That's all kids want from you. I expect she thought her mum would answer. As it was me, she'd know better than to ask. There was no point giving her any because she was a wasteful cow."

Whenever he saw people like John Taylor, Dylan despaired for the state of the country. What chance did Caroline or any other child have when their parents, or stepparents, didn't give a damn? Where did it end? If Caroline had children, how could she love them when she'd never been taught what love was?

"What about Child?" Dylan asked. "I assume he was questioned?"

"Yes. He couldn't have been more cooperative," Rhodes said. "Even said we could search the premises if we wanted. All we had to do was say the word."

"And did you say the word?"

"Too right we did. A fat lot of good it did us, though. We found nothing."

Child wasn't stupid, not when it came to hiding stuff from coppers.

"You got a warrant?"

"Yes, and that's another thing," Rhodes said. "We have to do everything by the book, Dylan. He's an expert at dodging the law, so—"

"Don't worry. I won't mess up the chance of securing a safe conviction. I'd love to see Child behind bars."

"Good. We want you to find out exactly what's going on at that commune. There must be something there that we missed." Rhodes returned to the table and handed over the folder. "I suggest you read through this. Any questions, just ask. Then it will be up to you. By the way, Frank Willoughby's on his way. He'll be here shortly."

"I'll look forward to it."

"He was your boss, wasn't he?" Miller asked, clearly curious as to why ex-Detective Chief Inspector Willoughby, a hero in this nick, would be spending time with a disgraced copper.

"For a while, yes."

"Get along well, did you?"

"Very well."

It was a lie, but Dylan didn't like the way Miller asked his questions. He was treating Dylan as if he were a criminal, not someone about to try to solve one of their cases for them. Besides, these days he and Frank were the best of mates.

"Right, we'll leave you to it," Rhodes said. "If you need anything, just shout."

Dylan looked straight at Miller. "Another coffee would be good."

"Of course. We'll see to it," Rhodes said.

When the two officers left the room, Dylan read through the pertinent facts. There would be file after file of paperwork, but this was Rhodes's copy of what he considered the most important facts in the girls' disappearance.

John Taylor's name cropped up repeatedly. Officers had been called out to his property several times in the past to sort out domestic disputes. It seemed as if Taylor's wife could give as good as she got, because Taylor had once ended up in hospital with a fractured skull after she found a more creative use for her saucepan.

A coffee arrived courtesy of an unsmiling Miller. "Room service is off duty now."

"Is that so?" Dylan replied.

"Yes. And don't think we all wanted you in on this case. Most of us can do without the help of bad coppers." He wrinkled his nose as if there were a rotten odour under it.

Dylan leaped out of his chair and grabbed the detective by the lapels of his jacket. "You call me a bad copper again, sunshine, and you'll have to shove your toothbrush up your arse to clean your teeth. Got that?"

A knock on the door preceded Frank's arrival. He did

a double take, but whether that was due to Dylan's appearance or the fact that he had his hands around Miller's throat was difficult to say. Probably the latter, because his eyes narrowed as he said, "Nice to see you're getting along so well."

"Wonderfully well," Dylan said. "We'll be exchanging bodily fluids next. Isn't that right, *Detective Sergeant* Miller?"

Dylan let the man go. Miller straightened his collar and, red-faced, nodded at Frank before leaving the room.

"What was that about?" Frank asked when they were alone.

"Just me taking exception to being called a bad copper. I suppose I should be used to it by now." Or if not used to it, he should be able to take it without resorting to violence. "It's fine. Forget it. How are things with you, Frank?"

"I'm in great shape." He patted Dylan on the shoulder. "It's good to see you. Even if you do look like a cross between a tramp and an eighties fashion guru."

"I tried to tell them that David Young wouldn't be sporting the same look these days. These glasses looked ridiculous years ago and they're even more out of place now. As for this beard—no way would he put up with it. I swear something's already taken up residence in it. My head's itching too. I think I've had a reaction to the dye." He gestured at the chairs. "Have a seat. I'd offer you a coffee but Miller said room service is off duty."

Frank sat down and Dylan wondered exactly how fit he was. A heart attack had forced him to retire from the force, and Dylan couldn't help thinking he looked a little frail. Or if not frail, then pale and weary. Still, there was no point pushing the issue because Frank would insist they go out and run a marathon before lunch.

"I suppose it was your idea to bring me up here," Dylan said.

Frank looked taken aback. "On the contrary. I was dead against it. I still am. Oh, no, don't think for a minute that you're getting tied up with Joe Child with my approval. I think it's a crazy idea."

Dylan frowned at him. "Why?"

"Because you're known in these parts, for one thing."

"But I—"

Frank waved away Dylan's interruption. "I'm not saying you're the celebrity you like to think you are, but you're known. It'll only take one person to recognise you and it'll get nasty. Child, in case you've forgotten, is one dangerous bastard."

"Allegedly."

"Have you forgotten Barney Fraser?"

Fraser, a thug who'd been known to have half of London living in his pocket, and one who'd trodden on the toes of drugs baron McCoy once too often, had been found with his tongue cut out. He'd bled to death in an old warehouse.

"Child had an alibi," Dylan said.

Frank snorted at that. "No. A bunch of crooks swore he was with them all weekend."

Dylan couldn't argue with that. Fraser's murderer had never been brought to justice. The clever money had Child down as the killer, but there was no evidence to secure a conviction.

"What brought him up north anyway, Frank?"

"I expect he'd made too many enemies down south. The force has nothing on him, or nothing new, but he'll have made enemies. Either that or the property prices brought him here. You get a lot more buildings and land for your freshly laundered money up here."

That was true. If you could afford a mansion in east Lancashire, you'd run to a broom cupboard in London.

"I thought both girls had vanished from Child's place," Dylan said, "but the second girl, Farrah, had returned home and had been living with her parents for a month. Maybe Child has nothing to do with her disappearance at all."

"It's possible."

"But unlikely?"

Frank thought for a moment. "I don't know. I do know that Child will be involved in some get-rich-quick scam."

"Aw, you've no heart. I was picturing him on his knees, begging forgiveness from his Lord for all sins committed."

"The bastard would be on his knees if I got my hands on him." Frank expelled his breath. "So what's your story?"

"I've supposedly come north because my girlfriend left me and because I did a job with a mate that got a bit too hot to handle. I caught the train to Manchester, fell asleep and ended up in Dawson's Clough. On being told I didn't have a ticket past Manchester, I got into an altercation with a ticket inspector and have been arrested for assault. As I need to kick my heels until my court case comes up, I'm begging for free board and lodging."

Frank nodded. "Child went along with it, did he?"

"He doesn't know what I've been arrested for, or that I'm due in court, but yes, he seemed convinced. Why shouldn't he be? As far as he was concerned, it was just a chance meeting in a bar. He was keen to make himself known to me. He gave me his card and said Doll—remember Doll?—would love to see me again."

"I remember Doll, yes. If you upset her in any way, three ugly brothers would make sure you lived to regret it." Frank shook his head. "I'm not in favour of arming Britain's coppers, but I wouldn't send a dog into that place. Watch your back."

"I will. What's the setup there? Any ideas?"

"It's a big place, an old farm with lots of barns and assorted outbuildings. He put down a deposit and took out a mortgage on it. It was almost derelict, but they're renovating it. We're supposed to believe everyone works together—cooking, cleaning, building, painting, whatever needs doing. There are about thirty people living there including Child, the lovely Doll and their two sons."

"How old are the sons now?"

"In their early twenties. Chips off the evil block, I suspect."

"So is it a family affair? Have they all found God?"

"So they'd have us believe."

They talked for another hour, speculating on what Child could be up to, but that's as far as they got. Speculation.

"Fair hair makes you look gay too," Frank said in a matter-of-fact way.

"Thanks. Any more compliments?"

"None for the moment." Frank chuckled before growing serious again. "Just be careful, Dylan. Child is an evil bastard. End of."

Chapter Four

DYLAN WAS KNACKERED. Since a ne'er-do-well like David Young wouldn't be forking out for taxis, he'd decided to walk to Child's place. Three miles had sounded nothing until he realised there was a steep hill to be climbed. Wind tugged at his spiky hair and his confounded beard, and a few icy spots of rain trickled down his neck. As rain and spectacles didn't mix, he'd taken off his glasses and shoved them in his pocket.

He was soon standing at the end of a curving lane about five hundred yards long. A wooden hand-painted sign welcomed all to Moorside Refuge and reminded those in doubt that God loved them.

Dylan leaned against a stone wall, removed one of his trainers and took out a sim card hidden beneath the thin insole. The wind immediately snatched it from his hand. Thankfully, he managed to put his foot on it as it landed on the ground, getting a soggy foot for his trouble.

With the card safely installed, he switched on his phone. Four messages waited—one from his mother and three from his wife. Usually, it was the other way round. It was his mother who called him a dozen times a day.

"Just calling for a chat," she said. "Speak soon."

As there was no point to that call, he deleted her message and called Bev.

"Hey," she said, "how's it going?"

"It's all good. I'm about to go in and get myself a bed. How are things down there?"

"Oh, so-so."

He waited for more, but nothing was forthcoming.

"Something wrong?" He hoped not. Sorting out a family crisis wasn't an option right now.

"No, not really." She sighed. "It's just that I've got that pain again and I don't feel great. What do you think it can be?"

"Bev, I love you to death, sweetheart, but my knowledge of female reproductive organs is zero and I'd like to keep it that way. Make an appointment now, while it's on your mind."

"Why should it be anything to do with my reproductive organs? Honestly, isn't that typical of a man."

And wasn't it typical of a woman to take offence when someone stated fact. "What else is down there, other than reproductive organs?"

"Well, I don't know."

"I don't either. I'm not a doctor."

She grunted something that he didn't catch, which was probably as well.

"Perhaps I will call the health centre. Well, I'll do it tomorrow. Your mum's having the kids tonight so I'm hitting the town with Lucy. I'll phone the health centre tomorrow when—"

"You've sobered up?"

"Probably," she said, and he could hear the amusement in her voice. "You know what Lucy's like."

He did. He also knew what Bev was like. A couple of glasses of wine and she was anyone's. She'd been known to throw up in taxis, pass out in hedges—

"Apart from that, everything's fine here." She

sounded brighter. "Luke's miffed because you won't be taking him to the football tomorrow. I've told him you'll probably be back for the next game. Do you think you will?"

"We'll see." Getting inside Child's life was one thing. Finding out what he was up to was something else entirely. Perhaps he was as innocent of any wrongdoing as he claimed. After all, Farrah Brindle hadn't lived at the refuge for a month before she went missing. "I'll do my best, but I've called Pikey and he's more than happy to take Luke. He said he'd call and collect Luke and the tickets around noon tomorrow. Is that okay?"

"Oh, that's good of him. Yes. Luke will be thrilled."

Pikey, or Detective Sergeant Pike, was a good copper, and an even better friend. If he and Dylan had been working together the night Dylan arrested that piece of scum—

They hadn't so it was no use going over it. Water under the bridge...

They'd remained good friends though, and Bev got along well with his wife. They should get together and catch up over a few beers.

"How's Freya?" he asked. "She okay?"

"She's good. As cute as ever."

He smiled at that. His daughter was noisy, wilful and demanding, but yeah, she was cute. "Okay. If you need me, leave a message. I'll check my phone as often as possible and I'll ring when I can, but don't worry if you don't hear from me for days. And make an appointment with the doctor."

"I will. Be careful, won't you, Dylan?"

"It's my middle name."

"Love you."

"Love you too." He ended the call, removed the sim card and returned it to his trainer. With David Young's sim card installed, he put on his glasses, slung his hold-all over his shoulder and walked up to Child's refuge.

The lane was thick with mud in places, which, given the amount of rain the region had seen recently, wasn't surprising. Deep, water-filled ruts would smash the exhaust on any low-slung vehicles.

Sheep grazed in a field off to his left. To his right was a smaller field. In front of him was a large stone house surrounded by sprawling outbuildings. Together the land and buildings, even taking into account the low property prices in Lancashire, had to be worth close to a million. Child must have taken out some mortgage.

Views were spectacular. From its vantage point high on the hill, the refuge peered down on the town of Dawson's Clough. Tall chimneys served as a reminder that the cotton mills had once brought great prosperity to this area. Behind the town loomed more barren hills that were breathtakingly beautiful on rare sunny days and, as Dylan knew from bitter experience, bleakly hostile when the rain and snow came, as it so often did to this corner of east Lancashire.

A woman with iron-grey hair and a face wrinkled with age was feeding chickens in front of the house. She was wearing a blue skirt, a multicoloured cardigan and purple Wellington boots. The chickens clucked around her feet as she tossed out food.

Welcome to Hippies R Us. His mother would have loved this place. She'd never shaken off her hippie tendencies. She'd never even tried. He could see her in this setting, smoking a joint while she fed chickens...

"Welcome," the woman said.

"Thanks. I'm looking for Joe. Is he around?"

"He's in the chapel. Come, I'll show you."

She threw the rest of the food to the chickens and, with the empty bucket dangling from her arm, set off for one of the buildings. She slid back a heavy wooden door and called out, "Joe, there's someone to see you."

She stepped back to let Dylan pass in front of her. He did so, and when he turned to thank her, she'd vanished.

"Davey!" Child rushed forward. "What a surprise. Good to see you!"

Half a dozen men of various ages paused for a moment to look at Dylan before continuing with their respective tasks.

The chapel was obviously a work in progress. Plasterboard was being fixed to the old stone walls. Cables dangled everywhere, and two freestanding halogen bulbs provided light. At the far end was an altar. Or, more accurate, an old trestle table covered by a heavily embroidered cloth that was held in place by two large brass candlesticks sitting at either end. Odd mixes of chairs, some wooden and some plastic, were stacked in a corner.

"You too, Joey." Dylan dropped his holdall at his feet. "I'm in a spot of bother."

Child rolled his eyes. "I'm not surprised. You can't go waving broken bottles at the filth, you know."

"It's not that. Well, yeah, it probably is. Resisting arrest and all that bollocks. But did I mention I fell asleep on the train and ended up here? I got into a bit of trouble with the ticket inspector. He was giving me hell for not having a ticket past Manchester, and I couldn't get him to see that I hadn't wanted to be on his bloody train past Manchester. To cut a long story short, we had a bit of a coming together and he's pressing charges. I've been in court this morning. A trial date's been set for February the fourteenth."

"Ah."

"I've got to stay in the area, I'm skint and I—"

"No one has to explain anything here," Child said. "You can stay as long as you like. We only ask that you help out with the chores. Okay?"

"Thanks. I appreciate it. Really."

"And no illegal activities, of course," Child added. "We're all Christians here, Davey, and we follow the commandments."

Child was a murdering bastard—allegedly—and this display of piety made Dylan slightly nauseous. "Right. Thanks."

Child slapped him on the back. "I'm glad you found us. We're a fair way out of town and there are only two buses a day. Did you walk?"

"I did, yeah. It gave me time to think, because I wasn't sure whether to come or not. I'm still not sure, to be honest. No offence, but all this God stuff isn't my thing. If you're happy to have me here, I'll give it a shot for a couple of days, but—"

"Of course we're happy to have you. Didn't I say you'd be welcome? The more the merrier. Now, come into the house and we'll sort you out a bed."

Chickens were still pecking for food as Dylan followed Child across the yard and into the house.

The main hallway was big and cold. Radiators that looked as if they'd been hanging there when Queen Victoria was on the throne were icy to the touch. Child carved his way through an obstacle course made up of tables, boxes and cycles, and Dylan followed.

"We'll get you a hot drink," Child said. "It's cold out there today."

It was cold in here.

Child pushed open a door and ushered Dylan into a large, cluttered kitchen. A dozen chairs clustered around a scrubbed pine table that had room for six. Utensils, papers and books littered surfaces. Pictures, photos and notes clung to a freezer door and, in the midst of this, two women were washing an enormous pile of dishes in a white porcelain sink.

"Meet Ivy and Sharon," Child said. "Ladies, this is Davey Young. He'll be staying with us for a few days."

"Pleased to meet you," the women said.

"Likewise."

"Ivy and Sharon come along for the Bible readings on Friday mornings," Child explained.

Dylan didn't know what he'd expected, probably nubile young things catering to Child's every sexual need, but as yet he hadn't seen a female under fifty. Ivy, still in the purple Wellington boots she'd worn to feed the chickens, was in her mid-sixties, he'd guess. Sharon was several years younger and had a far less colourful sense of fashion. She wore a brown tweed jacket and skirt and practical brown shoes that matched her brown hair.

Ivy put the kettle on and prepared tea for Dylan and Child.

"You don't live here then?" Dylan asked.

"Oh, no," Ivy said, "but we like to help out with the readings. And the soup kitchen."

"We go into town and take soup and blankets for the homeless," Child explained. "It's not much, but it all helps."

The door opened and a woman walked in who Dylan did recognise. Just.

Years ago, when he worked undercover, he'd met Child's wife half a dozen times. Back then, she'd sported straw-coloured hair, worn fake leopardskin skirts and tottered around on shoes with spikes for heels. Now she preferred black hair. Long fingernails were painted the same red as her lips. In deference to the low temperature, she wore a black cardigan over a tight T-shirt that showed off her impressive cleavage. An equally tight skirt said she ate more and exercised less than she used to.

"Bloody hell, as I live and breathe," she said. "When Joe said he'd bumped into you, I couldn't believe it. What the hell are you doing up here, Davey?"

"Oh, it's a long story, but I'm stuck up here for the foreseeable. I've got a court case coming up." He gave her a rueful smile. "It's good to see you again, Doll."

"You, too." She wagged a long finger at him. "You still getting in trouble with the law then?"

"I try not to but—" He shrugged.

"They're some buggers, aren't they? Once your name's on their list, that's it. They won't leave you alone."

"Never a truer word, Doll. They've always had it in for me and I'm sick of it."

Dylan put his backpack on the floor as Ivy handed him a large chipped mug filled with strong tea. "Thanks."

"You'll have to come to my show tomorrow night," Doll said. "We're off to Leeds. Joe does readings from the Bible and then I do my bit."

"Oh?"

"Yeah. Sometimes the spirits talk to me and some-times they don't."

"Spirits? What, like dead people?" He'd heard it all now. Child had found God and Doll was talking to dead people—people her husband had probably hastened on their way to those pearly gates.

"Those who haven't yet passed over," she corrected him. "You'll have to come along. Who knows, some of your late relatives might want to talk to you."

"I doubt it. They didn't when they were alive."

Ivy snorted with laughter. "I'd pay well to make sure none of my lot came back from the grave for a chat. The buggers drove me mad when they were alive, and I'd hate them to get a second chance."

"You might find them filled with forgiveness," Doll said.

"And I might not." Ivy took a packet of cigarettes and a lighter from her pocket. "Right, I'm off for a ciggie break. Meanwhile, if you see any of my relatives, Doll, don't tell them where I am."

Chuckling to herself, Ivy went outside to enjoy her smoke.

"No one will change Ivy's idea of the afterlife," Child said. "She's too set in her ways."

Or perhaps Ivy was simply sane.

Frank was worried that this assignment would be dangerous. The biggest risk, as far as Dylan could see, was ending up as crazy as Child and Doll.

"I'll come along to the show if I can beg a lift," he said. "Who knows, perhaps a rich relative will tell me where he buried the loot, eh?"

"Ah, that would be good," Doll said.

"Too true, it would. I'm sick of being skint. I could

do with a job—a good job. A foolproof one." He gave Child a knowing look but there was no response.

"There's no such thing. You need to forget all that nonsense, Davey. It's honest work that puts a roof over your head and food on your table. Come along tomorrow. We'll be taking the van, and you're more than welcome to come with us."

People came and went as Dylan drank his tea, but there were no hints as to what this place was actually used for. Perhaps, after all, Child had found God.

"Let's get you a bed sorted for the night," Child said when Dylan put down his empty mug.

He was given a grand tour of the premises and then shown his bed. *Oh. My. God.* He'd slept in a tent in the desert (don't ask), he'd shared a hotel room with a family of mice and he'd slept in a bath because he'd been too drunk to climb out, but he'd never slept in a small garden shed with five other people.

It was a shed. A bloody garden shed. There were three bunk beds on two sides and twelve inches of space between them. *Bed* was too generous a description. Planks of wood had been attached to the shed's sides and a ridiculously thin mattress had been laid on top.

"It's humble," Child said, "but I'm sure you'll be comfortable."

Humble? The prison cell he'd spent last night in had screamed five-star luxury compared to this.

"Thanks," he managed.

"We have better accommodation in the barn at the back," Child said, "but we feel it's only fair that the women have that."

"Of course. Thanks, Joey. I appreciate this."

It would be an incentive to get to the bottom of Child's

game, find out where Caroline and Farrah were, if indeed their disappearances were connected to Child, and get the hell away from here.

"The blankets are kept inside," Child added. "We'll collect those and I'll introduce you to the others who'll be sleeping here."

The others were those he'd seen working in the chapel when he arrived. Two men, Adrian and Pete, were both in their sixties and had shaggier beards than Dylan. Another, Gerry, was about forty. The last and youngest was Colin, an eager young chap in his late teens or maybe early twenties.

"We usually eat at six," Child said. "Tomorrow, because we're off to Leeds, we'll be sitting down earlier, at about five o'clock. We'll sort out your chores rota in the morning. Meanwhile, make yourself at home and get to know everyone."

It was already dark, and bitterly cold. They were walking back to the main house, where the temperature might be a couple of degrees warmer, when a man stepped outside.

"There you are, Joe."

Hands were shaken and introductions made by Child.

Bill Owen shook Dylan's hand. "Pleased to meet you, David." He was wearing a dog collar beneath his overcoat, and for some reason he was frowning at Dylan.

Shit. They'd met before. It had been brief, just a few words at a funeral, but Dylan could see from the spark of recognition that Owen had a good memory for faces and was currently wondering why Dylan Scott, private investigator, had decided to dye his hair, grow a beard and call himself David Young.

Shit!

This, of course, had been Frank's worry, that someone would recognise him. If Owen uttered so much as
a word about ex-coppers or private investigators, Dylan
would be dog meat.

His mind was racing but before he could say anything, a pair of headlights came up the lane and a patrol
car stopped yards from them. Two uniformed officers
got out.

"I wonder what they want," Child said, scowling.

"Me, probably," Dylan said.

"You two go inside," Child said. "I'll deal with them."
Shit!

Chapter Five

MALCOLM BRINDLE STEPPED off the Blackpool train and joined the crowd of people exiting Dawson's Clough Station. The bag slung over his shoulder had been heavy with flyers that morning, but now it was empty and it flapped against other passengers. He'd posted the flyers in shop windows, in pubs and phone booths. He'd stuck the rest to lampposts.

He'd planned to take a taxi home but he walked past the rank, turned right out of the station and wandered through his hometown, looking for the flyers he'd posted last week. Many had been torn down or blown down, and those that remained were tatty and difficult to read. He'd print out more tonight and circulate them tomorrow.

At least work wasn't too much of a problem. The teachers looked at him pityingly and were too unsure and too embarrassed to say anything if he didn't show up for a lesson. The headmaster had made it known that people had noticed his "um, distraction," but Malcolm had held his gaze until finally Potter had said, "Anything we can do to help, just let us know," and with a sympathetic smile had gone on his way.

The pupils didn't give a damn if he was there or not. None of them wanted to learn history. They simply didn't care. No matter how interesting or relevant to today's world he tried to make the lessons, he couldn't hold their attention for more than five minutes. Since Farrah's disappearance, he'd stopped trying.

The kids wouldn't care that he'd walked out of the school and spent most of the day tramping the streets of Blackpool, and staff members were too polite and sympathetic to comment. They would shoulder his workload, make soothing, meaningless noises and thank whatever god they worshipped that it wasn't their kid who was missing.

He knew it wasn't fair on them though, and he vowed to do his full workload next week. Tomorrow, and probably Sunday too, he'd post more flyers in Dawson's Clough. He'd print out a fresh load this evening. He'd make them more noticeable too. With lots of red ink, and perhaps a bigger photo of Farrah, people would pay them more attention.

He walked past a fish-and-chip shop, and the smell seeping into the early evening air reminded him that he hadn't eaten since breakfast. He wasn't hungry.

A hundred yards farther on, light from the Jolly Sailor spilled onto the pavement. Several smokers stood outside, shivering as they puffed on cigarettes.

He might not be hungry but he needed a drink. He was drinking quite a bit lately but it wasn't a problem. He could stop whenever he wanted. He'd never drink again when Farrah came home. It was just that tonight he needed—no, *wanted*—one.

He squeezed past the smokers and pushed open the door. He couldn't remember having been in the pub before. It wasn't his sort of place. It was big and barnlike, dingy too. Drinkers crowded around the bar and looked as if they'd been there most of the day. They probably had. He'd guess that work was too much effort for them.

They'd find it far easier to cash their benefit cheques
and spend the money in the boozer. They looked like
tough men. Hard men. He wouldn't want to pick a fight
with any of them.

A big dark-haired woman behind the bar looked at
him enquiringly. He wouldn't want to pick a fight with
her either.

He almost walked out but decided that as he was here,
he might was well have a quick one.

"A pint of your guest beer, please." He took out his
wallet and handed her a five-pound note.

While the glass filled, she checked the note under a
UV light. Perhaps they had a lot of forgeries changing
hands here.

"There you go." She handed him his change, topped
up his glass and set it on the bar.

"Thanks." He took a sip and thought it tasted sour.
He supposed they didn't sell many of the guest ales. The
drinkers here looked as if they counted the pennies and
opted for the cheap stuff. What they didn't spend here,
they could squander in the bookies.

A couple of pool tables sat at the far end of this vast
pub and a dozen or so men crowded round them, cheer-
ing on those playing or simply watching the game while
they drank.

A loud burst of laughter had Malcolm turning his
attention to the darts players to his left. One of them
looked familiar. He was tall and lanky with greasy dark
hair. Malcolm was sure he knew him. He racked his
brain as the man stood at the hockey and threw his darts.
When the man laughed again, Malcolm's blood ran cold.
It was that Taylor chap.

Malcolm had never met him but he'd seen his face in

the local paper and on the TV news. His stepdaughter had disappeared and police had questioned him. Malcolm had thought at the time that there was something sinister about him. Police wouldn't have taken him in for questioning without reason, would they? They must have had something to go on. Malcolm would bet it was a case of them knowing he'd been involved in her disappearance but being unable to prove it.

Taylor was an arrogant-looking individual. He was laughing again and had his arm round some loud-mouthed, overweight female. It might have been his wife, but Malcolm didn't think so. She didn't look like anyone's wife.

What the hell did he have to laugh about? His daughter, stepdaughter at least, was missing, just as Farrah was, and yet he was laughing. Malcolm wondered if he'd ever laugh again.

At first, police had been adamant that Farrah's disappearance wasn't linked in any way to Taylor's stepdaughter's. Malcolm could remember the young detective telling him that many, many people vanished each year. Usually, they took off for a better life in London, he said, or even abroad. Farrah hadn't. Malcolm didn't know where she was but he knew she hadn't taken off without a word to her parents. She wasn't that sort of girl. True, she'd changed. She could be moody and sullen at times, but she still knew the difference between right and wrong. It wasn't in her nature to let him and her mum worry like this.

Besides, she wouldn't have left her dog behind. Penny meant the world to her.

From the age of eight, Farrah had begged and pleaded for a dog. Not just any dog, but a Border collie. They'd

finally given in when she was twelve, and one bright,
sunny June day they'd brought home an eight-week-old
bundle of black-and-white fur. Farrah had been smitten
and had named her beloved puppy Penny. True to her
word, she'd taken Penny to training classes and, after a
lot of hard work, had ended up with a dog that was devoted to her. They were inseparable. No way would she
have left Penny to mope.

With the help of an old farmer she befriended, she'd
trained Penny to work with sheep. Only a week before
she vanished, she'd sent off her entry for a local sheepdog trials. She'd been as nervous as she'd been excited
about it. The trials had been and gone—no, she wouldn't
willingly have missed the event.

Malcolm hadn't been one hundred percent happy
about it, mainly because he didn't like Walter Topham,
the morose farmer who'd got her interested in working
the dog with sheep. Farrah thought he was amazing, a
real magician with sheepdogs, she'd said, but he was an
odd man. He lived alone, in a farmhouse where chickens were equally at home in the kitchen as they were
in the barn and where the smell of sheep lingered. He
might know all there was to know about sheepdogs, but
he possessed no social skills whatsoever. Farrah hadn't
cared about that though.

Seeing his glass was empty, Malcolm ordered a refill.

"I haven't seen you in here before, have I?" the barmaid asked.

"No. It's my first time. Thanks." He lifted his pint
glass and turned his back to her. He didn't want conversation. He wanted to know what Taylor had to laugh
about.

He was pulling his darts from the board. "The best of three, is it?" he asked his companion.

"Okay. And the loser buys the winner *two* pints?"

The pub was warm but Malcolm's blood still ran cold through his veins. Taylor was worrying about a darts game, of all things. He looked happy and carefree, as if he didn't care about anything, including his missing stepdaughter. If the original suspicions of the police were correct, what was he? A rapist? A kidnapper? A killer?

If he *had* done something to his stepdaughter, who's to say he hadn't done the same to others? Who was to say he hadn't done the same thing to Farrah? Perhaps the police weren't quite as clueless as he'd thought. Maybe there *was* a link between the girls.

Malcolm was finishing his third pint when Taylor took a dirty padded jacket from a hook and shrugged it on.

"See you tomorrow night," he said, slapping various mates on their backs.

As he headed out of the pub, Malcolm drained his glass, thanked the barmaid and set off in pursuit.

He didn't know where Taylor lived. His address could have been in the local paper when the police had released him, but Malcolm hadn't paid attention. He'd had no need to because Farrah, his beautiful Farrah, had been safe and well. Taylor's detention at the police station and the whole saga of his missing stepdaughter had been nothing more than a news item that hadn't touched him in any personal way.

It was only this evening that he'd thought Taylor *might* be guilty of something, that he *might* be responsible not only for his stepdaughter's disappearance but for Farrah's too.

Taylor walked into the fish-and-chip shop. Malcolm lingered outside, pretending to look at the small ads posted in the adjoining newsagent's window.

Taylor left the shop, tucking in to a mountain of chips, and walked slowly along Packer Street. Malcolm followed from a safe distance. This part of town was well lit so it was easy enough to see him. There were plenty of people about heading for a night out.

Malcolm had no idea why he was following him. Confronting him was out of the question because men like Taylor had a habit of talking with their fists. He'd find out where he lived, he supposed. That would be something.

One of Malcolm's neighbours was the crime reporter at the *Chronicle* so a word with him might be in order. He might know more about Taylor and his brush with the police than had been reported in the local press.

Taylor finished his chips, crumpled the paper into a ball and kicked it into the gutter. Filthy pig. There was a litter bin less than fifty yards away.

They walked on, past that bin and onto the Derby estate. Some of Malcolm's pupils lived on this local-authority housing complex, so he knew all about the residents. Most were on benefits, many fraudulently, and police were called out to break up fights or carry out drugs raids on an almost daily basis.

They passed a house that had been splashed in graffiti. Grass that hadn't been mown for years was littered with kids' toys and empty beer cans. A wooden fence at the side had been smashed. Malcolm shuddered and slowed his pace. There was no one around, and he was glad of that, but he didn't like being in this area.

Taylor turned up a pathway and let himself in to a

house at the end of a row. Malcolm hung around at a safe distance, watching lights go on inside.

After a minute, Malcolm walked on and stood outside number 16 Carston Avenue. There were no children's toys to be seen in the garden, no plants or pots. Again, the garden was an overgrown mess. People like Taylor would wait for the council to mow the grass. If the council didn't do it, it wouldn't get done. Simple.

Malcolm began the walk home. He lived a couple of miles from Carston Avenue, in an area where lawns and hedges were immaculate, and where new or nearly new cars waited on driveways to be washed and polished every Sunday.

He could have taken a taxi from the town centre but he preferred to walk and think. It was easier than going home and seeing the pain and despair etched deep on his wife's face.

Almost an hour later, he let himself into his home, flicked on the light switch and received a halfhearted greeting from Penny. Realising he was alone, Penny padded into the kitchen and lay on her bed.

Clare was out, thank God, so he didn't have to face her yet. She must have gone to her library group. She insisted it wasn't his fault, but he couldn't stop blaming himself. Farrah was his little girl, the child he'd held close on the day she was born and promised to take care of. He'd let her down.

He went straight to the drinks cabinet, poured himself a large whisky, threw himself down on the sofa and closed his eyes. Penny wandered into the room and let out a soft whimper. The dog was lonely, bored and lacking in exercise. It was impossible to wear her out and the walks he and Clare gave her weren't appreciated by the dog. She wanted Farrah's company and that was that. Malcolm had thought of visiting Topham and asking for his help and advice, but he kept putting it off. He wanted as little to do with the farmer as possible.

Police now believed, or said they believed, that Farrah's disappearance was connected to that refuge. They were wrong, Malcolm was sure of it. No, he'd bet his life that Taylor was involved in some way.

Malcolm knew where he lived and where he drank. The police might have failed but he wouldn't. Somehow, he'd get the truth out of him.

He'd planned to print out more flyers, but instead he switched on his computer and searched the internet for information on chloroform. That was the answer. If he could get enough to somehow render Taylor unconscious—although he had no idea how he'd get Taylor to a place where this might be feasible—he could tie him up and beat the truth from him. He needed to get a gun. That should be easy enough if he asked in the right places. After all, criminals had no trouble getting them. With a gun held to his head, Taylor would talk.

Of course, he didn't want to kill Taylor—

A ripple of anger burned through him. That was exactly what he wanted to do. He wouldn't though.

He glanced across at the bureau, where three silver-framed photos of his daughter sat. She looked happy, laughing and carefree. In one, she had her arm round her beloved dog. Penny was wearing a rosette she'd won at a local agility competition, and Farrah couldn't have looked happier. Her eyes shone. She looked content in the knowledge that all was right in her world. Or that her dad would make everything right in her world.

"I will, sweetheart. I will make it right. I promise."

Chapter Six

BILL OWEN CLEARLY knew his way round the refuge, because he went straight to a room that had to be used as an office by Child. Dylan followed, trying and failing to come up with a reason why private investigator Dylan Scott might be calling himself David Young. He needed a reason good enough to stop Owen blowing his cover.

The office was as cold as the rest of the house. A crucifix hung on the only wall that had been plastered. The other walls were bare stone and they looked damp. A cheap wooden desk sat near the window, and four chairs clustered around an empty fireplace. A bookcase held a selection of tatty paperbacks. A black leather-bound Bible, not particularly well thumbed, had been abandoned on a small pine table.

It was dark outside, but thanks to the patrol car's headlights it was easy enough to see Child talking to the two officers. The conversation looked to be friendly.

"What did Joe say your name was again?" Owen sat in the chair closest to the window. "David, was it?"

"That's right. David Young."

Owen was around sixty, tall and gaunt, with dark hair and steel-grey eyes. His face was long and his teeth large. Dylan would bet those equine features had earned him the nickname Trigger at some point in his life.

"And what brings you here, *David*?"

The emphasis on the name was clearly to show that

Dylan wasn't fooling him. He'd have to tough it out and deny all knowledge of private investigators.

"To tell the truth, I'm a bit down on my luck. I've run into a spot of bother with the law and I need to stay in the area until my court case comes up. Joe and I go way back—we used to work together down in London and he offered me a bed here."

"That was good of him."

"Yeah. He's a good mate. Mind you, no offence, but this God stuff isn't for me. Each to their own, of course, but it's not my scene."

"Perhaps Joe will change your mind."

"Not a chance." He smiled at the vicar. "What about you? I can see from the dog collar what you do for a living. Do you work round here?"

"Yes. I've been here for fourteen years."

"Really?"

"Yes, I've married and christened many people in the Clough. Buried a few too, of course." His gaze locked with Dylan's.

Shit. He knew damn well that they'd met at Kevin Mills's funeral. They'd only spoken for a couple of minutes, ten at the most, yet Owen recognised him despite the hair, the beard, the glasses and the scruffy clothes.

"I'm sure you have." Dylan nodded toward the police officers. "What can that be about?"

"The missing girls, I imagine."

"Girls?"

"Haven't you heard?"

Dylan shook his head. "I only arrived in the town yesterday and I've spent most of the time since stuck in the local nick. What girls are these then?"

"A young girl stayed here for a while and simply vanished. More recently, another girl who'd spent a month here before returning to her parents is also missing."

"Both girls missing? From here? That's a coincidence, isn't it? No wonder the filth are sniffing around."

Owen's knees were pressed tight together. "Many people who come here have problems so it's not that much of a surprise. Youngsters are searching for something and older people are running from something. They're a bit like you, David. You're only here because you have problems in your life, aren't you?"

"I suppose so. Did you know either of them?"

"One, yes. Farrah comes from a good family, but I'm afraid she went off the rails as teenagers are wont to do. She used to be a regular at my church with her parents, but that stopped. I suppose, like many teenagers, she was feeling stifled and wanted a taste of freedom. She was only here a month before she returned to the safety of her home."

"And then vanished?"

"So it seems."

"But the police are asking Joey about her?"

"I imagine so. I suppose they think that if she's in trouble, she'll return here. Of course, I could be wrong and they could be here on other business."

As he spoke, the patrol car fired into life and drove slowly away from the house toward the main road.

Seconds later, Child joined them. He was rubbing his hands together for warmth and Dylan wondered why he didn't think about heating this godawful building.

"Bill here has been telling me about girls who've gone missing," Dylan said. "Is that what the filth were here about?"

"Were you panicking, Davey?" Child smiled. "Don't worry, they didn't so much as mention your name."

He noticed Child hadn't answered his question. "Good. I'm sick of having them on my back all the time. So what were they here for?"

"They were asking about poor Caroline and Farrah, and sadly, I couldn't tell them anything. I'd like to think that the girls would get in touch with me if they had problems, but there's been nothing so far."

"Were they friends with each other?" Dylan asked.

"No. They never even met. Caroline upped and left and didn't say a word to anyone. She was a quiet, secretive girl though. She didn't say a lot to anyone. Farrah, of course, had already left here and gone home, thank goodness. That kid has a bright future ahead of her, so I'm glad she saw sense and returned to her parents."

Child sat down at his desk and looked enquiringly at Dylan. Whatever business he had with Bill Owen was clearly private.

"Right," Dylan said, getting to his feet, "I'll go and get myself settled in. Good to meet you, Bill."

"You too, David. Come and see me sometime."

It sounded like a threat of the "tell me what you're up to or I'll tell everyone exactly who you are" variety.

"Thanks. I will."

Chapter Seven

DYLAN WISHED HE were a smoker. If it weren't for the price of the things, he'd take it up tomorrow. He was convinced smokers had better social lives than more healthy mortals. They huddled together, united in their habit, and struck up conversations. He'd watched his mother stroll off to smoke a joint, and within minutes she'd make lifelong friends with like-minded druggies.

He didn't smoke though, so he'd have to put on a convincing performance as a lover of fresh air. And the air didn't come much fresher than this. It wasn't raining but the sky was heavy with cloud and no stars were visible. A gusting north wind was moaning.

He'd seen the man currently puffing on a hand-rolled cigarette earlier. He'd been working on a large vegetable plot, but Dylan hadn't had a chance to speak to him. He was late fifties or early sixties, thin and gaunt, and wore waterproof overtrousers and what looked to be a filthy black coat. As the only light came from a grubby lantern by the front door, it was difficult to tell.

"David Young." Dylan put out his hand, but after looking at it long and hard, the chap gazed up at the night sky and ignored both hand and Dylan.

"I'll be staying here for a few days." Dylan tried again, but there was no response. "Have you been here long?"

"Ugh." Whether that was a yes or no, Dylan had no

idea. He wasn't about to find out either, because the chap tossed his cigarette butt to the ground, used a heavy boot to extinguish it and began walking away from the house and up the lane.

He must have been carrying a torch because a spot of light soon danced in front of him as he walked.

Dylan was about to go back inside when another man came out for a smoke. This one he recognised. It was Adrian, one of the men he'd be sharing that confounded shed with.

Dylan nodded at the tiny dot of light moving along the lane. "I tried to start a conversation with him, but he wasn't interested."

"He doesn't speak. He nods and he'll grunt a bit, but that'll be your lot. He's not all there in the head, if you know what I mean."

"Ah. What's his name?"

"Kennedy. Whether that's his first or last name, I have no idea. He doesn't live here, but he comes and helps out now and again. He turned up one day and started working in the garden. Just like that. Joe let him stay. He arrives when he feels like it, does a few hours' work and then buggers off again. I don't know if Joe pays him or if he does it for the love of it. He doesn't speak to anyone and no one speaks to him. As I said, he's an odd bugger."

Yet another stray welcomed to the fold by Child. "I won't take offence then."

"So what about you, Davey? Is it Davey or Dave?"

"I'll answer to anything. Joey calls me Davey. He always has."

"Of course, you two go way back, don't you?"

"Yup. We worked together years ago. We had some times, I can tell you."

"So what brings you here?" Adrian asked.

"Didn't Joey tell you? I had a spot of bother with the law." Dylan stamped his feet to try to bring warmth to them. "I ended up here by mistake—fell asleep on the train to Manchester—and bumped into Joey. I had no idea he'd moved to this godforsaken place."

Adrian smiled at that. "It's not so bad. Do you like hill walking?"

"Nope."

"That's a pity. It's perfect round here for a long hike. I enjoy it. You get some fantastic views from the top. It's good for you too."

"I'm sure it is." In Dylan's experience, things that were good for you were unpleasant in the extreme. Tramping these barren moors would be no exception. "What's your story, Adrian? How did you end up here?"

"My wife and I split up. She went off with another bloke and I ended up living alone. I hated it and was spending all my time in the pub. That's no good for you, is it?"

Dylan smiled and nodded sympathetically, but it didn't sound such a bad life.

"One night, I was in a bar in town, Tempo—they do cheap drinks until ten—and I got talking to Joe."

"Yeah? Me too. I went into Tempo because of the cheap drinks. That's where I bumped into him."

"He's there every Thursday night. Anyway, he told me about this place and it sounded great. It *is* great. A week later, I moved in. I'm an electrician by trade so I'm helping turn that old barn into a chapel." He drew in a huge lungful of cold night air. "I love it."

"It's all the religious stuff that puts me off," Dylan said.

"I wasn't too keen at first. I'm a Christian, but I only used to go to church at Christmas and maybe Easter. It's okay though. Joe doesn't ram it down your throat all the time."

"That's something, I suppose. I'll see how it goes before I decide how long to stay. I hear Joe takes soup and blankets to the homeless in town. I wouldn't want to be sleeping on the streets in this sodding weather."

"Me neither. Yes, Joe does a lot of good work."

Saint Joe? No, Dylan couldn't swallow that one.

"I'm only surprised he can afford to be so generous," Dylan said. "I know everyone helps out with the chores, but there's no money coming in, is there?"

"That's where you're wrong. We sell fruit and vegetables at the local market once a week. Some of the women bake bread and cakes, and those are sold too. It's quite the cottage industry."

Even allowing for Child's aversion to heating, it would cost more than the profit from fruit, vegetables and cakes to keep this place going.

"We get plenty of donations too," Adrian went on. "We often set up the soup kitchen when the football team's playing at home, and that way we get around twenty thousand people walking past. They're generous, especially if the Blues have won. When Joe gives talks—there's one in Leeds tomorrow night—we always have a collection. We get by and Joe's very good with the finances."

Child was a tight-fisted sod, always getting the best price for jobs no one else wanted—illegal jobs. He'd probably accumulated thousands over the years but Dylan couldn't see him giving it to the poor. Child looked out for number one. He always had and he always would. There was a saying about leopards never changing their spots and Child was exactly the same. He'd never change his ways. Never in a million years.

"We had a big donation not so long back," Adrian said. "A celebrity—I can't remember his name but he was on one of these reality TV shows, *Big Brother* or something like that. He heard about the work Joe was doing and donated a few thousand."

"Really? How did he hear about Joe?"

"Dunno." Adrian shrugged. "We hand out leaflets when Joe gives talks—like the one tomorrow night in Leeds—so perhaps he saw one of those. We stand outside whatever building we're in and give them to passersby. That was probably it."

"Ah well, it's good if it pulls in the money." Dylan wasn't convinced. "Hey, I was hearing about the two girls who went missing. That's a strange lot of it, isn't it?"

"I don't know what to make of it. One of the girls, Caroline, vanished from here, you know. The other one, Farrah, I don't know much about. She wasn't here long, and you could see she didn't fit in. She had a dog with her for a start. It's no place for a dog, is it? It was no trouble, but even so. Reading between the lines, I think she'd had a row with her parents and was proving a point. She soon went back home."

"I wonder where they went."

"They could be anywhere. You know what kids are like." He stubbed out his cigarette. "It's time I turned in. I want an early start in the morning."

"I'll do the same soon," Dylan said.

"We've all got two blankets each but I'll warn you now, it can get a bit cold at night."

"I'm sure it can."

"I like to keep busy all day. That way, I'm asleep before I know it. Ah well, see you later, David."

"See you."

Dylan was about to head for that shed when the front door opened and another smoker emerged.

"You're here late, Ivy. I thought you'd gone hours ago."

"I was busy baking and then I got talking." She lit her cigarette and inhaled deeply. "My husband's always telling me I talk too much. Mind you, if I didn't get out of the house, I'd lose the power of speech. He wouldn't know what a conversation was if it stepped up and punched him in the face."

Dylan smiled. "So you went for the strong silent type?"

Ivy's laughter wheezed its way up from her chest. "You're almost right. He's retired now and I never know if I follow him around clearing up his mess or if he follows me around making a mess. Either way, it's better for both of us that he doesn't say much."

Dylan had warmed to Ivy on first meeting. She was one of those what-you-see-is-what-you-get women that Lancashire bred by the score. He'd guess she would speak her mind but would also help anyone in need. She was loud and waved her hands around as she spoke, a hangover from the days when women worked in the cotton mills and shouted or used hand signals to make themselves understood over the racket of the huge looms. Those days were long gone, but the habits remained.

"I was chatting to the vicar earlier," he said, "and he was telling me about the two missing girls. That's an odd lot of it, isn't it? Did you know them?"

"Oh, I do worry about them." She took a long pull on her cigarette, which induced a brief coughing fit. "I didn't know Caroline so well because she didn't have much time for us old folk. Farrah was different again though. We had a few laughs. She wasn't here long, about a month, but I liked her. She was good fun. I was so pleased when she went back to live with her mum and dad. She had a dog with her and it followed her everywhere. One of those collies. My sister has one and I sometimes babysit the thing for her. Well, it's crazy. It barks when you get the vacuum cleaner out, it barks at people walking past the window. It even barks at the TV. Farrah's dog did everything she told it. She'd tell it to lie down and there it would lie until she told it to move." She sighed. "Farrah was a good girl."

"Did you see her after she left here? When she went back to live with her parents?"

"Only twice. The first time I was hurrying to the dentist, so I couldn't stop for a chat. She told me that if I kept on smoking, all my teeth would drop out. Well, I told her, most of them already have." Her face crinkled into a smile. "The second time was about a week before she vanished. She was her usual happy self. Very happy, in fact. Told me how good it was to see me and dragged me off to the coffee bar, where she insisted on buying me a coffee and a cake. She had the dog with her, of course, but it lay outside and waited for us. She was in good spirits."

"She didn't mention going anywhere?"

"Not a word. Looking back though, I think there was a man involved. Only a man can put a smile like that on a girl's face." She pulled a face. "Young girls don't re-

alise that these handsome men soon turn into miserable
buggers you can't get a word out of."

A car turned up the lane.

"This'll be my taxi." She ground her cigarette stub
into the ground. "Are you sleeping in that shed tonight?
Rather you than me. It'll be cold enough to freeze your
bits off." She was still laughing as she climbed inside
the taxi.

Dylan watched until the taillights vanished from his
view and then he headed toward that shed.

He was reminded of the well-worn expression "What
goes around comes around." He'd taken this job to get
one up on the police force. He'd had so much confidence
in his own ability that he'd been sure he'd soon get to the
bottom of Child's scam and find the missing girls. So
here he was, more than two hundred miles from home
and about to spend the night not in a warm bed with
a warm wife, but in a freezing shed with five snoring
males. It served him right.

At home, Bev would have the central-heating boiler
working overtime. Luke would be lying in bed listening
to the rubbish teenagers called music, and his beautiful
baby girl, Freya, would be sleeping with her arms out-
stretched in happy oblivion.

Thank God he'd had the good sense to put half a bottle of whisky in his backpack. It was the cheap blended
crap that a bloke like Davey Young would drink, but it
was better than no whisky. And he couldn't imagine
there being much left in the morning…

Chapter Eight

THE TORCH SPLUTTERED, the light almost fading to nothing. Kennedy gave it a good shake. The darkness was total, and he'd twist his ankle in a pothole or fall headlong into a ditch without his light. It flickered again, then settled itself. The light wasn't brilliant, but it was better than nothing. Once he got to the outskirts of Dawson's Clough, he wouldn't need it.

He enjoyed walking round here in daylight. The air was always fresh, and the scenery spectacular. In London he rarely walked anywhere, but here it was energising. The six miles a day to Moorside Refuge and back was keeping him fit.

There was a new resident at the refuge. David Young. About forty, maybe younger, in fairly good shape but as scruffy as everyone else at the place. Spiky fair hair, untidy beard, dirty clothes—he was a good fit. Kennedy wondered what *his* story was. He'd soon find out. He was good at that.

A car sped past him. Young kids loved racing along these curving roads at a breakneck pace. Only a couple of weeks ago, a seventeen-year-old who'd only just passed his test had lost control of his car and crashed into a stone wall. The impact had killed him and his three passengers instantly.

A couple of sheep grazed on the verge and took no

notice of him as he passed. They were used to traffic and walkers.

He stepped out at a good pace and soon reached the edge of town where he was able to switch off his torch. He'd stayed late at the refuge tonight, curious about the new chap, and he was ready for his bed.

The town centre was busy. Youngsters were falling out of pubs and clubs, and several police officers were patrolling the streets, but everyone was good-natured. One girl, dressed in a sleeveless short black dress, completely oblivious of the biting cold, reached up and stole a policeman's helmet. Laughing, she put it on her head and posed as her girlfriends snapped photos with their phones. The officer joined in with the fun and soon had it back on his head.

Kennedy walked on. The fish-and-chip shop near his flat was still serving, and he dived inside, welcoming the warmth and the smell of food. He'd eaten his sandwiches at one o'clock, ten hours ago, and he was starving.

He was third in line, and when his turn came, he pointed at a board that read Haddock & Chips £3.95.

The woman behind the counter took a fish from the heated cabinet, put it on paper and scooped out a generous portion of chips.

"Salt and vinegar?" she asked, and he nodded.

He would have liked more vinegar, but he'd got some at home.

"Three ninety-five, love."

He handed over the ten-pound note Child had given him. She examined it closely and, satisfied it wasn't a forgery, put it in the till and gave him his change.

He nodded his thanks and left the shop with the hot parcel in his hand.

He rounded the corner and quickened his pace. A couple of minutes later, he was letting himself into his flat. All was quiet in the building. It usually was. The occupants of the other two flats were retired people who lived alone. It was one reason he'd chosen it.

He took off his coat, washed his hands and put his food on his plate. He sat down and flicked through the TV channels, finally settling on a current-affairs programme as he ate. The answering machine was blinking at him, telling him he had three messages, but they could wait.

The news ended, the weather report promised more rain for the area, and then a quiz show came on. Contestants were eager to win a few thousand pounds, but Kennedy wasn't paying attention.

When his plate was empty, he carried it to the kitchen and left it in the sink. He grabbed a can of beer from the fridge, walked back into the lounge and prodded a finger at the answering machine.

"Just reminding you about the presentation in Brussels. The flights are booked, and driver and car are on standby, but I need to know if you can make it. I've said I'll confirm your attendance tomorrow morning…"

Chapter Nine

DYLAN HAD SURVIVED what had to be the coldest night on record in that shed. At least he'd been wrong about one thing. There had only been three snoring men present. The other two had tossed and turned all night. Perhaps, like him, they'd been trying to stave off hypothermia. The late arrival of the dawn had been welcome, until he'd been told that he must spend four hours banging nails in plasterboard as payment for that torturous night. He had a throbbing thumb for his efforts.

Having walked the three miles into town, most of it downhill, thankfully, he could finally feel his feet again. The wind was gusting from the east today, straight from Siberia, and the ground still glittered with frost in sheltered corners.

He was about to call on Reverend Owen and find out how pally the vicar was with Child and, more important, if he intended to blow Dylan's cover. He hadn't made an appointment because he wanted to catch Owen off guard. It meant the vicar could be out administering to the sick or whatever it was they did these days.

The vicarage was a massive stone building standing square in a large, well-tended garden where holly trees maintained privacy. The property would belong to the diocese, but even so, it would be no hardship living in it. He wondered what sort of salary a vicar commanded these days.

Dylan didn't believe in God, and he loathed crimes that were committed in the name of religion, but apart from those minor details, he reckoned he could stand up in church and read a sermon, sing a hymn, carry out the odd wedding, funeral and christening, and visit those in need of a chat. It was easy money.

A polished blue Nissan sat on the neat, curving driveway, so that was promising.

He walked up stone steps and prodded a round bell push set in stone by the front door. After a few moments, he heard a shuffling from inside and the heavy door swung open.

"Ah. Welcome," Owen said as if he'd been expecting him. "Come in."

"Thank you."

Dylan had thought that if nothing else came from this visit, he would at least get warm. That seemed a forlorn hope, as it was no warmer inside than out. Perhaps this aversion to heat was a Lancashire thing.

The wide hallway was empty, apart from two small low tables. A few dark and depressing paintings tried, and failed, to bring cheer to the walls.

"I'm working in the kitchen," Owen said. "Come on."

Dylan was taken into a large icebox at the back of the house. One small radiator was warm—he touched it to check—but it had little effect on this high-ceilinged room with its single-glazed windows.

A table strewn with papers sat in the centre of the room. A grand's worth of MacBook was open.

"I'm working on Sunday's sermon," Owen said, nodding at the computer.

He was dressed for warmth and comfort in thick corduroy trousers, a chunky sweater and a green padded body warmer. "Can I offer you tea or coffee?"

"Tea would be welcome, thanks. Milk and two sugars, please."

While Owen made the tea, Dylan took in the rest of the room. A wall calendar was crammed with appointments, all written in a neat forward-sloping hand. A digital radio was plugged in but silent. A small portable TV sat on the worktop in a corner. Tea, coffee and sugar canisters were lined up with military precision. He couldn't see any religious artefacts.

The morning's newspaper hadn't been opened. The front page was taken up by news of the dead body Rhodes and his chums had found in an unlit alley close to the river. The man was still unidentified and the reporter had clearly struggled for enough information to fill the space.

"I don't know your real name," Owen said.

"David—Davey will do." If he didn't know it, there was no point telling him.

"It was your voice I recognised. We spoke at a funeral—young Kevin Mills's funeral." When Dylan didn't comment, he said, "I'm something of an expert on accents and I've had a couple of books published on the local dialect."

"Really?"

"Yes. I know you're an investigator of sorts, but that's all. What you're doing here is your business, of course. I imagine it's something to do with the disappearance of Caroline and Farrah?"

It seemed churlish to distrust a man of the cloth, but it was safer to trust no one.

"What do you know about them?" He took the cup of tea Owen offered him. "Thanks."

"Sit down." Owen gestured to one of the chairs clustered around the table. It was the farthest from that radiator. He'd made himself a fresh cup of tea and he took a noisy sip. "I know Farrah very well—I expect you've heard. She used to come to my services with her parents. She's a bright girl, and always seemed happy enough. The other girl, Caroline, I don't know. Her parents aren't churchgoers, more's the pity. If they had faith, it would be a great comfort to them at this difficult time."

What crap. "Is it helping Farrah's parents?"

"I'm sure it is."

"You haven't seen them?"

"I've called on them several times, of course. I've assured them that we're praying for Farrah. And for them, of course."

"But they haven't been to church?"

"Not for a while, no."

Dylan drank his tea. It was hot but he welcomed the burning sensation as it slid down his throat.

"What is it you're wanting from me?" Owen asked.

Dylan liked people who came straight to the point. He still didn't feel able to trust him though. Perhaps the cold was making him more cynical than usual.

"If you're worried I'll tell Joe who you are—" He frowned. "Joe said you were old friends. Is that true?"

"Acquaintances," Dylan said. "We once worked together."

"But he doesn't know you're an investigator, does he?"

Dylan sighed. "No, and I'd rather he didn't find out."

"He doesn't know your real name either, does he?"

"No."

"You can trust me." Smiling in a somewhat superior way, Owen tapped long fingers on the table. "I'm used to keeping confidences."

"It would be safer for all concerned, including you, if that's the case."

Owen's eyebrows shot up and Dylan shrugged. Owen could take the veiled threat any way he chose.

"What business do you have with Joe Child?" he asked.

"I suppose you could say I've been doing a little investigative work of my own," Owen said. "I was a little uneasy when I first heard about the setup there. Religious cults can be dangerous beasts, and I wanted to reassure myself that Child wasn't—a fanatic."

"And have you reassured yourself?"

"Oh, yes. From what I've seen, he's doing invaluable work. As he says himself, he's giving back to society. That's so commendable, isn't it? People could learn a lot from him."

Saint Joe.

"His wife—" Owen paused for a long moment to choose his words with care. "She's more difficult to fathom, I find. She claims to have a gift."

"Dead people talk to her." Dylan nodded.

Owen quirked a dark bushy eyebrow. "You believe that?"

"No, of course not."

"Have you seen her at one of her—performances?" He said the word *performance* with obvious distaste.

"No. Have you?"

"No." Owen gazed into the depths of his teacup. "I believe people pay to see her. The money's ploughed back into the refuge and to ministering to the town's homeless, so that's good, of course, but even so, it doesn't feel right. I'm not completely happy with that."

"How else are they going to fund the refuge?" Dylan asked.

"Well, I don't—"

"I'm serious. Where does the money come from? I know they grow their own vegetables, but there's a huge property to maintain, big cars to run, people to feed and clothe, the homeless to feed... Exactly where does the money come from?"

"Donations mostly, I believe. We had a joint fundraising event—half the proceeds for the church and half for the refuge—and it was hugely successful. As you'll know, Joe would make a great salesman. He has the gift of the gab and people give generously. Even with half the proceeds, the church has benefited more than ever before."

"Selling cakes? A bookstall? That wouldn't cover the costs of running the refuge."

Owen shrugged that off. "He has a benefactor, I gather. An old friend—an old wealthy friend."

"Who's that?"

"I don't know. It's none of my business, so I haven't discussed it with Joe. It's hearsay." He'd been frowning, but his expression cleared. "Look, David—whatever your name is—Joe is doing a lot of good work. He helps those with problems and I can only commend that. I wish there were a few more like him around."

Dylan was glad there weren't. "You said you knew Farrah very well. How come?"

The frown was back. "She used to attend my services with her parents."

"So you'd have a couple of words with her at the church door as the family was leaving? How would you know someone well from that?"

There was a slight hesitation. "We were trying to start up a choir, and Farrah was involved with that. There were meetings—we were keen to get the choir up and running for the Christmas carol concert. The school's music teacher was helping to organise it."

"Right. And you got to know her well through that?"

"Yes." There was a slight hesitation. "Also, she came to me—to chat. Her grandmother and her aunt passed away in the space of six months and she sometimes called in to talk about that."

"Ah. So you spent time alone with her?" That made more sense. "Was she close to her grandmother and aunt?"

"Yes. Their deaths hit her quite hard. Death is difficult for youngsters to deal with. She spoke of death a lot, and of course she wanted answers that I couldn't give her. She wanted guarantees that her relatives would be watching over her, that they'd be together in heaven and that she'd see them again when she died. We talked a lot. I tried to offer what comfort I could and talk through her concerns."

"So she wasn't as happy as people claim, was she? If the deaths of close family members hit her so hard, she couldn't have been."

"She was a clever, sensible girl. She was happy enough. Sad about such a tragic loss, especially one coming so soon after the first, but I'd describe her as happy. She certainly wasn't depressed."

"In your opinion."

"In my opinion, yes."

"Did she see anyone else? A doctor perhaps?"

"Not that I know of."

"What made her turn to you?" Dylan asked.

"People do. That's what I'm here for. People come to me every day with spiritual problems."

"How did they die?"

"Both had cancer. Her grandmother was in her sixties but her aunt was only forty-three. It's hard to take."

"But you believe you helped her?"

"I do, yes."

Had he? Dylan could imagine him offering his religious spiel, spiced with fitting Bible quotes, and assuming the young girl was taking every word as gospel.

"What else did she talk about when she visited you?"

"Many things. Her dog mostly. She was besotted with the creature. She used to spend time with Walter Topham. He's an old farmer—has a lot of success at sheepdog trials. She was training her dog to work with sheep."

"You said many things. What did she talk about other than her dog?"

"Schoolwork, music, fashion—the usual things on a teenager's mind."

Owen was old enough to be the girl's grandfather, so why in hell's name would she discuss such things as music and fashion with him?

"How does she get on with her parents?" Dylan asked.

"Very well. As I said, she's a good girl."

"Yet she moved out and went to live at Joe's refuge."

Owen smiled at that. "Just a silly phase she was going through. They had the usual parent-teenager rows. Farrah wanted more freedom. Given the choice, I think she would have moved in with Walter Topham. He had dogs and sheep—she would have been happy enough with that. Her parents didn't approve. Also, her friends were partying, whereas her parents insisted, quite rightly in my opinion, that she was too young. Farrah moved to the refuge, where she was perfectly safe, made her point and then returned to her home comforts."

"Did she visit you during her spell at the refuge?"

"Several times, yes. She used to walk over the hills with her dog."

"Did she talk about the place?"

"She did. At first she found it fun and exciting. She was treated as an adult and she made friends there. The novelty of having chores to do soon wears off though." Owen smiled again.

"You say she made friends. Who with?"

"I don't remember names, but the women, or girls, were all friendly. You'll discover for yourself that everyone gets on well."

Dylan emptied his cup, aware of Owen watching every breath he took.

"Look," Owen said at last, "I don't know what you're doing here, but if you're looking into the disappearance of Caroline and Farrah, there's nothing I can tell you. There's nothing Joe can tell you, either. You're barking up the wrong tree. You have to remember that Farrah had nothing to do with the refuge at the time of her disappearance."

"I haven't forgotten." Dylan wasn't sure how much more time he could spend in these subzero temperatures. "What's your theory then, Bill? Where do you think the two girls might be?"

"I don't know. They won't be together—they didn't know each other and they're as different as chalk and cheese—but I have no idea. Teenagers being teenagers, I imagine they've headed off for the bright lights and will scurry home when the gilt wears off."

"Where's the dog?"

"Sorry?"

"You said she was besotted with her dog. Is it with her?"

"No. No, it's with her parents."

"So you believe that despite being besotted with the animal, she's abandoned it? You're not worried about the girls at all?"

"Of course I'm worried. Teenagers are easily led astray. Let's face it, all sorts of horrors come from life in the big cities. Drink, drugs, prostitution—of course I worry for them. I pray, as does my congregation, for them every week."

If praying did any good, Dylan would offer up a quick one and save himself the discomfort of more nights in that freezing shed.

He was getting nothing from Owen. As far as the vicar was concerned, Child was a saint and the two girls were enjoying the high life in some unknown city. Dylan remained unconvinced. On both counts.

It was time to go. He'd find himself a nice warm pub and a long cold drink, and chat to the locals. Someone would know something. They always did.

Chapter Ten

BEV HELD THE phone to her ear and rolled her eyes at the health centre's recorded announcement. "Press One for urgent, on-the-day appointments…" That was a waste of time because you needed to be near death to get an on-the-day appointment, especially on a Saturday. Even if it were possible, she couldn't face seeing a doctor today. He'd probably tell her she had liver poisoning after last night's outing with her best mate, Lucy. They'd demolished a couple of bottles of wine too many.

She eventually opted for option three and listened to the phone ring out at the other end. She could imagine the receptionists filing their nails, discussing what they'd watched on TV last night or—

"Grosvenor Medical Centre. Helen speaking. How may I help you?"

"Oh, hi. Could I make an appointment with a doctor for as soon as possible, please?"

"Just a moment." Helen tapped on a computer keyboard. "Monday at two-thirty with Doctor Cavanagh?"

At two-thirty on Monday she'd be trying to make thirty pupils fall in love with the works of Tolkien. She had more hope than expectation. "Is there anything later? With a female doctor, if possible?"

"Just a moment, please." More tapping on the keyboard.

"Five-thirty on Monday afternoon with Dr. Singh?"

"That's fine. Thanks." With any luck she'd be pain-free by then and could call and cancel. She hated visiting the health centre. Everyone looked germ-ridden. Colds and coughs were rife. She refused to even pick up one of the magazines in the waiting area for fear of catching some bug or other.

"What name is it, please?"

"Mrs. Scott. Beverley Scott."

Having confirmed her address, Bev scrawled *Monday at 5:30* on the back on an envelope and returned the phone to its cradle.

Right. She'd push it from her mind until Monday. There was no point getting in a state about it. It was probably nothing. Perhaps she'd pulled a couple of muscles, one in her stomach and one in her back.

She sifted through mail that sat on the kitchen table, awaiting Dylan's return. It was mostly junk and she knew he wouldn't bother to open it. She might as well cut out the middleman and throw it straight in the recycling box.

She wished she had company. Usually, she longed for solitude, but today she would have liked to have the kids around. Luke was at the football with Dylan's ex-colleague though and Freya was fast asleep.

She should make the most of the quiet and do something constructive. And she knew just the thing.

She made herself a coffee, carried it upstairs to their bedroom, set the cup on the dresser and opened Dylan's wardrobe. She'd been threatening to sort it out for months. Every time she mentioned it, he said he'd do it himself. He never had and never would. She'd make the most of his absence and gather up a load of his clothes to throw out. He never wore half the stuff in there but he refused to throw anything out. Some items were so awful that he wouldn't dare wear them in her presence.

She took out the lot and spread everything across the bed. This would be fun, far better than worrying about odd pains or checking lists of symptoms online. Health forums on the internet were great for putting your mind at rest. They were also awesome at convincing you that you had any or all of the rare terminal diseases mentioned. She'd forget it.

The first item to end up on the pile to throw out was an old blazer. She'd always hated it. He wasn't a blazer sort of man. Next was a woollen jacket that she couldn't remember seeing him wear. He had enough suits to clothe the entire population of Shepherd's Bush. On the rare occasions he needed one, usually for weddings, funerals or christenings, he always bought a new one on the grounds that his others were old. If that was the case, and it might be, although they'd be old and unworn, they needed throwing out. It was the same with ties. He had dozens of the things, all taking up space and all seldom worn. He was a jeans, shirt and jacket man.

She was pleased with her progress and she'd stake her life on his not noticing they'd vanished.

Satisfied that she'd set aside as many clothes to discard as she dared, she turned to the shoes, all thrown haphazardly on the wardrobe's floor. She could be even more ruthless here.

A white box shoved in the far corner caught her eye and she grabbed it. She hadn't looked at their wedding photos for years. The expense—and she'd insisted they hire a top photographer—should have had her looking through the album every day. During the first year of their marriage, she'd probably looked through it a dozen times. Then, on the first couple of anniversaries, she'd refreshed her memory. Since then, it had lain here, shoved out of the way and forgotten.

She pushed Dylan's clothes aside and sat on the bed to open it. The first photo, taken as Dylan pushed her ring onto her finger, took her completely by surprise, not so much because they looked ridiculously young, but more because they were deliriously happy. Young and in love—it was as if nothing in the future could possibly blight those beaming smiles.

Almost seventeen years on, they didn't smile so much. They were happy, she supposed, but life was a merry-go-round of paying bills, acting as Luke's unpaid chauffeur and fitting life and work around Freya's odd sleeping patterns. There was little time left to smile.

They should get out more. Dylan's mum, their chief babysitter, was only a short bus ride away and she was more than happy to spend the night if necessary. They should make the most of her, go out and smile as they used to, enjoy life…

They could have a romantic weekend away. Dylan wasn't the most romantic of men—in fact, he wasn't in the least romantic—but even he couldn't fail to be moved by a weekend in Paris. Freya would be celebrating her first birthday in March, so she was old enough to stay with her grandmother for a night.

Forgetting photo albums and the clothes strewn across the bed, she went to her computer to research hotels in Paris that offered romantic getaways. Hopefully, Dylan would soon be home again and they could take off for the City of Love.

She was mentally enjoying an evening in a Parisian wine bar when the phone rang.

"Hello?" There was no answer but she had the feeling that someone was on the other end. "Hello? Is anyone there?"

There was a click and the line was dead. She dialled 1471 but the number had been withheld. A lot of call centres had withheld numbers. Perhaps someone had been phoning from a switchboard, realised they had the wrong number and were too shy, or too rude, to say so.

She forgot about it and returned to that wine bar in Paris.

Chapter Eleven

DYLAN HAD BEEN in some dives in his time but the Jolly Sailor beat the lot. It had two things in its favour. One, it sold beer. Two, it was showing the Arsenal versus Manchester United game on a huge TV screen.

Other than that, it was a dark, dingy, soulless place. Trade was brisk, so the landlord had to be doing something right, but it was one of those places where you wiped your feet on the way out. The carpet, grubby and badly worn, hadn't seen a cleaner since Moses was a lad. The bar was sticky with spilled beer and the glasses had long forgotten how to sparkle. Still, the place sold beer and it was showing the Arsenal game (no score yet). And he only had time for a very swift pint.

He'd ended up here because it was the first place he came to that promised warmth after leaving the vicarage. He wasn't sure he'd achieved anything from his meeting with Bill Owen. More important, he couldn't be certain that Owen wasn't friendlier with Child than he let on. He didn't trust either of them.

It was a pity he couldn't watch the full game, but at least Luke would be enjoying it. His lucky son would see the game and return to a warm comfortable home. Dylan, on the other hand, had to miss even the televised game to get back to the refuge in time to set off for Leeds with Child, Doll and whoever else was going to the meeting.

He'd be interested to see how much money they made from tonight's outing. He'd be interested to see Doll talking to dead folk too. If Dylan were dead, she'd be the last, the very last, person he'd chat with. Her main interests were, or had been, sinking gin and seeing how short she could wear a skirt.

He was engrossed in the game (still no score) when the man on the stool next to his swung round and spilled his beer all over Dylan's jeans.

"I'm terribly sorry. Here—" The man was about to dab the excess from Dylan's legs but clearly thought better of it. "Excuse me. Could we have a cloth over here, please?"

The barmaid eventually threw a grubby grey cloth at them.

"Thanks." Dylan lightly mopped up the beer. Even in this state, his jeans were cleaner than the cloth. "It's nothing to worry about. They'll soon dry."

"Let me get you a pint," the chap said.

"No, really. It's fine. It was your beer, not mine."

"Go on. It'll make me feel better."

"In that case, thanks." He had time for *two* quick pints. Just.

As his companion ordered their drinks, Dylan thought how out of place he looked when compared to the other customers. He was too well spoken and too well dressed for the Jolly Sailor.

"Thank you," Dylan said as a full pint was put on the bar in front of him.

"My pleasure. And I'm sorry. It was clumsy of me."

"Think nothing of it. And thanks again." Dylan was curious about this well-spoken stranger. "I'm new to these parts but I thought I'd see if I could find a decent pub. I can't say this one's my cup of tea. No offence, but it's a bit too—"

"I know what you mean. I've lived in the Clough for years but I'd never been in here until last night." He gave a tired smile. "There are better pubs in town so don't despair. I can recommend the Dog and Fox."

Dylan knew it well. He'd recommend it too. There was a slim chance he'd be recognised there though.

He fished in his pocket and took out one of the refuge's leaflets and a pen. "What was the name again? The Dog and Fox? I'll give it a try."

His new friend didn't comment. He was too busy staring at Dylan's leaflet.

"I'm staying there," Dylan explained.

"Really? My daughter—" His companion took a breath and tried again. "My daughter stayed there too. Just for a few weeks. About a month. Some time ago."

Dylan had hoped that the refuge's leaflet might prompt conversation, but he'd struck gold. "Really?"

"She's a teenager and went there in a state of—well, you know what teenagers are like."

"Only too well."

"I—" His companion's voice cracked. "I have leaflets of my own. Will you—look—" He reached down to a briefcase that was propped against his stool and pulled out a sheaf of papers, all asking for information about the missing Farrah Brindle. "Will you take a look at this? Perhaps you've seen Farrah. My daughter. We have no idea where she is, you see. The police—they're still looking, of course, but they're getting nowhere. Have you seen her?"

So this was Malcolm Brindle. And the poor bastard

was so distraught, he was struggling to force words out.
Damn it, Dylan wished he wasn't in such a rush.

"I haven't seen her," Dylan said, "but I'm sure I've
heard her name mentioned."

"You have?" Brindle's face sparked with brief hope.

"Yes, someone—" Dylan pretended to think. "Ah, it
was the vicar. Bill Owen told me about her disappearance."

"Oh, him. Yes, I suppose he would. I haven't seen
him in a while." Brindle's face dropped before he forced
it into a more composed shape. "Will you take one of
these anyway? Show it to people?"

"Of course." Dylan folded one of the flyers and
tucked it in his jacket pocket. "What made you think I
might have seen her? Are you expecting her to return
to the refuge?"

"No. Not really. I was clutching at straws. Do you
have children?"

He did. Davey Young didn't. "No."

"Then you couldn't understand."

Oh, Dylan could understand. He'd want to die if Luke
or Freya vanished. He didn't know what he'd do—well,
yes he did. He'd do all in his power to find them and
bring them home safely.

"The police think there's a link between the refuge
and Farrah's disappearance, you see. There isn't. She
went off the rails a little, rebelled, stayed there for a
month and came home. If anything, she seemed better after her stay there. More like her old self. It was a
month later when she—she just vanished."

"I'm sorry." Dylan quaffed his beer. "Why do the police think there's a link?"

"Because another girl who was staying there disappeared. That was months ago, and there's no connection. The other girl comes from a bad family—her stepfather drinks in here. I saw him last night. It's his sort of place. The police took him in for questioning when his daughter—stepdaughter—disappeared, so it's obvious they know something that they're not telling us."

So that was why Brindle was paying his second visit to the Jolly Sailor.

A loud groan went up from those watching the match. There was clearly a strong contingent of United supporters in the pub because Arsenal had scored. Dylan watched the replay of the goal, a beautiful curling shot from a free kick. He'd bet Luke had enjoyed that one.

He missed his kids when he was away for a few days so God knows how Brindle was coping.

"Bill Owen thought Farrah had probably taken off for the bright lights—London perhaps. Is that likely?"

"No. The man's a fool." He looked as if he regretted the outburst. "He's well-meaning, but getting involved with the local Girl Guides group doesn't give him any real knowledge of young girls, does it? He's never been married, never had children. No, Farrah didn't take off for London. Even at her worst, and teenagers can be difficult, she knew the difference between right and wrong. She wouldn't let her family worry. She wouldn't have left her dog either."

"Ah yes, he mentioned a dog."

"Something happened to Farrah," Brindle said with certainty. "She didn't go anywhere willingly."

"I'll ask around and show people this." Dylan tapped the flyer in his pocket. "Someone might know something. If I find out anything—"

"Yes, yes." Brindle reached into his briefcase for a

pen and square of paper. "Call me, will you? Anytime. Day or night." He wrote down his name, address, and landline and mobile numbers and handed the paper to Dylan.

"I will." Dylan put the paper in his pocket with the flyer. "I'm David, by the way. David Young." He was also in a hurry. If he didn't find a fast taxi, he'd miss his lift to Leeds with Child and the gang. "I have to go," he said. "But I promise I'll ask around. Will I see you again?"

"If you come here again, I might be here. Otherwise, call me. Anytime. And thank you, I appreciate it. Good to meet you, David."

Chapter Twelve

DYLAN HAD EXPECTED to see around a dozen people interested in hearing what Child had to say about repentance, doing God's will or whatever else he decided to tell them. The reality was row after row of occupied chairs. A very quick calculation suggested that more than a hundred people were crammed into this small hall.

There was no admission fee but people were encouraged to make a donation. Ten- and five-pound notes were weighted down by one- and two-pound coins. The sight of the cash surprised him, but there was probably no more than two or maybe three hundred pounds there. Out of that had to be taken fuel costs and hire of the hall, so Child's profit wouldn't be great.

Dylan sat on a plastic chair near the back of the hall and waited until, finally, Child, dressed all in black with a large crucifix hanging from a chain round his neck and reminding Dylan of Johnny Cash, bounded onto the stage and stood in front of the microphone. He didn't need to say a word. The sight of him silenced the audience. Even Dylan had to admit that he had a certain stage presence.

"Why me?" Child smiled at his audience. "That's the question I ask myself every single day. Why me? Why has God chosen me?" He put his hands deep in the pockets of his black trousers. "I'd like to tell you a little about myself. My father was a bad man and spent most of his life in prison. My mother was a drug addict who rarely knew what day it was. When I was taken into care at the age of four, I thought my life would get better. It didn't. Perhaps the staff did their best, but food was scarce and I was regularly beaten for some misdemeanour or other. I ran away at eleven, was dragged back, ran away again, and at fifteen, when I finally escaped, I lived rough on the streets of London."

Someone in the audience cleared their throat. Other than that, there wasn't a sound. People were hanging on Child's every word as if he were about to give them next week's winning lottery numbers.

"Oh, yes, I know what it's like to be cold and hungry. I've slept on the freezing streets and known nights when an hour's rest in a shop's doorway is a luxury. I know how it feels to have cold, wet feet all day because there's no money for shoes. I know the humiliation of scouring waste bins outside cafés and restaurants for scraps of food."

Bill Owen had said Child possessed the gift of the gab. He was right. The audience couldn't have been more enthralled.

"Looking back, I suppose it was no surprise that I ended up in prison," Child said. "I had to steal food to eat. I did bad things, ladies and gentlemen, and quite rightly, I served my time."

Pah. Child had got away with a lot more than stealing a few scraps of food. Probably murder. If he were convicted for every crime he'd ever committed, he'd take his final breath in jail.

"I've known hard times," Child said, "but, although I didn't realise it at the time, God was my constant companion. He stayed with me. Everyone else gave up on me, but he never did."

He beamed at his attentive audience.

"It was in prison that God spoke to me. One night, an inmate, a cold-blooded killer, a drug addict, came to my cell. Prison warders had found his stash of cocaine and he was convinced, wrongly I must add, that I'd tipped them off. He had a knife in his hand and he was about to kill me." Child paused for dramatic effect. "I was innocent, ladies and gentlemen, but I had a man—a killer—holding a knife to my throat." Another long pause. "What happened next can only be described as a miracle. Just as that knife was about to slice through my throat, this man, this killer, fell to the floor in front of me."

A wave of shocked gasps rippled through the audience.

"I shouted for the guards and tried to revive this man who'd wanted to kill me but, sadly, there was nothing we could do. A massive heart attack had claimed his life."

Utter bollocks. There had been no such deaths during Child's relatively short spells in a cell. Two inmates had committed suicide but there had been no heart attacks.

"It was much later, with the man's death still haunting me, that I questioned the evening's sequence of events. Why did he die at that precise moment? Why not five minutes later, when he'd done the job he'd come to do? What instinct made me try all I could to resuscitate him? I asked myself those questions, and many more, over and over. The answer to all three? God. I have no doubt of that. God didn't want my time to be over. God had plans for me."

Again, Child paused for dramatic effect. Instead of

turning to crime, Child should have gone on the stage. He was a natural actor. He moved across the small stage, meeting and holding the gazes of a select few sitting in the front rows.

"Why me?" he asked them. "Why would he choose a nobody like me?"

He looked to the audience for answers but they had none.

"Perhaps it was because I understood that, for many, life isn't easy. I don't know. All I know is that I was chosen. And I know this because God spoke to me. He told me to go out into the world and help people. There were people on the streets, he said, just as I'd once been, who needed my help. There were many, many others who were strangers to God and who needed to hear his word. Yes, ladies and gentlemen—" Another dramatic pause. "I have been chosen by God."

Spontaneous applause burst out like gunfire. People were on their feet to applaud, cheer and stamp their feet.

Dylan couldn't believe people were so gullible. How could they swallow such crap? After leaving prison for the last time, not having come close to saving anyone's life, Child had worked for the leader of one of the biggest drug rings in the country. Thanks in part to Dylan's spell undercover, most had been arrested. Child, unfortunately, had got lucky.

Child's talk went on and on. The audience loved him. He was more popular than Jesus would have been—although sadly, he hadn't yet demonstrated his ability to turn water into wine.

When he'd milked the audience for all he could, he got to the important stuff.

"Of course, helping those less fortunate doesn't come

cheap. They need food and a bed, for starters. To give them that, to help these poor souls, we need your donations. If you can spare anything, no matter how small, please give it. I know you'll all rest easy in your warm beds knowing you've given a nourishing meal or a blanket to some poor lost sheep." His audience was treated to a beaming smile. "Remember this from Matthew 6:24. 'No one can serve two masters. Either he will hate the one and love the other, or he will be devoted to the one and despise the other. You cannot serve both God and money.' Thank you."

This was turning into an expensive night out for members of the audience but they were past caring. They loved Child. As Owen had said, he'd make a good salesman. Notes and coins were being thrown in bowls that residents of the refuge were carrying from row to row.

Dylan was clearly in the wrong business.

When the noise died down and every spare penny had been lifted from the audience, Child made a cringeworthy speech of thanks and introduced Doll.

Dressed in a long skirt, flowing top and scarves, she looked more like Gypsy Rose Lee than the wife of an East End thug. Actually, she didn't scrub up too badly. Dylan had seen her looking worse, a lot worse.

"I can't tell you how proud I am of my husband and the wonderful work he's doing," she said. "There are so many troubled people in the world, so many wondering if life is worth living, if it's worth spending another cold night on the streets with only more cold nights to look forward to—it's truly heartbreaking. But just as God spoke to Joe, I know the Lord is watching over me too. I often think—" She broke off, as if she were listening to something only she could hear. "Wait. Sorry, I'm hear-ing— Is there a Phil in the audience? Phil?"

Audience members turned in their seats to see if they could spot Phil. No one could. No hands flew into the air. *Bad luck, Doll. Try John.*

"Just a minute. It's not Phil. Perhaps it's—Phyllis? Is Phyllis here tonight?"

Doll had struck lucky. An elderly lady's hand shot up. She looked embarrassed as everyone turned to stare at her.

"I'm Phyllis," she said, her voice little more than a whisper.

"I have a message for you." Doll's eyes were closed. She was shaking her head, swaying from side to side. "Something about—I can't quite make it out—some-thing about waiting for you. Someone's waiting for you."

Jeez! There should be a law against this.

"Is it Vic?" the lady asked.

"Vic, is that you?" Doll continued to sway. "It's faint. I'm sorry. If it was Vic, and I can't be sure, he says he's waiting for you. He says he's never left you and he never will."

"Oh." Phyllis had to reach deep into her coat pocket for a handkerchief. She dabbed at her eyes. "That was Vic. It must have been. Thank you, dear. Thank you so much."

Oh, please.

"I'm getting a message for Mary," Doll said, and three women stuck up hopeful hands.

"That's me," one of them cried.

"This is from Bob. Bobby? Does the name Bob or Bobby mean anything to any of you?"

"Yes, yes," another woman said, and she began sobbing. "Poor old Bob. My dog. We lost him just before Christmas. Is he all right?"

For some reason that escaped Dylan, this had people gazing at Doll in awe. Bob was all the proof they needed that Doll was genuine. If dogs were willing to send messages through Doll, she was truly special. She was the chosen one.

After twenty minutes spent listening to Doll toss out names—common names, he noticed—he wanted to vomit.

"I'm sorry," Doll said, "but I don't have time for more. I'll be back in Leeds on Wednesday though, if anyone wants to see me privately. I do have to charge for one-to-one sessions, to cover the cost of hiring the room. See one of us before you leave, if you need to speak to a loved one."

Doll left the stage looking weary, as if the weight of the dead lay heavy on her shoulders.

Child, however, literally skipped onto the stage. "Thank you all for coming. We'll be here for another hour, so if any of you have problems, come and chat. We'll do our best to help. If any of you haven't made a donation to our refuge or to the work we do with the homeless, please do so." He smiled a winning smile. "We take cash, cheques, blankets, bread—anything at all."

He gave a slight bow and left the stage to thunderous applause.

Dylan expected everyone to make a swift exit, but no, they wanted to speak to Child in person. Better still, they wanted to touch him. They shook his hand, they touched his sleeve and they gazed at him in wonder.

Eventually, people began, very reluctantly, to don coats and scarves and leave the building. It was the younger people who stayed behind. They watched Child, but mostly hung back from him, as if they were too in awe of him to approach. They were teenagers mostly. Impressionable young people. Young people who believed they had all life's answers and yet wanted confirmation from a man like Child. If only they knew.

Dylan got roped into stacking plastic chairs, and when he finished, Child was in deep conversation with a girl— well, she was a teenager doing a great job of pretending to be twenty-five. A short skirt showed off legs that went on forever. Long dark hair fell down her back. Whatever were her parents thinking about, letting her leave the house dressed like that? Sex on legs, and he'd bet she wasn't even sixteen.

She was looking up at Child, talking animatedly one minute and smiling coyly the next.

Dylan sidled over.

"We're a long way away from you," Child was saying, "but, naturally, you'd be made welcome. Everyone is welcome. That's what we're all about. Anyone who has problems can find a safe place with us."

"Thanks." Her broad smile lit up perfectly made-up eyes, the lashes heavy with thick black mascara.

"You don't look as if you have problems," Dylan told her, smiling.

"Like you wouldn't believe," she said. "Do this, do that, you can't do this, you can't do that. I had to get away from him before he killed me. I'm staying with a mate here, but it's only temporary."

"Before who killed you?" Dylan asked.

"The bastard of a boyfriend I had. Honestly, I always end up with the wrong ones. Still, it's good. He doesn't know where I am. I'm okay up here."

"How old are you?"

"Eighteen."

Never in a million years. Sixteen, possibly. Fifteen, more likely.

"And your parents are happy about you being up here?" he asked.

"Are they hell," she scoffed. "My life will be over if and when I ever go home."

"Are they violent too?" Child asked with a concerned frown.

She shrugged, but Dylan could see she was shocked by the suggestion. "Yeah."

This, he'd bet his life, was a girl who'd never had so much as a gentle smack from her parents. She probably needed one too.

She turned to Child and gave him that winning smile. "I'll be in touch, Joe. And thank you so much."

As she skipped off, Dylan saw that she was clutching one of Child's cards in her hand.

"Kids today," Dylan said to Child. "They believe it's their right to have constant happiness handed to them on a plate. How old do you reckon she was? Fifteen? Sixteen?"

"Eh? No. She said she was eighteen. Looked it to me. Anyway, what does it matter? The thing is, Davey, we don't know how bad things are for her. An abusive boyfriend, possibly abusive parents—she's got nowhere to go, has she?"

"Bollocks. She looked like a spoiled little rich kid to me."

Child shook his head as if Dylan were the child. "We can't judge—which is why we have to let people know that there's always a safe place for them."

Oh, yes. Come to the refuge and vanish into thin air...

The spoiled little rich kid hadn't got far. She was currently by the hall's exit, deep in conversation with Child's younger son, Hank.

There was little to choose between Child's sons, Gary and Hank. Gary was twenty-two, two years older than Hank. Both were tall, dark-haired, good-looking men. Dylan hadn't exchanged more than half a dozen words with either of them—they considered themselves far too superior for such things—but he got the impression both could be sullen and arrogant.

He was about to intervene yet again, but the young girl gave Hank a smile that was rewarded with a hand put lightly on her left buttock before she skipped off. She was now clutching two of Child's cards.

Chapter Thirteen

SUNDAY MORNING WAS cold and gloomy. Just like Dylan.

The day started badly, with everyone informed they must attend the prayer meeting. Unfortunately, Dylan wasn't given time to conjure up a sudden heart attack so he followed everyone to the chapel. Some were lucky enough to have a chair. Others, like Dylan, were forced to sit on the floor.

Child had an identity problem. He couldn't decide if he was Johnny Cash or the pope. He read from his Bible—on and on he went—and then suggested they all pray for those less fortunate. People who'd spent a night on the streets, and those who'd lost a loved one, were apparently in need of a prayer.

There was no heating in the chapel and Dylan had reached the stage where he'd kill for a warm bed. Before he climbed into it, he'd luxuriate in shaving off his beard, getting his hair cut, having a hot bath or shower and generally feeling *normal*. Or perhaps he should be grateful for the beard. It had to offer a little extra warmth.

Everyone else looked happy enough, as if there was nothing like a good prayer session before breakfast. Correction. Neither Gary nor Hank looked particularly pleased with life. They looked bored rigid, and Dylan could sympathise.

Child read Psalm 23. Even Dylan could have stumbled his way through "The Lord is my shepherd" without needing it written down.

"This afternoon," Child said, "we'll all be going into the town. We'll set up the soup stall and give out leaflets. Everyone got that?"

It was an order, not a request, and Dylan would need to think up a good excuse. Perhaps it was commendable, but he'd bet those sleeping rough in Dawson's Clough would prefer crack cocaine to soup and blankets.

After droning their way through "Rock of Ages," a hymn Dylan always associated with funerals, they had another prayer. This was one of thanks to the Lord for bringing them all safely to this place.

Finally, just as Dylan had lost the will to live, it was time for breakfast.

Unfortunately, he was in the third sitting, so he still had time to kill. Sunday, it seemed, was a day of rest. Apart from cooking duties, no one was expected to do chores. Dylan was on the washing-up rota and he'd be grateful to get his hands in hot soapy water. Always assuming they had hot water in this place...

His stomach was grumbling at the thought of sizzling sausages, bacon and fried eggs. His head was telling his stomach to wise up.

He was deciding how to pass the time when the sound of a car coming along the drive had him turning around. It was the new Bentley Continental V8. Five-hundred-brake horsepower. Eight-speed gearbox. About a hundred and thirty thousand pounds' worth of car. Dylan let out a whistle as its tyres crunched the gravel and its suspension bounced over the potholes. The driver must surely be lost.

Curious, Dylan wandered over to the front of the

house and watched as the driver leaned across to the passenger seat, picked up a large brown envelope and put it in the inside pocket of a black overcoat before climbing out of the car.

"Good morning," the chap said.

"Morning." Dylan nodded at his car. "You have to be lost, right?"

A chuckle. "Not at all. I'm Gordon Riley, a friend of Joe's."

"Oh, right. Well, me too. I'm David, by the way."

"Good to meet you, David. Any friend of Joe's is all right in my book."

Riley headed to the steps but, before he reached the door, Child pulled it open. "Gordon, you're up bright and early."

"Yes, I have a lot on today. How are you, Joe?"

"I'm good. You've met Davey, have you? Me and him go way back, don't we, Davey?"

Dylan joined them. "Way back," he agreed.

"Not quite as far back as me and you though, eh, Gordon?" Turning to Dylan, Child explained, "We were in the same bloody care home for years. Hell, wasn't it, Gordon?"

"It was."

"Gordon did all right for himself though," Child went on. "He was the nerd. Always had his head stuck in a book. I used to call him Einstein, he was that bloody clever, and I was right."

"Joe!" Riley's smile looked a little uncomfortable. "Joe used to fight my battles for me, David. The clever kids, the nerds like me, were bullied. As I was short and wore glasses, I was a natural target. Joe looked after me and we became good friends. Still, it's a long time ago and the bullies have all moved on."

"Come on then," Child said. "Let's get in the warm. See you later, Davey boy. Don't miss your breakfast, will you?"

"I won't." Dylan watched the two men disappear inside.

He could imagine Child being happy enough to fight another boy's battles. He'd always enjoyed a good fight and if he couldn't find one, he'd start one. It was a brave man who picked a fight with Child.

Child had also loved to be the leader. If a group of people were discussing anything, Child had to take charge.

Half an hour later, Dylan was sitting down to breakfast. His plate held sausage, scrambled egg, fried tomatoes and two rashers of bacon. There was also as much toast as he could eat. He could hardly believe his good fortune.

He felt better after he'd eaten, warmer too, and was soon joining Adrian at the sink to do the washing up.

"It always looks endless," Adrian said, "but we'll soon get through it. I find it quite therapeutic."

Dylan would tell that to Bev the next time their dishwasher threw a wobbly. *I'd wash the dishes, darling, but I'm sure you'll find it therapeutic...*

"Did you see that car?" Dylan plunged his hands into hot soapy water. "A chap just arrived in a Bentley, the new Bentley. Wow. It costs around a hundred and thirty grand."

Adrian nodded. "Gordon Riley. I'm not into cars but I know that's a nice one. He's only had it a month or so. He calls here quite often."

"Yeah? Why's that?"

"Him and Joe were at school together—or something like that. Gordon has his own business and has done well for himself. He's made a couple of generous donations to the refuge."

"Good for him. How generous?"

"Oh, I don't know the figures, but I do know Joe was very grateful."

"I wish I could afford a car like that," Dylan said. "Still, not much hope of that. I'd do the lottery but I can't afford the ticket. What business is he in, this Riley chap?"

"Computer games. You know how these kids play shooting the baddies on their Xbox consoles and suchlike? His company does the games. I don't know much about them, but they're popular in the U.K. and America."

"Where does he live? Locally?"

"No. He has a place in London, but he flies a lot. He has business meetings in New York and Germany that I know of."

"I always knew I should have done better at school," Dylan said with a rueful smile. "What I'd give for a car like that."

"All cars are expensive to run these days," Adrian said.

"True. I had an old banger but that had to go. The price of fuel is bloody ridiculous."

"And then you've tax and insurance on top of that."

"Yeah." A plate slipped out of Dylan's hands but he managed to catch it before any damage was done.

"Steady on," Adrian said. "We don't want any breakages."

"It's okay. I got it." He took more care as he cleaned the next plate. This job *did* seem endless. "We've got free time now, haven't we?"

"Yes. Why?"

"I fancy a walk into the town. I haven't seen anything of it so I thought I'd go and have a look round. I can meet up with everyone when we set up the soup stall, can't I?"

"Yes, of course. So long as you're on Baker Street at three o'clock, you'll be fine. I'll see you there. You can come with me and take the leaflets round the town."

"Okay, thanks. I'll set off when we've finished here and I'll see you at three."

They ploughed on with plate after plate, mug after mug, until only the cutlery remained. Dylan refilled the sink with clean hot water, threw the cutlery in and began washing knives, forks and spoons.

Finally, it was finished.

Dylan dried his hands. "See you later, Adrian."

"Don't be late!"

Dylan stepped outside in time to see the Bentley disappearing into the distance. Damn, he would have liked another word with Riley. The brake lights flashed red briefly and then the car was lost from view.

He walked round the back of the house and saw the gardener, Kennedy, hard at work. The ground must be waterlogged but he was making easy work of digging a portion of the vegetable patch.

Dylan wandered over. "Good morning."

Kennedy shoved the spade in the ground and turned over the soil.

"You're doing a great job," Dylan said.

Kennedy grunted in response.

"You live in town, do you?"

There wasn't so much as a grunt this time.

"One thing I like about this place," Dylan said, "is the breakfasts. I've just had bacon and sausage. It was great. You should move in."

For a brief second their gazes locked. Kennedy's expression seemed to say "When hell freezes over," but as he couldn't or didn't want to speak, it was impossible to know.

Kennedy continued to turn over the soil with his spade. The sodden ground had to be heavy but he wasn't even out of breath. He didn't look strong, quite the reverse in fact, but he was clearly fit.

The spade suddenly paused. Dylan followed Kennedy's gaze and saw that Gary Child was pacing outside the old barn with his phone held to his ear. It was impossible to hear what he was saying, but he looked angry.

"You can tell he's Joe's son, can't you?" Dylan said.

Again, Kennedy looked at him. And again, his expression was impossible to fathom.

Dylan was about to give up with Kennedy. Or more accurate, he was about to wander off and see if he could hear what Gary was saying. But Child rounded the corner and headed straight for them.

"Ah, you've met Kennedy then, Davey," he said.

"Well, we haven't had much of a chat."

Child snorted with laughter. "No, you don't do chit-chat, do you, Kennedy?" He spoke loudly, as if Kennedy was deaf. Perhaps he was. Either way, Child got no response from the man.

"Here—" Child held out a small box for Kennedy. "Fresh eggs."

Kennedy put down his spade and took the box. He opened it, inspected the eggs, and grunted his thanks.

Child reached in his pocket and pulled out a crisp ten-pound note. "Take this, too. You've worked hard and we're all grateful."

Kennedy looked at the note for long moments before finally taking it from Child and putting it in the pocket of his trousers. Again, he grunted his thanks. At least, Dylan presumed it was thanks. How could you tell?

Child shook his head in amused despair. "Help me carry the leaflets down to the garage, will you, Davey?"

"Of course."

As they walked to the stable block, Dylan wondered if he was losing his grip. He'd always considered himself a good judge of character, but Child was as big a mystery to him as Kennedy. The Child he'd grown to know and despise wouldn't put so much as a penny in a charity box. A tenner and a box of eggs was nothing, but he'd had no need to give anything to the gardener…

"What's wrong with Kennedy?" he asked.

"You tell me. I'm not sure if the poor sod is deaf and dumb or simply retarded. He turned up here out of the blue one day with a scrawled note asking if I'd allow him to work in the gardens. No payment necessary, the note said, but he wanted a garden to work on. It was signed Kennedy. No one knows if that's his first name or last."

"Where does he live?"

"In the town, I imagine. He always walks home in that direction. And don't knock him. He's a bloody miracle worker in the garden. You wouldn't believe how untidy the vegetable plot was before he started. As crazy as he is, I'd hate to lose him."

Child pulled open the stable door. Inside were several stacked cardboard boxes.

"We need to load up the Transit with these," Child said. "We'll be giving them out in town later today."

"Okay."

A leaflet was taped to one of the boxes and Dylan had a quick read. It described the work they did—helping the homeless—and assured everyone there was a bed at the refuge for them. A tear-out direct-debit form was conveniently provided so that people could help Child carry out his good work by making regular donations.

They picked up a couple of boxes each and carried them toward the garage.

"That's some car your mate's got," Dylan said. "I always saw myself driving around in a bloody great Bentley. Lucky sod."

"Money's not everything, Davey boy."

"It's not? Bloody hell, you've changed your tune since we worked together."

"I've seen the light."

"Hey, and what about that bloke who tried to knife you while you were inside? I never heard about that. Who was that?"

Child grinned. "That was a little white lie, Davey." More serious, he added, "I want to raise millions for the homeless—not only those in Dawson's Clough but in the whole country. We need donations, so I have to convince people, don't I?"

"Con folk, you mean?"

"No—just make them give more generously."

"Ah."

"There shouldn't be anyone sleeping on the streets in this day and age, should there?" Child spoke as if he cared. "The government keeps letting in all these bloody immigrants but that's no good, is it? How can we take care of them when we can't even take care of our own?"

Dylan was reminded of a night in London when Child, with half a bottle of whisky inside him, had picked a fight with a young Somalian. "I've done nothing," the young man had cried as Child had kicked him.

"You've come to my country, you fucking black bastard, that's what you've done." Child had once described himself as "racist and proud of it."

Seeing him handing over eggs and cash to Kennedy, it was easy for Dylan to forget how much he hated him.

"Dunno," Dylan answered his question. "By the way, I thought I'd walk into town now. I haven't had chance to see the place and I'd like a look round. I've arranged to meet up with Adrian at three. That's okay, isn't it?"

"Yes, but don't be late. There's a lot of work to be done today."

"I won't."

When they'd finished stacking boxes in the large white Transit van, ready to be showered on the town, Dylan made his excuses and escaped. He didn't go far. He walked down to the end of the lane as if he were heading for the town, then doubled back on himself. He kept close to the side of a high wall, where the trees hid him from view, until he was at the back of the refuge. His boots were caked in mud, and a black cloud threatened a downpour that would soak him to the skin.

He waited.

And waited.

He'd hoped Child and his band of followers would set off early—they had a soup kitchen to set up, after all—but it was almost two o'clock when the van and the battered Ford minibus carried them down the lane. From his vantage point, Dylan tried to count heads. He wouldn't put money on it, but he thought he was the only one on the premises. Except for Kennedy, that is. The bloke had finished one patch of digging and started on another.

Dylan gave the vehicles five minutes, in case they returned for something forgotten, and then walked up to the house. The front door was locked and bolted, as he'd expected, but the lock on the back door only took him five minutes to open. Not bad going, that. With practice, he'd be great at breaking and entering.

He wandered around the building to make sure he really was alone.

Satisfied he had the place to himself, he went straight to the bare drab room that was Child's office. The Doll he'd known wouldn't have lasted ten minutes in this building. It was too drab, too uncomfortable and far too cold. They'd both need a good pot of gold at the end of this particular rainbow.

He pulled open drawers but found nothing of interest. There were no wall safes hidden behind pictures. The books were exactly that—books. He searched every inch of the room. Nothing.

Rain lashed at the window and he was thankful he wasn't doling out soup and leaflets in town.

He was about to leave Child's office when a floorboard creaked beneath his foot. He dragged the table aside and lifted the corner of the worn grubby carpet. Eureka. A length of floorboard, about a foot long, was definitely loose. He lifted it, put his arm down into the void and moved it around until his fingers touched something. He grabbed the package and pulled it through the gap.

Unless he was very much mistaken, this was the same brown envelope he'd seen Riley put in his coat pocket.

The envelope was sealed and it was difficult to tell what was inside—a brick of heroin maybe.

Still listening for sounds of anyone who might have returned to the building, he took the package to the kitchen and put an inch of water in a pan to boil on the stove. Steaming open envelopes, especially the self-seal varieties like this one, was never as easy as it looked on TV, but it was his only option.

He held the envelope over the steam. It soon went damp and soggy, and the flap started to lift. With great care, he eased it open.

Nice.

Without disturbing the package, it was impossible to say how much money was inside. He could see no smaller denomination notes than fifty pounds. At a rough guess, he'd say the envelope contained around one hundred thousand pounds.

Very nice.

He resealed the envelope and, confident it was as good as new, threw away the hot water, dried the pan and returned it to its hook. He returned his find to Child's office.

With the cash back in its hiding place, he pulled the rug into place, dragged the table across and, satisfied that the room was as he'd found it, closed the door behind him.

He went upstairs, where there were six bedrooms. One might have expected such a god-fearing family to adorn the walls with crucifixes, but there were no religious items on show.

He checked his watch. He'd be late meeting up with

the others in town but, hopefully, not too late. So long as he could get a cab…

The largest of the bedrooms had to belong to Child and the lovely Doll. A dressing table was covered in creams and lotions, lipsticks, perfume bottles, hairbrush and every other thing required to make Doll look more beautiful—or less old.

He searched cupboards, wardrobes and drawers. He went through the pockets of clothes hanging in the wardrobes. He looked for dodgy floorboards. He moved various awful paintings aside to check for hidden wall safes. The ceiling had what looked to be original beams—too old and too substantial to be hiding anything.

He found nothing incriminating in that room or any of the others. There were enough condoms in Hank's room to keep a super stud going for ten years, but that wasn't a crime.

Still confident he was alone in the building, he changed the sim card in his phone and called Detective Inspector Rhodes.

"How's it going?"

"Okay," Dylan said. "I've found a load of cash—probably a hundred grand, it's difficult to say—and I have a feeling it was given to Child by an old mate of his, a businessman, one Gordon Riley."

"Riley? Yes, he's one of the refuge's benefactors. A hundred grand, you say?"

"Difficult to tell, but yes, probably."

"Riley's aboveboard. He's as rich as Croesus, thanks to some new computer game his company has unleashed on the world. He donated fifty grand this time last year. Child had a big piece put in the local paper about it. It's probably another donation."

"Hidden under the floorboards?"

"If Child has no safe on the property, and we couldn't find one, it's probably the best place until he can bank it. You can't trust anyone these days."

Dylan wasn't convinced. "Okay, that's it. I thought you might be interested."

"We are. Good work."

Dylan ended the call and hit the quick-dial button for his ex-boss, Frank.

"How are you getting on with that murdering bastard Child?" Frank asked.

"Okay, and I'll have to make this quick. There's a vicar, Bill Owen, who's recognised me. He says he won't tell Child, but I don't know if I can trust him. Do you know him?"

"The name rings a bell, but that's about all."

"Find out what you can about him, will you, Frank?"

"Will do. I think he's legit. He's been in the town quite a while. At least, I think he has. I'll check him out."

"He claims to have been here for fourteen years. Also, I've just called Rhodes and told him about a stash of cash I've found—about a hundred grand. I think a chap called Gordon Riley gave it to Child. Rhodes says the bloke's clean—rich from his computer-games company—but find out what you can about him, will you, mate?"

"Will do," Frank said. "Anything else?"

"That's it. And I need to get out of here so I can serve soup or dish out leaflets in the town. I'll call you when I can."

"Take care, Dylan."

"Will do."

Dylan changed sim cards in his phone, let himself out of the house and locked the door behind him.

He was about to head off down the lane when he heard a voice. He kept in tight against the house wall and moved silently and slowly to the side elevation.

"It looks like you're eating for six or more," the male voice said. "Here you go. Better than chasing mice, yes?"

Puzzled, Dylan risked a look round the corner of the house. There, sitting on the rickety bench under the apple tree, was Kennedy. He was feeding a heavily pregnant cat from an open pouch.

"Don't eat it all at once," Kennedy said.

So much for being deaf and dumb...

Chapter Fourteen

BEV WAS SHAKING so much, it took her three attempts to fasten the buttons on her shirt. Then she realised the buttons weren't in the corresponding holes and had to start over. Finally she was dressed, and she emerged from behind the screen to see Dr. Singh tapping away at her computer.

The doctor looked up and smiled at her. "Take a seat, Beverley."

Bev sat by the desk but couldn't see what was being typed into her file because the screen was angled away from her. She took a few deep breaths to recover from what had been a shockingly thorough internal examination.

A wall poster designed for health professionals showed the correct way to wash hands. *God help us all.* A box in the corner of the room was crammed with toys, presumably for toddlers needing vaccinations. White walls, a small wash basin, green couch with matching green curtains, doctor's desk and chair, two other chairs, shelves stacked with syringes, cotton wool and disposable gloves—the room gave Bev the creeps.

"Right," Dr. Singh said, "that all seemed normal, but we'll book you in for a scan to check everything out. While we're waiting for that, we'll get a CA-125 blood test done."

"A what?"

"Sorry." The doctor smiled in a way designed to re-assure. It didn't work. "CA-125 is a protein found in the blood. It's not a completely reliable test for ovarian can-cer because other things can produce raised levels, but we can hopefully rule it out. And don't start worrying that I think you have ovarian cancer, because I don't. I simply want to rule it out."

"I see." She didn't. She'd only heard one word. The *cancer* word ricocheted around her head.

"We'll book you in for an abdominal ultrasound and a transvaginal ultrasound, but your appointment could be four weeks away, so we'll do the blood test while we wait. Are you happy with that?"

Ecstatic.

"Fine," Bev said. "Thank you."

"I'll refer you for the scan but you'll need to make an appointment for your blood test on the way out. The next available one will be on Wednesday or Thursday."

"Thank you," Bev said again.

"Meanwhile," Dr. Singh said, "try not to worry. I couldn't find anything untoward. The pain will prob-ably go away of its own accord."

With an encouraging smile from Dr. Singh, Bev grabbed her bag and left the surgery.

She stood, third in line, at the reception desk. She'd never heard of a transvaginal ultrasound, but it didn't sound like the most fun a woman could have.

The receptionist looked up. "Yes?"

"I need to make an appointment for a blood test."

"Is it a starvation one?"

"I have no idea. It's a—" she'd forgotten already, "—CA something or other."

"CA-125. No, you don't need to starve for that. Wednesday afternoon at five o'clock?"

"Yes, that's fine, thanks."

Clutching the small printed appointment card in her hand, Bev strode out of the building and along the street to the nearest coffee bar. She ducked inside and dropped down onto a chair at a table by the window. She was still shaking when the waitress appeared by her side.

"A cappuccino, please."

"With chocolate?"

And crystal meth. "Please."

Dylan's mum was at the house looking after Luke and Freya, so there was no need to rush. She simply wanted a few minutes to herself. Just enough time to calm herself and get her thoughts into a logical order. The doctor had said the pain might go away of its own accord. She'd said everything had felt normal during that internal examination—and God, she'd been thorough. She'd said she didn't think it was ovarian cancer, she was merely ruling out all the nasty stuff. That was good, yes?

Yes. That was good.

"There you go, love. Enjoy." The waitress put a large cappuccino in front of her.

"Thanks."

As Bev spooned the chocolate and froth from her coffee, she wondered why she was worrying about this so much. She'd become a worrier lately, ever since Freya was born. Luke had grown into a tall, sturdy teenager and she hadn't imagined that after trying for a baby for years and finally admitting defeat, he'd ever have a brother or sister. But Freya had come along—an unexpected but wonderful gift—and Bev had been worrying ever since.

Even before this pain in her abdomen developed, she'd wondered what would happen if she became too ill to look after her daughter. Dylan thought she was mad, but he humoured her. He said he and his mother would cope between them. "And how ill would you have to be not to be able to play with her? You're unlikely to be bed-ridden for months on end…"

He was right, of course. She didn't want to be ill though, not even for a couple of days. She wanted to be fit, and healthy enough to run and play with her daughter.

Worrying herself sick because she had a vague abdominal pain wasn't an option. It was self-indulgent crap. It was ridiculous.

She'd push it from her mind, not mention it to anyone, and hope it went away.

If her mate Lucy had been in this state, she'd laugh at her and tell her to pull herself together. She had to look at the whole thing logically. There was no point inventing horrors to worry about.

With that decided, she finished her coffee, returned to the health centre for her car and drove home.

Dylan's mum was sitting at the kitchen table, reading a glossy magazine. Bev had to stifle a grin as she spotted the iPod and earphones. She'd bet her life that Vicky was listening to her hero, Bob Dylan. Vicky had some strange ways—the hippie clothes and lifestyle, the marijuana smoking—but Bev couldn't have wished for a better mother-in-law. She wasn't protective of her son as some women were. She was kind and always ready to lend a hand. Her sense of humour never faltered. She was crazy, but Bev adored her.

"Hello, love." The earphones were yanked out. "How did it go?"

"Fine," Bev said. "She's sending me for a scan and a blood test to make sure, but she didn't think it was anything to worry about. Is Freya asleep?"

Vicky nodded. "About five minutes ago. Luke—"

"—is watching TV. Yes, I guessed." Why he had to have the volume so high, Bev had no idea. There was nothing wrong with his hearing. Although there would be if he kept this up.

She went into the lounge. "Turn it down, Luke. It'll send you deaf."

He grinned up at her. "Sorry? Did you say something?"

"Ha-ha. Very funny." He was like his dad in every way imaginable.

The volume was turned down and she went back to the kitchen. "Fancy a glass of wine?"

"No, thanks, love. It would be wasted on me."

Bev opened a bottle and filled a glass right to the top. She deserved this.

"Any news from Dylan?" Vicky asked.

"No." Bev hated it when he worked away and she especially hated knowing he was working undercover. When he was kicked off the police force, she'd believed that was one nightmare they wouldn't have to go through. "He'll ring when he can, but I don't know when that'll be. I'm sure he's all right though."

"Of course he is. He's big enough and ugly enough to take of himself," Vicky said in a matter-of-fact way.

"True."

Vicky filled a cup with boiling water, showed it a

teabag and added some milk. "I'll drink this and get out of your way."

Bev smiled at that. "You're never in the way."

"Thank you. But I have a lot to do, so I'll go anyway."

They talked of how well Luke was doing at school and how he loved his football, and of how utterly adorable Freya was. They spoke of the weather and dreamed of sitting outside with long cold drinks when summer came.

"If it ever comes," Vicky said. "Summers in England are rare these days. What did we have last year? Those two weeks in March?"

"I remember it well. I put away all my warm clothes and spent the rest of our so-called summer freezing."

"That'll teach you." Vicky rinsed her cup under the tap and put it on the drainer. "Right, I'm off, love. Give me a shout if you need anything."

"I will, and thanks. I appreciate it."

Bev poured herself another glass of wine. She'd relax if it killed her.

Surprisingly, it was late that evening, when Luke and Freya were both asleep in their beds, before she switched on her computer. She'd have a quick look at CA-125 blood tests, transvaginal ultrasound scans and ovarian cancer, and then she'd settle down and watch a good film. She would not under any circumstances spend hours on health forums...

Chapter Fifteen

"You're going into town?" Dylan said. "That's great. Can I beg a lift in your taxi?"

Hank and Gary Child looked at each other, both waiting for the other to dream up the excuse of the decade. It clearly defeated them both. Their father was listening in, so that probably didn't help.

"Sure," Hank said with obvious reluctance.

"Which part of town are you making for?" Dylan asked.

"We're going to Tempo," Gary said. "No offence, Dave, but I don't think they'll let you in. The last I heard, you were threatening coppers with broken bottles."

"Yeah, well. I ought to show my face and apologise. A lift to Tempo would be great. And don't worry, I won't cramp your style." He winked at them. "I'll apologise for my less-than-admirable behaviour, enjoy a couple of their cheap drinks and make my own way back. The walk won't seem so far with a couple of whiskies inside me."

Hank shrugged. "Suit yourself."

The moon was throwing its light on the brooding hills when the taxi pulled up outside the refuge. The sky, dotted with stars, promised another cold night.

Gary jumped in the front seat and Hank and Dylan sat in the back.

"Tempo," Gary said.

The driver was as quiet and disinclined to chat as the Child boys.

"I can't believe you two are grown men," Dylan said. "When I used to work with your dad, he was always talking about you. Back then though, you were just teenagers."

"That's a long time ago," Hank said.

"Yes, a lot of water's passed under the bridge since then. Mind you, I was even more surprised to find him in a setup like this. He'd be the last person I'd have expected to find God and start doing charity work."

"Yeah, well."

"What about you two? Do you like living up north? Are you enjoying life at the refuge?"

"Would you?" Hank asked. "I'm out of here when I can get some cash together. I'll be heading back to civilisation."

"London?"

"Yeah."

"So all this God stuff isn't for you either?"

"It's not that, it's just that it's so dead up here. There's nothing to do. I'm heading back to London as soon as I can. I'll get a decent job down there, somewhere to live—"

"I don't blame you. It would be too quiet for me too. I can't understand how your dad copes with it, or why he'd want to. When I first found out he was living here, I thought the heat must have been on in London. That was the only reason I could think of why someone would be here. When he said it was through choice, well, it beats me."

"There's money in it," Hank said with a smirk.

"There's talk of him doing a TV show. There'll be a lot of money in that."

"TV? Great. Doing what? This Bible-bashing stuff?"

"Yeah. Folk lap it up."

Maybe they did, but there had to be more money in drug dealing or contract killing, and Child had always been a greedy bastard.

"Not me," Dylan said. "I shall be glad to get away. Not from your dad, we've always got on great, but from the north, the cold and all the God stuff. I've done four days now—that's enough."

More than enough.

The taxi slowed to a stop outside Tempo. The club's neon sign flashed blue-and-red stripes on Gary's face as he paid the driver.

"Thanks," Dylan said. "I appreciate it. See you both tomorrow. Have a good night."

"You, too," Hank called over his shoulder as he and Gary strode into the club.

Dylan followed at a more leisurely pace. Gary was right. There was a fair chance he wouldn't be allowed entry.

He gave the two bouncers a confident smile and walked straight past them into the building.

Four uniformed men and a long-haired young girl were serving drinks. There was no sign of the barman who'd been on duty when he was "arrested." He made the most of it and ordered a drink from the young girl.

He hated clubs like Tempo. The drinks might be cheap but the noise levels made it difficult to strike up a conversation with anyone. He'd have a quick pint and then try the pubs and speak to a few locals. As yet, he had no idea why Child had suddenly turned to God, why that bundle of cash had been sitting beneath the floor-boards, if Bill Owen was genuine or involved with Child, how long he had until his cover was blown, why Kennedy refused to speak to anyone but a cat...

He sat at the bar, trying to block out the raucous music and enjoy his drink, and watched Hank and Gary Child. They were deep in conversation at a table on a raised platform. Perhaps they'd chosen the seats to give them the best view of the dancers when they appeared. Gary was talking earnestly, but Hank was continually watching the door to see who came into the club.

Half an hour later, a chap walked in and, instead of going to the bar to order a drink, went straight to the toilets. Hank immediately followed him.

Gary was watching so Dylan feigned ignorance for a couple of minutes and then strolled toward those toilets. The stranger came out and collided head-on with Dylan.

"Watch where you're going, mate."

Dylan flinched, not at the aggression oozing from this big man, but from the garlic on his breath. He was well over six feet tall, broad too, and had several body piercings. A chain was tattooed around his neck.

"Sorry—didn't realise someone was coming out." Dylan, confident he'd recognise the bloke again—who wouldn't?—pushed open the door marked Gents.

He was in time to see Hank emerge from one of the cubicles.

"You buying or selling, Hank?"

"Eh? I don't know what you're talking about."

Dylan pointed to his nose. "I'm not daft enough to believe you've been snorting talcum powder."

Scowling, Hank checked in a mirror above one of the washbasins and rubbed away the cocaine with his finger.

"So?" Dylan asked. "You buying or selling? I could do with something. I've been clean for a month, but—"

"Then stay bloody clean. I bought, okay? I'm not selling and I don't have any to spare." Furious, Hank pushed past him and left the room.

Dylan lingered for a minute and then walked back to his seat at the bar.

If Child was involved in drugs, his sons wouldn't be buying cocaine from Tattoo Man. Or perhaps Child didn't know his son was using.

Dylan felt like bashing his head against the bar in frustration. What the hell was Child up to? No way could he or his refuge be as squeaky-clean as he was making out. No way. Police believed they'd searched every inch of that place but they must have missed something.

There was the bundle of cash hidden beneath the floorboards. Dylan had to cling to that as evidence Child was involved in some scam or other. Gordon Riley had to be involved too. Unless Dylan was mistaken, he was the one who'd handed over that cash.

He glanced across to the table where Hank and Gary had been sitting. It was empty.

"Excuse me—" He attracted one of the barmen's attention. "I came in with a couple of young men. They were sitting over there. You didn't see where they went, did you?"

"The Childs, you mean?"

"Yes, that's them."

"I didn't see them leave, but I assume they've gone to Manchester." The barman tested the cleanliness of a glass he was polishing. "They often call here for a quick drink and then get a cab to Manchester. Were you supposed to be going with them?"

"No, nothing like that. I just remembered something I needed to tell them. Oh, well, it doesn't matter. Manchester you say? What takes them there?"

"No idea." The barman put the glass on the shelf and picked up another to polish. "Better nightlife, more people, more fun—I'd rather be in Manchester than the Clough, wouldn't you?"

Smiling, Dylan nodded. "Yes, I suppose so."

Manchester was a vibrant city, true, but it was twenty miles down the road and that was expensive and time-consuming in a cab. There had to be something more than the nightlife to attract Gary and Hank to the city on a Monday night.

"Do you know the Childs well?" Dylan asked. "I know their dad from way back, and I'm still trying to accept that Gary and Hank are grown men."

"I wouldn't say I know them. They call in quite often, sometimes stay to chat up the girls and sometimes go into Manchester. Ah, yes, I know their father. He sometimes calls in here. He runs that place—hippie commune out of town."

"That's him, but I don't think he'd like you calling it that. It's a safe refuge for the town's waifs and strays. I'm staying there at the moment."

"Yeah? I've heard all sorts of rumours about the place—witchcraft, black magic, cannabis farming—you name it, I've heard it."

"That's crazy. We're just harmless people who want to help those in need. Do unto others as you would have done unto yourself, that's what I always say." Or something like that. "Where have the rumours come from?"

"Everywhere. But he's a southerner, a bit like you, if I'm not mistaken, and the locals get suspicious. Christ,

I'm from the Midlands and you'd think I'd landed from
Mars. The locals are a funny lot. They're not comfortable away from their own sort and will invent all sorts
of crazy stories about newcomers to the area."

"There's nothing to fear from anyone at the refuge."
Apart from the odd missing tongue.

Damn. He was about to be recognised. The barman
who'd helped the police cuff him must have been on a
break. He was heading straight for Dylan's side of the
bar.

Dylan drained his glass and went in search of some
nightlife of his own. He walked past the Jolly Sailor,
then doubled back and ducked inside. It wasn't his sort
of pub, not by any stretch of the imagination, but Malcolm Brindle had been drinking there on Saturday and
John Taylor was a regular.

Like a lot of pubs, the Jolly Sailor was almost empty.
Monday nights were low on trade because people had
spent their money over the weekend. If they had a few
quid left, they'd spend it at Tempo on cheap drinks.

The barmaid was a big, dark-haired woman who
clearly didn't believe in warm smiles to welcome her
customers. In fact, she looked as if she resented everyone
who walked through the door. She banged his pint on the
bar, managing to slop some across the dirty mahogany.

"It's quiet tonight." He might as well attempt conversation with her. "I was in here on Saturday and it was
packed then."

"It's Monday," she said as if he were a moron.

"Well, yes. Even so—"

"If you want company, you need to drink at Tempo.
That place will be heaving."

"I've just come from there. I fancied a change of scene."

Bored, she picked up a copy of the *Sun* and turned to the TV pages.

"When I was in here on Saturday—" no one could accuse him of lacking perseverance, "—I was talking to a chap whose daughter had vanished. How awful must that be? Can't think of his name—"

"Johnny? Johnny Taylor?"

"No. No, I'm sure it wasn't that. It was—his daughter was called Farrah, I do remember that."

"Brindle?"

"Yeah, that's it. Malcolm Brindle."

She closed the newspaper, more eager to talk now. "I've never seen him in here. Thinking about it though, I probably wouldn't recognise him. I've seen his picture in the paper, but that's all."

"So who's this Taylor chap you mentioned?" Dylan supped his pint. "Oh, wait—I heard something about two girls disappearing. Is he the father of the other one?"

"Stepfather."

"Ah. It's a strange lot of it, isn't it? Two girls vanishing. What do they reckon? The police, I mean? They must have some idea what's happened to them, mustn't they?"

"Bloody hopeless, them lot. But—" she leaned in close, "—the last I heard, they reckoned there was something going on up at the funny farm. Well, we all know that. You wouldn't catch me within a mile of that place. God knows what they get up to."

"The funny farm?" Dylan felt obliged to ask, but he knew what the answer would be.

"Yeah, there's some sort of cult up on the Burnley Road. Moorside Refuge, it's called."

"A cult?" He feigned shock. "What happens? What do they do?"

"It's rumours. Apparently, they all dance naked and make a sacrifice—"

Dylan managed to stop himself laughing. But really—

"That's what I heard," she said. "Some say they drink blood from chickens. Others—" she dropped her deep voice to a whisper, "—others reckon they make human sacrifices. You don't need a degree to know where those two girls have gone, do you?"

Before Dylan could comment on that, another customer arrived and she turned to serve him. "The usual, Dennis?"

The chap nodded and hunted in his pocket, finally producing a crumpled five-pound note.

"We were talking about the bleedin' funny farm," the barmaid told him. "What d'you reckon's going on up there?"

"Who knows? Money laundering, I shouldn't wonder. Or drugs. They've probably got a cannabis farm—something like that."

"If you ask me," she said, "they're into black magic. I was just saying, there were rumours of human sacrifices. Two girls disappear from there—"

"One," Dennis said. "The other was living at home."

"But she probably went back. I expect she made friends there, went back to see them and ended up with a knife through her heart. It wouldn't surprise me, not one little bit. There's a strange bloke goes up there quite often too. He's a right bloody oddball—doesn't speak, just stares at you. I was driving back over the hill at about ten o'clock the other night when I saw him walking toward the town with a torch. What the hell was he doing out and about at that time of night? Some claim he works in the gardens but no one in their right mind does gardening in the pitch bloody dark, do they?"

"They don't," Dylan said.

"They're all bloody oddballs up there," the barmaid said. "There's something sinful going on up there, you mark my words." Scowling, she went away to serve someone else.

Dennis sidled closer to Dylan. "The chap who runs it has come up from London." Dennis clearly wasn't impressed by southerners. "You'd think he could do his Good Samaritan thing down there, wouldn't you?"

"I suppose he wanted somewhere more rural. Besides, a place big enough to house the local strays would cost millions down in the city."

"Aye."

"And perhaps he feels there are plenty of people looking after the homeless in London, whereas up here—"

He broke off to see what had attracted his companion's attention, turned around and saw none other than Doll Child walk in. This evening, she looked nothing like Gypsy Rose Lee. Her skirt was little longer than a belt, a black see-through blouse left nothing to the imagination, feet were perched on six-inch heels, and her makeup was immaculate, if heavy.

She saw Dylan, frowned a mixture of surprise and annoyance and, smiling broadly, rushed forward. "Well, Davey, fancy seeing you here. Are you buying?"

Damn it. He'd been enjoying chatting about the funny farm. No chance of that now. Dennis had moved away to sup his pint. He was probably wondering how the stranger in the pub, the one who hadn't admitted to knowing anything about the funny farm, knew Doll Child.

"Of course I am. What brings you here then, Doll?"

"Oh—" She waved her hands as if grasping for inspiration. "I had to nip into town to see a friend, but she must have got the date muddled or something. She wasn't there so I thought I may as well call in here and have a quick drink while I waited for a taxi. The rank was deserted."

"Great. I'll share that taxi with you."

"Well, yeah. Okay."

"What are you having, Doll?"

"A gin and tonic. Thanks." She sat on the stool beside him and made futile attempts to pull down her skirt.

"I wouldn't have thought this was your sort of place," he said.

She took a small sip of her gin and leaned toward him, thrusting her cleavage at his pint. "It's closest to the taxi rank."

That was true.

"It's dead tonight, isn't it?" he said. "I had a quick one in Tempo. I don't suppose that's your sort of place either." The young dancers would show up Doll's signs of ageing. She wouldn't like that.

"I hate the place. It's always full of old men ogling tarts. Joe doesn't like the place either. He goes in every Thursday but he finds it a chore."

He lifted his glass, took a swallow and grinned at her. "You wouldn't believe the rumours that are flying round about the refuge."

"I bet I would. I reckon I've heard 'em all."

"Black magic? Human sacrifices?"

She snorted with laughter. "I think all sacrifices call for the blood of a young virgin, don't they? You'd be hard pushed to find one of those in the Clough."

"I expect it's with the two girls going missing. Something like that happens—well, it's bound to start all sorts of rumours."

"Tarts—both of 'em. The silly little sods could be anywhere. That Farrah—I told Joe at the time that he was too soft with her. Fancy letting her bring a bloody dog to the place. She was a right stuck-up little thing too. Thought she was a cut above everyone else."

"Pretty, wasn't she?"

"We were all pretty at that age, Davey."

"Speak for yourself."

Laughing, she nudged his arm and thrust her cleavage ever closer. "You always were a ladies' man."

He'd tell that to Bev. She was forever accusing him of being a chauvinist and a misogynist.

"That chap who called—the one with the flash car—Gordon, wasn't it? How does a bloke afford a car like that? It was a bloody Bentley, of all things. I bet there wasn't any change from a hundred and thirty grand."

She winked and tapped the side of her nose. "Gordon could afford a whole fleet of the things. He's a self-made multimillionaire. Clever, he is. Real clever. There was a piece in the paper about him not so long ago and they reckoned almost every kid in the country owned a computer game that his company sells. He's rolling in money. It just goes to show that honesty sometimes pays."

"Not in my book, it doesn't."

"It worked for Gordon."

"Him and Joey were in the same care home, I gather."

"Yeah. Joe had to fight his battles for him. He was

clever, so the other kids always picked on him. He's having the last laugh though. He could buy the bleedin' lot
of them now. Every single one."

"It's all right for some. Where's he live? London, I
suppose."

"Yeah. He's got a place in Florida too. Me and Joe
went out there once. I'd quite like a house out there—all
we did was sit by the pool all day. That's the life, eh?"

"It certainly beats freezing your balls off running a
soup kitchen."

"Tell me about it. I wish—"

She broke off as the door opened, turned to look and
gave the man who walked in a slight shake of her head.
The chap ignored her, walked to the other side of the bar,
ordered his pint and went to join three others in front
of the darts board.

"What do you wish?" Dylan asked.

"Aw, nothing. It's time I rang for that taxi. D'you
want to share it, Davey, or are you staying for another?"

"I'll share it. Thanks."

Doll was quiet on the short ride home. Dylan wasn't
in the mood for conversation either. He was too busy
wondering why Doll had warned off John Taylor back
in the Jolly Sailor.

Chapter Sixteen

DYLAN WAS ON washing-up duty again. He'd started the never-ending task with company, but Adrian had been summoned by Child to do electrical work in the barn that everyone chose to call the chapel.

The breakfast had been good—a hot full English—but he would have preferred to eat in town and let someone else do the washing up. That way, he'd be free to ask questions.

During last night's taxi ride with Doll, he'd spotted what he suspected was Walter Topham's farm. It was a run-down-looking place with a huge sign outside offering kittens and Border collie puppies for sale. He planned to see what the farmer knew about Farrah Brindle.

Meanwhile, no matter how many plates he washed, the pile didn't lessen. As for the cutlery, he swore everyone used half a dozen knives. On and on it went.

The door opened and he turned, hoping Adrian had returned to help. It was Doll and someone else—the girl who'd been talking to Child and his son at that meeting in Leeds. The girl who claimed to be eighteen and was closer to fifteen.

"You on your own, Davey?"

"Yeah. Adrian's gone off with Joe to do something in the chapel."

Doll nodded at her companion. "This is Anna Woodward. She'll be staying for a while."

"Hi, Anna. It's a surprise seeing you again."

Doll didn't looked surprised or pleased to see Anna. She gave her a light shove in the back and said, "You may as well help with the washing up while you're here. We'll sort you out later."

"Okay." The girl gave a beaming smile and joined Dylan at the sink. "Where's the tea towel?"

"Bottom drawer," he said.

Doll looked as if she wanted to linger but she turned on her high heels and was heard walking down the hall and out of the building.

Anna was as good at drying plates as Dylan was at washing them. Which wasn't very. She was a hell of a lot more enthusiastic though.

"Why have you come here?" he asked.

She shrugged. "Why have you?"

"I got into a spot of bother with the law and needed a free bed for a few days."

"Me too. Well, I'm not in trouble with the police, but I need a bed. I was staying with a mate in Leeds but she didn't have room for me. I thought I'd give this place a try, so I hopped on the train and here I am." She looked as if she expected fanfares. She was out of luck.

"You'll find it boring."

"I can do boring."

Dylan doubted that. "Cold, too."

"I've brought plenty of sweaters."

"How old did you say you were?"

"Eighteen."

"And how old are you really?"

"Eighteen."

Dylan's hands stilled in the soapy water as he looked at her more closely. This morning, she was wearing skin-tight jeans and a thick grey-and-white sweater. Long dark hair was tied back with black ribbon. Small gold earrings sparkled and her watch wasn't cheap. She was well-spoken and obviously came from a good family.

"I'd guess sixteen," he said.

"Well, you'd guess wrong, wouldn't you?"

"What year were you born?"

There was the usual pause that people lying about their age always took to do the calculation. "Nineteen ninety-five." She looked smug.

He let it go, but he'd still bet his life that she was fifteen or sixteen.

"What have you heard about this place?" he asked as he scrubbed the remains of fried egg from a plate.

"Only what Joe and Hank told me. Why?"

"Just curious. You haven't heard about the two girls who vanished from here?"

She frowned. "No. What—what about them?"

"Put it this way, if I was a sixteen-year-old—or even an eighteen-year-old—girl, you wouldn't catch me dead in this place. Two girls stayed here, Caroline and Farrah, and then vanished into thin air. The locals think they were used as human sacrifices. The police don't have a clue what's happened to them."

She'd visibly paled. That was good, but he doubted he'd done enough to shock her into going home to her parents.

"I'd be careful if I were you," he said.

"What really happened to them?" she asked.

"Who knows? Perhaps the locals are right and this place offers up human sacrifices to the devil every second Tuesday."

She carefully dried the plate she was holding and added it to the pile. "You're trying to scare me."

"Nope. I'm saying I wouldn't want to be in your shoes. I'd go home, if I was you. I'm sure your parents would welcome you back with open arms."

"That shows what you know." The defiance was back. "I'm better off here."

"If you say so."

"What did she say your name was?"

"Davey. Or Dave. Whichever."

"What did you do then? Why are you in trouble with the police?"

"Nothing serious. I don't suppose Anna is your real name, is it?"

"That's for me to know and you to find out, isn't it?" Grinning at her wit, she nodded at the sink. "That water needs changing. These plates are coming out dirtier than when they went in."

She was right. Dylan let the water escape and refilled the sink with fresh.

"I'm looking forward to giving out soup to the homeless," she said suddenly. "That must be cool, mustn't it?"

"Not so much cool as downright freezing. It was minus two last night."

She rolled her eyes at what she thought was a joke. "It still must be good though. I've done a couple of nights on the streets. It was great."

His initial impression was right. She was a spoiled little rich kid. He'd bet she'd been given everything her heart desired and thought it would be fun to see how the other half lived. She'd imagine the have-nots partying the days and nights away. It was easy enough to do when you had a rich daddy at the end of a phone.

He thought of his own kids. Freya, not yet a year old, was too young to know anything, but he hoped they'd instilled the right values in Luke. He thought they had. He couldn't imagine Luke thinking it fun to sleep on the streets. Like a lot of youngsters these days, though, he had an easy life. He was ferried from football practice to cinema to fast-food outlet without question. He owned every gadget imaginable. All the same, he was a good kid. He knew the difference between right and wrong and he knew that fun didn't come from any drug-induced high.

He saw that her attention was on something outside. Correction. *Someone.*

Hank Child was coming toward to the house with his usual arrogant swagger.

"I suppose he's another reason you've come here," Dylan said.

"Who are you? My bloody dad?"

"I wouldn't think so. Nineteen ninety-five—no. Not unless your mum's an exotic dancer from Peckham."

She wrinkled her nose in distaste.

"Hank's a good-looking young man," he said.

"Gorgeous," she said. "Nice with it."

Dylan wouldn't go that far, but he declined to comment because the door swung open.

Hank's face lit up when he saw Anna. "So you decided to come after all? Hey, that's great. When did you get here?"

"About an hour ago. I caught the early train. It's good to see you, Hank." She fluttered long lashes at him.

"You too." Hank switched on the kettle and rested one hip on the worktop while he waited for it to boil.

"Things are definitely looking up round here. Are you on your own?"

"Yes."

"Better and better." He winked at her. "D'you want a coffee?"

"Please." She smiled coyly.

"Here—" Dylan slung clean cutlery on the drainer. "These won't dry themselves."

Still smiling at Hank, she picked up the cutlery and started to dry it.

When the task was over, Dylan left her in the dubious hands of Hank. As she was only having a coffee with him, and as the place was buzzing with people, she wouldn't come to much harm.

There were probably more chores waiting for him, but he needed to escape.

As he stepped outside, he wished he *could* leave the country. Egypt appealed to him. Anywhere warm was attractive. Lancashire was pretty, with white frost glistening in the weak sunlight, but the last word to describe it would be *warm*.

He was about to head down the lane when Child appeared in front of him. "Where are you going?"

"Didn't I tell you? I need to check in at the local nick."

"Ah, right." Child found that amusing. "Off you go then. We don't want you upsetting the law, Davey."

"It won't hurt them to wait. Did you want me for something?"

"No. Go and keep the boys in blue happy. I'll see you later." Child was already hurrying into the house.

Dylan walked at a brisk pace too. It was the only way to keep vaguely warm. He stepped it up and was soon jogging down the hill, being careful to avoid lethal patches of black ice.

The sign outside what he assumed was Walter Topham's farm still offered kittens and Border collie puppies for sale. Dylan walked up to the house and hoped he didn't leave with a kitten in his pocket.

"Yes? Did you want something?"

Dylan turned to see a man in his sixties standing with his hands on his hips and a scowl on his face. Two black-and-white dogs stood by his side looking as if they fancied Dylan for lunch.

"Hello." Dylan walked closer. The bright-eyed dogs didn't take their eyes off him. "I saw the sign for the Border collies. A friend of mine is looking for one and I wanted some more information. Are you the man to see?"

The chap's shoulders relaxed. "I am. Walter Topham. Know a bit about the dogs, do you?"

"Not really, but my friend does. He's had them for years."

"Not much point you looking at them then, is there? They're from good working stock. Is that what he's after? They're not for pets."

"He has a smallholding." Christ, it was early for the third degree. "Quite a few sheep."

Topham still looked suspicious. "How much land does he have?"

"Fifty acres." Dylan had no idea what fifty acres of land looked like. It was the first figure to enter his head. It seemed to satisfy Topham though, and that was the aim.

"I can show you the bloodlines. You can pass it on. You'd better come inside."

"Thank you."

"Away!" At the sound of their master's voice, the two dogs ran off out of sight.

"Do you keep many sheep?" Dylan thought he might as well try to make conversation as they ambled toward the house.

"I do." Topham clearly wasn't a great conversationalist. "You'd better give me a minute."

He went into the house, closing the door firmly on Dylan. Seconds later he was back. "Come on then."

They were greeted by yet another collie, this one old and grey around the muzzle. Dylan had assumed Topham had needed those few seconds to secure a dog that took objection to strangers, but this animal couldn't have been more friendly. It licked Dylan's hand with the gentlest of touches. Topham ignored it and walked into the untidiest, dirtiest kitchen—

A goose, a bloody goose of all things, wandered into the room, ambled past the dog and waddled out of the room to God alone knew where. A goose!

Topham paid it no attention.

Dylan wasn't a great believer in housework himself, but there had to be limits. The room was warm, thanks to an old black stove, but that was all it had going for it. A black kettle sat on the stove and two dirty towels hung from a rail at its side. A couple of chipped brown mugs waited to be washed. An old dresser thick with dust showed off equally dusty trophies and rosettes.

"You may as well sit down," Topham said as he hunted through drawers in the dresser.

"Thank you."

Topham pulled out a ledger and opened it on the table in front of Dylan. He turned pages and then pointed.

"That'll give you the bloodlines. They'll be good workers." He pushed a grubby used envelope at Dylan. "You can make a note for your friend."

"Right." He took a pen from his pocket and scribbled down what could have been a foreign language. He paused. "Sorry, did you say your name was Topham?"

"I did."

"Ah, I've heard it mentioned. You were helping Farrah Brindle with her dog, weren't you?"

There was a long pause. "She brought her to work with the sheep a few times, yes."

"I don't suppose you've heard from her since she vanished."

"Why should I?"

"People think she's taken off for the bright lights. I thought she might have worried about her dog—she might have contacted you for advice."

"No."

"It seems odd that she'd leave her dog, doesn't it?"

"Folk are odd. Give me dogs any day. You know where you are with dogs. Why are you so interested?"

"Just curious. I'm staying at Moorside Refuge for a few days—"

"We can do without places like that in the Clough."

"Oh? How do you mean?"

"There have always been a few bad 'uns in the Clough, but we know those. We don't want people like that coming in and taking over with their strange goings-on."

"I haven't seen any strange goings-on. I've only been there a few days, but even so, it all looks okay to me. I think they're doing a good job, helping the homeless and suchlike."

"Ay. Well, maybe they are." He nodded at the envelope. "Have you got all that?"

"Nearly." Dylan copied down more dogs' names and numbers. "And like I was saying, I heard about Farrah because she stayed at the refuge for a while."

"She soon saw sense and went home. Right, they're six weeks old so they won't be ready to leave for another fortnight. I've got two dogs and two bitches left. Six hundred pounds each."

Dylan folded the envelope and put it in his pocket with his pen. "Can I see them? I can take pictures on my phone and send them to him."

"Suit yourself." He put the ledger safely in the drawer and, without a word, walked out of the kitchen and down a long dark hallway to the back of the house.

Leaning against the wall on a small shelf, their edges curling, were two black-and-white photos of a young girl with long blond hair falling around her face. In both, she was laughing into the camera and had her arm around her dog, a black-and-white Border collie.

"Are you a photographer, Mr. Topham?"

"What? No."

Dylan peered more closely. He'd thought the photos were of Farrah Brindle, but he was wrong. The girls could be twins but these photos had been taken years ago. Cars in the background were models from the seventies and eighties.

"They're very good," he said.

"A chap from the local paper took them. My daughter came second at a local trials. She should have come first but she dropped points at the pen. She was good with a dog." He seemed to lose himself in a different world.

"Does she still work with dogs?"

"No. Right, it's this way, if you want to see these pups."

There was no more time to study the photos of Topham's daughter, but she was the image of Farrah Brindle.

He followed Topham across a frozen yard to a ramshackle stable block.

Topham pulled open an outer door and they stood at the edge of a small enclosure where a collie was fending off eight black-and-white puppies. Correction, there were seven black-and-white puppies and one white one.

"I'm not selling him." Topham pointed to the white puppy. "I think he might be deaf." He picked up a stick and prodded two puppies. "Those are the males and these—" He pushed the adult dog out of the way with his stick and poked two more. "These are the bitches. The other three are sold. Six hundred pounds. They'll be good workers. I'll have no trouble selling them."

It was dark inside the stable and Dylan doubted that anything would be recognisable in his photos, but he went through the motions for his fictitious friend. The pups posed obligingly and Dylan knew Topham was right. He'd have no trouble selling them. They were as cute as only puppies can be.

"That everything?" Topham asked. "You've got my phone number, have you?"

"No, I don't—"

"It's on the sign on the gate. Right, good day to you."

Topham stomped back to the house, leaving Dylan to find his own way back to the road. He paused to make a note of Topham's phone number before walking slowly back to the refuge.

Chapter Seventeen

KENNEDY STIFLED ANOTHER yawn. He'd worked all day in the garden, walked home to eat his fish and chips—he'd soon look like fish and chips—and walked back to the refuge. It was almost two in the morning and he was tempted to go home to his bed.

Half an hour ago, Joe Child had left the building. He'd walked round the side of the house and then down the lane to the main road. It was unlike Child to walk anywhere when he had several vehicles at his disposal. Where the devil could he be going at this time of night? And why hadn't he wanted to risk alerting anyone to his departure by firing a car's engine?

Child had been alone, walking quickly, and Kennedy would have followed but a light had come on in the chapel and he'd been too interested in that.

His eyes were accustomed to the darkness, so he'd had no trouble creeping across the yard and to the chapel. He'd been standing there—listening for half an hour—and a couple of coughs and a single curse made him think that Hank Child was inside.

Perhaps the Child family suffered from insomnia.

Kennedy stifled another yawn. All was silent in the chapel and he was about to give up and walk home when the sound of the refuge's front door being carefully closed alerted him. He pressed himself close to the chapel wall, out of sight, and saw the new girl—Anna, they called her—running across the yard and to the chapel.

She let herself into the building and Kennedy heard muffled voices. He couldn't make out the words but he recognised the voices. Anna and Hank Child must have agreed to meet. She was giggling. He was talking in a low, coaxing voice.

There were no prizes for guessing what they were up to.

Hank Child was insatiable. Kennedy wondered if he'd been the same at that age, but he knew he hadn't. Chance would have been a fine thing. He'd thought about sex a lot, like any other young man, but he hadn't gone through women the way young Child did. He hadn't had the looks that Child did, for a start. Women of all ages liked to look at Child. The more they looked, the taller he stood and the more arrogant he became. And they loved it. Often, he'd bring women back to the chapel after a night on the town. He'd call a taxi for them early the next morning. The young women would be all over him, demanding to know when they'd see him again. He liked to play hard to get. "I'll call you," he'd say as he bundled them into the waiting taxi. Kennedy doubted he ever did.

He listened more closely. He heard Anna's voice raised. Child's voice was petulant. Moments later, there was moaning—

The cat slunk by, too intent on a good night's hunting to pay him any attention. The possibility of a fresh mouse was far more tempting than a stroke behind the ears.

Another half hour ticked silently by. The chapel

door opened and Child and Anna emerged, their voices hushed.

"Tomorrow night?" Anna asked in a whisper.

"Maybe. I'll see you around."

"Don't I get a good-night kiss?"

Kennedy didn't hear Child's response, but she didn't get her kiss. She had a smack on the bottom before he strode off, and she hurried across the yard and let herself in through the front door.

Kennedy might as well go home. Waiting for Child senior to return was pointless because he could be out all night.

A dark shadow moved. All was quiet but a figure—a man—was striding across the yard and to the lane. The new chap. Davey Young. Where was he sneaking off to?

Kennedy followed at a safe distance. Like Young, he could move silently. Unless he tripped on one of the lethal holes in the track.

Young walked purposefully down to the main road, unaware that Kennedy was watching his every step. Instead of turning to the left and in the direction of the town, Young turned right. About six miles of open countryside stretched that way. All he'd see—if it hadn't been too dark to see anything—were the forbidding moors.

Curious, Kennedy followed. The distance was difficult to gauge, but he'd guess they walked no more than half a mile. A car was parked in the lay-by. Its lights flashed briefly. Young quickened his pace and got in the car.

The engine fired and drove off.

Kennedy made a mental note of the registration plate and watched the taillights vanish round a bend.

Chapter Eighteen

"DID YOU GET out all right?"

Dylan leaned back in the passenger seat and relaxed. Frank's car was clean, comfortable and blessedly warm. Bliss. "Yeah. If anyone says anything, I'll tell them I couldn't sleep and decided to go for a walk."

"Have a look in the glove box," Frank said. "There's a treat for you."

It was enough of a treat to be warm until he found the half bottle of single malt whisky. "Hey, you're a star."

"Can't have you soft southerners drinking the cheap shite, can we? Help yourself. I'll drive over the hill and park at the back of the football ground."

There were no glasses so Dylan took a swig from the bottle. It ran down his throat, generously warm. It was like nectar, compared to the cheap blended crap Davey Young drank.

"Do you want some?" He offered the bottle in Frank's direction.

"No, I'm driving." He grinned. "I might spill some."

Dylan smiled at the old joke. It felt good to be comfortable, and to be himself.

Frank drove into the car park behind the football ground and killed the engine and lights. No one else was around at this late—or early—hour.

Frank took the bottle and enjoyed a quick drink.

"I have an interesting snippet," he said as he handed it back, "but tell me how you're getting on first."

Typical of Frank. He always liked to keep you in the dark.

"I'm getting on depressingly slowly. Do you know a farmer called Walter Topham? He breeds and works sheepdogs."

"I know of him, yes. Why do you ask?"

"I have a feeling that he's not all he claims to be. Farrah Brindle used to visit him to get help training her dog to work with sheep. I called on him, on the pretence of being interested in puppies he has for sale, and while I was there, I spotted a photo of a girl who's a dead ringer for Farrah. He claims it's his daughter."

Frank nodded. "I expect it is. I heard that Farrah had spent time with him, so I checked him out. I can't remember his daughter's name now, but she was killed. Car accident. She'd passed her driving test a fortnight earlier and was showing off with her friends. She and a girlfriend were killed instantly. Two lads in the back survived with cuts and bruises."

Dylan winced. Given that to cope with, Topham was entitled to be a moody, curmudgeonly old bugger.

"He's married then?" There had been no signs of a woman's touch at the farm.

"Divorced. His wife went off with someone else not long after the accident."

A double whammy. No wonder Topham found it easier to deal with dogs than people. All the same—

"He wasn't keen to talk about Farrah. He wasn't keen to talk about anything, even the puppies he was selling. And there was a bloody goose wandering about the kitchen as if it owned the place." He stretched out his legs and pushed Topham from his mind. "Did you manage to find out anything about Bill Owen?"

"Nothing exciting," Frank said. "He seems okay. Been here for years, well respected, popular, will probably end his days here. There's never been a hint of scandal about him. Not so much as a parking ticket."

"Farrah used to call on him. She lost an aunt and a grandmother to cancer, apparently, and used to visit him for spiritual guidance. He also claims that she talked of her dog, and about fashion and music. Seems a bit odd, doesn't it? He's old enough to be her grandfather. Why the hell would she talk music and fashion with him?"

Frank shrugged. "People treat vicars differently. They see them as one step down from God. For some people, talking to the vicar is almost as good as having a chinwag with the Almighty."

Dylan snorted at that. "Has he any links with the refuge or anyone there? I know the church and the refuge held a joint fundraising event, but that's all anyone will admit to."

"None that we could find. Rhodes and the boys are checking more thoroughly, but I don't think they'll find anything. It's the same with Gordon Riley. There's nothing of interest there either." Frank paused as a set of car headlights lit up the car park. The driver was merely turning round though and soon vanished from sight. "Riley was at the same care home as Child. A grim place it was too, by all accounts. Riley was there first and was bullied constantly. Child arrived, an angry little sod, and took on the bullies. I gather Riley used to do his schoolwork for him by way of payment."

"Child has always loved a good fight."

"I know. Riley left at about the same time as Child

ran away. He did well for himself. He's a clever bloke and now owns one of the biggest computer-games companies in Europe."

"The education in the care home was that good?" Dylan was sceptical.

"I doubt it. No, I think Riley had the good sense to sniff out top experts in their fields."

"So he and Child have been mates ever since?"

"Ah well, that I don't know. It seems unlikely."

"It does. And if Riley's as respectable as he makes out, why would he want a friend like—"

"—that murdering bastard Child? Exactly. I don't know. I do know that he's made a healthy donation to the refuge in the past. Perhaps he's still haunted by all that bullying and wants to repay Child for fighting his battles for him."

"Perhaps."

They lapsed into silence. Dylan took another swig of whisky. "Do you know anything about a bloke called Kennedy who works at the refuge? He's a gardener. The story is that he pitched up one day with a note asking if he could work in the gardens. Child gives him a tenner and half a dozen eggs now and again, and that's that."

"The name means nothing to me. Why do you ask?"

"He doesn't speak. People told me he's not quite right in the head."

"And?"

"And I heard him talking to a cat. He sounded well-spoken, well educated."

"Kennedy? Is that his first or last name?"

"No idea. No one seems to know anything about him. I only overheard him talking to that cat when I should have been doling out soup to the homeless. He must have thought he had the place to himself."

"That's interesting. I'll see what I can find out. I'll put Rhodes onto it."

Yes, let Rhodes and his sidekick do some work. While he was risking frostbite in that confounded shed, they left their lovely warm offices for their lovely warm beds.

"Also, a young girl arrived at the refuge today. She claims to be eighteen, but I reckon she's closer to fifteen or sixteen. Home Counties accent. She calls herself Anna Woodward but I doubt that's her real name. She met Childs senior and junior at that meeting in Leeds. I'd say she was a spoiled little rich kid. She says she's escaped a violent boyfriend and has been staying with a friend in Leeds. I'll try to take a picture with my phone and send it to you. Get them to check out missing persons, will you?"

"Will do. Meanwhile, keep an eye on her."

"I'll do my best. I don't want anyone disappearing while I'm on watch." He took a long, slow swig from the bottle. "So what do you have, Frank?"

Frank rubbed his hands together like a conjurer about to pull a white rabbit from a hat. "The night you arrived—when you met Child at that nightclub?"

"What about it?"

"There was a body found in a nearby alley."

Dylan nodded. "I know. Rhodes told me—I gather it inconvenienced them. I've read about it in the paper, too. So?"

"He's finally been identified. You remember Barney Fraser?"

"Sure do. Had his tongue removed, beaten to death possibly, *probably*, by our hero, Joe Child."

"The very one. Well, the dead body found in the alley? One Christian Fraser—youngest son of Barney."

"You have got to be bloody kidding me."

"No. They found out who he was a couple of hours ago."

"And Child hasn't been arrested yet?"

"I'm not sure he's even been spoken to. There's a bit of a problem there."

There would be. "Go on."

"The barman at Tempo confirms that Child arrived at the club at seven-thirty. Fraser junior was killed between about nine and ten o'clock."

"I was with him at about ten-thirty."

"Exactly. But just because Child has a neat little alibi, it doesn't mean he isn't involved in some way."

"Why does Child go to Tempo every Thursday night anyway? What's the attraction there?"

"It's full of smackheads," Frank said in a matter-of-fact way. "He likes to be around people with problems, to see if he can help."

"That's bollocks."

"I know that and you know that, but that's his story. Perhaps he likes to give himself an alibi while his henchmen beat people to death."

"No way. It would kill him to miss out on giving someone a good send-off." Child would do his own dirty work—and enjoy every brutal second.

"What was Fraser junior doing in the Clough?"

"No one knows yet. They only got an ID a couple of hours ago. He and his two brothers live in Manchester these days, so it's not far from home for him. I'll let you know when I hear anything more."

"Do that. I'm curious." Another car pulled into the

car park, turned and drove out again. "I'd better get back before I'm missed. Back to that bloody awful shed. Still, at least the breakfasts are good."

"There you go then." Frank fired the engine and drove out of the car park. "You can't have everything, you know. That's the trouble with you soft southerners, you struggle to cope with a little hardship."

"Ha."

"Oh, did I tell you my good news?"

"No. What's that?"

"The lovely Esme is moving out on Monday." Frank smiled his satisfaction.

Esme was Frank's neighbour, the woman who had longed to become the fourth Mrs. Willoughby.

"Has she given up on you then?"

"Seems like it," Frank said. "Of course, I'll miss her fruitcakes. And her apple pies. It'll be nice to walk round the garden without her lying in wait to thrust her cleavage in my face though. Just keep your fingers crossed that her house sale doesn't fall through."

"I wonder who'll be moving in. Maybe you'll get lucky, Frank."

"Pah. As you're so often telling me, there are two sorts of luck. I'm better on my own now. I've done the matrimonial stuff and it's hard work."

Dylan couldn't argue with that.

"I'd better drop you here." Frank slowed the car to a stop. "No point getting too close."

"Thanks. I'll be in touch."

Dylan left the warm comfort of Frank's car and huddled deep inside his coat for the cold walk back to the refuge.

Chapter Nineteen

DYLAN KNEW HE should get a kick out of helping those less fortunate, but all he got was bored and frozen. Most of those queuing for the hot potato-and-leek soup merely wanted to save themselves a trip to McDonald's. None looked as if they'd spent the night shivering on a park bench. Most were better dressed than he was.

The "soup kitchen" was a Transit van with a hob powered by a noisy, smelly generator. Ivy and Sharon were busy ladling the soup into polystyrene cups from a huge pan.

Child stood to the side, behind a small table almost hidden by leaflets telling people how God loved them and how they should give themselves to God. He was doing his usual speech about how God had chosen him, and a good crowd had gathered. Coins chinked satisfyingly as they landed in a large bucket on the table.

A couple of uniformed police officers strolled past. They took no notice of Child, presumably because they were used to seeing him there. Perhaps they were grateful that he had such an attentive crowd. While people were listening to Child they weren't shoplifting or mugging old ladies.

A man strode past, hesitated, dug in his pocket and threw a five-pound note in the bucket.

"God bless you, sir." Child broke off from his speech to thank the stranger.

Dylan was handing out leaflets that offered shelter at the refuge and prayer to anyone in need. They also begged for donations, of course. He thrust a leaflet at a passerby.

"Why, thank you, David."

Dylan looked up into the long face of Bill Owen. "Oh, hi. Are you here for the performance or the free soup?"

Owen smiled. "I had no idea Joe would be here today. I've been up at the hospital, visiting a member of my congregation."

"Well, today's soup is potato and leek. I can recommend it."

"Thank you, but I'll save it for those in need."

"Can I have a quick look?" Dylan nodded at the newspaper tucked beneath Owen's arm.

"Of course. Help yourself."

News of Christian Fraser's murder filled the front page. Dylan quickly scanned it but discovered nothing he didn't already know.

"Thanks." He handed it back. "By the way, I meant to ask you about that farmer, the one Farrah Brindle went to with her dog. Topham's his name, right?"

"That's right." Owen wore a puzzled frown.

"I heard his daughter died in a car accident."

"Indeed she did. That was shortly before I arrived in the parish. A tragedy, to be sure. What makes you ask about him?"

"I met him," Dylan said. "I thought he was a miserable old devil and I was quite rude to him. Then someone told me about his daughter and I felt guilty. This chap said his wife left him soon afterwards."

Owen nodded, still wearing that frown. "So I believe."

"I don't suppose he's much of a churchgoer."

"No. I'm afraid not."

"Well, look who's here." Child gave a smiling bow. "Reverend, how about we lead these people in a hymn?"

"What? Oh, yes, of course." Owen walked to stand beside Child, who muttered something in his ear.

"Ladies and gentlemen," Child said, "please join us in singing 'Rock of Ages.'"

Not again. Dylan wondered if Child knew any other hymns. *Murdering bastard.*

At least Child could hold a tune, which was more than could be said for Owen. Given that it was a bitterly cold late afternoon in a shopping centre, the crowd did an impressive job. People enjoyed singing along, and when it was over, they dropped donations in the bucket and went on their way with lighter hearts.

Dylan's own heart would be lighter when this charity stint was over. There was still some way to go though. Before they could leave the town, they had to search out those sleeping rough and give them blankets that had been bought from a local wholesaler and were almost useless. They were far too thin to keep the cold Lancashire nights at bay.

He'd thought Owen had gone when the singing ended, but the vicar was in deep conversation with Child. They were both looking at Dylan as they spoke. They had to be talking about him.

The soup kitchen closed, and Ivy wandered over to Dylan for a quick smoke. She took a deep pull on her cigarette and sighed with pleasure as she exhaled.

"I keep meaning to give them up," she said, "and I will. Just not today."

"They're not cheap these days," Dylan said. "Very bad for your health too, of course."

"I know. Still, something's got to kill you, hasn't it? I'd hate to give up the ciggies and then get knocked down by a bus. What a tragic waste that would be."

Dylan smiled at her logic. "Joe's got a good singing voice, hasn't he? I was impressed. Better than the vicar's, at any rate."

Ivy snorted with laughter. "My cat's got a better voice than the vicar's."

"He seems a nice enough bloke though, and he gets on well with Joe. They were having a right old chin-wag."

"Were they?"

Ivy had been standing fairly close to Child and Owen. Close enough to hear their conversation, unless they'd kept it deliberately hushed.

"Yeah. I wondered if they were talking about Farrah. I gather the vicar was friendly with her."

"I think she did see quite a bit of him, yes." Ivy put her cigarette to her lips and inhaled. "A lot of the town's youngsters see a lot of him. He helped raise money to keep the Girl Guides group going. He used to help out with the local youth club too. Not many kids went to it. Well, you wouldn't, would you? Not much chance of a quick snog behind the bike shed, with the vicar looking on." She wheezed with laughter. "I can see that vicars have to get on well with the youngsters these days. After all, they're the congregation of the future. I think he takes it all a bit too seriously though. He likes to make out he's young and trendy when, really, they'd have far more respect for him if he was just himself."

Smiling, Dylan nodded.

"I'd love to know what happened to Farrah," she said.

"She could be a little madam, like most her age, but she was a good girl. Like I told you, I reckon there was a man. Isn't there always a man?"

"Any idea who it might have been?"

"Me?" She seemed surprised by the question. "None at all. My guess is, he was married. At that age, us girls like to shout about our conquests. If we're tight-lipped, you can bet your life he's married. Men like that have it easy, don't they? They promise young girls the moon and the stars, and they're daft enough to fall for it hook, line and sinker. For all that, I would have thought Farrah had more sense. I suppose I can't claim to have known her well, but I liked her a lot." She chewed on her bottom lip. "I do hope she's all right."

So did Dylan.

He also hoped everyone's favourite vicar hadn't blown his cover. If Owen had squealed to Child—well, he didn't know what would happen. He only knew that life without a tongue wouldn't be a laugh a minute.

He handed out more leaflets and wondered if there could be a more pointless task. Most of them would end up blowing around the streets with the discarded burger wrappers.

"Hello there. It's David, isn't it?"

Dylan was surprised to see Malcolm Brindle and even more surprised to see the attractive woman with her arm linked through his.

"Hello. Good to see you again." Dylan looked at the woman and waited for an introduction.

"This is my wife, Clare. Clare, this is David Young, the chap I told you about, the one who's staying at Moorside Refuge."

Her face lit up and she put out a slender hand. "Good

to meet you, David. You're doing such good work at the refuge."

Dylan made appropriate noises, but he was still surprised that Brindle was married to this beauty. Tall and elegant, she was wrapped in a knee-length red woollen coat and black boots. Fair hair was short and well cut. A pair of small gold studs adorned her ears. Only if you looked closely could you see the shadows beneath her eyes and the tenseness around her mouth.

"Malcolm has a dental appointment," she said, "and I'm nipping into the coffee shop to wait for him. Would you join me? I'd love to hear about the refuge."

He'd wanted an excuse to talk to Clare Brindle and he was being offered it on a plate. "Of course. Thank you, I'd love to."

Brindle glanced at his watch. "I'd better get a move on, darling. I'll see you in about half an hour." He gave her a quick peck on the cheek. "Good to see you again, David."

"You too."

He strode off and his wife smiled fondly. "Rather him than me. He needs an extraction and the very thought makes me shudder. Quick, let's get out of this wind."

The coffee bar was only a short distance away, and they were soon sitting at a table by the window. A young girl came to take their order.

"Cappuccino for me, please," Clare said with an enquiring look at Dylan.

"I'll have the same. Thanks."

"So tell me about the refuge," Clare said when they were alone. "As Malcolm told you, our daughter spent a few weeks there. I think she found it an eye-opener, but she enjoyed herself. You're doing such marvellous work. If there were more Christians in the world, we'd live in a much better place, wouldn't we?"

"Without doubt." She looked fragile. Elegant and attractive, but fragile, like a rare piece of porcelain that could so easily be smashed into a million pieces.

"I always think it sad that the parable of the Good Samaritan is known by all yet understood by so few," she said. "The lawyer asked Jesus, 'And who is my neighbour?' and still people don't understand, do they?"

Bollocks. They needed to get off the religion talk before Dylan was rumbled. She'd probably studied theology, and Dylan's recollection of the Good Samaritan story he'd been told at primary school had dimmed to almost nothing over the years. Hadn't some bloke been robbed and left for dead, and been ignored by lots of people until someone, the Good Samaritan of the story, took pity on him?

"There are still too many priests and Levites, aren't there?" she said.

Priests wore long black robes and got involved in child-abuse scandals. But Levites? Dylan didn't have a clue. They sounded like little hairy creatures with sharp teeth and long tails.

"There are." Best to agree with her and change the subject. "What made your daughter choose to stay at the refuge? Was it simply the chance to help those less fortunate?"

"She met someone who told her all about the place, and the lifestyle appealed to her. She's always loved a cause. If there's anything to protest against, like fox hunting, roads being built through open countryside, animals being used in experiments, Farrah's there. She has strong views on everything and it infuriates her to think that she lives in a country where people aren't provided with food and shelter."

The waitress put two coffees in front of them. "Is there anything else I can get for you?" On being told there wasn't, she gave them a beaming smile and left them alone.

"She had her dog with her," Clare went on, "and I gather she used to skip the Bible study classes and the services. Penny's a collie and she needs a lot of exercise, so I suppose Farrah would deal with her dog when study classes were on. She's a practical person. She'll do whatever it takes to help the homeless but—well, it was the same with church services. She thought them a little self-indulgent and believed people should spend their time raising money for sick children, the homeless and the elderly rather than sit in church and talk about it."

"She has a point."

"I've made her sound like a saint and she isn't that. She's just a normal teenager with a normal teenager's hopes, dreams and tantrums." She smiled at the latter, then seemed to hug herself. "The night she vanished—she said she was meeting up with a couple of friends and would be home by eleven. Of course, we checked with her friends and they'd made no plans. We think—we think she was meeting a boyfriend that she hadn't told us about."

She spooned the chocolate dusting from the top of her coffee with a hand that trembled.

"What about internet chat rooms?" Police would have checked, but he like confirmation. "Did she spend a lot of time on Facebook or Twitter?"

"No. She had a Facebook page, but it was just a means of keeping up with friends. She didn't use it often because she didn't have time. She took Penny for long walks before and after school, she sometimes worked at the town hall when there were functions on—oh, and she spent a fair bit of time with a local farmer. He's a strange one but Farrah adored him. He's an experienced sheepdog handler and Farrah hoped he'd help her train Penny to work with sheep. She was an outdoors type and didn't spend much time at her computer. The police took it away to see if they could find anything, but they couldn't."

Dylan nodded. "She's thought of fondly at the refuge. There's a woman, Ivy, who worries about her."

"She mentioned Ivy. Said she was lovely."

"She is. How did Farrah get along with the others? How about the family—Joe, Doll, Hank and Gary? Did she like them?"

"I think so, yes. She wanted more freedom than we're prepared to give her. Her friends are allowed to stay out late and do as they please. Farrah isn't. It came to a head when she wanted to go to a dog show in London on her own and stay the night. She'd already checked out a hotel that allowed dogs. We wouldn't let her go, there were a few arguments and she moved to the refuge. We couldn't stop her, and between you and me, we thought it would do her good. And, of course, we knew she'd be safe there."

That was more than Dylan knew. No one was safe at that place.

"When she came back, she was more like her old self," Clare said. "We thought any problems had been solved."

"You say you believe she was meeting up with a boyfriend. Can't her friends come up with any names?"

"No. Her friends are a sensible bunch, and I know they realise how serious this is and would tell us, but no. If there was a boyfriend, she kept him secret from everyone."

"Even the vicar?" Dylan asked. "We were chatting and he said he and Farrah were close. I'm surprised she didn't mention anyone to him."

Clare stirred her coffee round and round before she answered. "I don't think they were as close as he likes to believe. She always thought him something of a fuddy-duddy. She felt a little sorry for him because so few people turned up for his services, but I don't think they were close."

"Ah."

"People are reluctant to turn up for his services," she went on with a forced smile, "because they're long, drawn-out and totally uninspiring. I should go, I know I should, especially as he keeps Farrah in his prayers, but I just don't have the heart right now."

"I'm sure he understands."

"Sorry," she said with another smile that clearly took tremendous effort, "you don't want to hear about our problems. I wanted you to tell me about the refuge."

"Don't apologise. I've heard a lot about Farrah, so of course I'm interested. It must be so difficult for you. But as the Lord says—" *Bugger.* He'd forgotten. Something about God never giving us more problems than we can bear? Nope, it had gone. He gave her a beaming smile. "The Lord says many things that offer comfort. Farrah is in our prayers at the refuge. As are you and your husband, of course."

"Thank you. It means a lot. Faith is a great help in

times like these. It's funny but whenever I pick up my Bible, I'm constantly drawn to Luke 15, verse 9."

She waited expectantly, but all Dylan could do was pretend to ponder. They'd be here till Christmas if they waited for him to guess what little gem Luke 15 offered. "And that is—?"

"The lost sheep, of course."

"Of course. It's one of my favourite passages too. I'm no good at the numbers though. Dyslexic," he added.

"Oh, really. I have a friend who's the same. She's fine with letters but the numerals give her problems."

"That's it exactly. Luke 15," he said. "I'll remember that. I'll read it at our next service at the refuge."

"Thank you so much. I suppose the repentance of sinners isn't relevant, but it's the whole idea of straying and being welcomed back to the fold that appeals to me."

"I fully understand."

The coffee bar's door opened and Brindle strode inside. Pleasantries were exchanged, with great difficulty on Brindle's part because his mouth was numb, and the meeting was over.

"It's been lovely to meet you," Clare said as they parted. "I hope we'll see you again."

"Likewise. I hope you have good news about Farrah soon too."

He strode back to the soup kitchen, hoping he hadn't been missed and hoping the job was over for the day. He also hoped Child wasn't sharpening a knife.

IT WAS DIFFICULT getting Child alone but, that evening, at a little after eight o'clock, Dylan finally managed it. He'd been watching and waiting, and when he saw Child cross the yard to the chapel, he grabbed the newspaper he'd bought and followed.

His breath clouded in front of him. Above, a clear sky dotted with millions of stars promised yet another cold night.

Child was doing nothing when Dylan stepped into the dimly lit chapel. Nothing. He was simply staring at the back wall. Deep in thought maybe? Wondering what he should do about Owen's little bombshell? Deciding on the best way to dispose of a private investigator who was pretending to be his best pal? There was only one way to find out.

"Hey, Joey."

Child spun around. Light from a couple of flickering candles made him look grotesque. "Davey."

The greeting gave nothing away.

"Have you seen this? My God, I couldn't believe it." Dylan waved his newspaper in front of him and moved closer to a candle. "It's Christian Fraser. You know who he is, don't you?"

"Of course I do. I've been a friend to those boys for years." He glanced at his watch. "In fact, I'm heading over to see them now—to see if there's anything I can do. Those three—two boys have known tragedy, haven't they? First their father, now their kid brother."

"Heading over there?"

"Yes. They live in Manchester these days. As they're less than an hour away, I often see them."

Dylan reached into the pocket of his jacket and brought out a half bottle of whisky. "Fancy a drop, Joey? I had a flutter on the horses and thought I'd celebrate."

"Still gambling?" Child sneered. "You'll never learn, will you?"

"I never get in over my head, you know that. Here, have a drop." He thrust the bottle at Child. "So you're friends with the Fraser lads? Until I saw this in the paper, I didn't even know he had any sons."

Child took a swig of whisky from the bottle, wiped the top and handed it back. "Thanks. They were only kids when you were around. They're a few years older than Gary and Hank. I took them under my wing after their dad was murdered."

"Wow. I didn't know that. I didn't realise you and Barney were mates."

"We weren't. How could we be, when we worked for different sides? I felt for those boys of his though. You didn't go to Barney's funeral, did you? I did. I thought I should. It was a sad do. Three boys left without a father. They had their mother, of course, but a boy needs a man in his life, don't you think?"

As an only child who'd been brought up by an unmarried mother, a crazy unmarried mother at that, Dylan couldn't argue with him. The Fraser boys' mother was probably a bit more normal though.

"Well, yeah. So you still keep in touch with them?"

"Yes."

"I always thought our old boss, McCoy, had something to do with Barney's murder. Didn't you?"

Child shrugged. "I've no idea who was behind it. No one was ever caught."

"No." And if Dylan were a gambling man, which he wasn't, he'd bet he was standing opposite Barney Fraser's killer. The brutality of it, the removing of the bloke's tongue while he was still alive, boasted Child's trademarks. "I always assumed though. Didn't you ever hear anything?"

"Not a whisper."

"And now this," Dylan said, shaking his head. "Someone has it in for that family. What's it all about, do you reckon?"

"No idea."

"You must have some inkling. Did the sons take over where their father left off?"

"Drugs? No, they're clean. They own a chain of nightclubs in the North. Some in London too—well, Barney owned most of them, but these days, they're clean." Child glanced at his watch again. "And now I need to offer a quick prayer for those boys. If you'll—"

"Yeah. No worries." Dylan turned to leave, then stopped. "According to this—" he tapped the newspaper, "—he was killed while we were at that nightclub. It was the night we met."

"I know."

"Makes you think, doesn't it?"

"It does. And now I need to pray."

"Of course."

Child was a cagey sod. In the past, Dylan had managed to hold conversations with him. Not now.

He still didn't know if Owen had blown his cover. Child had given nothing away, but he wouldn't. He wasn't that stupid.

He left Child to his prayers—yeah, right—and walked back to the side of the house. He kept watch and when, ten minutes later, Child set off—presumably to console those poor boys—he returned to the chapel.

He had no idea what Child had been doing in there, but he'd stake his life on it not involving praying for anyone's soul.

He lit the biggest candles he could find and searched

every centimetre of that chapel. It didn't take long, because the place was little more than an empty shell. The
floor was concrete, so no hidden floorboards. Nothing
had been hidden beneath the plastic chairs or under that
makeshift altar. Toolboxes contained—unsurprisingly—
tools. There was nothing.

So what was Child's game?

Chapter Twenty

"HE'S ON HIS way."

Ben looked at his brother. His only living brother, he thought with a sickening thud in his gut. "Okay, and this time, we need some answers from him."

"Yeah."

"Maybe Chris was right," Ben said. "Perhaps he has lost his bottle."

"He hasn't."

"How can we be sure? I say we ask someone else to find out what the fuck is going on."

"There is no one else." Mark reached for the whisky bottle and refilled his glass. His hands were shaking. Not surprising, really. Receiving death threats, then hearing that your kid brother had been beaten to death, did that to a man.

Ben took the bottle from him and refilled his own glass. "We need to do something now—before *we're* found dead in an alley."

"I know, I know."

It was no use. Ben couldn't sit here and wait for Joe to arrive. He needed to be doing something. Anything. "I'll go and see what's happening downstairs."

"Nothing's happening."

"I'll go anyway."

After draining his glass, Ben left the office and went down the stairs to where life was carrying on as if everything were normal, as if his kid brother hadn't been murdered on the street. Music blared out, and people were dancing, laughing or chatting, and it was possible to believe that Christian would walk through the door and say, "Joke!"

He'd always been the comedian in the family. As the youngest, he'd been spoiled rotten by their parents. To their mother, he was the baby. Even their father, knowing that Ben and Mark would take over the business, had treated him differently. It was if he'd been put on the earth merely to be indulged. He'd never been scolded or nagged. They'd all loved him and they'd all spoiled him.

Ben strode across to the bar. Trade was brisk, mainly thanks to a stag night. The groom-to-be was clearly a popular bloke as he had around a hundred friends enjoying his last night of freedom.

For all Ben knew, Christian's killer could be in this room. It must have been someone who'd known Christian well, someone he'd confided in, someone who'd known he was going to Dawson's Clough to see Joe. But who could have known? It had been a spur-of-the-moment decision.

Ben went over and over their last conversation. It had been ridiculously brief because Christian had been on the train coming home from London.

"I'm going straight to see Joe. You will not believe what that bastard did." The connection broke.

A minute later, Christian phoned again. "Bloody tunnel."

That was all Ben had heard clearly. It was the last time he spoke to his brother. It was the last time he ever would speak to him.

His kid brother was dead. Every time that thought hit

him, he didn't know whether he was going to be sick or drop to the floor and weep.

He didn't want to be in the club with all the raucous laughter mocking his sadness. Nor did he want to be in the office with Mark. He wished he were a million miles away from all this. When this was over, he would be. He didn't need to be here. It wasn't as if he needed the money. He could sell up, catch a plane to Brazil and enjoy life. That had to be better than waiting for the next threatening note to arrive. Mark could say what he liked but Ben was out of here.

He took the stairs back to the office, where Mark was staring into his empty glass. If getting drunk solved anything, Mark wouldn't have a care in the world.

They said little as they waited for Joe. What was there to say? Their kid brother, the one who'd spent his life looking up to his brothers, had been murdered in cold blood. And for what? Why? What the fuck had any of them done to deserve this?

The anger lodged in the pit of his stomach but he knew it was preferable to the grief. Anger faded. The loss of his brother would haunt him for the rest of his days.

The phone rang and Mark snatched at it. He looked at the display and Ben saw the flash of pain in his eyes.

"Hey, Mum, how are you doing? Do you have people with you?"

Her sister and brother-in-law were staying with her. She'd be okay. Their mother was a lot tougher than she looked—and acted. Living with their father for so long had taught her to take the knocks.

"We're catching the first train tomorrow," Mark told her. "We'll be with you by ten o'clock. Yes, yes." He threw a quick glance at Ben. "Yes, he's doing okay."

Ben stood on the far side of the room but he could still hear her sobbing. He was grateful he hadn't picked up the phone. He was struggling with his own grief too much to deal with hers too. Tomorrow would be soon enough for that. They'd be travelling to London to be with her and also to discuss the funeral arrangements, arrangements that couldn't be carried out until the police decided to release the body. That could be weeks away yet.

Ten minutes later, the club manager called to say that Joe had arrived, then escorted him up the stairs and into the office.

"Thanks," Ben said, effectively dismissing him.

Did Joe look wary? He seemed to hesitate as if expecting them to say something. The moment was fleeting and he was soon giving them a hug. "I am so sorry. Whoever's done this will pay, you have my word on that."

"But who has done it, Joe?" Ben demanded. "And why?"

"I don't—"

"Exactly, you don't know. How long have we been paying you? Over a year now. And for what? You're no further forward than you were at the start."

Joe patted his shoulder. "Take it easy. I know how hard Chris's death has hit you. Believe me, I feel the same. I think of you boys as my own, you know I do."

"Yes, calm down, Ben," Mark said. "Here, Uncle Joe, have a drink. Ben's just a bit wound up. We both are— it's bloody hard."

"I know. You don't have to apologise to me, you know that. We're all shocked by Chris's death. None of us can be expected to think straight."

Mark nodded, filled a glass for Joe and refilled his

own. Ben could easily have drunk himself to blessed oblivion, but first he wanted some answers.

"So what have you got, Joe?" He'd dropped the *Uncle* long ago.

He often wondered what his father would have thought of Joe stepping in to take care of them. That their father had made his money from drugs was no secret. It was also common knowledge that Joe had worked for his biggest rival, McCoy. Yet Joe said he'd always respected Barney Fraser, and true to his word, he'd stepped in to see Barney's widow all right and taken care of the three of them.

What was he doing for them though? Christian hadn't trusted him. He'd thought Joe was taking the money and not bothering to look into anything. Ben had dismissed that as nonsense, but now he too was wondering if Joe was actually working for his money.

What had Christian meant during that last phone call? *You will not believe what that bastard did.* What had he done?

"The word on the street is that it was a random mugging," Joe said.

"What?" Ben didn't believe what he'd heard. "So we get death threats, one of us ends up dead, and it's a fucking coincidence? Get real!"

Joe threw himself down in a chair. He always acted as if he owned the place, and tonight Ben found that irritating.

"I'm telling you what the word on the street is. But if you think about it—first off, his wallet and phone were taken. That's the sign of a mugging. Maybe, instead of handing over his wallet and having done with it, he put up a fight. Second, no one knew he was coming to see me. He only called me a few hours earlier. Whoever's threatening you couldn't possibly have known he'd be there."

"What exactly did he say when he called you?" Ben asked.

"I've told you. He wasn't happy, and I could see his point, to think that you were all paying me and getting no answers. I wanted to talk about it there and then, but he insisted on coming to see me. He was like that, you know he was. Once he got a bee in his bloody bonnet, that was it. He had to thrash it out. As I was on my way to Tempo, we decided we'd discuss it there and make a night of it. When he didn't turn up, I assumed he'd cooled off and decided he didn't need to take me to task after all."

Ben had heard it all before. "So we get notes from someone who wants us dead. Chris is murdered and you're trying to tell me that it was a mugging? That's crap."

Joe shrugged. "Look, I've been paying the best noses in London to get to the bottom of this. We're fairly certain that someone's out for revenge—your dad made a lot of enemies in his time."

"When you say *we're* fairly certain, who do you mean?" Mark asked.

"I can't tell you—yet. But as I was saying, your dad made enemies. We have a few suspects. But—" he stressed the word, "—*but* we know that those involved weren't aware that Chris was coming to see me. Also—" He broke off.

"What?" Ben asked.

"It wasn't their style," Joe said softly. "Your dad—

well, you'll know this—had his tongue removed. Chris was simply beaten to death."

And that was supposed to be consolation?

"Look, sons," Joe said, "I know this is a difficult time, but I'm telling you again to maintain the tightest security, okay? This place, your homes—they need to be tighter than a duck's arse. Make sure you have people around you when you go out. Take no risks at all, got that?"

Ben nodded impatiently. Mark swallowed more whisky.

"Manchester is crawling with people I count as friends," Joe assured them. "It's expensive, yes, but if anyone connected to you, or anyone who was connected to your dad, makes a move, I'll know about it. I even have prison guards on my payroll. Yes, really, I have a couple in Strangeways listening and watching for anything."

Ben walked a circle of the office. They were between a rock and a hard place. Joe had contacts, they knew that, and it was strangely reassuring to know they were out on the streets. They couldn't stop paying Joe, or he'd have to stop paying them.

But what had Christian meant? *You will not believe what that bastard did...*

"Why was he angry?" Ben asked. "He phoned me. He was on the train going straight to meet you."

"What did he say?" Joe asked.

"Not a lot because the connection kept breaking up. He was angry with you though. He said, 'You will not believe what that bastard did.' Those were his exact words."

Joe laughed. "How the devil would I know? Chris was

in one of his moods, you know he was. I expect he was annoyed because I told him I always go to Tempo on a Thursday night and said I'd meet him there. He certainly wasn't happy about meeting in a club."

Was that all? No. Christian had been *really* angry. There had to have been more to it than that.

"You said, 'suspects,'" Ben reminded him. "Who are these suspects of yours?"

"It's safer for you right now not to know," Joe said. "You've heard nothing from anyone?"

"No."

"That's another thing," Joe said. "If it had been personal, someone would be gloating. As unlikely as it sounds, it is possible that Chris's death was a horrible, tragic coincidence."

He gave them a moment for that to sink in, and possibly for them to draw comfort from it. Ben couldn't. His kid brother was dead and he didn't think he'd ever take comfort from anything ever again.

"How's Susie doing?" Joe asked.

"She's okay," Mark said. "She was on the phone ten minutes ago, and yeah, she's doing okay. She has people there—family—and we're travelling down to be with her tomorrow."

"Good. Good. I've phoned her to offer my condolences, of course, but although she sounded as if she was bearing up, it's difficult to tell over the phone. You tell her from me that, if there's anything she needs, anything at all, she must get in touch with me, okay?"

"Yes, of course," Mark said. "Thanks, Uncle Joe. Here, have another drink."

"Better not." Joe was all sympathetic smiles. "I'm

driving and I don't want the law on my back—not till we've got to the bottom of this."

He stood, ready to take his leave, but Ben wanted answers. "It seems to me we'd be one hell of a lot safer if we did know the names of your so-called suspects. We need names, Joe!"

Joe stood completely still, thinking. "Okay," he said slowly, "does the name David Young ring a bell?"

The name meant nothing to Ben. He looked to Mark, who shook his head. "Why do you want to know?"

"It's probably nothing. Me and him used to work together—for McCoy. When McCoy was busted, Young got sent down. Did eight months, I think. But the night Chris was supposed to be meeting me—"

"The night he was murdered," Mark said.

"Yes," Joe agreed. "That night, Young ended up in Tempo, the club where I was supposed to meet Chris. Things had got too hot for him to handle down south so he'd got a train up here, to Manchester. Except the prick fell asleep, got into a fight with a ticket inspector and jumped off the train in Dawson's Clough. We were still in Tempo, catching up on old times, when the law arrived to arrest him. He's got no money and a court case coming up, so he's staying with me temporarily."

"And you don't trust him?"

"I did," Joe said slowly, "but him showing up the same night that Chris was killed struck me as a bit of a coincidence. And tonight, before I came here, he was asking about Christian. He said he'd seen it in the local paper and was talking about your dad's murder."

"Fucking hell! He must be our man," Ben said.

Joe grimaced. "I don't know. The police are watching his every move, so it would have been difficult for him.

But I'll get someone to keep an eye on him. Of course, it won't be cheap—"

Mark went straight to the safe, struggled with the combination and finally managed to open it. He pulled out several bundles of cash, about fifty grand.

"Do whatever it takes," Mark said. "If that bastard killed Chris—"

"He's a dead man," Joe finished for him. "Don't you fret about that, boys. If Davey Young's involved in any way at all, he'll wish he'd never been born. You can trust me on that one!"

David Young. Ben would remember that name. He'd do some digging around himself.

Chapter Twenty-One

BEV DIDN'T KNOW what to blame for her sleepless night, the pain she was in or worrying about the pain she was in. Either way, it was four-thirty and she hadn't slept above ten minutes all night. She switched on the bedside lamp, reached for her phone to see if any messages had come through from Dylan—nothing—and picked up her book. If she couldn't sleep, she might as well read.

She was halfway through a romantic suspense novel that was well written and had the best hero ever, yet she couldn't concentrate on the heroine's plight. After several minutes, her eyes feeling as if she'd bathed them in gravel, she realised she'd done nothing but read the same paragraph over and over again. She put down the book, switched off the lamp, gave her pillow a heartfelt thump and closed her eyes.

She wasn't one of those needy women. She had her own fulfilling life, she had the children, she was independent and she was used to Dylan being away—but right now, she missed him like hell. She'd love him to be here, to tell her with his own brand of impatience that she was worrying about nothing.

A distant ambulance raced to an emergency, and when the siren faded away there wasn't a sound. No cars, no birds, no wind—more important, no children. They'd soon be awake though, and yet again she'd feel like death. She didn't cope well when deprived of her sleep. It made her edgy and irritable.

She began counting backward from 500 but lost her place at 489. Tomorrow—today, she corrected herself— she'd go for a good long walk. She needed more fresh air and exercise. Certainly at the weekend, she'd drag the kids outside for a walk.

She turned over and lay on her back to stare at the ceiling. Not that she could see the ceiling. Not a peep of light penetrated these blackout blinds.

For the hundredth time that day, she asked herself exactly what she was worrying about. People walked around with all sorts of aches, pains and nasty ailments. They didn't panic that they were on the verge of death, so why was she constantly worrying? There were hundreds of complaints that could cause the pain she was getting. She should know, she'd spent enough hours on the internet investigating them all.

She had a bad feeling about it, that was all. Come to that, she had a bad feeling about everything right now. She hated Dylan working undercover. It could get dangerous if his identity was discovered. He wasn't living with saints, he was living with a possible—probable— killer.

She switched on her phone to check the time. A cheery message told her the alarm would be sounding in exactly one hour and seven minutes. Great.

Tomorrow, as well as treating her body to some physical exercise, she'd make sure she'd had a few glasses of wine before she crawled into bed. If the exercise didn't help, the alcohol would have to.

She eventually drifted off and was woken by the shrill

screeching of her alarm. She felt worse, if that were possible, than she had before she fell asleep.

Miraculously, the children were still sleeping, so she went straight to the shower and let the hot water wake her. With her body clean and her hair washed, she felt better. With a strong cup of coffee inside her, she felt almost human.

The chaos that followed gave her no time to think. Getting Luke ready for school had been easier when he was five. These days, he'd be engrossed in his music, or talking instead of eating breakfast. Freya was in one of those moods when she would only stop grizzling if she was picked up and carried.

Dylan's mum arrived at her usual time, and Bev breathed a relieved sigh. "You'll have fun with madam today."

"I always do." Vicky beamed at her granddaughter and happily carried her around the room while Bev grabbed everything she—and Luke—needed for the day.

"Right, we're off. If you have any problems—"

"I'll call," Vicky said. "Off you go. Have fun."

"Fun?" Luke scoffed. "At school?"

"You never know."

"I do."

Bev grabbed her handbag and car keys just as the phone rang. She crossed the room to inspect the display, ready to ignore it, but it was the health centre. Her stomach did an impressive backflip. They never phoned. If you'd had blood tests done, you had to badger them to make certain the results were back and, more important, that they'd been checked by a doctor.

"Hello?"

"Mrs. Scott?"

"Yes." Bev expected her heart to burst through her rib cage at any moment.

"This is the health centre. I'm calling to let you know your blood test results are back. There's nothing to worry about, but Dr. Singh would like to see you as soon as possible. Can you come in today?"

Nothing to worry about. Nothing to worry about.

"Well, yes. What sort of time?"

"As soon as possible."

Nothing to worry about.

Bev tried to think about the day's schedule but her mind was too busy panicking to think straight. "I can make it around eleven."

"Let me see—how about ten past eleven?"

"Yes."

"Excellent. Right, Mrs. Scott, that's ten past eleven with Dr. Singh."

Bev returned the phone to its cradle.

"Everything all right, love?" Vicky asked.

"Yes, fine." Bev forced her face into something resembling a smile. "Just the health centre calling to say my blood test results are back. They want to see me this morning."

Something flashed across Vicky's face but was gone before Bev could analyse it. "I'm sure there's nothing to worry about."

"That's what they said. Nothing to worry about. Anyway, I'll have to go or I'll be late."

"Good luck," Vicky called after her.

Nothing to worry about.

Of course there was something to worry about, Bev thought as she climbed in her car, fired the engine and slammed it into gear. If there was nothing to worry about, the receptionist could have given her the results. There was no need for a doctor's appointment when there was nothing to worry about.

Perhaps she was overreacting but she was damn sure there was plenty to worry about.

Chapter Twenty-Two

DYLAN HAD FINISHED the Everest of washing up and was sneaking a quick coffee before his allotted two hours of manual labour when Doll strode into the kitchen. This morning's outfit was the trademark short skirt—it was a wonder she didn't get frostbite—and tight blue blouse.

Apart from a few brief moments on Tuesday morning, when she'd brought Anna Woodward to the kitchen, it was the first time he'd seen her since Monday night. And the more he thought about that, the more convinced he became that she would have met up with John Taylor if he hadn't been there.

"How are things with you, Doll?"

"Oh—" She sighed. "Okay, I suppose. They'd be a damn sight better if that Woodward girl would keep her hands to herself. If she thinks she's getting hooked up with Hank, she can think again. The last thing he needs in his life is a little slut like her."

Such a welcoming Christian attitude warmed your heart.

"She's a kid, Doll. I'm sure she's harmless enough."

"Pah." She poured herself a coffee, and spilt half of it on the counter. "I've warned her about coming on to him. If she tries it on again, she'll be out. Joe can say what he likes, but she'll be gone."

"Gone where? She doesn't have anywhere else, does she?"

"I don't care where she goes, so long as it's away from here." She took a sip of coffee that must have scalded her lips. "The young ones are the worst. They have great bodies—" She gave a bitter laugh. "Didn't we all at that age? They think it's their duty to flaunt them and catch the most eligible male they can."

It wasn't in Doll's nature to age gracefully. She'd see the flaws, the odd wrinkle here and the sagging there. Age wouldn't be welcomed or accepted in her world.

"I expect it's a bit of fun to her," he said.

"Pah," she said again.

Hell hath no fury like a woman ageing and jealous.

"I don't suppose you're going to town tonight, are you, Doll?"

Her scowl deepened briefly. "I might be. Why?"

"I wondered if I could share a taxi with you. Or with Joe, if he's going. I thought I might go in that club and have a couple of cheap drinks."

"Tempo?"

"That's the one. I met Joe there last week."

"I know." She sighed. "Yes, I'll be going in. I'm meeting up with my friend, the one I should have seen on Monday. If she's better, that is. She's had a stinking cold."

"Fingers crossed then. Can I beg a lift?"

"Sure." She didn't look happy about it.

"Thanks. I appreciate it."

She took her phone from a skirt pocket. "Don't you need to be at the chapel?"

He grinned and gave her a mock salute. "I do, yeah. I'm on my way."

He rinsed his cup and put it away, then left her to her phone call. He closed the kitchen door behind him,

walked away with a heavier tread than usual, then crept
silently back to the door and listened.

"No, no," Doll was saying. "I'll have to see you somewhere else, that's all. How about the Rising Sun?"

The Rising Sun. As Dylan crept off again, he pic-
tured the faded sign hanging outside a pub. He simply
couldn't place where that pub was.

He made his way to the chapel, ready to begin work.

"Have you done any plastering before?" Child asked.

"What? No, of course not."

"There's a first time for everything." Child grinned at
him. "It doesn't have to be a professional job. It's good
that we all chip in though, don't you think?"

"I don't have the first clue about plastering."

"It's easy enough. The mix details are on the bags of
plaster. We've got an old electric mixer out the back, so
you don't have to do it by hand. Then spread it on the
walls as evenly as possible. Adrian's helping. Between
you, you'll do a great job."

Dylan went outside to where Adrian was studying
the instructions on a bag of plaster. "You done this before, Dave?"

"No. You?"

"No. Between you and me, I don't think it's as easy
as it looks."

"I'm damn sure it isn't."

"Ah well, I suppose all we can do is give it our best
shot."

Their best shot was going to be a disaster, but Dylan
had far more important things on his mind than the inside of a building that might or might not be used as a
chapel. He'd searched the damn place and found nothing,

but he wasn't convinced that the old stone barn didn't have a far more sinister purpose.

As they mixed the plaster, he was aware of Kennedy working on the ever-expanding vegetable plot. Their mysterious gardener had been absent for a couple of days, and Dylan would love to know what he did in his spare time. He'd love to know why he watched everything and said nothing too.

The plastering, thanks to Adrian's persistence, wasn't too bad at all. Obviously, if you'd paid someone to do a similar job in your home, you'd demand your money back, but it was passable. Even Child was impressed.

"See? I told you so. The Lord gave you talents you aren't even aware of."

Dylan wished the Lord had given him a few more talents—like X-ray vision.

Their work stint was soon over, and instead of joining Adrian at the house for a well-earned lunch, Dylan crossed the yard to the vegetable patch where Kennedy was moving the earth.

"Hi," Dylan greeted him. "We met before, but it was dark. Dave Young."

There was no answer.

"And you're Kennedy. Is that first or last name?"

No answer. There wasn't so much as a blink.

"I'd love to know why you won't talk to anyone," he said. "People believe you're deaf and dumb, you know. I know that's not true because I've heard you talking to the cat. You're well-spoken and I'd bet my life you've had a good education."

Kennedy's gaunt face was dominated by slate-grey eyes that seemed to look straight through Dylan. He stood motionless, the metal fork idle. For a moment,

Dylan thought he was about to get an explanation, but after a minute or so, Kennedy lowered his gaze and turned over more ground.

"I suppose you'd have a lot of explaining to do if people knew you could talk," Dylan said. "Joe Child would certainly want to know why, instead of chatting, you preferred to spend your time watching everyone and everything. He might be a bit angry and, as you may or may not know, he's not a bloke to cross. It could be the last tenner and half dozen eggs you get from him."

The fork was idle again. Kennedy leaned on the handle, those eyes of his burning into Dylan's. "So what are you going to do about it? Tell him I'm working in his garden under false pretences?"

Even knowing he could speak, and speak well, Dylan was still surprised by the sound of his voice. "No. I'd rather hear what you've seen going on in this place."

"Oh, I'm sure you would." That piercing gaze became more thoughtful. "I've seen Anna Woodward meeting Hank Child in the chapel for a late-night sex session. I've seen Gordon Riley turn up at all hours of the day and night."

"Really?"

"Yes. Really."

"So—what exactly are you doing here?" Dylan asked.

Kennedy smiled at that and the weariness seemed to slip away from his face. "What exactly are *you* doing here? What are you? A police officer? A private investigator? I'd guess at the latter. Am I right? Are you a private investigator?"

Dylan didn't answer that. "What else have you seen?"

"I've seen you creeping out at night to meet up with ex-Detective Chief Inspector Willoughby."

Chapter Twenty-Three

"THANKS, DOLL! SEE you later." Dylan left the taxi and ambled up to Tempo's front doors. He stood to watch the taxi disappear into the night, and then he approached the two bouncers who guarded the entrance to Tempo. "Can you tell me where the Rising Sun is, mate?"

"Yeah. I can tell you it's a dump too. It's at the back of the old bingo hall on Cavendish Street."

"Of course it is." Dylan could remember passing it one night and seeing a drunk comatose at the bus stop opposite. "Thanks."

He went inside and shuddered. Tempo looked tackier than usual, if that were possible.

There was no one in sight that he recognised, on either side of the bar. Certainly no one behind the bar would recognise him as the drunk who enjoyed threatening coppers with broken bottles.

Child, according to Doll, wouldn't be arriving until later as he had a "spot of business to attend to." Dylan would love to know what that was about.

More important, he'd love to know how in hell's name Kennedy had guessed he was a private investigator and how he'd known he'd met up with Frank. Dylan was slipping. He should have known he was being followed. He'd got no clues from Kennedy, because just as he opened his mouth to pose the question, Child had appeared.

"You may as well talk to yourself as talk to him," he'd said. "Isn't that right, Kennedy?"

Kennedy had grunted and returned to the task of turning over soil.

"Davey, I need you to come with me. The window in the back stables has finally disintegrated and I want to get it boarded up. It'll be easier with two of us."

Dylan had no choice but to walk with Child to the stable block. He'd gone with an extremely uneasy feeling.

Dylan had done little poking around at the refuge during the night, as he'd considered it too dangerous. Kennedy had no such qualms. Who the hell was he, and what was he up to?

Before ordering himself a drink, Dylan crossed the crowded room to the toilets. He dived inside one of the cubicles and removed his boot. Nestling beneath the insole was his sim card. He swapped it with Davey Young's and listened to his messages.

The first was a torrent from Bev. She was talking too loudly—and hysterically—for him to take it in at first, and he had to listen again. Even then, all he caught was "doctor" and "scan" and "Oh, my fucking God, Dylan."

Frowning, he played his next message. Another from Bev. "Sorry, I panicked. I expect it'll be okay. Give me a call though, will you? Hope you're okay."

The third and fourth were from prospective clients and they'd have to wait. If Child discovered his real identity, he wouldn't be needing any clients. All he'd need was a tag round his big toe.

He swapped sim cards again, left the toilets and went to the bar. While he waited to be served, he looked around him. Most customers were young, either late teens or early twenties. If this was Child's hunting ground, and if he was hunting teenage girls, preferably blonde ones, it was an excellent choice of venue.

Coloured bulbs flashed impressively but provided more shadows than light. Most people were watching the girls dancing on stage or around the tables. If you were so inclined, you could get up to mischief without being noticed.

Dylan had only intended to have one quick drink to pass enough time to allow Doll to get nicely settled in the Rising Sun, but as he drained his glass, in walked Child. He wasn't alone. Walking on his right was Gordon Riley, and Riley's arm was resting lightly on Anna Woodward's waist as he ushered her to the bar. Both men were smiling. Anna was giggling at something Riley had said. She was wearing heavy makeup, ridiculously high heels and a sophisticated black dress. She'd easily have passed for eighteen, but Dylan still thought she was closer to sixteen.

Dylan watched them at the opposite end of the bar as they ordered their drinks. Riley was paying. Anna ordered a triple vodka. He wasn't close enough to hear what was being said—the music was too loud anyway—but Anna was batting her eyelashes at Riley and obviously pleading with him for something. Finally, he gave in and allowed himself to be led to the dance floor. It just proved that money could buy anything. Riley was nothing to look at and Anna wouldn't have spared him a second glance if it weren't for his wallet. Who said size didn't matter?

Dylan ordered himself another drink and wandered over to where Child was watching his friends.

"Hey, Joe, how's things?"

"Davey, boy! I wondered if we'd see you here."

"I'm only having a couple. The price will be going up in a minute, so I'll go and have a look at the local pubs." Smiling, he nodded across at the dance floor. "I think your friend's a bit old for Anna."

"It's only a bit of fun and at least we can see that she gets home safely. Believe me, she's better off with Gordon than some of the idiots in here."

"It's probably Gordon you need to worry about."

Child gave a hearty laugh. "Probably. He won't get too carried away and she'll soon grow tired of his computer jargon. He's a great mate, of course, but believe me, he could bore the balls off a buffalo when he talks computers and software."

"She probably won't be able to hear him over this racket," Dylan said as the volume was cranked up a notch.

"True."

Dylan sipped at his whisky. He wondered if the staff knew that watering down drinks, even if they were cheap, was against the law.

"Did you see Barney Fraser's boys last night?" he asked.

"I did." The smile was replaced with a sympathetic sigh. "They're bearing up. Nothing else they can do, is there? It's their mother I feel for. She's done nothing to deserve this. The boys are travelling down to London to be with her, and I'll probably pay a quick visit too, just to see if there's anything I can do. They're like family to me."

"Have they any idea who killed him?"

"None at all. As his phone and wallet were missing, we can only assume it was a mugging. If someone pulled a knife on me and asked for my cash, I'd hand it over. No question. Christian wouldn't. He'd act first and think later."

"Was a knife used?"

"Well, no. But you know what I mean."

"Yeah." He knew exactly what he meant. By nature, Child was a suspicious bastard, and if he was pimping the mugging theory, it was odds-on he knew who'd ended Christian Fraser's life.

It seemed to Dylan that the more questions he asked, the more questions he needed to ask. Answers, on the other hand, were sadly lacking. He had no idea what was going on in Child's life, and he certainly had no idea what had happened to Caroline and Farrah, but he knew the two were connected. Until he could get to the bottom of Child's sordid lot, he stood no chance of discovering the whereabouts of the two girls.

"Do you want a lift back later, Davey?"

"No—unless it's in Gordon's Bentley."

Child snorted with laughter. "You and your cars."

"I know, I know. Thou shalt not cover thy neighbour's ox or donkey, or anything else that belongs to thy neighbour. James 14."

Child looked impressed. "Very good."

It would have been even better if Dylan could have remembered the whole quote, and it sure as hell didn't come from James 14. He didn't know where it came from. And neither did Child.

"For your information though, Davey, Gordon's staying in a hotel and travelling back in the morning. I'll get a taxi and drop him off." Child looked across to where Riley and Anna were dancing. "And don't worry about Anna. I'll make sure she shares that taxi."

"Good idea. I'll wander off in a minute. If I'm stuck for a lift, I'll call back here and see if you're still around."

"Suit yourself."

They were joined by a red-faced Anna and an extremely satisfied-looking Riley. Dylan supposed any bloke's ego would be given a stroke if they had an eighteen—or sixteen—year-old fawning over them. Sadly, Dylan's bank balance never ran to such luxuries.

Talk was general, and boring, so Dylan said his goodnights and left them to it.

The temperature had dropped dramatically and a stiff wind swirled snowflakes around his face. He walked quickly, hands deep in his pockets, and was grateful to push open the door of the Rising Sun.

This pub was slightly more appealing than the Jolly Sailor. Slightly. There were six customers inside, but unfortunately, Doll was nowhere in sight. Sod it, he should have gone with his instincts and followed her.

The young barmaid looked bored as she stared at a silent TV. Adverts for wash powder clearly didn't interest her. She looked as if she didn't even have the energy to chew her gum.

"A double whisky, please." He might as well make the most of his visit.

She didn't answer, but she did slowly reach for a glass and put it to the optic. "Anything in it?"

"No, thanks. As it comes." He handed her a ten-pound note. "It's quiet in here tonight."

"It's quiet every night."

"I was hoping some friends of mine might have called in."

"Oh? Who might they be?"

"Joe Child. Do you know him? Or his wife, Doll."

"She's been in." Her expression said she wasn't Doll's number-one fan. "She met up with Maggie Cummings. They had a gin and tonic each and then left."

"Ah, right. Oh, well, never mind." He felt deflated. He'd been sure she was meeting Taylor. "I'm only stopping for a quick one myself. It's not much fun drinking alone, is it?"

She shrugged and returned her gaze to the TV.

He wished now that he'd stayed at Tempo. Not that he expected to learn much from anyone there. If there was one thing Child was good at, it was keeping up appearances. Whatever he was up to, everything on the outside would be squeaky-clean.

He soon left the Rising Sun and made his way to the Jolly Sailor. There was no sign of Doll or Taylor in there either, but Malcolm Brindle was at the bar. Judging by his bleary-eyed expression, he'd been propping it up for a while.

"Oh, hello there, David. Good to see you. Did you ask around? Did you ask people at the refuge if they'd seen or heard from Farrah?" Brindle was an image of despair. His hair was sticking up as if he'd tried to pull it from his head.

"I did. Sorry. Here, let me get you a drink."

"Thanks."

The barmaid was her usual unfriendly self, but she soon had their drinks in front of them and was handing Dylan his change.

"I even asked Walter Topham," Dylan said. "I thought—well, I thought that if she didn't feel able to contact you for some reason, she might have spoken to him. I expect they were quite close, given that he helped her with her dog, I mean."

"He's a miserable so-and-so."

Dylan couldn't argue with that. "I heard his daughter had been killed in a car accident, so I suppose he has good reason to be."

"Yes, she was. I don't think he ever got over it. No one would, would they?"

"Unlikely. Did Farrah go to his farm often?"

"More often than I liked," Brindle said. "She thinks he's wonderful. It always amused her that dogs and chickens were free to roam the kitchen together. He lives in a pigsty but he doesn't mind, and Farrah didn't either. Sometimes, she'd be there all weekend. Not overnight, of course, but she'd get to his place around seven and help him around the farm, with the sheep, you know, until seven at night. Then, the next day, she'd be there again."

"Do the police know that?"

"Yes. We gave them a list of names and addresses of people she spent time with. I know they spoke to him. Why do you ask?"

"No reason. I just wondered if they were checking everyone she might get in touch with. Your wife thought she might have been meeting up with a boyfriend that she hadn't mentioned. Is that likely?"

"That's all we can think," Brindle said. "We never knew. She said she was meeting up with friends, but they knew nothing about it. We think there was a boyfriend. To be honest, we thought there must be something wrong—we thought he might be married or something." He was silent for long moments. "If she's dead—" He broke off, unable to continue.

Dylan wanted to offer a few platitudes but could force none through his lips. If Child was involved in her disappearance, she probably was. If not, she'd probably be wishing she were.

"I'll keep asking around," Dylan said. "People come and go at the refuge. You never know."

Brindle nodded his thanks, but there was no hope left inside him. "That woman from your refuge was in earlier."

"Which one?"

"The cheap-looking one. Married to the chap who owns the place, I think."

"Doll? Black hair, long fingernails, short skirt?"

"That's her. She came in, had a quick drink, took a phone call, met up with another woman and then left."

"What about that chap you saw in here? Taylor, is it? Has he been in again?"

"Yes, he's here most nights. That's why I've taken to calling in. He left about two minutes after that woman from your refuge."

Interesting.

"I was going to have a word with him," Brindle said, "but he was gone so fast."

"I don't suppose he knows anything," Dylan said. "If he did, I'm sure he'd tell the police. After all, his step-daughter is missing too."

"He's not worrying about that. He's always laughing with his chums. He plays darts as if it's the most important thing in the world. I don't know what I was going to say to him, but I know he's involved, I just know it. I'll get the truth out of him though, you can be sure of that."

"And how do you intend to do that?" It was probably a waste of breath talking to Brindle because he'd clearly been drowning his sorrows for a few hours. "The police couldn't get anything out of him, so why do you think you'll succeed?"

Brindle leaned in close, so close that Dylan almost choked on whisky fumes. "Can I trust you?"

Trust me, I'm a private investigator. "Of course."

"I'm going to get something to put in his drink. At first, I thought I'd get hold of chloroform, but it's not easy to find—not without raising suspicions."

Dylan felt his eyebrows shoot up. "Chloroform?"

"I dismissed that. Instead, I'm going to put some Valium or flunitrazepam in his drink. That's the stuff they use—this date-rape thing."

Dylan nodded slowly. "I know what it is."

"I'll see him here, slip something in his drink, then make some excuse to get him to come outside with me." His voice dropped so low that Dylan struggled to hear him. "I've got a gun. An Asian chap that I'd heard about sold it to me. I'll threaten him with that. I'll make him talk."

Holy crap. Dylan sucked in a breath. "I don't think that's a good idea. I'm sure he's innocent, but even if he isn't, he's not the sort of bloke to argue with. He's a hard case. He's been in trouble with the police for domestic violence and ABH—actual bodily harm. At least, that's what I heard."

"He won't argue with a gun held to his head."

Give me strength! Dylan had heard it all now. The mouse that was Malcolm Brindle wouldn't stand a chance against a thug like Taylor.

"Tell you what, Malcolm. You've got my phone number, right? You tell me when you're going to confront Taylor and I'll come along. You'll be safer that way. He'll think twice about taking on two of us. Besides, one can hold him and the other can do what's necessary."

Brindle leaned back on his stool. "Would you? Would you do that?"

"Why not? If he is hiding something, you need to know. I won't do anything bad. I certainly won't hurt him—"

"Oh, no. I only want him to talk."

"Then I'm with you. Just let me know when and where, okay? And try to give me a couple of hours' notice."

"I will." Brindle reached for Dylan's hand and clasped it tight. "Thank you so much. That means a lot to me."

"I still say it's a crazy thing to do. But if you're determined, it will be easier with two."

"Thank you. Truly, I mean it." He looked slightly more hopeful now, as if there was something he could do to find his daughter. "It's time I went home. Clare, you know. I don't like to think of her being alone. Good to see you again, David. And thank you."

"If I hear anything, I'll be in touch."

"Thank you."

Brindle drained his glass, pushed himself away from the bar, staggered for a couple of paces, got his bearings and walked out.

Brindle was a ticking time bomb but Dylan felt sure Taylor could take care of himself. Not that anyone could argue with a bullet. Jeez.

Dylan ordered another drink. He needed something to cheer himself up.

He'd only been in Dawson's Clough a short time though, so it was madness to despair. A week ago tonight, he'd met up with Child and spent the night in a police cell. A week was nothing. It wasn't too surprising that he'd made no progress. He *would* find Farrah Brindle and Caroline Aldridge, come hell or high water he'd find them, but he had to remember that Rome hadn't been built in a day.

"You'd better make it a double," he told the barmaid.

Chapter Twenty-Four

DYLAN LEFT THE Jolly Sailor and went back to Tempo for a quick drink. There was no sign of Child and he soon left the still-rowdy club.

The taxi rank was deserted. It was cold but at least it wasn't snowing, so he hung around for a few minutes before deciding the walk would do him good. Given that it was all uphill, he'd stand half a chance of being warm when he fell into his makeshift bed.

A half-moon was shedding a little light, and his eyes soon adjusted to the darkness. Car headlights dazzled him occasionally.

When he was a mile from town, he leaned against a precarious stone wall and swapped his phone's sim cards. He hit the button for Bev.

"Hi!" She sounded sleepy, but pleased to hear from him.

"Sorry. Did I wake you?"

"No. I couldn't sleep. How's it going up there? And why are you out of breath?"

"Uphill. And slowly," he said. "But never mind that, tell me in words of one syllable what's going on with you."

"Okay. I'm sorry I panicked but—" She took a breath. "I had that blood test to see if I had raised levels of CA-125, right? If levels are normal, you can more or less rule out ovarian cancer. Well, the health centre phoned me this morning. I had to see the doctor and she told me my levels *aren't* normal. They're unusually high."

"Right. So what are they going to do about it?"

"They'd already booked me in for a scan, but unless it's an emergency, appointments for those usually take about six weeks to come through. As I have these high levels of CA-125, they've rushed it through and I'm going for a scan on Monday."

"That's good then." It was frighteningly efficient for the NHS. "You'll hopefully know more then."

"Yes." She was silent for a moment. "What if it's cancer, Dylan?"

"It won't be. You're far too young for that."

"I don't think cancer has much respect for age."

"It could be one of a hundred things. They always start by ruling out the bad stuff. You'll be fine. You're healthy enough—you've had a bit of pain, Bev, but you can't say you've felt ill. If it was cancer, you'd be feeling terrible."

"That's what I keep telling myself."

"And even if the worst came to the worst, they can sort stuff like that so long as they find it early enough. You'll be fine."

"I hope so."

He could hear the tremor in her voice and wished he were with her. "You will. Trust me, I'm a private investigator."

"Oh, yeah. For a minute there, I'd forgotten." Her voice was lighter. "So how's it going with you? Have you any idea where those girls are yet?"

"Not yet, but when I have, you'll be the first to know. You can have the honour of shaving off this sodding beard. It's driving me mad."

They chatted about the kids and life in general for a couple of minutes and then Dylan had to go. "I'll call you tomorrow, sweetheart. Try not to worry, okay?"

"I'll try."

As Dylan swapped sim cards again, a sudden gust of icy wind made him shiver. He'd had an uneasy feeling since arriving in the godforsaken north, and worrying about Bev wasn't helping matters. Not that he was planning to worry *too* much. Even if she was diagnosed with ovarian cancer, it wasn't the end of the world. A quick operation would soon remove her ovaries. It wasn't as if they were needed.

They were fortunate in that his mother was fit and healthy, so if Bev did need treatment, the doting grandmother would be more than happy to take charge of the kids.

He'd soon get to the bottom of whatever it was Child was up to, he'd soon find the missing girls, and then he could go home and be there for his family.

He carried on walking and managed to reach the turn-off for the refuge without falling in a ditch and breaking an ankle. All he had to do now was negotiate the potholes in the lane. That would be easier if the moon didn't insist on disappearing behind clouds every few seconds.

He'd almost reached his shed when he heard a sound. It could have been anything, a fox out hunting or a cat on the prowl. He stood still. There was nothing to be seen or heard.

A distant owl hooted and then he heard that sound again. Had someone stood on a dry twig?

He moved slowly and quietly to where he thought the noise had come from. He had the distinct feeling he wasn't alone.

Kennedy emerged from the shadows and Dylan's heart skipped a shocked beat.

"Well, well. It's a bit late for planting potatoes." Dylan spoke in a whisper so as not to alert anyone else to their presence. "A perfect night for spying on the residents though."

"Indeed."

"So what are you up to?" Dylan asked. "What exactly are you doing here?"

"The same as you, I imagine. What exactly are *you* doing here?"

Dylan hated these cat-and-mouse games, but he wasn't inclined to tell Kennedy anything. At least nothing he didn't already know. "Staying with an old friend—temporarily," he replied.

It was impossible to read the expression on Kennedy's face in the near-total darkness, but a soft snort told him the chap wasn't impressed with his answer.

"What about you?" Dylan asked. "And who are you?"

"That doesn't matter."

"What are you doing here at this time of night?"

"Spying on the residents. Trying to find out what's going on. As I said, the same as you."

"What have you found out then?"

Kennedy tapped his foot silently on the ground for a moment. Then, surprisingly, he spoke. "Joe Child is as Christian as Satan himself. One of the sons is on drugs and fancies himself as a ladies' man. The other is gambling heavily. Gordon Riley turns up at all hours. He arrives in style, driving his Bentley when his visits are official, and he gets a taxi to drop him off halfway between here and town when his visits are—what shall we say?—unofficial."

"Does he indeed? How often does he visit?"

"Twice this week. Three times last week."

Interesting. "When you say Child is as Christian as Satan himself, what do you mean? What's he doing that's so bad?"

"He's getting money out of people by threatening them. I've overheard two phone conversations he's had. In both, he told the person on the other end that they had no choice but to pay up. In one, he said, 'Pay up or wind up dead, it's your choice.' I don't know who he was speaking to. It could have been the same person or two people. Even around me, dumb half-wit that I am, he was trying not to be overheard."

A car's headlights lit up the sky as a vehicle turned onto the lane.

"Get back," Dylan said, urging Kennedy into the dark safety of the bushes.

They both watched in silence as Child and Anna climbed out of the taxi. Child paid the man and, laughing, he and Anna hurried inside. The taxi drove off into the night.

There had been no sign of Child or Anna at the nightclub, and it had taken Dylan the best part of an hour to walk back to the refuge. Where had the two been between leaving Tempo and getting out of that taxi?

"Child's wife arrived half an hour ago," Kennedy said, his voice low. "Different taxi. Alone."

Kennedy sniffed the air, much like a wild animal seeking its prey. "It's time I was off."

"I'll walk to the end of the lane with you."

They set off, careful to keep to the uneven verge at the edge of the lane where the hedge and occasional tree gave them cover.

"Why?" Dylan asked. "Why are you so intent on finding out what's going on here?"

"Why are you?"

As Kennedy had shared his information, it seemed only fair that Dylan do the same. "Two girls with connections to this place have vanished into thin air. I want to know what happened to them."

"Ah." Kennedy was almost dismissive. "I gather those connections are a little tenuous."

He was right. Dylan was convinced Child and the refuge were involved in their disappearance though.

He was so lost in thought that they reached the end of the lane without him noticing.

"Good luck," Kennedy said. "And good night."

He set off at a smart pace in the direction of the town.

Dylan wanted to follow, to grab Kennedy by the throat and demand to know exactly what he was doing at the refuge. It would be a pointless exercise though.

He removed his boot and swapped sim cards in his phone again. He found Frank's number and hit the button.

"Yes?" He sounded half asleep.

"Sorry, did I wake you?" Dylan spoke in a whisper.

"You did, but only because I'd fallen asleep in front of the TV. What's up, Dylan?"

"What's not? Malcolm bloody Brindle, for starters. He's decided that John Taylor did something to his step-daughter and then did the same thing to Farrah to cover his tracks."

"What's given him that idea?"

"God knows. He doesn't believe that CID would have questioned Taylor without reason. He's convinced they suspect him but don't have enough evidence to charge him. The good news is that when I met Brindle tonight, he was so drunk he'll probably have forgotten everything by morning. The bad news is that he's got a gun. He's planning to put something in Taylor's drink and then hold a gun to his head to make him talk."

"Bloody hell."

"Exactly. He needs watching, Frank. I've said I'll do the deed with him, so long as he gives me notice, but if he decides to go it alone—"

"We'll have another corpse in the Clough. Brindle's probably."

"Yeah." Dylan didn't have time for a chat. "There's something else. Riley is a more frequent visitor than I thought, it seems. Can you send me names and addresses for anyone who knows him and Child from way back? Send stuff to this phone and I'll pick it up when I can."

"Will do. Anything else?"

"Not yet. You go and enjoy your warm bed. Have a wee dram of Scotch and think of me shivering to death in that bloody shed."

Frank chuckled. "Take care."

Trying not to think about Frank's warm, comfortable house with its well-stocked drinks cabinet, Dylan returned Davey Young's sim card to his phone and trudged back along the lane to the refuge. He didn't know what he wanted most—a stiff drink, a hot shower, a shave or a warm bed.

A light was on in the kitchen and he went to investigate. Anna Woodward was sitting at the table, nursing a mug of hot chocolate. Her eyes were red and a little moist. Unless Dylan was mistaken, she'd been crying.

"Everything all right, Anna?"

"Yes, great, thanks."

"Did you have a good evening?"

"Yes. It was lovely, thanks."

"Do you want a sandwich?" he asked, pulling open the fridge door. "I can offer you cheese and tomato or cheese and onion."

She smiled but looked as if she was going to start crying again. "Cheese and tomato would be good. Thanks. I think I've had too much to drink. It might help settle my stomach."

"You need a good fry-up to do that. Make sure you eat lots for breakfast."

"I will."

As he made sandwiches, Dylan revised his opinion of Anna. She might be a spoiled little rich kid, but she was also a little lost and lonely. Her bravado had deserted her this evening. She was too busy being sad to put on her sophisticated woman-of-the-world act.

He put a sandwich in front of her. "Thanks."

"So why have you been crying?" He sat opposite and bit into bread that could have been fresher. "Nothing's that bad, is it?"

"It's my nan's birthday today. Or should have been. She died a couple of months ago."

"I'm sorry. Were you close?"

"Yeah. She was the nicest person I've ever known. I used to call on her every day. She lived near us and I'd call in on my way home from school." She flushed with colour. "That's when I was going to school, of course."

"Of course."

"I'd often stay with her for the weekend too. That was fun. She used to make her own lemonade, you know." Anna spoke with a kind of wonder. "Nothing she ate or drank came out of a box or a bottle. She was always laughing too. And she had endless patience. She taught me to crochet and knit. And she taught me to cook. Only simple stuff, but I do a mean roast dinner and apple pie. She even said my pastry was better than hers."

She bit her lip and Dylan saw that she was struggling to keep her emotions in check. The alcohol wouldn't have helped. He didn't know how much she'd had but he'd seen her order that treble vodka.

"I was glad to go out tonight," she said. "It took my mind off it for a bit. As soon as I got back though, it hit me again. I know it sounds silly, but the fact that I'll never see her again keeps taking me by surprise."

Dylan nodded his understanding. "What would she think if she knew you were here?" he asked casually.

She gave a little shrug but didn't answer.

He swallowed the last bite of his sandwich and picked a couple of slivers of cheese from the plate. "Who was she? Your mum or your dad's mother?"

"My mum's. She was a lot different to mum, though. Mum's always busy. She runs her own shop, vintage clothes, which takes up all her time. She sells stuff all over the world and I bet she'd die if she lost an internet connection for five minutes."

"It's hard work, running a business."

Anna shrugged again.

"What about your dad?" he asked. "What does he do?"

"He's an architect. He spends all his time drawing boring plans."

"I bet you live in a nice house though, eh?"

"It's all right. Big. Flash. My friends are all envious."

"Where is it?"

"You ask a lot of questions."

She was right. "I know. I'm curious about people. And I'd bet my life that your dad isn't drawing plans at this minute. I bet your mum isn't on the internet either. I bet they're lonely, scared and worried to death about you."

She took a crumpled tissue from her bag and blew her nose.

"Shall I tell you something, Anna? You'd be a really nice kid if you acted your age and didn't pretend to be someone you're not. I bet your nan would agree with that, too."

"And shall I tell you something, Davey Young? You'd be a half-decent-looking bloke if you shaved off your beard and ditched those glasses."

"Why, thank you."

She stood and grabbed her bag. "Thanks for the sandwich. And the chat. I feel a bit better now."

"Do me a favour, Anna. Go home, eh?"

She looked at him for long moments. "Good night."

Chapter Twenty-Five

IT WASN'T LIGHT when Joe jumped out of bed but he still went to the window, pulled back the curtains and looked out. Distant lights showed that the town of Dawson's Clough was slowly waking. A few early-morning commuters were beginning their journeys. Other than that, all was quiet.

His dinner jacket, still in the cleaner's polythene bag, hung on the back of the door waiting patiently for the evening's banquet at which, it seemed likely, he would be named Shining Light of the Year.

Shining Light. Every time he heard the award mentioned, its name made him smile. Who dreamed that up?

There was no money on offer—well, there was none that Joe would get his hands on. The charity of the winner's choice would receive ten thousand pounds. Joe—assuming he won, and he had it on good authority that he'd received the most votes—would be presented with a glass trophy. He'd also have his photo splashed across all the local papers. Reports would say what a great bloke he was and donations would come flooding in. It would be a win-win situation.

Last year's winner had, with some of his own money and a few donations, set up a riding school for disabled kids. Some minor royal had said what a great job he'd done, and the next thing, he'd been named as the town's Shining Light.

Doll stirred but didn't wake. It would probably be another couple of hours before she opened her eyes.

He watched her. And wondered.

As a kid, all Joe had wanted was a normal family. An attractive doting wife and a couple of kids, boys preferably. Well, he'd wanted money, obviously. Not for what it could buy him but for the security it offered. So long as you had money, no one could touch you. You could buy your way out of anything.

Now, he had it all. He had his family and he was a millionaire. And yet—

He had doubts about Doll. Nothing he could pinpoint, but there were times she seemed too eager to get away from him, and times she couldn't look him in the eye.

Joe had enjoyed plenty of women during their marriage, the younger, prettier and more willing to please the better, but he'd always been discreet and he was damned if Doll was going to make a fool of him. He'd be a laughingstock if anyone knew she was having an affair. Perhaps she wasn't, perhaps he was being paranoid. He didn't know.

He intended to keep a very close eye on her.

The first hint of light appeared on the horizon and soon began to glisten on frost-covered grass, fences and hedgerows. Growing up in London—not that he'd seen much of it outside the care home—he'd longed to live in the country. He'd thought the sense of freedom must be wonderful. This was his first taste of rural life and it had come as an unwelcome surprise. Life was lived 24/7 in the city, but here nothing happened for hour after hour. There was little traffic, just the sound of cows or sheep to break the monotonous silence. Everywhere was dirty too. It was impossible to get from A to B without getting caked in mud.

Even the people were different. In the city, people from all continents, speaking their own languages, co-existed and accepted each other. Here, they liked to live in their own tiny world and were suspicious of outsiders. Everyone thought northerners were friendly, and while it was true that they had all the time in the world to stop and chat, it was only because they were nosy. They had to know your business, and what they couldn't find out, they invented. As far as Joe was concerned, country life had nothing whatsoever going for it.

Doll rolled over and woke with a frown. "What are you doing up at this time of the morning?"

"I couldn't sleep. I'll get you a coffee if you like."

"Yeah?"

His unusual generosity took her by surprise. He felt generous because it was going to be a good day. A good night, at least. He'd soon be the town's Shining Light.

There was no one in the kitchen but he did see Kennedy plodding up the lane. The ground was frozen solid so there could be no work for him to do. That was one crazy man.

When Joe returned to their bedroom with two coffees, Doll was sitting up and checking stuff on her phone. She put it down on the table, but Joe wondered what she'd been doing. He'd get hold of her phone later and have a look at it. Not that she was stupid enough to keep incriminating messages on it.

"The taxi will be here at seven tonight," Joe said.

She nodded. "Another fun-filled evening to look forward to."

Her sarcasm irritated him, but he knew what she meant. It was sure to be a dull affair.

"How much longer, Joe?" Her voice turned to a whine. "I can't stomach much more of this place."

She'd been keen to get away from the day they arrived. If she was seeing someone else, she'd be happy enough to stay. Wouldn't she?

"Twelve months tops," he said. "By Christmas. Before Christmas."

"Promise?"

"Promise." He didn't want to stay here for any longer than necessary either. "And that'll be it, Doll. We'll be set up for life and enjoying a life in the sunshine."

"You keep saying that, but then you always want more. Keep on like this and we'll be collecting our pensions before we're set up for life."

It was all right for Doll. She'd never been homeless, never been without a family. She hadn't grown up surrounded by riches, but one thing had always been constant in her life—security. She had no idea what it was like to fend for yourself, to rely on your wits and have to beg, steal and kill for security.

"I mean it this time. A few more months, that's all. We'll celebrate Christmas in our new home under a warm sun."

"I hope so. I haven't recovered from last Christmas yet and I never, but never, want another like that."

Joe thought it had been fun. It had certainly been lucrative. He'd felt like God as he'd given to the poor and helped those less fortunate. Of course, he'd helped himself more. "Tell you what, Doll, we'll have a weekend down home. How about that? We'll leave tomorrow morning and come back on Monday."

"Yeah?" Her face lit up.

"Yeah," he said. "You can shop till you drop and we'll take in a show."

While they were there, he'd call on Susie Fraser and offer his condolences. It was a damn shame about Christian. Of the three Fraser boys, he'd been his favourite. He'd been overshadowed by Mark and Ben all his life, yet he'd been the most intelligent of the brothers.

Rage bubbled up inside him as he thought about Christian and those damned photos.

"I need a whole new wardrobe," Doll was saying. "It's ages since I saw decent shops."

"We'll put that right this weekend. You can treat yourself, Doll."

While Doll spent his money, he'd ask questions. He had ways of making people talk and he'd soon find out who'd been chatting to Christian…

Chapter Twenty-Six

ON SATURDAY AFTERNOON, Dylan, miraculously, had the refuge to himself. Well, Kennedy was probably out in the garden, but he didn't count.

He planned to search every inch of the building and outbuildings. No doubt the police had conducted a thorough search, but they'd been at the refuge on Child's invitation. Anything incriminating would have been moved a long, long way away.

It was probably the same today because Child, Doll, Hank and Gary had all taken off for London for the weekend. According to Child, Doll needed to see the bright lights and he wanted to offer his condolences to Christian Fraser's mother. Child had looked full of sympathy for the woman, but Dylan would still bet his life that her husband's tongue had been removed by one Joe Child. Still, no point thinking about that. He had more important things on his mind. He needed to discover the whereabouts of Caroline Aldridge and Farrah Brindle. There had to be clues at the refuge. He couldn't have looked in the right places.

The other residents had set off for town. They had soup kitchens to run and the homeless to minister to. Dylan should have been helping but he'd claimed feverish symptoms, said he felt too weak and nauseous to be out on the streets. Given that he'd slept in that sodding shed for over a week, it was a wonder he'd had to lie.

He'd locked the doors. It was unlikely anyone would turn up, but if they did, he'd have advance warning.

He started his search in the Childs' bedroom. Doll must know the sort of man she'd married, so Child would feel safe hiding any evidence in a room he shared with her. The carpet was fitted—there was nothing under that. Wardrobes were filled with clothes, expensive clothes, and had no false backs. Drawers contained more clothes. There were enough lipsticks, face creams and other paraphernalia to keep a brothel's staff looking good for a decade.

Two phones lay lifeless in a drawer. Neither boasted a sim card or any battery power, and there were no chargers in sight. Next to them, in a green box, was a Rolex watch. It was showing the correct time and looked to be genuine. It was a lot classier than the cheap, although flashy, watch that Child wore.

Tuesday's newspaper sat on a chair by what had to be Child's side of the bed. Dylan flicked through it—and stopped. A word had been cut carefully from a headline. Dylan read the article, a piece of late news, and guessed the headline should have read Two Men Killed in Motorway Crash. The word *Killed* was missing.

He sat on the bed, pondering this, and gave a start as his phone trilled out. "Yes?"

"Is that David?" a well-spoken voice asked.

"It is." It was Malcolm Brindle. "What can I do for you?"

"It's me. Malcolm. I've decided to do it tonight. No point waiting, is there? I thought—well, you said you'd come along."

Dylan stifled a groan. He'd hoped Brindle's bout of insanity might fade as the alcohol wore off. Obviously not. "I did, yes, but I'm more convinced than ever that it's not a good idea. Tell you what, why don't you go to the police and ask them what they have on Taylor? It could be—"

"They won't tell me anything. They call on us every now and again to reassure us that they're doing all they can, but really, they don't know what to do. They're clueless. They don't even know where to start. I have to do this myself."

In Brindle's shoes, Dylan would feel exactly the same. He wouldn't be able to sit around waiting for the police to come up with something. "So what's the plan?"

"He'll be drinking in the Jolly Sailor tonight. He's sure to be there. I'm going to go along, slip some fluni-trazepam in his drink—"

"And what do you intend to do when he's passed out in front of a pub full of drinkers?"

"I won't give him time for that. When he's taken a drink, I'm going to get him outside—"

"How?"

"Now this is the clever part—"

Dylan very much doubted that.

"I've heard," Brindle said, "that he sells cheap ciga-rettes. I'm going to ask if I can buy some from him. By that time, he'll be feeling unwell—he'll be conscious, but I gather he won't remember anything that happens after-wards. I'll hold the gun to his head and make him talk."

There was silence as Brindle waited for congratula-tions. Dylan despaired.

Brindle was a desperate man, and he could fully un-derstand that, but spiking Taylor's drink, giving him some cock-and-bull story about wanting to buy illegal cigarettes, and then pulling a gun on him wasn't the way to get the information they needed.

"Okay," he said, resigned. "What time?"

"You're coming along?"

"Why not? It'll be easier with two."

"Thank you. Thank you *so* much. Shall we say seven o'clock at the Jolly Sailor?"

"I'll be there."

Dylan tried to push Brindle from his mind. He'd cross that particular crazy bridge when he came to it.

He continued with his search and found half a dozen DVDs, all showing an American preacher in full flow. Like Child, he was dressed in black. A huge gold ring on his finger twinkled beneath the camera's lights. He might have found Child's hero but it wasn't any help.

None of the bedrooms produced any clues. Hank's was a pigsty, which meant that Dylan didn't have to be too careful about putting things back. Burglars could arrive and turn the place over and no one would be any the wiser.

Gary's room, in complete contrast, was neat. Everything was in its rightful place. No clues though. Not even a sniff of recreational drugs.

In Child's study, nothing struck him as odd, other than a pair of protective gloves wrapped around a small pair of scissors and a pair of tweezers. If he were sending blackmail letters or threatening notes, he might cut telling words from a newspaper—

Blackmail? Child would enjoy such a lucrative pastime, there was no doubt about that, but who could be his victim? And how might teenage girls fit in?

Dylan didn't have a clue.

His next stop was the kitchen. It was preposterous

to think anything discriminating might be in the room because the world and his wife used it, but all the same, he checked everything—from the sink's waste pipe to the cereal boxes. Nothing.

He was wasting his time. Child wasn't naive enough to leave any clues lying around.

Whatever Dylan was looking for, and he didn't have a clue what that was, was somewhere else. Child and the clan were in London. Why? Where did they stay?

This place was a smokescreen, he was sure of it. The truth, he'd bet, was closer to London.

Chapter Twenty-Seven

THE JOLLY SAILOR was more depressing than usual. This Saturday night's entertainment was an ageing rock band that belted out hits from the seventies and eighties. Badly.

Brindle, looking deathly pale, walked through the main door at seven-twenty. Dylan was already halfway down his first pint.

"Thanks so much for coming, David." Brindle's hands shook alarmingly as he reached into his pocket. Dylan thought for one awful moment that he was going for his gun and was relieved when he pulled out his wallet. "Can I get you one?"

"No, thanks. We'd better not have too much."

Brindle nodded at the wisdom of that, but still ordered himself a double whisky. "Dutch courage," he said in a low voice.

When his drink was in front of him, he looked around the crowded pub. "There's no sign of him yet then?"

"Not yet," Dylan said.

"He'll soon turn up."

"Meanwhile, let's go into the other room. It'll be quieter. We'll be able to hear ourselves think." Impossible to do that with Johnny and the Weavers killing one of Slade's old hits.

"We don't want to miss him."

"We won't."

The smaller bar was quieter but still fairly crowded. Here, people were watching a talent show on a big-screen TV.

The Jolly Sailor might be the town's biggest dump but it was doing a good trade tonight.

"There's still time for a rethink," Dylan said when they'd settled themselves in a corner.

"There's nothing to think about."

"I think there's plenty. For one thing, the police would have taken far more interest in Taylor if they'd had anything to go on. He must have convinced them of his innocence."

Brindle snorted at that. "That shows how much you know about our police force."

Dylan knew a whole lot more than Brindle but he kept silent.

"If they don't have evidence," Brindle said, "or if the evidence hasn't been obtained or kept in the correct manner, they can't bring a conviction."

Dylan was aware of that. "There must be other suspects though," he said. "That farmer, for a start. You didn't approve of Farrah's relationship with Walter Topham. I've met him and I have to agree that he's an oddball. His daughter died—"

"I know. I know all that, and it did cross my mind. He was more interested in the dog than Farrah though."

Dylan was clutching at straws. Topham was an oddball, and his dead daughter was a ringer for Farrah Brindle, but there was nothing to suggest he'd ever known Caroline Aldridge, or that he might bear a grudge against young teenage girls. Except, of course, that they were alive, whereas his girl wasn't. A shrink would have a field day with that theory but Dylan couldn't get too excited about it. Topham spent his days on a farm where animals lived and died, where one was constantly reminded of life and death and all nature's circles. Topham was too grounded in reality.

Maybe.

Brindle kept patting the inside pocket of the large woollen overcoat he wore.

"You need to give me the gun," Dylan said in a whisper.

"What?"

"You're going to approach Taylor and ask him if he'll sell you some cheap cigarettes. Even if he is semicomatose, he might be suspicious. He'll check you out and be far from happy to find that you're carrying a weapon."

Brindle patted his pocket again.

"As soon as we know he's harmless and we have the upper hand, you can have it back," Dylan said. "You can be the one who threatens him."

Brindle thought about it for a moment. "Okay."

"Go to the toilets and hang up your coat. I'll go as soon as I see you coming back. I'll bring your coat back for you, okay?"

Brindle was getting nervous now. He wasn't thinking straight. However, he nodded, put down his drink and walked slowly, anxiously, in the direction of the toilets.

Dylan spent the few seconds he was out of sight wondering what he'd got himself into. This was madness.

Brindle walked quickly back to the bar. Without saying a word, Dylan went to the toilets and found his coat. Inside the deep inner pocket was a Kel-Tec P-11. It was small and lightweight enough to stay hidden in his jacket, but would do the job.

He sauntered back to the bar. "You forgot this, mate."

Brindle took his overcoat and shrugged it on. "Yeah. Thanks." Beads of sweat had broken out on Brindle's forehead and across his top lip. "There's a chap over there who keeps watching us," he said.

Dylan had already spotted him. He was sitting at a table with an untouched pint in front of him. Short hair, leather jacket, jeans, black boots. "There's not much else to do in here if you're on your own. Ignore him."

The pub was getting busier. Young people called in on their way to one of the clubs. It was noisy and crowded, but there was no sign of Taylor. It would be typical of the bloke not to turn up. It was his usual drinking hole though, and it would be unlike him not to be out and about on a Saturday night. There was still plenty of time.

Dylan tried to make conversation with Brindle but the chap was too nervous. Dylan guessed he was one of those who would rather spend an hour catching a moth to put it safely outside than kill the creature.

Brindle nudged his arm, managing to spill some of Dylan's beer. "He's here. He's here."

Dylan didn't turn round to look. He could see Taylor reflected in the smeared glass behind the bar. He strutted with confidence, smiling at those he knew, scowling at those he didn't. He stood close to Dylan's seat to order his drink and, with that in his hand, walked across to a group of people he knew at the darts board.

"Excuse me." Brindle rushed off.

For one awful moment, Dylan thought he was going to confront Taylor, but instead he dived into the toilets. When he returned, he was dabbing at his mouth with a handkerchief.

"Sorry," he said. "I just—I was sick. Nerves." He gave an anxious smile.

"Why don't you go home? This isn't going to prove anything, you must know that. All it will do is land you in trouble."

Brindle shook his head. "I have to find out what he's done."

"And if it's nothing?"

"Then—I don't know."

Taylor wandered over to the bar and ordered a second pint.

"Let him enjoy this one," Dylan suggested, "and then we'll move in. Okay?"

Brindle nodded and looked as if he was about to be sick again.

"So—" Dylan was determined to make conversation. "How's your wife coping?"

"Badly. She doesn't blame me but—"

"Blame you? Why should she?"

Brindle thought for a moment. "Husband, father—it's a given that you take care of people, isn't it? That's your main task in life, to keep them safe, happy and healthy."

Dylan supposed it was. It was a task he wasn't doing very well right now. He was two hundred and fifty miles from home while his wife was worrying herself sick and taking care of his kids. There was the financial side of things though. To keep a family safe, happy and healthy cost money, and someone had to earn it.

He wasn't heading off on a guilt trip though. He'd leave that for Brindle.

"I don't know," he said. "I don't have a wife or kids but you can't keep them safe all the time, can you? Accidents happen—shit happens. There's no way anyone could blame you. Is there?"

"I suppose not."

"You hadn't argued with Farrah, had you? You hadn't done anything that might result in her—"

"No. No, of course not."

"Then it can't be your fault." Dylan scratched at his beard. The sooner he could shave it off, the better. It had gone to the shaggy, filthy stage now. He loathed it. "What about her siblings? Are they doing okay?"

"They both live in London," he said. "Her sister, Sandra, is worried. She's at university, doing a PhD in economics. She calls us every couple of days to ask if we've heard anything. She comes home once a month. As for Matthew—he keeps his feelings hidden, always has. He doesn't talk about Farrah often, but I'm sure he thinks of her all the time."

"What does he do?"

"Matthew? He's teaching French and geography to inner-city teenagers who couldn't give a damn." Brindle managed a weak smile. "A bit like me, I suppose."

A bit like Bev too, although the kids who attended her English and drama lessons came from more prosperous backgrounds.

"Christmas was awful," Brindle said.

"Oh?"

"The children came home and—well, I suppose it's understandable. They wanted to enjoy Christmas, but Clare and me—well, we couldn't. Obviously. Matthew and Sandra must have felt unimportant, as if we didn't care about them, as if only Farrah mattered. It was—difficult. Also, Sandra had split up with her boyfriend, so she was alternating between anger and distress. I think we were all glad when the holiday was over."

His voice dropped to a whisper. "Taylor's coming over to order another drink. This is it."

Dylan looked across the room to where the chap with the untouched pint was still watching them closely. Dylan nodded at him. There was no response.

"Okay," he said to Brindle. "When Taylor's settled back at the darts board, don't take your eyes off his drink. I'll collide with him on my way to the slot machine. While I'm busy apologising, you tamper with his drink. Right?"

Brindle licked his dry lips. "Right."

"We'll give him a couple of minutes."

"Yes."

Brindle's hands were shaking so much that he struggled to pick up his drink. He'd never make a criminal—

Front and back doors to the pub burst open and eight uniformed police officers stormed inside. "No one leaves."

"A fucking raid," the barmaid snapped. "That's all we need."

"What will we do?" Brindle looked close to tears. "The gun."

"You keep quiet. We've never met, okay? You have drugs in your pocket because you're depressed. We've never met."

"But that's not fair. I can't allow—"

"Shut up!"

Only seven arrests were made. As Dylan and Brindle joined the other five in the van bound for the local nick, Dylan thought that was good going for a place like the Jolly Sailor. Taylor had passed his search easily enough and would be happily enjoying his fourth pint of the night by now…

Chapter Twenty-Eight

LEAH COULD HEAR his footsteps coming ever closer. Slow, thoughtful, cunning footsteps. Then they stopped. She held her breath. All she could hear was the blood pounding in her ears.

She mustn't make a sound. He'd give up eventually, he had to, and then she could make a run for it.

She had no idea where she was, only that this derelict old building was home to rats that scurried in annoyance at having their peace disturbed.

She could outrun him. She must cling to that fact. She could outrun most people. There was no need for this terror that gripped her.

"Anna? Come on, sweetheart. Don't be silly now."

She had no idea why she'd chosen the name Anna. She'd thought it sounded grown-up and sophisticated but now she hated it. Stupid, stupid name.

"Anna, where are you?" He was close. Too close.

She'd escaped from him and raced along a hallway where doors led to empty rooms. Then she'd found this cupboard and thanked God that it had two old bolts that, with a little force, had creaked into place. There was no light. No air. Behind her, she was aware of the occasional scratching sound. Rats probably. She'd rather face a rat than him.

"Anna, darling, I'm sorry I lost my temper with you. And I'm sorry this place isn't what you were expecting."

He gave a hollow laugh. "It's not where I was expecting to spend the night either, but I told you, something cropped up." His footsteps moved right past her door and then stopped again. She could hear his breath coming in small jerky gasps. "Don't let this silly quarrel spoil things. I'm sorry. Truly, I am. I know you're not like the others. I don't know what made me say such a ridiculous thing."

Leah felt a single tear slide down her face and onto her neck. She was too frightened to make even the slightest movement.

All she wanted was to go home. At the moment, even her mother's nagging and her father's refusal to admit she existed seemed appealing. At least it was familiar. Her bed with its childish cover would be waiting for her with freshly laundered sheets. Why had she given it up? For what?

To be hiding from a maniac in a cupboard where rats had made their home?

I want to go home. I want to go home.

"Anna, sweetheart, I have champagne. A present for you, too. Don't you want to see?"

I want to go home.

He'd promised her a weekend in the best hotel in London, but midway through the journey, when they were still an hour from the City, he'd taken a phone call that had put him in a bad mood.

"A change of plan, sweetheart," he said. "There's something I have to deal with so London will have to wait a while. I know a place though. We'll spend the night there and go on to London tomorrow."

He drove on for about half an hour and brought her to

this creepy old building that looked as if it hadn't seen a human for half a century.

"We can't stay here." She was appalled that he could even suggest such a thing. "It spooks me. I won't stay here."

"Where will you go?" A cold note of steel crept into his voice. "You have no money, no friends—you have nothing."

"I'd rather sleep on the street than spend a night here."

"Oh, you would, would you?"

Despite the nasty tone, she stood her ground. "Yes, I would. Sorry, but you're on your own."

She strode away from him, not having a clue where she was or where she was going, but he caught up with her, lifted his hand and delivered a stinging blow to her face.

"I've spent many a night here, and if it's good enough for me, it's good enough for you, Miss High and Fucking Mighty. Christ, you're all the same. You flash your tits in the hope that some sucker will pay for it. Well, dream on, darling. I've had better than you. A lot better."

"I'm sorry, but I'm not—"

His second blow split her lip. She attempted to mop up the blood but he grabbed her by the hair and dragged her toward the building. "You're spending the night with me, you little whore, and you're spending it here. Now, shut the fuck up."

"I won't stay here."

He laughed at that before shoving her against the cold stone wall and taking a large key from his pocket. When the old door swung open, he pushed her inside and locked the door behind him.

He tore at her blouse and laughed again. "Cheap little whores like you are ten a penny and don't you ever forget that."

He'd gone crazy then. Anger had spewed out of him in a relentless torrent. Punches had rained down on her until, finally, she'd managed to raise her knee—hard. While he'd been bent double and retching, she'd made a run for it and ended up in this filthy old cupboard...

"I know every inch of this place," he said, "so I will find you. You may as well come out now and we'll pretend nothing happened, okay? I know you're not a whore, I know that. I've told you that you're special. You know you are. You're the one for me. I knew it the moment I saw you. Come on, sweetheart. Don't let one silly little quarrel spoil our evening. We'll spend the night here and leave for London early in the morning. I promise."

His footsteps receded and Leah let out her breath. She heard him opening and closing doors.

"I know you're up here." He kicked something—a door or a wall.

Something had come up, he'd said. That must mean he had to deal with the mysterious something. Meet someone perhaps? All she had to do was keep quiet until he left and then run like hell.

She wanted to cry. Her lip was bleeding and every inch of her face was hurting from his punches. Her ear was bleeding and her right eye was swollen and closing.

She had to keep calm. At least, she had to stay as in control as she was now—which wasn't great.

All was quiet. Perhaps he'd gone. She hadn't heard his car, but she probably wouldn't. This was an old building and perhaps the walls were thick. She didn't know. It was too dark to see her watch, but she'd give it about five minutes and then creep out.

She began counting off the seconds—

A noise stopped her. Something heavy and made of metal was being dragged along the hallway. It was coming closer and then stopped right outside her door. The handle turned but the bolts held.

"I'm going to count to ten, Anna. If you don't open the door, I'm going to smash it down. If I have to do that, you're going to wish you hadn't been born..."

Chapter Twenty-Nine

DYLAN SAT IN interview room 3 opposite Detective Inspector Keith Rhodes and found himself wondering again if Rhodes was on the take. The only coppers Dylan knew who could afford to dress so well were dodgy. He pushed the thought away. Maybe Rhodes spent his entire salary on Armani's finest.

"Where's Brindle?" he asked.

"Along the corridor, being interviewed. So far, he hasn't said anything. If he keeps that up, we'll release him in an hour or so. Mind you, he looks terrified enough to spill the beans and tell all. If he does that—" Rhodes left the sentence unfinished.

If he confessed, the daft sod would be facing all sorts of charges.

It had worked out well, really. Before setting off for the Jolly Sailor, Dylan had phoned Rhodes to arrange a raid that would see them both arrested before Brindle had time to do anything stupid. A plainclothes officer would be present, just in case. Dylan had spotted the officer immediately. Even Brindle had remarked on the man sitting watching them with an untouched pint in front of him.

The best part was that, as Dylan was under arrest for possession of a firearm, he could vanish for a couple of days. He fancied going home.

"So what have you got for me?" he asked.

"Not a great deal, I'm afraid." Rhodes slid a short list of names across the desk. "The only link from the past between Child and Riley is St. Lawrence's, and kids who wound up there are difficult to trace. Troubled kids from troubled backgrounds—most of them left there with nothing and haven't been heard of since."

"Child kept in touch with Riley all these years," Dylan pointed out, "so maybe he's still pally with some others."

"Maybe." Rhodes was doubtful. "It's such a long time ago. It's more than thirty years since Child left St. Lawrence's."

Dylan was well aware of that.

"Also," Rhodes added, "records weren't kept like they are these days. Nothing was on computer. The place closed down fourteen years ago, and all records were moved to a new place set up by the local council. Except they've been lost. There was a fire at the offices and it's assumed that all files went up in smoke. No one knows for sure though."

Dylan read the short list of people who'd attended St. Lawrence's and known Child, but nothing leaped out at him. He hadn't expected it to. Contact details were available for two of those people—two who were currently locked up, one for armed burglary and one for manslaughter.

"This is it? There's nothing else? Nothing at all?"

"We have the address of the woman who was in charge of the place at the time. She's in a nursing home now, suffering from dementia."

Dylan rolled his eyes. A lot of use she'd be.

"She isn't too bad, I gather," Rhodes said, handing

over another piece of paper. "She has good days and bad days, but in between the bad days they say she's lucid."

"Right."

It wasn't much, but it was a start. Dylan would bet that Child had been one of those kids you'd remember. If these people remembered Child, they might remember others he'd been involved with.

He typed the details into his phone, his own phone, and then changed the sim card to Davey Young's.

"There is one slight snag," he said.

Rhodes's eyebrows beetled together. "What's that?"

"Child's in London."

"What? Why in hell's name didn't you say so?"

"It didn't seem important." It was a lie, but so what?

"Not important? You're heading to London to ask about him and you don't think it's important?"

"It'll be fine. He's driving back on Monday morning. I gather he and Doll are taking in a show and visiting Christian Fraser's mother to offer their condolences."

Rhodes snorted at that. "That's big of him."

"A heart of gold, that's Child. Anyway, I'll watch my back."

"You need to," Rhodes said with a hint of a smile. "I'm sure life gets a bit tricky when your tongue's been hacked out."

"And on that note—"

"Watch what you're doing, Dylan."

"I will. You'll make sure Davey Young gets a good piece in the local rag so that everyone knows he's banged up in a cell?"

"We will."

"You'll go easy on Brindle?"

"Of course. Mind you, the stupid bastard needs a

bloody good wake-up call." He gathered up his paper-work and stood to indicate the meeting was over. "The car you've stolen is parked out the back—next to the bins. The key's in the ignition."

"Thanks." Dylan got to his feet and opened the door. "Be seeing you."

"You'll be able to spread the word as you drive," Rhodes called after him.

Dylan didn't have a clue what he meant and he didn't stop to ask. The sooner he reached London the better.

As he strode out of the building, he thought how ci-vilised it was to have a set of wheels at his disposal. He'd never been a fan of public transport and never used it unless absolutely necessary. He liked the freedom a car gave him.

He stepped outside, pulled his woollen hat low on his head and looked for the bins. They were lined up in a row. Next to them sat a—

No, it couldn't be. Davey Young might not be the brightest bloke on the planet, but if he were nicking a car, he'd choose one that looked as if it stood a slim chance of moving.

It couldn't be. Yet there was nothing else in sight. The—Dylan did a quick calculation—twenty-three-year-old rust bucket was the only vehicle there. Fingers crossed, he walked over to it and opened the door. The key was in the ignition.

Dylan sat inside the heap of junk. It smelled of stale booze and vomit. God knows where they'd found this little gem.

And then he saw it. In the rear window, a large sticker read Jesus Saves.

"Sod it."

He tried the ignition and was surprised when it coughed into life. If it got him to London, he'd start to believe in miracles.

Chapter Thirty

BEV CAME TO with a start. She wasn't sure what had woken her but it wasn't the dawn chorus. It was only two-twenty, and even the birds needed their sleep.

She lay still and listened. All was quiet. Eerily quiet.

She got out of bed, grabbed her dressing gown from the hook on the back of the door and padded across the landing to Freya's room. Her daughter was lying on her back, arms thrown out, fast asleep. It must be wonderful to be so relaxed. Bev envied her.

She walked across to Luke's room and pushed open the door. She wouldn't have been surprised to find him sitting up listening to music through headphones, but he too was fast asleep. Unlike his sister, he was frowning and his hands were curled into fists.

Bev returned to her bedroom and was about to take off her dressing gown when another noise, a soft footfall, had her heart leaping in fright. There was someone in the house.

She looked round the bedroom and picked up the only weapon she could see—a bedside lamp. Careful not to make a sound, she tiptoed to the top of the stairs.

She heard a faint click that sounded like a window in the kitchen being closed. Another footstep.

"Who's there?" She was surprised at how strong her voice sounded and how it didn't so much as hint at the terror coursing through her veins. "I'm armed!"

"That's just the way I like my women, sweetheart."

"Dylan?"

When she saw him at the bottom of the stairs, she almost threw herself headlong down them. There was no need though. He took them two at a time.

"What calibre lamp do you have there, ma'am?" He took it from her, put it on the floor and wrapped his arms around her.

"What are you doing here? Why didn't you tell me you were coming? And what the hell is that smell?"

"Ah, sorry. That smell is me. I'll run a bath." His hand tight around hers, he led her to the bathroom. "Care to join me?"

"No. I wouldn't let a dog share your bathwater right now. And that beard is revolting." But she was smiling. It was so good to see him, even sporting the shaggiest, filthiest-looking beard she'd ever seen. "Why are you creeping about?"

"I had to get in through the kitchen window—you should keep it locked, Bev. I've told you about that before."

"But—"

"David Young doesn't have a key to this place, remember? All he has is a stolen car that stinks of—well, you'd rather not know." He turned the bath tap on full. "So," he said. "How are you doing?"

She was doing crap. Complete crap. If she went a full ten minutes without bursting into tears, it was a minor miracle. No matter how many times she told herself there was nothing seriously wrong with her, the panic refused to give her a moment's peace.

"I'm okay. I'll be glad to get Monday out of the way and see what the scan picks up, but I'm okay."

He sat on the rim of the bath and squeezed her hands. "You'll be fine. I'll try to be there—or here. No promises, but I'll do my best."

Tears stung the back of her eyes. "Thanks."

The panic eased slightly. She felt the weight of it leave her. There was no point discussing it. Besides, until she'd had the scan, there was nothing to discuss.

"So what would you have done if I'd locked the kitchen window?" she asked. "And why couldn't you call me? I could have let you in."

"I wanted it to be a surprise." He grinned a little sheepishly. "A *nice* surprise. I didn't mean to scare you. Sorry."

He pulled off his clothes and dropped them on the floor. From the neck down, he looked like her Dylan. From the neck up, however, he looked awful. His hair was overlong and untidy, his beard was disgusting and he looked tired. She preferred to look at him from the neck down. He looked good. Very good.

"Luxury." He lay back in the bath and then submerged himself for a full minute. Water cascaded from his head as he emerged. "You cannot believe how good that feels."

She picked up his clothes and held them at arms' length. "I'll put these in the washer."

"No point. I'll have to leave early. I can only stay a few hours."

"They'll be done by then." She left the room before he could argue. No way was she having those stinking the house out.

When she returned to the bathroom, the bath was empty and he was in the shower. The bath might be filthy but at least she'd be sharing her bed with a clean body. She couldn't wait.

Chapter Thirty-One

If Dylan had nothing better to do with his days than wait for the grim reaper, he'd choose to do it here.

The Tall Pines was home to the elderly, the infirm and dementia sufferers—those who could afford it, at least—and it was easy to imagine dukes and duchesses of a bygone age attending grand balls or playing croquet on the lawns.

The massive stone building was approached by way of a long curving driveway flanked with—surprise, surprise—tall pine trees. Well-manicured lawns stretched out on either side. To Dylan's left was a lake where a swan glided majestically. To his right was a circular rose garden dotted with wooden benches.

His battered, stinking car looked out of place among the upmarket vehicles. Dylan had toyed with the idea of donning a suit and driving his Morgan, but like it or not, he had to play the part of David Young, just in case.

Thanks to Bev, his clothes no longer smelled as bad as the inside of the car.

Her surprise at the sight of him had been nothing compared the shock he'd experienced on seeing her. She couldn't have lost weight in the ten days he'd been away, but she looked thinner, almost gaunt. Dark circles beneath her eyes told him how much sleep she'd had—or not had.

She was a worrier though, always had been. Like a

dog with a bone, she'd focus on one particular problem and be unable to think of anything else. She'd worry away until the problem was solved. For a while she'd be fine, but then something else would crop up. As she was worrying enough for both of them, and as worrying had never solved anything, Dylan was determined to push all thoughts of her approaching scan from his mind. She was young, fit and healthy—and getting everything out of proportion, as usual.

He parked the car as far away as possible from the imposing building and headed for the main entrance. He looked an unkempt mess, but at least he didn't smell.

The spacious reception area reeked of money. Large modern paintings adorned the walls. In the centre was a circular counter. The young woman sitting behind it gave him a toothpaste-ad smile as he approached. She didn't so much as blink at his appearance. "Can I help you, sir?"

"Yes, I phoned earlier to see Belle Watson."

"Ah yes, of course. Mr. Young, is it?"

"That's right."

"Just a moment." She picked up a phone, pressed a button and waited a second. "Karen, would you come to the front desk, please? A Mr. Young is here to see Belle. Could you show him to the conservatory, please?"

She replaced the phone and repeated the toothpaste-ad smile. "Someone will be with you in a moment. Karen will take you to Belle."

"Thank you. How is she today?"

"I haven't seen her, but she's usually cheerful when she knows she has a visitor." She lowered her voice. "She doesn't have too many, I'm afraid."

"No family?"

"No. She never married, you see. Her sister visits three or four times a year—she lives in Scotland so it's quite a trek for her—and a neighbour comes when she's up to it. She's elderly herself though, so it's very difficult."

Sadly, there were no advantages to age, or none that Dylan could think of. He'd hate to be left to rot in this place, as luxurious as it was.

A young woman with another toothpaste-ad smile walked into the reception area. "Mr. Young? I'm Karen. Please, come with me."

Like her doppelgänger behind the desk, Karen didn't look twice at him. Perhaps scruffs like him were regular visitors. Nah, he couldn't believe that.

He followed her along thickly carpeted hallways where yet more modern works of art hung from the walls in black frames. The paintwork was a spotless pale blue.

Karen pushed open double doors and a welcome warmth seeped out. "Belle, you have a visitor." She spoke in a loud cajoling voice, much as one would to an errant teenager who belonged to someone else and was therefore untouchable. "That's nice, isn't it?"

She touched Dylan's arm and added in a quieter voice, "I'll see that you aren't disturbed."

"Thank you."

The huge Victorian conservatory was home to a few tall potted ferns, some expensive but tasteful furniture and a grey-haired elderly lady who was hunched over a newspaper with a pen in her hand. If she was lucid enough to attempt the crossword, perhaps all wasn't lost after all.

She carefully folded the newspaper and laid it flat on the table, where an empty teacup and saucer sat, then turned her sharp gaze on him. "Who did they say you were?"

"I'm David Young." He put out his hand but it was ignored. "I'd like to ask you about your time at St. Lawrence's, if I may."

"Are you Molly's boy?"

"I'm afraid not. No, I used to know a couple of people from St. Lawrence's—Joe Child and Gordon Riley—and I'm trying to find some friends of theirs. I wondered if you remembered them—and if you remembered the names of people they were particularly friendly with."

"You look like Molly's boy."

"Do I?" He rustled up a smile but this was going to be hard work. "Sorry, I don't know any Molly."

"She was a one, wasn't she? I remember her getting married, you know. I knew it would end in tears, but there, she wouldn't be told." She frowned at him. "Are you sure you're not her boy?"

"Quite sure."

"What was his name?"

"I'm sorry, I don't know. I don't know Molly." It was time to chalk this particular chat up as a waste of time.

"She looked fat, didn't she? On her wedding day, I mean?"

Dylan stifled a groan. One minute she thought he was Molly's son and the next she thought he'd been at the mysterious Molly's wedding. "I'm sorry," he said.

"St. Lawrence's is closed now," she said, taking him by surprise.

"Yes, so I believe."

"It merged with St. Thomas's."

So she knew that much. "That's right. Do you remember your time there?"

"Of course." She peered at him over the top of her glasses. "I may be old, Mr.—I may be old, but I'm not stupid."

"Sorry. And it's David."

"David." She thought for a moment. "Molly didn't call her boy David, did she? No, I'm sure it was something else. It was one of those silly fancy names, wasn't it?"

"I don't know."

Karen came into the conservatory bearing a tray laden with white porcelain teapot, sugar bowl, cups, saucers and biscuits. "How are you two getting along then? Would you like another cup of tea, Belle? I'll leave it here and you can make up your own mind. You can be mother." Smiling, and not giving either of them chance to respond, she silently left the room.

No wonder Belle was a little crazy. Dylan would be too, if he had to live in a place where the staff treated you like an idiot—in a polite way, because of the vast sums of money you paid for the privilege, of course.

"He came from the devil's own sperm," Belle said, lifting the teapot.

Dylan wasn't sure whether or not to risk asking. "Who's that?"

"Joseph Child." She poured tea into two cups, added sugar to her own, stirred it and helped herself to a biscuit. "The devil's offspring, he was."

"Joe Child? You remember him then?"

"It was Zac."

"Sorry?"

"Molly's boy was Zac. I'm sure of it. What sort of name's that for a child? Ridiculous. Why can't people stick to proper names—like Andrew, Peter, James, John? Even David, for that matter."

"Indeed." This was going to be a long, slow process and patience wasn't one of Dylan's virtues. He wished Belle had never heard of Molly. "Do you remember Joe Child well?"

"The devil's offspring."

"Yes. So I believe. Do you remember Gordon Riley?"

"You'll come to a sticky end, I used to tell Joseph Child. Do you know what he did? Laughed in my face. The devil's offspring."

"What about his friends? I know he was pally with Gordon Riley, but were there others?"

"I was good at my job. I quite enjoyed it. It was just— some of the children were hard work."

Dylan smiled. "I can imagine."

"She died anyway."

"Who did?" He guessed the answer before it came from her lips.

"Molly."

"Did she? I'm sorry to hear that."

"She committed suicide." Belle helped herself to another biscuit and chewed thoughtfully. "I don't approve. God has to decide who lives and who dies, don't you agree? If we all gave up when the going got a little tough, there would be precious few of us left in the world. What about that boy of hers? She had it tough, I know, but even so—" She broke off as a blackbird landed on the grass outside. "I wonder if they're feeding the birds. I keep reminding them but they're hopeless. They forget. They're too busy deciding what to wear to ensnare some unsuspecting man."

"Ah."

"What was I saying?"

"You were trying to remember anyone Joe Child was friendly with," Dylan said.

"Yes." She looked at him long and hard. "You need a haircut, young man."

"I know. I'm sorry."

"Are you married?"

"No."

"I never walked down the aisle either. In my day, a woman had a career or a family. One couldn't have both. I chose my career."

"At St. Lawrence's, yes."

"What did you say your name was?" she asked again.

"David. David Young."

"You've come from St. Lawrence's?"

"No. I'm trying to find someone—anyone—who was friendly with Joe Child or Gordon Riley."

"Ah, yes. The devil's offspring."

"Why do you call him that?"

"He was evil. I wonder what happened to him."

"He's safe and well, and living in Lancashire," Dylan told her. "He helps the homeless, runs Bible classes—he's married with two children."

She shook her head, smiling. "No. You're getting confused."

She was probably right.

"The trouble he was mixed up in—" She broke off. "I always thought Raymond Mair was involved in that."

Dylan's ears pricked up. Mair was on the list of names Rhodes had given him. He was meeting him later today. "What trouble was that?"

"Did Molly send you?"

Dylan felt like screaming. "No. I don't know Molly." And hadn't she committed suicide?

"What did she call her boy?"

"Zac."

"Did she? What sort of name's that for a boy?"

"A very silly one."

Dylan stayed for another hour but he was none the wiser. He shouldn't have expected any more, he supposed. He'd had a decent cup of tea and a couple of biscuits. He'd also been given Raymond Mair's name, and he knew there had been some sort of trouble. That wasn't surprising. Trouble followed Joe Child everywhere.

"How did you get on?" the receptionist asked as he was leaving.

"Not too well. She was too busy talking about someone called Molly. Who was that? Do you know?"

"Ah, the mysterious Molly. We know nothing about her, I'm afraid. We've asked her sister and her neighbour but they have no idea. If Belle's right, the poor woman committed suicide and I suppose that preys on her mind. And unfortunately, she has so few visitors—well, I say that, but she's had more lately."

"Oh?"

"Yes. Her sister came down to London for a week and visited her every day. Her neighbour Alice has been twice this month, and then another gentleman came." She offered him a regretful smile. "I don't think he got much sense out of her either."

"Who was that? It wasn't Alan Bishop, was it?" He invented the name, threw it out there and received a frown in return.

"No. No, I'm sure that wasn't it."

"I'm curious because three of us are trying to find old friends we've lost touch with. It was Alan who suggested coming here to see Belle. Was it Geoff perhaps?"

"No." She ran her finger down signatures in the visitors' book.

"If it's Geoff, you won't read his signature." He gave her his best smile. "We always say he should have been a doctor because his handwriting's so bad."

She returned the smile. "Here it is. Three weeks ago. I don't think it's Geoff—" She bent her head over the sprawling ink and turned it slightly so that Dylan could see. "Is that Mather? Chris—Christopher Mather?"

"It's Christian Fraser. He told me he might call on her. Hmm, I'd better go and have another quick word with her."

He strode back to the conservatory, wondering what in hell's name Fraser had been doing here. There had to be a connection between his visit and his subsequent murder. Had to be.

He reached the conservatory to find Belle studying the crossword. She looked up, immediately folded the newspaper and put it on the table.

"I thought you'd gone," she said.

He sat opposite her. "I've just heard that someone else came to visit you, Belle. A chap called Christian Fraser. Do you remember him?"

"Of course." She gave him a scornful glance. "I may be old, Mr.—I may be old, but I'm not stupid."

She'd forgotten Dylan's—Davey's—name already.

"I know you're not. Sorry, Belle."

"He wore a lovely suit and looked really handsome." She didn't add "not like you" but it was implied.

"Have you met him before?"

"Of course not. I thought at first he must be Molly's boy. I don't think he was though."

"No, he's not Molly's boy. His father, Barney Fraser,

died." There was no flicker of recognition at the name. "Joe Child took Christian and his two brothers under his wing, I gather. They're close friends."

Belle shook her head and wagged a finger. "No, he wasn't friendly with Joseph Child."

"Really? Did he ask about Joe—Joseph?"

"No. He didn't mention him."

Dylan found that hard to believe. The trouble was that although Belle sounded fairly lucid, it was impossible to tell.

"A man saved my life once," she said. "I was stepping onto a train at Paddington Station and collapsed. It's strange, you know, but I don't remember getting to the station. I don't remember leaving the house, even. I remember nothing until I woke in hospital, three days later. I'd had a heart attack and this man saved my life. I can show you, if you don't believe me."

She yanked at the bell pull behind her chair. A small red light flashed above it.

Karen appeared in the conservatory as if she'd been waiting outside. "Is everything all right?"

"I'd like my special box, please. Would you fetch it for me?"

"I'll have Phillip bring it to you."

Karen swept out of the room and Dylan tried to bring the conversation back to more important matters. "About Christian Fraser—"

"I don't know why that girl speaks as if I know who she's talking about. She said Phillip would bring my box as if I know him. I've never met him and I'm not sure about the idea of a stranger rifling through my belongings. But what can you do? I can't carry it myself. I used to, of course. That box has been everywhere with me."

"I'm sure Phillip and the rest of staff are trustworthy."

"You hear of such terrible things. Once you get old, you're very vulnerable."

Dylan nodded at the truth of that.

Phillip came into the room carrying a wooden box about two feet square and a foot deep. "Hello, Belle. How are we feeling today?"

"I can't answer for you, young man, but I'm feeling fine. Put my box on the table, if you would."

"Of course. There you go." With a wink for Dylan, he left the room.

Belle looked at Dylan. "What did I want this for?"

"You said a man saved your life. You were going to show me the evidence, I believe."

"Ah, yes." The box was unlocked and she pushed back the lid. It was crammed to the top with papers.

A long hour passed during which Belle discussed the merits of every scrap of paper she uncovered, from her medical notes to an invitation to a wedding in 1990.

"Here," she announced, brandishing a newspaper clipping. "This is the man who saved my life."

Dylan took it from her, looked at the grainy photo of a slightly younger Belle and a man. Then he looked again. He recognised that face.

He read the few paragraphs that told how Belle Watson, aged eighty, had suffered a heart attack while boarding a train at Paddington Station. A Richard Winters had been about to board and had immediately started CPR. He'd managed to establish a pulse until a defibrillator and medical staff arrived. The photo showed Belle meeting her saviour a month or so later.

Ricky Winters. Well, well, well.

"That's quite a story, Belle." Quite a knight in shining

armour too. "Does it have anything to do with Christian Fraser coming to see you?"

She snatched the newspaper clipping from him. "Of course. He'd seen this—it's on the internet apparently—and he was trying to find Mr. Winters."

"Why?"

"I've no idea, but I expect he found him. He found me so I'm sure he found Mr. Winters."

"You don't happen to know where Mr. Winters is living, do you?"

"Of course not. That's his business." A bell rang somewhere in the building. "It's time for lunch, Mr.—Mr. Young." She smiled her satisfaction at having re-membered his name. "Goodbye."

"Goodbye, Belle. And thank you."

As Dylan exchanged the comfort of the Tall Pines for the wreck of a car he was driving, despair settled around him. What he had to do was find Caroline Aldridge and Farrah Brindle, and he wasn't sure that no matter how deeply he delved into Child's murky life, he was any closer to doing that.

Chapter Thirty-Two

DYLAN HATED PRISONS. He'd always thought them far too luxurious for the scum that ended up there, but since his own spell behind bars, he loathed them with a passion. As soon as he stepped inside, feelings of claustrophobia had his heart pounding. They all spewed out the same smell and the same noise levels. The smell he could cope with, just, but the noise jangled on his nerves.

Thanks to the efforts of DI Rhodes, he would shortly be talking to Raymond Mair. Even Dylan had been surprised at how quickly permission had been granted.

Mair had been convicted of a list of crimes as long as the M1 but they were all fairly minor. Most of them included assault but Mair only turned nasty if he had his eye on something worth being stolen. At least, Dylan hoped that was the case. The general opinion was that he felt happier on the inside than out in the real world. As he'd spent more of his adult life in jail than out, it wasn't surprising that he coped better with the familiar.

Visiting was allowed only between two and three o'clock, which meant that Dylan couldn't be with Bev while she had her scan. He'd see her afterward though. Perhaps they could share a bottle of wine and celebrate her good news. He hoped so.

After his surprising chat with Belle, he needed to find Ricky Winters too. He and Winters had put the world to rights over many a pint and a burger in the past.

He joined several other visitors, mostly women, and was searched far more thoroughly than he'd expected before finally being allowed into the visiting room, where tables and plastic chairs were fixed firmly to the floor. Dylan shuddered and took a couple of deep breaths to slow his heartbeat.

Prisoners strolled into the room and sat opposite their visitors. Dylan waited. And waited.

Finally, a tattoo on legs walked into the room. He stood completely still to stare at Dylan. A prison officer gave him a nudge and he, reluctantly it seemed, came over to the table and threw himself down opposite Dylan.

Mair was tall, thin and covered in tattoos. A spider's web completely covered his neck, a snake curved around the fingers and wrist of his left hand, and some sort of cross covered a right hand that was missing a finger.

"Who the fuck are you?"

As far as any of them knew, Mair and Child had had no contact since their days at St. Lawrence's. If they were wrong though, if the two men were involved in something, and if the two were pals, this could get awkward. Belle's mention of Mair had given Dylan an uneasy feeling. Perhaps he and Child were more friendly than any of them knew.

"David. David Young. I was—"

"What do you want with me? And how the hell did you get a pass? Why wasn't I told you wanted to see me?"

"It seems there was a bit of a mix-up." Dylan gave him a shrug that managed to insult the entire staff of HM Prisons. "I put the request in two or three weeks ago and—"

"So what do you want with me?"

"I'm trying to find someone and—"

"Who?"

"I'm trying to tell you." *Christ!* "There's a bloke who owes me some money. Serious money. But he's done a runner. Leastways, I can't find him."

"What? You reckon he's hiding in my cell?" Mair gave a scoffing laugh.

"No, I reckon he's being hidden by his mates. I want to find out who those mates are and I'm thinking you can help me."

"What's his name? And hey, what's in it for me?"

"That depends on whether you deliver. His name's Joe Child. Remember him? You and him were at St. Lawrence's together, weren't you?"

"What?" Mair's surprise burst out on a laugh. "Fuck me. That's years ago, pal."

"I know. But you can probably help. I know he was pally with Gordon Riley, but there were a couple of others he was friendly with, wasn't there? It's them I'm after. Do you have any idea who they might be?"

Mair clearly didn't feel obliged to speak.

"You did know Joe Child, didn't you?" Dylan asked.

"Sure."

"Mates with him, were you?"

Mair sneered. "He only kicked the shit out of me twice, so yeah, I suppose you could say we got along pretty well. Funny I didn't get a Christmas card from him, when you stop to think about it." His eyes narrowed to dark slits. "So what's going on? Why the questions? What's it to do with me?"

"It's nothing to do with you," Dylan said. "I told you, Joe owes me money from way back but he's done a runner. I want to know if his friends are hiding him."

"He never had friends."

"Gordon Riley was a friend, wasn't he?"

"The fuck was he. So you're going after Joe?"

"Yep."

Mair sneered again. "You don't stand a chance, mate."

"We'll see. Now, are you telling me I'm wrong about Joe and his chum Gordon? They weren't big chums?"

"'Course they weren't. Like I said, Joe didn't have chums."

"I thought—well, I know they're in touch these days."

"Yeah?" That clearly took Mair by surprise but he shrugged it off. "Perhaps they are. You're going back a long, long way. We were kids then. Everyone's moved on. All the same, there's no way Joe would be chummy with Gordon."

"But I thought—"

"You thought wrong," Mair said. "Joe Child was a piece of shit then and I don't suppose he's changed. He controlled us kids. We all did as he said, Gordon included, or we had the shit kicked out of us. Simple choice. Gordon got off a bit more lightly because he was useful. He'd do Joe's schoolwork—he was a clever little sod—and he'd cover for Joe. If there was the slightest hint of trouble, Gordon would provide Joe's alibi. Gordon hated him but was too scared to stand up to him. And Joe—that mad fucker hated everyone."

"Perhaps things have changed. From what I've heard, they're big mates these days."

"Then I'll bet you've heard wrong." Mair shrugged. "I don't know why you're even here. I haven't seen either of 'em since I left that shit hole, St. Lawrence's. Don't want to either. They can both fucking rot for all I care."

"You said Gordon used to provide Joe's alibi if there was any trouble."

"So?"

"So what sort of trouble was there? Did something happen?" He knew it had. Belle had told him that much. She'd also believed the man sitting opposite him had been involved.

Mair was a long time answering. "Yeah. Something happened."

"What?"

"It was all hushed up, but shit, I swear some of 'em thought it was me. As if I'd do something like that." He bristled with indignation. "As I said, it was hushed up. Everything was hushed up there. Kids were locked in the cellar for days if they were caught running in the building, and that was hushed up. Another punishment was three days without food, and that was hushed up. Fucking shit hole. They should bulldoze the place. Perhaps they have by now. Who knows? The last I heard, it was crawling with squatters. Who the fuck would want to sleep there?"

"What happened?"

Again, Mair thought long and hard before answering. "A girl was raped."

Dylan waited for more but there was no more. "Which girl?"

"Us kids knew that Joe and Gordon had done it, but of course they stuck up for each other, swore they were somewhere else. Us boys were questioned for days. We were locked in the cellar, we went without food, we were beaten—and we knew Joe and Gordon had done it. Sick fuckers."

"Who thought you might have been responsible?"

"The old biddy who ran the place, for starters. Miss Fucking Watson."

The lovely Belle. Back then, she wouldn't have been an "old" biddy. She'd have been in her forties or fifties perhaps, which to kids would have seemed ancient.

"Why?"

"Why? Because she wanted someone to punish and she picked on me. She wouldn't pick on Joe, that's for sure. They were all scared of him, even her."

"Even when he was a kid?"

"Yeah."

"How do you know Joe and Gordon were responsible?"

"It had Joe's name written all over it. It was brutal. Fuck me, I'll give a woman a slap now and again if she pisses me off, but what they did—" He spat on the floor. *Nice.* "It happened in the sports room where tennis, cricket and rounders bats were kept. They raped her and then they used a rounders bat on her."

Wincing, Dylan leaned back in his seat.

"She'd been cut too. She nearly bled to death," Mair said in a matter-of-fact way. "One of her friends found her the next morning."

"Was she all right?"

"No, she was never all right. They got a doctor to her. That was another thing, no kid there got to see the inside of a hospital. This creepy old doctor used to be called in if there was an emergency. I suppose they didn't want us going to hospital in case anyone noticed all the bruises we'd got. Anyway, he came out to her. She stayed in a room on her own for a couple of weeks and eventually was fit enough to return to normal. Well, as normal as possible. She never recovered though. She was always a little—crazy."

Dylan wasn't surprised. "Did she say Child and Riley were responsible?"

"She said fuck all. Not a word. Too scared, I expect."

"How old was she?"

Mair thought for a moment. "It wasn't long before we left the place. I'd guess that we were about fifteen and she was thirteen. She might have been fourteen, but no older than that." He drummed snake-covered fingers on the table. "She never said anything and no bugger pressed her too hard. They wanted it forgotten. Like everything else that happened at that place, it had to be swept under the fucking carpet. We all knew it was them, but no fucker was brave enough to say so. What good would it have done anyway? Joe would have kicked the shit out of us and it wouldn't have helped Molly, would it?"

"Molly? The girl's name was Molly?" *Oh, Belle, you're not as crazy as I thought...*

"Yeah. Molly Johnson."

"What happened to her?"

"How the hell would I know? I told you, I left that shit hole and never spoke to anyone from there again. Never saw anyone or spoke to anyone. And that suits me fine."

"And you can't think of anyone who might have been friendly with Child or Riley around then?"

"Nope. Believe me, if I could help, I would. You'd come off worse because Joe would probably kill you, but I'd like to see someone get the better of that piece of shit."

So would Dylan.

"While I'm here, do the names Caroline Aldridge or Farrah Brindle mean anything to you?" Dylan asked.

"No. Should they?"

As Mair had been in this place for the past five years, there was only one answer to that. "No. But thanks anyway. Be seeing you."

Chapter Thirty-Three

DYLAN CHECKED HIS messages—nothing from Bev—swapped his sim card for David Young's, returned his own to his shoe and caught a bus across London to the gym where Ricky Winters had once spent a lot of time.

The gym had been given a facelift since Dylan had last seen it, probably because it had featured on TV a couple of times. The owner, James Terry, was an ex-boxer who'd been given an OBE for his work in helping to keep youngsters off the streets. Dylan supposed it was better for them to knock hell out of each other than to sell drugs on street corners or knock hell out of unsuspecting passersby.

He walked inside and up a steep but narrow staircase to the gym itself, where the smell of curry and stale sweat lingered in the air. Two young men, both clad in protective headgear, danced around a ring, throwing the occasional punch. Away from the ring, a black man's muscles rippled impressively as he punched a heavy bag.

Dylan walked over to him. "Hi. I'm trying to find Ricky. Ricky Winters. Does he still hang out here?"

"Sure." The man carried on punching the bag. He wasn't even breathing heavily.

"Any idea where I might find him?"

The chap nodded toward the ring, where a man stood outside the ropes, barking orders. "Ask Winston."

Dylan crossed the room to the ring. No one paid him

any attention and he waited, impressed with what he saw. He wasn't an expert when it came to boxing but the taller of the two men looked useful. He was quick on his feet and his punches were delivered with lightning speed. Such talent could be an advantage in this particular part of London.

Eventually, Winston rang a bell and the fighting stopped. He turned to Dylan, looked him up and down and clearly found him wanting. "Are you looking for me?"

"I'm looking for Ricky. Ricky Winters. He used to hang out here."

"He still does."

"I'm an old friend," Dylan said. "I'm back in the City for a couple of days, so I thought I'd look him up. Any idea where I might find him?"

"I haven't seen him for a week or more," Winston said. "The last I heard, he was flashing the cash in the Feathers." At Dylan's blank look, he added, "The pub round the corner. Go out of here and turn right, go to the end of the road and then take another right. You can't miss it. If he's not there, someone will know where he is."

"That's great. Thanks a lot."

"Who shall I say was looking for him, if I see him first?" Suspicion was always uppermost in people's minds round here.

"Davey Young. He'll know who you mean."

He hoped Ricky would remember his time spent with Davey Young. Dylan had been taken on as a driver by McCoy, but McCoy hadn't fully trusted him. As Dylan had been a copper working undercover at the time, he'd been right to have his suspicions. McCoy had trusted

Ricky though, and he'd thrown the two of them together so that Ricky could keep an eye on his new recruit.

Ricky wasn't the sharpest tool in the box, and although he'd dreamed of riches, he'd never been likely to acquire them. He was a small-time crook who'd been loyal to McCoy and who'd done a couple of stretches in prison for his trouble.

Dylan pushed open the door to the Feathers and Ricky Winters was the first person he spotted. It was impossible to miss him. Ricky was six foot five and broad shouldered, but it was the way he was standing at the bar surrounded by an admiring crowd that drew the eye. Winston had said he'd been splashing the cash, which might explain his popularity.

Ricky looked at Dylan, looked away, and then looked back, his eyes narrowing. A smile lit his face as recognition dawned. "Holy shit! Will you look what the bloody cat's dragged in." He swept through the crowd to slap Dylan on the back. "Davey! Long time no see. I thought you must be dead."

"Alive and kicking, Ricky."

"It must be—what? Eight years?"

"Give or take. How goes it, Ricky?"

"Very well indeed, my boy. Here, the drinks are on me. What are you having?" Without waiting for a reply, Ricky, who'd obviously been propping up the bar for a few hours, slapped his arm round Dylan's shoulder and shoved him to the bar. "A treble whisky for my friend."

"Seems like you've come into some money, Ricky," Dylan said as the barman poured his whisky.

"I certainly have." He tapped the side of his nose and leaned in close to whisper, "I cashed in an insurance policy."

"Very nice. I wish I had one of those."

Ricky snorted with laughter. "So what are you doing here? And how come I haven't seen you around for years? The last I heard, you'd been arrested and slammed in jail."

"That's right." Dylan took the glass of whisky. "Cheers. What about you, Ricky? What have you been up to?"

"This and that. Nothing big. Just small jobs here and there. To tell the truth, there hasn't been much about since McCoy died." He looked Dylan up and down. "You're looking older. Still, I suppose it catches up with all of us. Are you dying your hair now?"

"No. Why? Does it look a bit—?"

"Girly?" Ricky snorted with laughter. "Yeah. It always did though."

They caught up on gossip for the next hour or so. Dylan had heard most of it from his newfound chums on the force, but it was better hearing it from street level. More drinks were bought for every customer in the pub and glasses were soon emptied. If Dylan wasn't careful, Ricky would pass out before dishing up any useful information.

"It's lucky you caught me," Ricky said. "I'm off to France next week."

"France? What d'you want to go there for?"

"My missus—hey, I bet you didn't know I'd gone and tied the knot, did you?"

"Married? You?"

"Yeah. Well, Trudi's always wanted a bit of sunshine so we're buying a place in France. Down south."

"Wow. How the other half live. This insurance policy you cashed in—can I get one?"

Ricky laughed. "It's been maturing for quite a while."

"Even so. It must be pretty big if you can afford a place in the sun."

"Yeah. Now then, let me get another round in. All this talking is thirsty work."

Never mind Ricky passing out, Dylan wouldn't be far behind him if he didn't take the treble whiskies more slowly. His head was already swimming.

"Remember Joey?" he asked when they had fresh drinks in their hands. "Joey Child?"

"'Course I do." The smile had slipped a little. Ricky licked his lips. "What made you think of him?"

"I've seen him."

"Yeah? I heard he'd turned into some Bible freak up north."

"He has. He spends all his time helping the homeless. Him, Doll and his two boys."

"I haven't seen him for years. Recently, are you talking?"

"I saw him last week," Dylan said.

Ricky looked decidedly uneasy. Either that or he was about to throw up the best part of a bottle of whisky.

"Hey, and there was someone looking for you?"

"Who?" Ricky was distinctly pale now.

"Remember Barney Fraser? His boy. Christian."

Ricky went perfectly still. He'd been swaying on his feet a little, but he was quite still now. "Here, let's go into the back room. It'll be quiet in there. Can't hear yourself think in here."

He paid for another round of drinks for everyone and then nudged Dylan in the direction of the back room. It was small and occupied by two old men enjoying the warmth from a spluttering gas fire.

"When was this?" Ricky asked in a whisper. "When was the Fraser boy looking for me?"

"A couple of weeks back. Three or four perhaps."

"Ah. Well, he found me, so that's all right, isn't it?"

"You've seen him?"

"Yes. Why? What's he saying?"

"He's not saying anything, Ricky. Dead men don't make great conversationalists."

"Dead?" Ricky put down his glass and leaned back on the leather-covered bench. He looked as if he regretted the drinks. "How did he die?"

"Beaten to a pulp up north. Do you know Dawson's Clough?"

"That's where Joe Child is."

"That's it."

"Fuck." Ricky's hands shook and panic flashed across his eyes. "I'm in trouble, Davey. Big fucking trouble."

"Why's that? What's going on?"

"Fuck."

"Anything I can do to help, mate?" Dylan asked.

Despite his massive build, Ricky had always scared easily. Now he looked terrified.

"We've got to get out of here." His drink forgotten, Ricky was already on his feet. "Come on. Follow me."

"What the—?"

"Come on!"

Dylan needed to check up on Bev, but the sooner he found out what was going on—or, better still, what had happened to Farrah and Caroline—the quicker he could go home for good. How Ricky could have anything that might lead him to the girls, he had no idea, but he was sure everything would lead back to them. Eventually.

Once out in the cold night air, Ricky stood quite still. "I don't know where to go or what to do."

Dylan didn't know what the problem was so he couldn't help. The fresh air would do them both good though.

"How about we get something to eat?" He was starving and wished now that he'd cleared the plate of biscuits on offer at Tall Pines.

Ricky nodded. "There's a place along here. Burgers, kebabs, pizzas—whatever you want."

"Sounds good."

Half an hour later, when they'd demolished a pizza each, Ricky looked slightly—and it was only slightly—more calm. "Right," he said, "when was he killed?"

"Christian Fraser? A week ago last Thursday night. What do you know about it?"

"I know who did it. Joey. Joey fucking Child."

"Nope. He was in a nightclub in Dawson's Clough."

"Bollocks was he. He killed him, all right. I'd stake my life on it."

It was possible, Dylan supposed. Child claimed to have been at Tempo all evening. He'd been seen arriving and leaving hours later. He could easily have left the building unnoticed though.

"Besides," Dylan said, "he's pally with the Fraser boys. He took them under his wing after their dad was killed, apparently."

"Ha. That's what you think, Davey. Shit, that's what *everyone* thinks. You're all fucking wrong."

"How do you mean?"

They walked along the street with Ricky looking over his shoulder every few paces. "The Fraser boys, all three of them, had been receiving death threats, right?

They were paying their big chum Joey to find out who was threatening them. Paying him a lot of dosh. Except Christian—the youngest—wasn't convinced. He didn't trust Joey. Christ, who in their right mind would trust that bloody maniac?"

Fair point, well put.

"Christian started asking questions," Ricky said. "Questions about his dad, questions about folk who worked for McCoy—like me and you. Well, probably not you because you weren't with us long. But when I heard that, I thought it was my lucky day."

"Why?"

"Because—" There was a long, long pause. Ricky was holding his breath and Dylan found that he was too. "Because I know who killed Barney Fraser."

Bingo. Dylan, along with most coppers working at the time, thought they knew too. They'd all have put money on Child being suspect number one. "Who?"

"Guess." Even now, when he was scared shitless, Ricky had to play guessing games.

"Joe Child?"

"In one."

"How do you know?"

A crowd was waiting for a late bus. Everyone ignored the bench provided, preferring to stand.

Ricky, as if his legs could no longer support him, sank down on that bench. People edged away and Dylan couldn't blame them. He had all the signs of a madman.

"How do you know that, Ricky?"

"McCoy—" He broke off and shook his head. There were too many ears in range.

Dylan sat beside him on the bench and was glad he'd

had those whiskies. It was bitterly cold and they had to be providing his body with some warmth.

Five minutes later, a bus trundled into view and ambled to a stop. Everyone got on—everyone except him and Ricky.

"How do you know that Child killed Barney Fraser?" Dylan asked for the third time, when they were alone.

"McCoy didn't trust Joe. Something had happened, I don't know what, and McCoy was wary. There had been a few leaks."

Dylan swallowed hard. Those leaks had come from him. He'd known McCoy would soon start to wonder how coppers were suddenly turning up at unexpected times.

"McCoy thought Joe had turned dirty," Ricky said, "and I had to follow him. I used to do a bit of photography and McCoy wanted pictures of Joe's movements. I followed him for weeks. Probably a couple of months. There was nothing to say that Joe was doing anything other than what McCoy told him." He tapped his shoes on the paving slabs as if trying to bring warmth to his feet. "But McCoy insisted I keep following him, and you know what he was like."

Dylan knew exactly what he was like. Mad, bad and extremely dangerous to know.

"One night, I followed Joe as usual and—Christ, I could hardly believe it. Did you know Barney Fraser had his tongue cut out?"

"I heard rumours, yeah."

"Remember how old Fraser used to go around with his minders in tow? Well, they'd been sitting in their car and someone, I don't know who, had tampered with it. They tried to start the engine but it was dead, so they couldn't meet Fraser. They phoned him and he said he'd walk. It wasn't far to his house. He set off walking and Joe ambushed him and dragged him into *his* car." Ricky shoved his hands deep in his pockets. "I followed. Just like McCoy had told me."

Ricky became lost in his memories. Dylan didn't have the time to waste. "Go on."

"Joe drove him out to that old factory. You know the one that McCoy owned? The one where the bloke got behind on his rent and was kicked out?"

"I know it." The tenant had received a few broken ribs during that "chat" with McCoy.

"Well, Child drove him there. He dragged him out of the car and into that factory. I followed—Christ, it was awful. Joe knocked him about a bit, then—then he cut his bloody tongue out. Why he did that, I have no idea. It was almost as if he enjoyed it too. Anyway, I hid behind a stack of boxes. The bloke had a shoe business and there were still piles and piles of shoe boxes there. I hid behind those and took photos. I did it automatically. Somehow, it didn't seem quite so bad with my camera to my eye. It was after, when I got home, that it hit me. I had nightmares for weeks afterwards."

"Why did Joe kill him though?"

"He was acting on McCoy's orders. Fraser was getting too big for his boots so he had to be—disposed of."

"So McCoy was happy that you'd taken photos of the whole thing?"

"He'd expected no less. Of course, I'd just changed to digital then and I printed out the pictures for him. There were only three or four that had come out reasonably well. I could hardly use a flash, could I? I was shit scared as it was that Joe would catch me and rip *my* fucking tongue out."

Dylan slapped his hand to his forehead. "Digital photos. You've had them on your computer all this time, haven't you?"

"Not on my computer, no. I'm not that stupid. I kept the files though, yeah."

"Your insurance policy?"

"Yeah. When the Fraser boy turned up, I told him I could give him proof about his dad's killer."

"At a price?"

"Christ, Davey, a bloke's got to live."

"Of course he has. How much did he pay?"

"Two hundred and fifty big ones." Ricky sighed. "I printed out the photos for him. I kept the file, just in case I could make some more cash out of them. The idiot was hell-bent on confronting Joe. I warned him—I told him to be careful."

"So you think he confronted Joe and Joe decided he had to be—disposed of?"

Ricky looked at him as if he were mad. "Give me another explanation."

Dylan couldn't. Child, however, could prove he was at Tempo on the night of Christian Fraser's murder. Someone would have to prove that he wasn't.

"Do you think he squealed?" Ricky asked, a pleading note in his voice.

"It's difficult to know. Joey will have wanted to know where Fraser got the photos, and violence can be a very persuasive weapon. In his shoes, I would have talked."

"Fuck. What the fuck do I do now?"

"That place in France—"

"That's no good. Everyone knows about it. I've told people. How could I have been so stupid?"

Poor Ricky. He'd always been a small-time crook and he always would be. He didn't deserve the wrath of Child on his back though. "Go somewhere else then. Scotland, Wales, Belgium—anywhere. If Child knows you have enough proof to give him a life sentence—"

"I'm a dead man," Ricky finished for him.

That was an accurate assessment.

"When did you last see Joe?" Dylan asked him.

"Years back. Probably three years ago. Why do you ask?"

"Just curious. You know and I know that the Bible-bashing God stuff is complete bollocks, so what can he be up to? Any ideas?"

"Apart from getting money from the Fraser boys for so-called protection, I haven't got a clue. Fucking son of a bitch."

"Yeah. I don't suppose anyone's mentioned any names to you, have they? Like Caroline Aldridge or Farrah Brindle?"

"Never heard of them. Why do you want to know?"

"I can't find them and I think Child's had dealings with them. I'd hate to think of them suffering at his hands."

"Look, I've got to go, Davey. I need to get the missus out. I need to run, don't I?"

"It might be a wise move."

Ricky didn't run, but he did stagger down the street at a good pace.

Dylan wished he could have asked for copies of those photos, but he couldn't. It didn't matter. Ricky would be easy enough to find. Police would soon track him and those files down.

Unless Joe Child tracked him down first.

Chapter Thirty-Four

IT WAS ALMOST one in the morning when Dylan crept into his house. He'd thought he'd have to break in again, but the place was lit up like Blackpool Illuminations and the back door was unlocked. Bev was always ready to complain about the number of burglaries and petty crimes in the area, but she couldn't get the hang of something as simple as locking the blasted door.

He walked into the sitting room, where the TV was on. No one was watching it. His mum was drinking a cup of her foul-smelling herbal tea and Bev was staring at a magazine.

"Sorry," he said, sitting down next to her. "I couldn't get away. How did it go?"

"Fine." She accepted his kiss and gave him a tight little smile.

If there was one thing he hated it was Bev saying she was *fine*. *Fine*, in his experience, meant "Everything's crap and you have to go through forty questions to discover what's most crap."

"What did they say at the hospital?"

"Oh, I'll tell you later. How did you get on?"

He gave her a quick summary of his day, but he was too restless to settle. He wandered across to the window, pulled back the curtain and glanced out. He couldn't stop a wistful sigh escaping. His Morgan, the most beautiful car in the world, shouldn't be sitting idle. Still, hopefully he'd soon be home for good. He could be Dylan Scott, private investigator, again, driver of a fine piece of British engineering. On his first day back home, he'd take the Morgan for a spin—maybe head to Brighton...

His mum finished her drink and stood up. "I'm away to my bed, folks. Late nights don't agree with me. Don't worry, Bev. I'll be up bright and early, so you'll have no need to rush."

Bev gave her another of those forced smiles. "Thanks, Vicky. I appreciate it."

"Are you staying the night, Mum?" Dylan asked.

"School trip," Bev explained with her usual lack of enthusiasm for such events.

"Right. I need to get away soon too," Dylan said. "I'll get myself a small drink and then get going."

What he wanted was an excuse for a quick word with his mum, and fortunately she followed him into the kitchen.

"What's wrong with Bev?" he asked in a whisper.

"I expect she's worrying about the scan results."

"So how come she was okay yesterday and not today?"

Vicky rolled her eyes at such a stupid question. "Because she hadn't had the scan yesterday."

"So having had a test, there's suddenly more to worry about?"

She gave him a small smile. "Yes."

That was female logic at its finest, and Dylan wasn't going to waste his time trying to make sense of it.

Vicky gave him a quick hug. "Take care, Dylan. Stay safe, okay? Family is the only thing that matters when it all comes down to it. Don't take any risks for something that's not important."

"I won't."

She gave him a long look, then sighed. "The sooner you get your hair cut and have a shave, the better. You look like a tramp. And blond hair makes you look— like a spiv."

"A spiv?"

"Yes. One of those flashy individuals who makes a living from profiteering rather than actual work. The sort who goes bankrupt from a dodgy deal but who still has fifteen luxury properties in his wife's name."

"I wish."

Smiling, she gave him a hug. A long hug, as if she might never see him again. It made him uneasy.

When she'd gone, he poured himself a very small whisky and returned to the lounge, where Bev was staring at her magazine.

She looked up at him. "When do you think you'll be home for good?"

"Oh, it shouldn't be too long now."

If he'd been any further forward than on the day he'd first arrived in Dawson's Clough, that claim might have had a ring of truth to it. But he wasn't. Or not much. He did know that he was on the right track. He had to be. And, if nothing else, he now had proof—at least, he could find proof—that Child had murdered Barney Fraser. Every copper in the land had believed it to be so, but it was unbelievably good to know that the proof existed. It was also more than likely that Child had ended Christian Fraser's life.

As to the whereabouts of Caroline and Farrah, he still didn't have a clue. Child had to be mixed up in it though.

Dylan wasn't sure that he knew much more about Child than he had on day one. It seemed likely, as both

Belle and Mair had mentioned the event, that a girl named Molly had been brutally raped during Child's time at the care home. She might even, as Belle claimed, have committed suicide. There was no proof that Child had been involved though. And just because Mair claimed Child had simply used Riley, that didn't mean the two of them weren't good friends these days. Riley made healthy donations to Child's refuge so Child was sure to be pally with him.

Round and round his thoughts went. The most infuriating thing of all was that, on the surface, Child was as clean as the proverbial whistle. There were some dark undercurrents though…

He sat next to Bev and nudged her magazine. "Are you going to stare at that page until morning? Are you fascinated by an ad for a new vacuum cleaner?"

He saw that the pages were wet. "Bev? What's wrong, sweetheart?"

She shook her head, too choked to answer, and buried her head against his chest.

"What is it?" A huge lump of dread wedged itself in the pit of his stomach. "Bev?"

She sniffed and sobbed and then choked out the word "Tumour."

That lump of dread shifted before settling again. He held her tight. "Talk to me."

"I haven't told your mum." The words came out in short, hysterical bursts. "I couldn't tell her. Couldn't say the word. But I have a tumour on my ovary."

"What—?" Dylan had to clear his throat and try again. He was trying to keep calm, but it was bloody difficult. "What sort of tumour? What exactly did they say?"

"They're booking me in for more tests. I'm having a MRI scan to see if there are problems elsewhere and I've got to have a biopsy. They should phone me tomorrow—today—and they say I'm to be ready for surgery on Thursday or Friday."

She buried her face again and began to howl.

Dylan held her close and made what he hoped were soothing noises. He knew nothing of medical matters, but he did know that Bev was young and fit. The idea of her having a serious illness was ludicrous. She'd had a bit of pain, that was all.

"A tumour isn't anything to worry about," he said. "They'll remove it and that will be that. You'll come home, recover and be fine. The pain will have gone and—"

"I'm scared," she whispered.

"I know, sweetheart." He pulled her closer and stroked her face. "I'm sure you're getting everything out of proportion though."

"What about Freya? Who will take care of my baby if I die?"

"I will. Mum will. Hell, even Luke will." She was about to argue, but he put a finger to her lips to silence her. "It's ridiculous to talk like this, Bev. You know it is. You're not dying. You're forty years old, for God's sake. People all over the country are having tumours removed right now. It means nothing. More tumours are benign than—than otherwise."

He had no idea if that was true or not, but he'd bet it was pretty accurate for forty-year-old women.

"Let's worry when we have something to worry about, yes?" he said. "Meanwhile, we have nothing. Everything's fine right now. Everything will be fine. Trust me, I'm a private investigator."

Her teeth had started to chatter. "I hope you're right."

He had to leave in a short while, and he hated that. She needed him here, and once again, he was spending his time at the other end of the country. Never again. The next time anyone mentioned a job in Dawson's Clough, or anywhere north of Watford Gap, he'd tell them to sod off. "Let's go to bed."

"When are you leaving?" she asked.

"I've got a couple of hours or so." He was bone weary and he'd had too much to drink with Ricky. The food had helped a little but he needed a nap. "Come on." He reached for her hand and pulled her to her feet.

He had a quick hot shower, which was luxury, and when he went into their bedroom, she was lying on her back, staring at the ceiling.

He climbed into bed beside her, switched off the lamp and wrapped her in his arms.

"I expect you're right," she said. "I'm probably getting everything out of proportion."

"No change there then," he said, and she chuckled.

She held his arm in a vicelike grip, but as the seconds passed, she began to relax. A few minutes later, her soft regular breathing told him she was asleep.

Dylan enjoyed the sensation of being in his own bed, and soon he too was asleep.

When he woke, his arm was numb and it took him a moment to realise where he was. It soon came back to him. He had to get in the heap of junk Rhodes called a car, assuming it hadn't been stolen or towed away as scrap, drive it back to Dawson's Clough and leave it outside a used-car dealer's on Peel Street.

He extricated his arm, flexed his muscles to bring back some circulation, and switched on the lamp.

Bev came to with a start. "What time is it?"

"Too early for you. Go back to sleep, love."

He really did have to go. There was no way he could throw in the towel now. Too much had been invested in this case and he had to see it through. Besides, as he'd told Bev, they had nothing to worry about at the moment. She would have a quick operation to remove the tumour and start the road back to full recovery. Everything would be fine, he was sure of it.

"I can't stay, Bev."

"I know."

She knew, but she didn't like it. He didn't either.

"I'll try to check my phone more often, okay? Leave a message the second you hear anything, and I'll call you when I can, okay?"

"Okay."

"Don't worry if it takes a while. It's a bit difficult."

"I know." She was a little calmer.

"Mum will be right here," he reminded her. "Lucy will come and keep you company. You have lots of friends so there's no need to be alone."

"I know. Perhaps you're right. Perhaps it's nothing to worry about. Remember Beryl? She had a tumour."

"A lot of people have them. A quick op and life returns to normal."

"They haven't actually mentioned the C-word," she said, "but I do have high levels of CA-125, which is an early indicator. And they wouldn't do a MRI scan if they didn't think—"

"Nothing's a hundred percent. Worry when there's something to worry about, okay?"

She nodded, but he knew she'd worry herself sick regardless. He would too.

"You go," she said. "I'll be okay."

He got out of the warm bed and pulled on his clothes. "I'll be home as soon as I can. I promise. Hopefully, it won't be too long now." He reached across the bed to kiss her. "I'll see you soon."

"Take care, won't you? And don't worry about me. I'll be okay."

He hoped so, but he wasn't convinced.

He had to go though. It was time to return to the dark shadows of Child's life.

No one had stolen the heap of junk DI Rhodes called a car, and miraculously it did the 230-mile journey from London to Dawson's Clough without skipping a beat. Dylan's Morgan would have done it faster, but he still managed it in under five hours and that included taking a half-hour break.

During the drive, he'd worked on his story for Child. He'd been arrested during a drugs raid for possession of a weapon, but police had been forced to release him because his claim about it having being planted during the raid had convinced them of his innocence. So he'd stolen a car and driven to London to see if the heat was still on. As it most definitely was, he'd returned to the safety of the refuge to lie low for a while. Hopefully Child would believe that. Maybe he wouldn't even have missed him. Maybe.

As instructed, he left the car, unlocked and with the keys in the ignition, outside Fletcher's, where a huge sign promised Class Cars at Bargain Basement Prices, and began the walk through the town. He'd be at the refuge in plenty of time for breakfast.

It was almost six-thirty and the town was slowly waking. A few cars yawned their way through the quiet streets.

He was opposite a fish-and-chip shop on a quiet street when a large dark car slowed to a stop outside an old terraced house that had been converted to flats. A tall, thin man wearing a classy overcoat and carrying a smart leather briefcase emerged from the back of the car, looked left and right, and let himself into the house. It was Kennedy.

Kennedy with a briefcase? Being driven around in an expensive car? Looking smart and businesslike? That didn't add up.

Lights came on in the second-floor windows of the house. Presumably, as he'd let himself in with a key, Kennedy lived there. It was probably rented, given that two identical properties in the row had Flat to Let signs outside.

A few yards on was a bus shelter, and Dylan settled there to watch the building. All was in darkness except for the second floor. He saw a figure, presumably Kennedy, moving behind curtains.

Minutes ticked by. At seven-thirty, all lights on the second floor were extinguished. A few seconds later, Kennedy emerged. The smart coat and briefcase were gone. In their place was a grubby waterproof coat and a carrier bag.

Dylan would love to get inside that house. He was proud of his breaking-and-entering skills, and if it were a private house, he'd go for it. With a number of tenants inside though, it was too risky.

For now, he had little choice but to follow Kennedy. Dylan suspected they were both heading for the same place.

Chapter Thirty-Five

LEAH RECALLED A book she'd read. She wasn't into self-help books, but a friend had given it to her, saying it was fascinating, and to pass a train journey, she'd read it. She couldn't remember too much about it, only that it kept banging on about living in the moment. Nothing, it claimed, was too bad in the present moment. If you stopped dwelling on the past, wishing you'd done or said something differently, and if you didn't worry about what *might* happen in the future, life was good. Dogs, the author claimed, were always happy because they didn't think about past or future. They had no idea they were going to the vet's next week or that the lump in their throat was leading them to a slow death. If they'd been in trouble last week for peeing on the carpet or chewing a favourite shoe, they'd forgotten.

That was crap though. Dogs abandoned by owners to take their chance at rescue centres weren't happy. Some were so stressed by a life of confinement that they bounced off the walls of their kennel 24/7 and went so crazy, they had to be put to sleep.

The book was crap. Life at this particular moment was about as bad as it got.

All the same, she supposed she was quite calm. She knew she was going to die in this hellhole and she'd accepted her fate.

She should have known that he'd get to her, that one

door wouldn't keep her safe. Those bolts had stood no chance when faced with an angry man brandishing a heavy fire extinguisher.

He'd dragged her, kicking and screaming, to this windowless room where the only piece of furniture was a bed with a filthy mattress. No sheets, no blankets, no toilet—nothing. Light seeped in from gaps around the ill-fitting door to tell her when darkness fell and when the sun rose.

Then—

Live in the moment, she reminded herself. There was no point reliving the pain.

Her left eye refused to open, two teeth were missing, the cuts on her arms, breasts and legs refused to stop bleeding, and the cigarette burns on her arms and legs—

Live in the moment.

She had no idea of the day, let alone the time. She'd guess it was Tuesday, but she couldn't be sure. It had been Saturday night when he drove her here, when she realised she wasn't spending the night in a top London hotel after all.

Sunday night, she'd been raped, cut and beaten. He'd set up a camera on a sturdy tripod so that every second of her pain was recorded. Her only respite had been the brief seconds during which he went to stand behind that camera and made sure it was capturing everything. Several times, he'd stopped to smoke a cigarette. He'd tossed the matches to the floor and stubbed out the cigarettes on her skin. He'd coughed a lot, as if he wasn't used to smoking.

Every time she thought of that night—

Live in the moment.

On Monday night, she'd been alone. That was last night. He'd left last night, so today had to be Tuesday.

"I'll be back," he'd said, but she was past caring.

She knew she was going to die here. She only hoped it was before he returned.

There was no escape. Whether the door was locked was of little consequence because a pair of thick metal handcuffs held her left wrist to the bed.

"Don't think you'll get away like that other ungrateful bitch," he'd said as he snapped the cuffs in place.

If she'd had the strength, she might have been able to drag the bed around the room. What was the point though? There was no way out.

Unless—

For a brief second, wild glorious hope surged through her. When he'd gone, she'd heard a key turn, yet there was no light shining through the lock. It was a big, old-fashioned lock and the key would be heavy. The floor-boards were uneven and there was a gap easily wide enough for a key beneath the door. If the key was in the door, she might be able to poke it out with one of his discarded matches.

There was a little light coming from the gaps around the door, but not enough to see the matches on the floor. She had to run her free hand over the floorboards. She soon found one and she gripped it between her teeth as she tried to drag the bed toward the door. It was easier to push it, and soon she was able to reach the lock.

Her heart was pounding so hard, she thought it might burst from her rib cage.

She pushed her matchstick into the lock. It stopped. The key was still in the lock. She poked it, she wriggled the matchstick in the lock. Nothing happened.

Tears rolled down her cheeks as she continued to work her matchstick in the lock. Minutes ticked by. Perhaps hours ticked by. Her matchstick was ruined, every bone in her body hurt and every inch of skin was bruised and bleeding, but she knew she mustn't give up.

She dragged the bed back a little and used her free hand to sweep the floorboards for more spent matches. She found another and pushed the bed back to the door. Her new match was soon useless.

It was hopeless. There was no escape. Deep down, she'd known that.

Perhaps the worst part was knowing that no one had a clue where she was. She'd walked out on her parents on impulse and hadn't told them she was going to Leeds to stay with Shelley. They didn't even know Shelley. Even if they had known her, Shelley and her boyfriend would simply tell them that she'd left Leeds to stay at the refuge. People at the refuge would believe she'd gone home or returned to Leeds. And what would they care? They didn't even know her real name. They might wonder in passing what had happened to Anna Woodward but that would be as far as it went.

No one knew where she was. Worse, no one cared.

All was silent. The only smell was her own body odour and her own filth. All she could taste was blood. She had no food, no water and no escape.

That book she'd read was full of shit. No dog, no matter how expert it was at living in the moment, would be happy to be chained to a bed and in so much pain it no longer cared if it lived or died.

Chapter Thirty-Six

WHEN DYLAN SAT down to breakfast in the refuge's kitchen, he wondered if the biting cold weather was responsible for robbing people of their sense of humour.

Ivy, usually a busy, smiling woman, was slamming plates around and banging them down on the table for this shift of diners.

"Everything all right, Ivy?" he asked.

"No." She placed her hands on her ample hips and sighed. "No. Everything isn't all right."

"What's the problem?"

Everyone in the room—all twelve of them—were quiet. Ivy could be relied upon to be bright and chirpy, to offer a smile for everyone and always look on the bright side. People were uneasy in the face of this angry Ivy.

"When I retired," she said, "I wanted something to do to get me out of the house. I didn't need the money—well, no more than anyone else—so I decided on voluntary work. Well, I wanted to get away from my Alf too, because he was under my feet all day, but that's another story." She eased herself into a vacant chair, the anger ebbing from her. "I worked in Oxfam's shop for a while, but that closed so I came here. I liked the whole idea of the place. As far as I could see, everyone helped those in need. I know I can swear like a trooper, but I'm a Christian and I like to help others. I wouldn't dream of slamming my religion down anyone's throat, it has to be their own decision, but I wanted to help those who wanted or needed help."

Dylan, along with everyone else, waited for her to go on.

"Well, pardon me for saying so, but I don't feel as if I'm helping anyone. All I seem to do is cook breakfasts and clean this place. What's the point of that? I thought we were setting up the soup kitchen today, but no. It's been cancelled again. All I am is an unpaid skivvy. I'm doing nothing useful."

There were murmurs of agreement from around the table.

"I agree," Sharon said. "We're certainly not getting out into the community as much as we used to, or as much as I feel we should."

"I've had the impression that Joe's losing interest lately." Adrian couldn't quite bring himself to be critical of Child. As far as he was concerned, the man was a saint. "Perhaps he's got a lot on his mind. That young man who was killed, Christian Fraser, that was a friend of his. Like a son to him, he told me."

People agreed and expressed sympathy for the family.

Adrian was behaving differently toward Dylan. He was edgy, reserved. Dylan wondered if he'd done or said something to upset the bloke. Or perhaps Adrian had seen the small paragraph in the local paper that told how David Young had been arrested during a raid on a local pub and released without charge. He would disapprove.

Hank Child stormed into the room and everyone fell silent. He helped himself to coffee, then turned around to look down his nose at them all. "I don't suppose anyone's heard from Anna?"

"Nothing. Sorry," Sharon said.

"Anna?" Dylan asked. "What's she doing?"

"Now there's a question we'd all like answered." Hank's voice was like ice. He looked at Dylan as if he were dog shit, shook his head in despair at the rest of them and carried his coffee out of the room. Dylan didn't take it personally. Hank considered himself a cut above everyone.

"What's all that about?" he asked.

"I think Anna's been leading him on," Sharon said, her voice little more than a whisper. "He was expecting to meet her on Saturday night and she didn't turn up. We haven't heard from her since."

"Someone saw her in Tempo—that nightclub in town," Adrian said. "She was dancing with a group of girls and having a laugh."

"She's taken her belongings," Sharon put in, "so she never had any intention of coming back here. You'd think she could have said goodbye, wouldn't you? Mind, that's young people for you."

"Did she have any belongings?" Dylan had thought she'd turned up with just a backpack.

"Oh, yes," Sharon said, "and it's all gone—iPod, phone and chargers, clothes, toiletries—all gone."

"Didn't she say anything?" he asked. "Was she meeting someone? Going back to her friends in Leeds?"

"That's just it," Sharon said. "She didn't say a word. We didn't get so much as a 'good to meet you.'"

Maybe she'd taken his advice and gone home. He hoped so. If that were the case though, he would have expected her to say goodbyes to them all.

Child stormed into the room then and Dylan decided the weather *must* be making everyone grumpy.

He looked straight at Dylan. "Can't you keep out of trouble for more than five minutes, Davey?"

"Seems not." Dylan shrugged. "It's okay though. There was a drugs raid—"

"So I heard. And you're the one found with a gun. Nice one."

Ivy gasped. Sharon's hand went to cover her mouth and she inched back from Dylan as if she expected him to put a bullet through her heart.

"I read about it in the paper," Adrian said, which explained his reservation.

"Except it wasn't mine," Dylan said. "I'd never seen it before in my life. When the coppers arrived, I wasn't wearing my jacket. I put it on, about to make a sharp exit, and the coppers searched me at the same moment I discovered it. Some rotten bugger had obviously been looking for a hiding place and my jacket was the best place."

"The coppers believed that?" Child's tone was scoffing.

"It's the truth."

"I don't want them sniffing round here," Child said. "They're here often enough as it is."

Was Child finally feeling uncomfortable?

"That's because of the missing girls," Dylan said. "It's nothing to do with me."

Child merely grunted.

"And now I hear Anna's taken off," Dylan said. "I hope she's okay."

"Of course she is. Christ, she's a grown woman."

"Is she hell. She's just a kid."

"I agree." Ivy sounded nervous, but people did when Child was in a bad mood. "The more I saw of her, the more I thought she was probably closer to sixteen than eighteen."

"Rubbish," Child said. "Anyway, she said when she came here that it was only for a day or two. I for one didn't expect her to stay longer. If you lot did, you're dafter than you look."

Charming.

"Right, you're all going into town today after all. I've had a change of mind. It's high time we set up the soup kitchen or the homeless will think we've deserted them. The leaflets are all ready to go—Simon's loading up the van. I'll be late getting there as I have a spot of business to attend to, but I'll join you early evening to see how it's going. Do you think you can manage without me?"

"Yes," Ivy said, looking relieved. "I was just saying we hadn't been out doing charity work for a while. It'll be good to get out."

Business to attend to? Dylan would love to know what that was. With luck, he'd find out. He'd go into town with the rest of them and sneak off on the pretext of going farther afield in the town to hand out leaflets. Then he'd double back to the refuge and see what Child was up to.

"Meanwhile, try to keep the noise down, will you?" Child added. "Doll's not feeling too great this morning."

"I'm sorry to hear that," Ivy said. "Is there anything I can do? Would she like—?"

"What she'd like is peace and quiet, Ivy. See to it, will you?"

Child stomped off, leaving Ivy red-faced with humiliation or anger. His footsteps were heard as he tramped up the stairs loudly enough to wake the dead. So much for peace and quiet.

"Men can be some miserable buggers," Ivy said to no one in particular.

"Joe's certainly not very happy," Dylan said. "I hope everything's okay. This business he has to deal with, I hope nothing's wrong."

"He does a lot of business," Adrian said. "He has to keep bringing in the donations to keep this place going."

"Of course," Dylan agreed.

After he'd eaten breakfast and helped with the washing up, Dylan went out into the gardens. Kennedy was in the shed, oiling an ancient lawn mower.

"Everyone will be going into the town today," Dylan said. "Everyone except Joe Child. He has business to attend to apparently."

"Is that so?"

"It is." Dylan stamped his feet to warm them. "You had a late night, didn't you?"

"Sorry?"

"I saw you getting out of a car early this morning."

Kennedy's eyes narrowed. "So?"

"So you looked very smart. It looked as if you had business of your own."

"No. I stayed with a relative and got back later than I thought. I do own a suit—not that it's any of your business."

He owned a suit and a very upper-class accent. Dylan would bet his life that Kennedy hadn't attended the local comprehensive school.

"None at all. Ah well, I'll catch you later." Dylan walked back across the yard to the front of the house. He couldn't remember the last time he'd been this tired. Years back, he'd been able to party all night and be fine the next day. These days, a missed night's sleep had him feeling like death for a week. All he'd done was sit in a car and drive. He must be getting old.

The cold didn't help. Temperatures had again fallen below freezing. It made for a charming frost-covered landscape, but it was hard work keeping warm.

He was about to go inside the house when Doll, dressed to kill in a grey woollen coat and matching knee-length boots, came out. He thought she must be feeling better, but looking closely, he wasn't so sure.

"Hi, Doll. You okay? Joe said you weren't feeling too good this morning?"

"I wasn't. A funny thing happened, Davey, and it's left me feeling—" she shuddered, "—unsettled."

"What was that?"

"I had this—vision." She put a hand up to stop him interrupting. "It was just after four o'clock this morning. I was wide awake and I hadn't been drinking. It wasn't a dream or anything. It was a real—well, it was a vision."

"I thought you had visions all the time. It's like dead people talking to you. It happens all the time, doesn't it?"

She shook her head, annoyed. "This was for real. I saw a dead body. A faceless dead body." Beneath the carefully applied makeup, she was a sickly colour. Her eyes were a little red and puffy.

"How do you mean? Come on, Doll. You don't believe that crap, do you?"

"Usually, no." She traced a circle in the frost with her booted foot. "It's crap. The stuff I do, it's all crap. It brings donations in—but this was for real and it was bloody scary, let me tell you. I saw the body as clearly as I can see you now."

"What was the body like? Any clue who it was?"

"No. I saw it from a distance first. It was sitting, and

it looked as if it was watching something. I went closer, walked in front of it, and it was a dead body. It had no face though." She wrapped her arms around herself for extra warmth. "I'm wondering if it was—Anna Woodward. Or perhaps one of the other girls. Farrah Brindle or Caroline Aldridge."

"What made you think that? Has something happened? Did someone mention the girls to you? Has something like that brought this on?"

"Nothing. No one's mentioned them. Well, Hank's annoyed because Anna walked out without a word to him, but other than that, no one's said or done anything." She rubbed her hands over her arms and took her car keys from her pocket. "You wouldn't understand, Davey. Joe doesn't either. He told me I needed to see a shrink. I told him that *anyone* married to him for this long would need to see a bleedin' shrink." She laughed at her own joke. "It's left me shaken though, I can tell you that. I'm trying to forget about it. I'm off to town to have lunch with my mate. Be seeing you."

Dylan watched her car until it vanished from his view. He had no doubt that Doll thought she'd seen something. He also had no doubt that something had put the idea in her head. Something she saw Child do perhaps? Something she overheard her husband discussing?

Or perhaps he was going as crazy as Doll.

He still couldn't believe that Anna would have left without a word to anyone. Beneath the brash exterior, she was a good kid. Her grandmother, probably her best friend, had died and her parents were too busy to pay her the attention she needed. Loneliness, and the belief that she could find happiness in the company of strangers, had brought her to the refuge.

He hoped the realisation that life didn't work like that had taken her home to her parents.

Chapter Thirty-Seven

DYLAN HUNG AROUND in town, dishing out soup and leaflets and watching people throw donations in the baskets,
until two o'clock. Then he wandered off and began the
three-mile trek back to the refuge.

He paused for a moment when he drew level with
Walter Topham's farm. There was no sign offering Border collies for sale, so presumably they'd all gone to new
homes. He was about to walk on when he realised the
farm wasn't as deserted as he'd thought. Dylan jogged
down the lane to the farm. He was right. Malcolm Brindle was standing at the door. A sorrowful-looking dog
stood next to him.

There was no knowing what Brindle had in mind.
He'd wanted to kill John Taylor. Maybe he thought he'd
be more successful at ridding the world of Topham.

"What are you doing here?" Dylan asked him.

"I—"

A loud bang, like a gun being fired, cut short Brindle's reply. They both turned to see an ancient Land
Rover bouncing down the lane toward them. The vehicle backfired again and spluttered to a stop a couple
of yards from them.

Topham climbed out, stood to look at them both for
a moment, then reached inside the Land Rover. He took
out two carrier bags that held bread, yoghurts, a magazine, tins of soup and baked beans.

He looked at Brindle, he looked down at the dog and then his steely glance rested on Dylan. "It's you, is it? I never did hear from your friend." He sounded suspicious, as if he doubted the existence of Dylan's puppy-hunting friend.

"No, that's why I'm here. Sorry I haven't been back sooner. The thing is, by the time I told my friend about your puppies, he'd found one somewhere else that same day. Sorry."

"It's no skin off my nose." He looked at the collie and then up at Brindle. "What do you want?"

"It's the dog," Brindle said, and Dylan noticed how old and tired the man looked. Tired of life. "We can't cope with her and I was wondering—" His voice cracked. "We'd pay you well, of course, but I wondered if you had room for her. She'll work with your sheep, you know she will."

"I've already got dogs that'll work with sheep, but I suppose I can take her off your hands."

Brindle fondled the dog's ears. "She's not to be sold or anything like that, just in case— If you can't keep her here, and give her the exercise she needs, I'll have to think of something else. She's bored, you see."

"Aye, she will be. Dogs like this need to work. They need a job to do. You can't expect them to sit around the house all day."

Brindle nodded like a man who'd heard the same thing too many times before. "Will you take her?"

"I'll want money for her food."

"Of course. A hundred pounds a month? Is that enough? Two hundred?"

"Aye, it'll do."

"You'll take good care of her, won't you?"

Topham took the lead from Brindle. "I've been around working collies since I was born. I've forgotten more about 'em than you'll ever know."

"I appreciate that. It's just that—"

"The dog'll be ready and waiting for her."

"Thank you," Brindle said.

"Is there anything else?" Topham asked.

"No." Brindle shook his head.

"Then I'll bid you both good day. Some of us have work to do." With the dog's lead in one hand and his groceries in the other, he went inside and shut the door behind him. A couple of bolts could be heard sliding into place.

Dylan and Brindle walked back up the lane to the main road.

"It's for the best," Brindle said, and his voice shook with emotion. "It's not fair on the dog to keep her. She's Farrah's dog. Without Farrah, she's got no interest in life."

"He'll take good care of her. She'll get plenty of exercise, running around after sheep."

"Yes."

Brindle looked a different man today. Before, he'd been wild-eyed and desperate. Now, he looked old, tired and very sad.

"Did you walk here?" Dylan asked.

"Yes. One last walk with the dog." He managed a weary smile that quickly vanished. "The police—they let you go okay? No charges or anything?"

"None," Dylan said. "You?"

"They kept me there for a few hours but that was all." He took a long shuddering breath. "It's lucky they turned up, isn't it? Like fate stepping in and bringing me to my senses. I don't know what had come over me. I think, I really think, I would have killed Taylor."

Dylan was fairly convinced of it too. "I'm sure he had nothing to do with Farrah's disappearance."

Brindle sighed. "You're probably right. The police are convinced he's innocent. I want—*need*—someone to blame. It's the not knowing that's the hardest part. I've reached the stage now when I need to know if she's alive or—"

He couldn't even whisper the word *dead*.

"I can understand that." Dylan wished there was something he could say, but there was nothing. It was possible, even probable, that Brindle's daughter was dead. Caroline Aldridge could have met the same fate. Dylan couldn't fill the man with false hope. He couldn't bring himself to utter the usual "I'm sure she'll turn up" platitudes.

"Meanwhile," Brindle said when they reached the main road, "I must try to get on with my life. Everything's falling apart around me—my marriage, my career. I need to get it together again."

"Yes."

"I go this way," Brindle said, pointing in the direction of the town.

"And I go to the refuge. You still have my number? If there's anything I can do—"

"Thank you. And thank you for your help with—the other night. The police. That gun. I appreciate it more than I can say."

"It was nothing. Be seeing you."

Dylan tried to figure out the conundrum as he walked on. He knew Child had killed Barney Fraser and he'd stake his life on his having killed Christian Fraser, too.

If Christian had confronted Child with the photographic evidence of his guilt, Child would have had no hesitation in silencing him. But what in hell's name did any of that have to do with the girls' disappearances? That Child knew what had happened to the girls, he had no doubt. Finding out, however, was proving a lot easier said than done.

It was no use getting angry, but the sight of Brindle handing over that sad dog had him longing to grab Child by the throat and beat the truth from him. There were a few flaws to that idea, of course. The main one being that Child would smash him to a pulp.

Thanks to his brisk pace, he was warm when he arrived at the refuge. There was no one around and he crept along the side of the wall toward the house where it was unlikely anyone would see him. All was deserted. Whatever business Child had to attend to was either done and dusted or could be done via phone or email. There were no visitors.

Or perhaps there never had been any business. If Bill Owen had told Child that Davey Young was a private investigator, Child would want to silence said PI. Knives and missing tongues would be involved. The best way to lure a private investigator to your den was to tell him you'd be alone.

He inched round the back of the building and had a look for Kennedy, but there was no sign of the gardener. No sign of anyone.

Child's car was in the garage so he was presumably in the building. If they stumbled over each other, Dylan would feign illness and say he'd needed to get to his bed and rest.

It was odd that Kennedy wasn't around though. Dylan

had told him Child was staying behind on the assump-
tion that Kennedy would watch for any comings and
goings.

He walked into the house and to the kitchen. There
wasn't a sound. The old building was eerily quiet.

He made himself a coffee and grabbed a slab of cake.
He'd think better with something inside his stomach.
He ate his cake and carried his coffee to the main sitting room, where everyone usually gathered. Darkness
was falling but the window still gave him a good view
of the grounds. The only movement came from a blackbird pecking at the frozen ground.

The phone trilled out, startling him. It rang and rang
before the answer machine kicked in. No message was
left.

Dylan swallowed the last of his coffee and ventured
along the hallway. Perhaps the business Child had was
with another woman. Everyone was in town, Doll was
at a friend's—

No, Child wasn't that stupid. If he was up to no good
with another woman, he'd be a long way from the refuge.
He knocked on the door to Child's office. There was no
response, so hoping he wasn't walking into a trap, he
pushed open the door.

Child was sitting behind his desk. His right hand
rested on the desk, as if he were about to reach for the
phone. His left arm hung loosely at his side.

His eyes were wide and staring and his mouth was
slightly open, but he looked almost normal—except for
the gaping hole in his forehead.

Chapter Thirty-Eight

THE REFUGE WAS crawling with coppers, and although it looked chaotic, Dylan supposed they knew what they were doing. He knew from experience how difficult it was when a crime scene was crammed with people. Forensics experts had taken over Child's office where, as far as Dylan knew, Child's body was still in that chair.

Doll, Hank and Gary were in an upstairs room and it sounded as if Doll had finally stopped screaming.

The rest of them were being questioned, or waiting to be questioned. Dylan was one of those waiting.

No one spoke. Two uniformed coppers were watching over them so perhaps people felt intimidated. Or perhaps they were simply too shocked to say anything. A few wondered aloud who could kill such a good man. Dylan could give them a list a yard long.

His initial shock was long gone. People like Child were sitting targets. When you tampered with people's lives, and certainly when you took lives, there was only so long you could escape a bullet.

It was picking one from the list that bugged Dylan. Who the hell had come to this place and killed him?

Would Ricky have been able to find Child so quickly? He'd been terrified, and planning to go into hiding, but perhaps he'd decided to put a bullet through Child's skull before Child had a chance to find him. If that were the case, Ricky might want to silence Dylan too.

Another question niggled away at him. Who was Kennedy?

He knew nothing about the bloke, only that he wasn't what he seemed. He was well-spoken, well educated, and he appeared to have money. He spent his time pretending to work in the garden while watching and listening. So why, when Dylan had told him everyone but Child was going into town, hadn't he stayed to watch for visitors Child might have?

There was an obvious answer to that, of course. Kennedy had made the most of the opportunity, put a bullet through Child's skull and legged it. For all Dylan knew, by telling Kennedy that Child would be alone, he'd signed Child's death warrant.

A female police officer came into the room. "David Young, please?"

At last.

He followed her out of the room, expecting to go to the library where he'd thought people were giving statements, but she looked at him with suspicion and said, "They want you in the dining room."

"Wherever."

She knocked on the door to the dining room and announced his arrival to the two men present.

When the door closed behind her, Detective Inspector Rhodes and Detective Sergeant Miller got to their feet. "What the hell happened?"

Rhodes looked as immaculately turned out as ever. His sidekick, Miller, looked his usual thuggish self.

"I've no idea." Dylan told how he'd returned to Dawson's Clough that morning, how Child had mentioned business he had to attend to, and how everyone had gone into town to dole out charity to the needy. "I planned to come back and watch the place," he explained, "but I was delayed. I saw Malcolm Brindle at Topham's Farm."

"You're kidding me," Rhodes said. "Surely he doesn't think—?"

"No. Apparently he'd gone to take Farrah's dog for the farmer to look after. He looked beaten. He's seen the error of his ways and is trying to get his life back on track. I wouldn't say he's accepted that Farrah could be dead, but he's getting there."

Rhodes and Miller both sat at the table again. Dylan preferred to stand.

"Who knew Child was going to be here alone all day?" Miller asked.

Dylan shrugged. "It's probably easier to say who didn't know. It was common knowledge. Everyone was told to go into town—everyone except Doll. She said she was visiting a friend in town. I can't imagine that she'd come back and kill him."

"We've already checked her alibi," Rhodes said. "She's in the clear."

"It seems to me that we're looking for someone from the refuge," Miller put in.

"Not necessarily." Dylan wasn't about to offer up Kennedy's name. Kennedy was his. "I strongly suspect it goes back a long time. While in London, I spoke to Ricky Winters."

"Who?" Miller was impatient. He probably saw this case as a good chance for promotion.

"He worked for McCoy when I was undercover. We spent quite a bit of time together."

"And?" Miller asked, scowling.

"He's come into some money." Dylan didn't feel the need to rush his story. Try as he might, he couldn't warm to Miller. He could take or leave his boss too. "Apparently, McCoy put out an order for Barney Fraser to be—disposed of. The man chosen for the job—"

"Child?" Rhodes asked.

"The very same. However, there was trouble in the camp at the time. McCoy had his doubts about Child so he had him watched. Ricky Winters was told to watch him. I don't know why he was chosen. Maybe because, although he wasn't very bright, he was loyal. Or maybe it was because he was a keen amateur photographer. I don't know. He spent some time watching Child and taking pictures of his movements. So on the night in question, he had photographic proof for McCoy that Child had indeed taken Barney Fraser to a disused warehouse and killed him."

"Bingo!"

"He kept copies on file," Dylan explained. "Now, with McCoy gone, he thought it was time to cash in. It seems as if one Christian Fraser—"

"What?" Rhodes almost choked on his cold coffee.

"Yes. It appears the Fraser boys had been receiving death threats. Death threats sent by Joe Child probably. Anyway, they were paying Child a tidy sum to find out who was threatening them. Christian, however, didn't trust Child. Hadn't for some time. So he started asking questions. He even ended up at Tall Pines, the nursing home where Belle Watson is ending her days. I don't imagine she told him anything useful, but he was trying to find people who'd worked alongside Child and he saw Ricky's picture in an old newspaper clip. In the photo, he was shown with Belle. So he trotted off to see Ricky, and Ricky was only too pleased to make some money from those old photos. He's been living it up and is plan-

ning to move to the south of France. Now, though, with
Christian dead—murdered—he's gone into panic mode.
He thinks Christian confronted Child, told him where
the pictures came from and ended up dead."

Detective Sergeant Miller let out a soft whistle.

"You need to find holes in Child's story for the night
Christian Fraser was murdered," Dylan said. "We know
he went to Tempo that night because it was the night I
met him, and we know what time he left. Between arriving and leaving, however, I bet he crept out and dealt
with Fraser."

"We need to talk to the Fraser brothers," Rhodes said.

"Then there's Gordon Riley," Dylan said. "I'm not
sure what the relationship is between him and Child—
other than the fact that Riley, for reasons unknown,
feels obliged to make generous donations to the refuge. There's a scam going on there. No one I've spoken
to believes they're friends, and I reckon it's blackmail
or some money-laundering scam they're involved in.
There's something odd about their friendship. I wonder
if the business Child was supposed to attend to today
had anything to do with him. It's a long shot but it might
be worth having a word with him."

DS Miller scribbled something in a notebook.

"Anything—or anyone else?" Rhodes asked.

Dylan thought of Kennedy. "Not that I can think of.
But Riley's involved somehow, I'm sure of it."

"We'll bring him in for a chat."

"So what happens now?"

Rhodes drummed his fingers on the table. "When
everyone has given statements, they'll be told to leave."

"When do you start to rip this place apart?"

"Who says we're going to rip it apart?" DS Miller asked.

"I do." Dylan really disliked Miller. "Who killed Child is irrelevant. Bloody annoying, but irrelevant."

"Annoying?" Miller said.

"Yes. With him gone, we might have lost all hope of finding Caroline and Farrah. What matters is finding out what Child was up to and how and why two young girls—maybe even three young girls, if Anna Woodward is involved—met Child and then vanished off the face of the earth. The explanation has to be here somewhere."

"Anna Woodward?" Rhodes asked, frowning.

"Yes. She's upped and left without a goodbye to anyone. Child was adamant she never planned to stay more than a couple of days. All her belongings have gone too. Hank Child is annoyed, or pretending to be annoyed, because she was supposed to meet up with him and didn't show. She may be living it up back in Leeds, or wherever she comes from. Then again, she may have met the same fate as Caroline and Farrah."

"Bloody hell," Rhodes muttered.

"Quite. You need to tear this place apart. There has to be something here. Some clue. There has to be."

"We'll be on to it at first light," Rhodes said.

"Good. Is there anything else, because I have things to do?"

"Like what?" Miller asked.

Like finding Kennedy. "Just things. I'll let you know if I hear anything."

"Stay close to people," Rhodes said. "If our killer is someone from the refuge, someone will know something."

Dylan didn't think their killer was close to the refuge. They could think what they liked though. "Will do. Where exactly are people going? You've got a few beds to find."

"We're working on it. We'll set up temporary accommodation—probably at the old mission hall on King's Road. As soon as it's organised, we'll let everyone know."

"Okay."

Dylan swung out of the room and worked out his best means of escape. Police were at the front and back doors of the building but they'd ignored the dilapidated conservatory. Although it was rarely used, mainly because half the glass roof was missing, it was locked. It took him two minutes tops to pick the lock and creep out.

He headed toward town and to the terraced house where he'd seen Kennedy that morning. Something told him Kennedy would no longer be there.

Chapter Thirty-Nine

BEV POURED HERSELF a generous glass of red wine. She wished she could drink the whole bottle, then follow it up with another. Right now, she'd give anything to fall into a drunken stupor and forget everything. Five minutes without worrying would be sheer bliss. "I'm going for a long bath."

Vicky was pouring hot water onto one of her herbal teabags, but she stopped, put down the kettle and came to give Bev a hug. Bev felt the sting of tears.

"I wish there was something I could say, love." Vicky pulled back to look at her. "We're all here for you, you know that. Whatever you do, don't worry alone. Talk to us. We'll be with you every step of the way."

Bev didn't trust herself to speak but she managed a wobbly smile.

Vicky patted her shoulder. "Go and lock yourself in the bathroom for an hour. Light some candles, drink some wine and relax. Shout if you need anything."

"I'm not an invalid." *Yet*, she thought. She smiled to take the sting from her words. "Thanks for being here, Vicky."

Vicky waved a hand in dismissal. "Where else would I be? I'll be here as long as you need me and I'll go as soon as you say. I won't overstay my welcome, so don't worry about that."

"I wasn't." This time, Bev's smile was genuine.

Taking Vicky's advice, she slid the bolt across and exhaled a long sigh. Alone at last. Alone with her worries.

She turned the tap on full and poured lashings of scented oil into the water. For a moment she watched the swirling water, then she took off her clothes and stood naked in front of the mirror. She looked quite normal. Well, normal for her. Despite having lost a little weight recently, she could still do with losing another few pounds, and her posture wasn't great thanks to spending too long hunched over a desk while trying to decipher kids' handwriting. When all this was over, she'd take better care of herself. She'd improve her diet and eat only healthy things instead of filling up on chocolate. Coffee could be cut down and replaced with water. There was no way she'd turn into an exercise freak but it wouldn't hurt her to fit more walking into her life. Her hair needed a good trim too and she might look better if she had it tinted a shade lighter. If she needed chemotherapy though, a trim would be the last thing on her mind. Her hair would fall out, and she'd be sick, really, really sick.

Some days, she marvelled at the miracles of modern medicine. Other days, she despaired at the crumbling state of the health service. Having said that, she couldn't fault the treatment she'd received so far. It seemed that, when it tried, the NHS could move quickly.

She turned off the tap, dipped a toe in the water and decided the temperature was perfect. She lit her candles, switched off the light and, with her glass of wine balanced on the edge of bath, climbed in and sank back in the soothing water.

This was usually her idea of bliss. When Dylan was home, she'd abandon the kids to his care and hide in the bathroom for an hour or so with a glass of wine and a good book. Usually, it was relaxing. Tonight, it was anything but that.

Whenever she tried to remind herself that many, many people survived cancer, she always came back to the huge numbers that didn't. The very word made her angry. People threw huge amounts of money into the research of this hateful disease and yet still people had their lives ruined.

If the worst came to the worst, it would be Freya who'd suffer most. The poor little mite wasn't yet a year old. She'd done nothing but bring joy to the world. She didn't deserve to go through her life without a mother.

As much as Bev loved Dylan, she knew he'd be a crap single parent. He was a great dad and would do anything for his kids, but he was too disorganised and laid-back to deal with the more practical matters, like making sure they ate properly, dressed properly and got the most from their education.

She drained her glass of wine and began to feel a little better. She knew she was getting everything out of proportion. The way her thoughts ran on and on, anyone would think she'd been given three days to live. She must stop being so pathetic and get on with life.

When the water had cooled to unbearable levels, she climbed out of the bath and wrapped herself in a huge towel. She felt better. More relaxed.

She pulled on her dressing gown, snuffed out the candles, and was crossing the landing when the phone rang. Seeing it was Dylan, she grabbed it before he hung up.

"Hi. How's it going?" he asked.

She'd always considered herself an independent type

but the sound of his voice brought a lump to her throat. She'd never missed him more than she did right now.

"Okay," she said. "I'm going in early on Friday morning for a MRI scan and a biopsy."

"Really? That's—fast."

"I know. I'll have to take back all I've said about the state of the NHS." She was determined to sound bright and chirpy—there was no point being anything else when he was hundreds of miles away—but she could tell that the speed at which things were moving had surprised him. It had probably worried him too, as it had her. "What about you? How's everything going up there?"

"Child's dead."

It took a moment for that to sink in. "How?"

"A bullet through the brain. It couldn't have happened to a nicer chap but I wish whoever did it had waited a while. Never mind that, how are you *really* doing?"

"I'm okay. Your mum's more or less moved in. We'll see what happens on Friday."

"Yeah. That's all we can do. Are the kids okay?"

"Fine. Well, Luke put a football through someone's shed window on the way home from school today. He knocked at the house but no one answered. He's going to return to the scene of the crime in the morning and apologise. So we may or may not have a shed window to pay for."

"It's only money."

"True." That was the one and only benefit of having something real to worry about. Normal stuff like paying bills became insignificant. When all this was over, Bev would never worry again. "How's Dawson's Clough?"

"Sodding cold."

"It's cold here too."

"Not this cold. I swear the Clough is the coldest place on the planet."

They chatted about the mundane—the weather, the kids, TV shows—and skirted round anything unpleasant. Bev would have happily talked the night away but Dylan was walking in the dark, cold countryside. He had a job to do and Bev knew she should let him get on with it. The sooner he found those poor girls, the sooner he'd be home.

"I miss you," she said.

"Yeah? Blimey, that's a first."

She smiled. "No, I always miss you. I miss the clutter, the arguments, the snoring—"

"I don't snore."

"Ha."

"Look, I'd better go."

She held the phone more tightly and wished she were holding him. "Yes, you go. I'll give you a ring when I hear anything. Be careful, won't you?"

"I will. I'll call when I can."

The line went dead, and the fear and the loneliness settled around her again. Another glass of wine would have to help her fight it off.

Chapter Forty

AS SOON AS Dylan had exchanged his phone's sim card for Davey Young's, he walked smartly on and hung around outside Kennedy's building. After about half an hour an elderly chap walked up to the front door, carrying a takeaway bag that smelled so good Dylan began to slaver like a dog. Chicken tikka, he'd bet. He'd kill for an Indian takeaway right now.

"That smells good," he said, and he followed the bloke inside without a problem.

"I hope it tastes as good."

Dylan followed him up the stairs to the second floor. There were only two doors and the chap with the take-away headed to one on the left. Kennedy's flat had to be the door on the right. Hoping he was right, he pressed an insistent finger to the bell.

He was completely taken aback when Kennedy opened the door a few inches. On seeing Dylan, he was about to slam it but Dylan's reactions were quicker. He wedged his foot in the gap.

"Either I come in or I chat with all your neighbours and see what they know about you."

Kennedy yanked open the door. "What do you want with me?"

He looked exhausted. Whether he looked as if he'd put a bullet through Child's head was difficult to tell.

"I want to know what you've been doing all day," Dylan said.

He followed Kennedy into a sitting room where a small TV was showing the early evening news headlines. Furniture was cheap and basic. On the table, however, sat a half-full bottle of Lagavulin. Single malt whisky on a gardener's wage? Kennedy didn't even earn a proper wage. He was offered a ten-pound note and half a dozen eggs now and again.

"I've been working in the garden at the refuge. I left at around two o'clock because I was tired. As you know, I had a late night." His voice was heavy with sarcasm.

"How was Joe Child when you left?"

"I didn't see him." He switched off the TV. "Why do you ask?"

"So you didn't put a bullet through his head?"

Kennedy looked so shocked that he almost dropped off Dylan's list of suspects. Almost. "Is he—all right?"

"No. Bullets and skulls don't mix too well."

"Good Lord." Kennedy dropped into a scruffy arm-chair. "Dead?"

"As the proverbial dodo."

"Well!" Was it shock that gave him a wide-eyed look? Or was it anger? Dylan couldn't be sure. "Suicide or murder?"

"Murder."

"Are you sure?"

"Men with bullets in their skulls tend to struggle to hide the gun. Yes, I'm sure." Dylan nodded at the bottle of whisky. "Are you offering?"

Kennedy thought for a moment. "Yes. Why not?" He was on his feet and he went to the kitchen. When he came back, he was carrying two expensive crystal whisky glasses.

"Thanks," he said as Kennedy handed him a very acceptable measure.

"What happened to Child then? Who killed him?"

"I was hoping you'd tell me."

"What?" His eyes narrowed. "Me? What makes you think—? Hang on a minute, you surely didn't think I'd killed him?"

"It crossed my mind, yes." It still was crossing his mind. Kennedy had managed to convince everyone he was a deaf and dumb gardener so convincingly, feigning shock at Child's death would be a walk in the park. "As far as I'm aware, you were the only person, other than Child, at the refuge today. I told you he'd be there alone."

"Well, yes, but—" Kennedy shook his head. "No, it wasn't me. He wouldn't have escaped so lightly if I'd had anything to do with it."

He looked as if he regretted saying so much. There was definitely anger in his expression. What had Child done to him, other than belittle him by offering him a tenner and some eggs for weeks of hard graft?

"That's come out of the blue, hasn't it?" Kennedy said. "Any other ideas who might have killed him?"

"No."

They sat in front of an old, spluttering gas fire that was throwing out a welcome amount of heat. If Dylan sat here much longer, he might even take off his jacket.

"I wish I'd stayed on now." Kennedy took an appreciative sip of whisky. "I was tired and there seemed no point, so I came home. I left about ten minutes after the vicar turned up. What's his name? Owen. Bill Owen."

"Bill Owen was there?"

"Yes."

Their gazes locked. Dylan didn't trust Owen, but a gun-toting killer? People's views on Owen differed. To some, he was the well-liked, well-respected vicar who'd settled well in the town. He claimed to have been close to Farrah, but Ivy thought that was stretching the truth. She'd said he helped with the Girl Guides group and the local youth club and liked to think he was close to *all* the youngsters. Clare Brindle had said Farrah thought him an old fuddy-duddy.

For all Dylan knew though, Owen might not have been near the refuge this afternoon. Kennedy could easily have thrown his name out to muddy the water.

"So what's happening now?" Kennedy asked.

"The refuge is a crime scene. All residents are being moved out to temporary accommodation."

"And you?"

"What do you mean?"

"What are you doing? More to the point, who are you?"

"Davey Young. An old friend—"

Kennedy rolled his eyes at that.

"Who are *you?*" Dylan asked.

Kennedy smiled at that. "Touché."

"So you saw nothing out of the ordinary today? Child didn't go anywhere, see anyone apart from Bill Owen?"

"No. Once you all left, everything was quiet. Nothing was moving. That's why I came home." He swirled whisky around in his glass. "Child's dead. That's a shock."

"You weren't his biggest fan though, were you?"

"No. So what's your theory. On his murder, I mean?"

"I don't have one. What's yours?"

"I wish I had one. What do you think he was doing?" Kennedy asked. "Apart from pretending to be Jesus."

Dylan smiled at the description. "I can't answer that one either."

Kennedy rested a thoughtful gaze on him. "Are you a police officer?"

"No." Damn it. Dylan always reckoned he could spot a plainclothes copper from a hundred yards, but he liked to think he'd never had that look. After all, he'd done pretty well undercover. "What makes you ask that?"

Kennedy shrugged. "You ask a lot of questions. You don't seem too concerned about your upcoming court case. You don't seem to mind that your life's a mess. It's as if it's all temporary to you."

Very observant.

"Then my earlier supposition was right. You're a private investigator," Kennedy guessed. "I've come across a few of those in my time."

"Really?"

"Yes." He didn't elaborate. "Switch off the fire if you're too warm."

"No chance of that. I doubt I'll ever be too warm again."

Kennedy smiled. "The weather's hellish up here, isn't it? So bleak and so cold. If it isn't raining, it's snowing."

"That about sums it up. Where do you originate from?"

"Oxfordshire."

"Very nice."

"Yes."

Dylan was enjoying the whisky and the warmth, but he didn't have time for the cosy chat. It was a waste of

time anyway. Kennedy could tell him any lies he chose.
The bloke was a talented actor.

"Caroline Aldridge and Farrah Brindle," Dylan said.
"What do those names mean to you?"

"Not a lot, I'm afraid. I know they're around the
same age, and very similar in appearance, and I know
they both vanished after having come into contact with
Child."

"The police haven't been able to find evidence of any
wrongdoing on Child's part."

"How closely have they looked?"

"Pretty closely, I gather."

Kennedy didn't look convinced.

"What about Anna Woodward?" Dylan asked. "Did
you see her leave? Did you see or hear anything that
might give a clue as to where she's gone?"

"Are you telling me she's missing too? Like Caroline and Farrah?"

"Not necessarily." Maybe she'd seen sense and returned to her parents. "What do you think has happened
to the girls?"

Kennedy considered this and took a sip of whisky
before answering. "I couldn't say. If there is any wrongdoing, however, I would guess that Child and his assistant are involved."

"His assistant? Riley, you mean?"

"Yes."

"You've seen him turn up at the refuge at odd hours,
haven't you? Sometimes he arrives by car and others by
taxi. Is that right?"

"Yes."

Was it? Or was Kennedy looking for someone to take
the fall for Child's murder? It could all be lies.

"Why would he do that?" Dylan asked, playing along. "Presumably, he didn't want his exceptionally flash car recognised. I assume he left it where it wouldn't be too conspicuous and visited the refuge in a battered old taxi that no one would look twice at."

Kennedy nodded but had nothing to add.

Dylan took his phone from his pocket and searched through his list of numbers for Nick. He hit the button and listened to it ring out for what seemed an age. Just as he expected it to go to voice mail, it was answered.

"David Young. Good to hear from you," Detective Inspector Rhodes said.

"Yeah, yeah. Have you spoken to the vicar, Bill Owen?"

"Owen? I don't know. Why do you ask?"

"It's possible he visited the refuge this afternoon. He could be the last person to have seen Child alive."

"I'll get onto it. Someone may have spoken to him. I'll check it out."

"What about Riley? Have you brought him in yet?"

"No, we haven't. We've hit a snag there. According to his personal assistant, he's in New York on business. She believes he left from Heathrow yesterday. However, he wasn't on the flight she gave us. He wasn't on any other flight that we've managed to find yet either. We've checked with neighbours at both his homes, and he hasn't been seen at either for the last couple of weeks. At the moment, we can't ascertain his whereabouts."

"Which means he's done a sodding runner."

"We can't say at the moment."

"Right. Okay." Dylan ended the call before he was subjected to more copper-speak.

Kennedy didn't ask questions, but Dylan could feel

his curious gaze resting on him. "Gordon Riley is no-where to be found at the moment."

"Interesting."

"Yes. You wouldn't have any idea, would you?"

Kennedy looked taken aback by the question. "No."

"What do you know about him?"

Kennedy rested his fingers beneath his chin to make a steeple. "He works hard. A workaholic, I'd say. He's an exceptionally clever man, an astute businessman who can spot trends early. He has a home in London and one in the Cotswolds that he rarely uses. He lives alone. A bit of a loner all round. He's made a fortune from computer games. His social life is almost nonexistent. In fact, I'd say it *is* nonexistent. Any engagements are always business related. He's charming when he needs to be. He has no family. His father was never involved in his life and his mother, who spent most of her time in prison on drugs-related charges, died four years ago. His grandmother took care of him for a while during one of his mother's prison spells, but she found him too difficult and he ended up in a care home. He's certainly done well for himself, when you think about it. He's one of those driven individuals. Too busy adding to his fortune to stop and think about loneliness."

Dylan knew most of that. He was impressed with Kennedy's summing-up though.

"And you've no idea where he could be?"

"None whatsoever," Kennedy said.

If Riley had anything to do with Child's murder, he could be close by. Still in Dawson's Clough perhaps.

"A refill?" Kennedy asked, raising his glass.

"Please." It would help him think.

While Kennedy filled their glasses, Dylan thought

how pleasant it would be to sit and idle the night away with that bottle of Lagavulin. It wouldn't help though. Besides, he'd rather be at home with his own glass and his own bottle. With his wife and his kids. Bev would be worrying herself silly, hopefully about nothing. Freya would be sleeping or giggling. She was always doing one or the other. She had an infectious giggle and they spent ages making her laugh. Luke—well, Luke would be busy being Luke. He'd be listening to music. And probably thinking up a good reason as to why he'd put a football through a stranger's shed window. What had Bev said? That he was returning to the scene of the crime in the morning?

Returning to the scene of the crime.

"Thanks." He took the glass from Kennedy and raised it to his lips.

Returning to the scene of the crime...

"I don't suppose you have a car handy, do you, Kennedy?" It was a long shot, but he needed to be doing something.

"Why? Where do you want to go?"

"London." Mair had said St. Lawrence's should have been bulldozed. The last he'd heard, the building was home to squatters. Squatters or people involved in a scam with Child and Riley? "There's an old care home. It shut down years ago—"

"St. Lawrence's?" He spoke as if the building represented his worst nightmare.

"Yes. What do you know about the place?"

"It was closed years ago. It's practically derelict now."

Kennedy had done his research. Why? Who the hell was he? "I thought I might take a look," Dylan said.

Although if it was almost derelict, there was probably little point.

Kennedy was a long time answering. "I'll come with you. I can have a car here in fifteen minutes."

Dylan needed a car, but he wasn't sure about Kennedy tagging along. It was all very well keeping your friends close and your enemies closer, but he didn't know which category Kennedy should go into. He could have killed Child this afternoon. He could be planning on doing the same thing to Dylan. "There's no need. I expect it's a wild-goose chase."

"I expect it is. But I'm coming with you. If you want a car—" He left the sentence unfinished.

Dylan wanted a car and it would be quicker to use Kennedy's than asking DI Rhodes to provide David Young with another "stolen" vehicle.

Less than fifteen minutes later, Dylan followed Kennedy down the stairs from his second-floor flat. Kennedy had had the good sense to don a heavy woollen overcoat. He also carried a small bag into which he'd put a full bottle of Lagavulin. If he was driving, Dylan might take advantage of that.

They stepped outside and Dylan stopped short. A man emerged from the driver's door of a large black Daimler.

"Good evening, Sir Angus."

Dylan looked around him, fully expecting to find that they'd stepped into the middle of a film set. "Sir Angus? You're kidding me."

"No. But you can call me Kennedy."

The driver held open the rear door and they both slipped inside the warm car.

"Sir Angus?" Dylan said again.

"Yes. I assume you'd rather travel in a less conspicuous manner, but as we've both been drinking—" He shrugged. "We wouldn't want to be pulled over on a drink-driving charge, would we?"

Dylan was more than capable of driving. He might be over the legal limit—correction, he *was* over the legal limit—but he was still capable of driving. All the same, having done the journey last night and having had no sleep since, he shouldn't complain.

After telling the driver their destination, Kennedy leaned back in his seat and closed his eyes.

Dylan should join him, as sleep might help his brain function more efficiently, but his mind was too busy. Questions chased themselves around and he kept coming back to the conundrum that was Kennedy. Who in hell's name was he? How did he know about St. Lawrence's? How did his driver know where St. Lawrence's was without having to ask?

No, he wouldn't sleep. It was too risky when he could be sharing a car with a cold-blooded killer.

Chapter Forty-One

KENNEDY'S CAR WAS warm and comfortable, and Dylan must have dozed off. When he woke, the Daimler was overtaking a line of trucks on a dual carriageway, and a sign confirmed that they were only about twenty minutes or so away from St. Lawrence's.

He stretched his limbs, thankful for the Daimler's generous legroom, and tried to get his brain in gear. According to the dashboard clock, it was ten past four. Daylight would arrive around seven-thirty.

"Where are we?" Kennedy had managed to sleep for the entire journey.

"About twenty minutes away. Look, I expect it's a waste of time, our coming here. It was only an idea. Just me clutching at straws." It was an idea that was sounding more ridiculous with every passing mile. An idea brought on by too much whisky probably. "St. Lawrence's, as you know, was where Child and Riley met, and where they lived for several years. They were just kids then though. I thought perhaps there might be some clues there, but it's doubtful."

"We're almost there so we may as well take a look."

"What exactly does St. Lawrence's mean to you?" Dylan asked. "How come you know so much about it?"

"I know as much as you do. Probably less. I happened to drive past it one day but I've never been inside the building. Have you?"

He was lying. No one would "happen" to drive past.

"No, but I heard it had been taken over by squatters and I'd be interested in talking to them. You never know, those squatters might be there at Child's invitation. They might be working for him. Or Riley." It sounded unlikely, but when you were fresh out of original ideas, you had to try the ridiculous. "Squatters aren't usually happy to see strangers though, so I suggest we leave the car at a safe distance and walk the rest of the way."

Kennedy checked his pockets. "Good idea."

"I have a better one. Why don't you stay in the car and wait for me? I doubt I'll be more than five minutes."

"I'm coming with you. You're right, you know. Anything could be going on inside that building. I hadn't thought of that."

It was a waste of time arguing with him. How could you argue when you had no idea what motivated a person or even who they were?

One thing was certain, he'd watch his back. Kennedy could be a killer and Dylan wanted to be ready for him.

As they neared St. Lawrence's, the streets became more run-down. It had started to rain and a stiff breeze blew litter along the road and pavements. Several shops were boarded up. Some houses had boards instead of windows. It wasn't a pleasant place to live—or to take a walk in the early hours of the morning. They passed a phone kiosk and a bus shelter. Both had been vandalised. Graffiti had been sprayed on a corner shop.

"I suggest I park here, Sir Angus." The driver looked less than enthralled at the idea of parking the Daimler in such a run-down area.

"Yes. And I suggest you lock the doors when we've gone."

"Will do."

"Is there a torch we can use?" Dylan asked.

The driver got out of the car, walked round to the rear of the car and returned with a large, heavy torch, which he handed to Kennedy.

"It's raining quite heavily now," Dylan said. "Why don't you—?"

"I'm coming with you." Kennedy—or whoever he was—opened the door and stepped onto the pavement.

Dylan climbed out and wished he were wearing Kennedy's coat. It was long and warm, whereas his own leather jacket offered little protection from the rain or wind. Kennedy also wore a cashmere scarf and leather gloves.

They walked quickly along dimly lit pavements. A couple of cars passed them, both driven by young males who liked a heavy foot on the accelerator.

"Here we are," Kennedy said eventually.

A high brick wall was the only evidence. They walked a few more paces and came to huge iron gates. Kennedy was right. This was St. Lawrence's. Only a single street-light shed any light on the building but Dylan recognised it from a picture he'd managed to find on the internet.

The gates were held firm with a rusty old chain and a padlock.

"Interesting." The chain might be rusty but the padlock was shiny with use. "It's unlike squatters to have a key." Perhaps they wanted to keep out visitors.

There was no way they could climb over the gate, and the wall was at least two feet taller than Dylan. No footholds were visible, and a curling line of barbed wire sat on the top, so it would be difficult to scale the wall too.

"Let's have a look round," he suggested.

The building occupied a corner plot. To the rear was a disused factory that didn't look as if it had seen life this century.

An ancient tree overhung the wall toward the rear of the property. If they could climb that, they might—and it was a big *might*—manage to drop onto the wall and into the grounds. It was their best option. Possibly.

"Let's have the torch."

Kennedy handed it over and Dylan shone it over every inch of the wall. The wall was around a hundred years old but the long-dead builders had done a good job.

"Right." He handed the torch back to Kennedy. "Give me a leg up. If I can reach that branch, and assuming it takes my weight, I might be able to drag myself far enough along to reach the wall."

"It doesn't look strong enough."

"I know." Dylan managed to grab the branch. The snap as he put his weight on it was deafening, and if it hadn't been for Kennedy breaking his fall, he would have hit the pavement hard.

"Sod it." Dylan took the torch again, crossed the road and searched the run-down properties for anything that might help.

Ten minutes later, he found an old wooden pallet that had been abandoned at the side of a closed-down newsagent's. He dragged it along the road and propped it as firmly as he could against the wall of St. Lawrence's so that he had a ladder of sorts, albeit a wet, rotting one.

It was enough. He was soon clinging to the top of the wall, with the barbed wire scratching at his chest. It was tempting to jump down the other side and leave Kennedy behind, but the bloke was sure to follow him, so he turned and put out an arm to give Kennedy a helping hand.

"It's a long way down," Kennedy said, stating the obvious.

"And a prickly landing." Beneath them were some sort of low spiky shrubs that Dylan didn't recognise.

Dylan lowered himself and let go. He landed in a heap, but with no bones broken. "Throw me the torch."

Kennedy took it from his pocket and dropped it. Dylan poked it with his toe out of harm's way and prepared to give Kennedy a helping hand. "Go for it. I'll break your fall."

Kennedy managed to land lightly and a lot more elegantly than Dylan.

"Right, let's go." Dylan was soaked to the skin and cold.

When they reached the Victorian four-storey building, Dylan was surprised by its size. It was massive. He'd known that over sixty kids had once lived here, but he was still taken aback. Half a dozen steps led to the main entrance. Dylan didn't even try the door. He wanted a look round first.

It was still early and squatters would probably be asleep.

A large window at the back of the building had been smashed, and only a thin piece of hardboard kept the elements at bay. That could prove their best way in.

A heavy metal crowbar lay nearby, probably the one that had been used to smash the window, and Dylan grabbed it. Squatters were usually too stoned to care about anything, but he wasn't sure that these were regular squatters. They could be working for Child. Hell, they could be doing a million things. He still wasn't sure what plans Kennedy had for him either. He'd definitely feel better going inside with a weapon to hand.

"Softly, softly," he whispered, and he saw Kennedy nod in agreement.

He tried the back door but wasn't surprised to find it locked. They walked around to the front of the house and tried the main door. Again, it was locked. As he'd thought, their best option was the broken window.

Someone had done a good job. All glass had been removed, and once the board was taken out, it was easy enough to climb inside. Dylan replaced the board so that the wind blowing into the building wouldn't alert any occupants.

There was no sign of life in this small room. Spiders—and probably rats—had made it their own. A door led to a large empty kitchen. No water ran from the taps. No food or crockery sat in the cupboards. This room hadn't been touched for years.

They crept from unused room to unused room and were about to mount a wide curling staircase when they heard footsteps.

Without saying a word, Dylan switched off the torch and elbowed Kennedy into the darkness at the side of the staircase. He gripped his crowbar tight.

The footsteps had been moving quickly, but they stopped. Dylan held his breath.

There was a light creak of a floorboard. Whoever was moving around was aware of their presence.

A beam of light suddenly swept down the staircase.

Dylan switched on his own torch and aimed the light at the high ceiling. It had the desired result. Heavy footsteps took the stairs two at a time.

The figure appeared and Dylan shone his torch straight at him. His light fell on a torch—and a gun.

Shit.

There were times when quick thinking was called for. In Dylan's experience, those times coincided with moments when your brain struggled to recall your own name.

"We're unarmed," he said.

Gordon Riley laughed at that. It was the manic sound of a man totally unhinged. "Good."

"Put your gun away."

"Now why would I want to do that?"

There was no good reason that Dylan could think of.

He was soaked and freezing, a torch was half blinding him and a gun was aimed at his face. This wasn't going to rank as one of his better days.

He was aware of Kennedy, rigid with tension, standing beside him. Kennedy had forgotten to breathe.

"Joe's dead," Dylan said, "but I assume you know that."

"Yes."

"I assume you killed him."

"Right again."

"Why?"

Riley put the torch on the floor and moved a couple of steps closer. "Why not?"

He was standing no more than six feet from them. A gun would inflict serious damage from that range.

Somehow, and Dylan had no idea how, he had to disarm him. Riley had lost the plot though. The slightest movement and—

No, Dylan had to talk their way out of this.

Kennedy wasn't saying a word, thank God.

"Why not indeed," Dylan said. "He killed Christian Fraser, I believe. I suppose you know that. He certainly killed Fraser senior. Apparently, the Fraser boys had been receiving death threats. In Child's office, I found a newspaper from which a word had been cut. No prizes for guessing who was sending those threats, then. No prizes for guessing who they were paying for protection either. I think he'd been getting money out of the Fraser boys for quite a while. I would also imagine, given your wealth, that he got quite a bit of money out of you."

Dylan was being deliberately wordy, playing for enough time to come up with a plan, but there was no reaction from Riley.

Dylan tried another angle.

"I thought Joe was for real. All the charity work, all the God stuff, I fell for it. I suppose we put him on a pedestal. He seemed such a good man. He was certainly good to me—giving me a roof when I needed one. I suppose he conned us all."

"He never conned me." Riley was insulted by the idea. "I've always known what he's like. Even as a kid— if he had five pounds and I had one, he wouldn't rest until he'd got his hands on my pound. All brawn and no brain."

"Yes, I've come to realise that. You used to be friends though, didn't you?"

"Never."

"So—what was it? Blackmail? We've all got secrets—"

"What are you doing here?" Riley cut him off. "How did you find this place? How did you know I'd be here?"

"We didn't." Dylan tried to keep his tone conversational. Riley had relaxed his grip on the gun and it now hung loosely by his side, which was slightly more encouraging. "The police are looking for you. I'm sure you're safe here though. It's the ideal hiding place. You could do anything here, couldn't you? Drugs—"

Riley shook his head, amused by the notion. "I have no interest in drugs."

"Ah well, even so, it's a great hiding place."

"If it were, you wouldn't be here. How did you find me?" he asked again.

"I was talking to an old friend of yours," Dylan said. "Remember Raymond Mair? He used to live here too."

"I remember him."

"He thought this place might have been bulldozed. He said that the last he heard, it had been taken over by squatters. I wondered if those squatters knew anything about the one-time residents like Joe."

"Squatters? There are no squatters here. Never have been." He looked up at the ceiling for a too-brief moment.

"Why now? Why, after all these years, did you kill Joe?"

A crazed smile curved Riley's lips. "He'd become too expensive."

"He was blackmailing you?"

"Why else would I give him money? It started when we were children. Something happened, and he used it against me. I was too young to—too young to deal with it then. I paid. All these years, I've paid up."

"For so long? So what's new? Why kill him now?"

"He grew greedy. He learned something new, you see. He thought he'd be set up for life."

"And that something new was?"

Riley laughed that crazy sound again. Dylan had

studied psychology and could offer up a reliable diagnosis. Fucking insane.

"I suspected blackmail," Dylan said. As well as a lot of other things. "I knew something happened when you were kids. This is where it all started, isn't it?"

"Oh, yes." The gun had been pointing at the floor but Riley raised it and aimed it straight at Dylan's chest. "Joe believed it was all my fault. It wasn't, it was hers. There was a girl—a silly young whore who gave me the come-on. A lot of girls did. She said she wanted to be my friend, but even then I knew she just wanted sex. So I gave it to her. Joe said he'd cover for me. Oh, yes, he covered for me all right, and I've been paying for that privilege ever since. What right did he have? What business was it of his what I did?" His voice was rising toward hysteria. "I was sick of him hanging around my neck. I'd had enough of his bullying tactics and I'd had enough of paying him to keep quiet. But then something else happened, something he thought would keep him in luxury until the end of his days. I'm no longer a child. I can fight my own battles now. So I killed him. Just as I'm going to kill you."

"What was the whore's name?" It was the first thing Kennedy had said and it took Dylan completely by surprise. So did Kennedy's voice. The steely anger was as unnerving as Riley's gun.

"Who cares what her name was?" Riley laughed. "She was a whore, a stupid little whore who meant nothing to anyone."

Dylan knew her name. "It was Molly Johnson."

"Something like that, yes." Riley looked surprised. And impressed. "Who cares what her name was?"

The answer to that was deafening. Dylan flinched as he waited to feel the bullet tear through his flesh.

Instead, it was Riley who fell to the floor. His expression was as shocked as Dylan's.

Another shot rang out. And another.

"What the fuck—?" Dylan grabbed Kennedy's arm and wrestled the gun from him. "What the fuck have you done?"

Chapter Forty-Two

LEAH HAD KNOWN it was dark outside because no chink of light was visible under the door. She'd thought she was safe from him until she heard his footsteps. She'd known it was him. She'd recognise those footsteps anywhere. Besides, who else could it be?

She'd hoped and prayed with every fibre of her being that he'd leave her alone. Or kill her. She didn't much care which.

It was a forlorn hope, of course. The key had turned in the lock and the door had swung slowly open. He'd been carrying a huge lantern torch that lit up his face and made his sneer more sinister. He also held a camera attached to a sturdy tripod.

"You stink." His tone was filled with disgust. "What sort of stupid whore can't even keep herself clean? Proud of it, are you? Proud of your own disgusting mess?"

She couldn't have answered him if she tried. Her throat was dry. Her lips were swollen from the last punch he'd delivered. Her flesh was covered in cigarette burns. All she could do was curl into a tiny ball and hug the pain to her.

He set up the camera, all the time muttering about the stench. When he was finally happy that it was set up to his satisfaction, he stood behind it and lit a cigarette. The first drag made him cough—it usually did. Leah wished it would choke him.

"So what have you been doing, Anna? Apart from shitting and pissing yourself?"

She'd started to sob. Despair overwhelmed her. She wished he'd kill her right now. He wouldn't, she knew that. He'd stub his cigarette out on her, cut her and punch her, rape her, light another cigarette—

Please God, let it end.

"Dirty stinking whore!" He walked close to her, the cigarette dangling from his fingers.

He took another long inhalation then brought the cigarette down to her breast. She heard him sigh as he stubbed it out on her poor flesh. She didn't even cry out. She wasn't really there—it was as if she were on the ceiling, looking down at this animal. She was so used to the pain that nothing hurt anymore.

He grabbed her legs and pulled so that she was lying straight on the bed rather than curled up in a ball. Pain from her wrist as the handcuff bit into her flesh had her close to passing out. She closed her eyes tight and prayed she might die. Right now.

"You're a—" He suddenly froze. "What was that?"

He tiptoed to the door and listened for a full minute.

All Leah could hear was the blood pounding in her ears. A silent scream was buried deep inside her.

He walked back to pick up the torch, then quietly opened the door and stepped outside.

She curled up into the foetal position, covered her head with her free arm and closed her eyes tight.

Muffled voices drifted up to her. Surely there weren't more like him?

The loud bang, followed by another and another, had her sitting up straight and clinging to the bed. He'd shot someone. The crazy bastard had shot someone. He would come back to shoot her.

It was then that the last shred of sanity left her. The scream buried so deep inside her had to be let out. She started screaming and she couldn't stop.

He came into the room but she couldn't look at him. Nor could she stop screaming.

He sounded different. "It's me…Davey. You're safe… I won't touch you…you're safe, Anna…ambulance on its way…"

She screamed until the darkness claimed her.

Chapter Forty-Three

THE FLOOR SWAM up to meet Dylan as he walked out of the police station, and he grabbed at the rail by the steps to steady himself. It was tempting to curl up on the steps, as wet as they were, and sleep for a week.

He was free to leave though. He'd soon be able to sink into a hot bath before falling into his own bed.

In the building he'd just left, having been questioned for hours, detectives were scurrying around looking for Gordon Riley's killer. They wouldn't find him because—

They wouldn't find him because he was sitting in a car that was parked a mere ten yards from Dylan.

Dylan wandered over to it and the rear window slid down smoothly.

"I wondered if you'd like a lift," Kennedy said.

Dylan had learned a lot during the past twelve hours. Kennedy was none other than Sir Angus Holmes, recently retired and widely regarded as one of the best judges the U.K. had ever seen.

He could call himself Kennedy or Sir bloody Angus, but Dylan was still pissed off with him. He tried not to be. He tried to remind himself that if he came face-to-face with his daughter's killer, he'd blow his sodding brains out too. It didn't help. With Riley dead, the chances of finding Caroline and Farrah were slim.

"Thanks." Dylan opened the door and climbed inside. There was no point being churlish. Riley was dead and nothing would change that. Besides, it was good to be out of the rain. "You talked your way out of it okay then? I suppose you did. Who would doubt the word of Sir Angus Holmes?"

"The same person who'd doubt the word of ex-Detective Sergeant Dylan Scott perhaps?"

"No one takes the word of a disgraced copper."

"Hmm." Kennedy ran a slender finger along his bottom lip. "I've spent the last hour reading up on your case. Why haven't you appealed?"

The answer to that was easy enough. "I don't have years of my life to waste on something so pointless. It was all politics, designed to make the force look good in the eyes of a public losing faith. Nothing would come of an appeal."

"How cynical. I'm a great believer in this country's justice system."

Dylan raised an eyebrow at that. "You didn't leave Gordon Riley to the country's wonderful justice system."

Their stories had been simple enough. They'd travelled to St. Lawrence's on a hunch, which was true enough, and had heard three shots ring out. They'd found Riley lying next to a gun, had heard someone running away from the scene but hadn't been able to give chase because Anna had started screaming.

Neither had mentioned that Dylan had taken the precaution of wiping that gun clean of any prints or that he'd made sure Kennedy dumped the gloves he'd been wearing.

"I owe you for that," Kennedy said. "Thank you. I was more than prepared to spend the rest of my life behind bars. However, I can't say the idea was particularly appealing."

"Why the interest in St. Lawrence's and Gordon Riley?" Dylan asked.

Kennedy tapped his driver on the shoulder. "Drive around for a while, will you?"

The engine purred into life and pulled into a slow-moving stream of traffic.

"My wife was ill—cancer," Kennedy said, and an icy shudder travelled down Dylan's spine. Cancer. It was all he heard at the moment.

"So I took early retirement," Kennedy said, "and devoted my time to my wife and our garden. My wife died six months ago and—" he paused to choose his words with care, "—I had plenty of time to fill."

"And you decided to fill it at the refuge?"

"I decided to find out all I could about ex-residents of St. Lawrence's," Kennedy corrected him. "I had good sources, as you might guess, but St. Lawrence's children were difficult to find until I came across Joe Child, who in turn led me to Gordon Riley."

"But why?"

Kennedy exhaled a long breath. "Many years ago, I had a brief fling with a young woman. We were little more than children. I was in my first year at university, the first time I'd lived away from home and—well, it was sex, drugs and rock and roll. I soon sobered up when she told me she was pregnant. That was the last thing I needed. I gave her money for an abortion and put it from my mind. You can do that when you're young."

"And?"

"I graduated, began my career, married—" He sighed. "One day, she met me outside court. I didn't recognise her, and for a few moments even her name didn't ring any bells. She handed me an envelope and said she thought I might like to see what my daughter looked like. She said she hadn't been able to go through with the abortion after all." He groaned. "What could I do? I had a good marriage and a very successful career. I gave her more money. A lot of money. Money to take care of the child, money to keep quiet—money to keep her out of my life. She was more than happy to take the money and run. I was glad about that. I couldn't have her in my life. We came from—"

"Different sides of the tracks?" Dylan suggested, and Kennedy nodded.

"She had a drug problem. She worked as a prostitute. What could I do?"

"Perhaps the child wasn't yours."

Kennedy reached into the inside pocket of his coat and took out a leather wallet. He opened that and took out a photo of a ten-year-old smiling shyly into the camera. The photo looked as if it had been taken in a supermarket booth.

There was no doubting the identity of the girl's father. She was Angus Holmes in miniature.

"I tried to forget that somewhere out there was a young girl of my own flesh and blood. I worked hard. I concentrated on my career and happily accepted all the accolades that came my way." He spoke with self-disgust. "Then, when my wife became ill, I retired to spend time with her. I thought we might travel, do all the things we'd never found time for, but sadly she didn't have long. When she died, I floundered a little. I also found it increasingly difficult to ignore the fact that I had a child. So I hired an investigator to find that child. I discovered that her mother died only a few months after she gave me that photo. An overdose—heroin and alcohol. My daughter ended up in St. Lawrence's."

"Oh, God."

"Quite. What happened from then on was more difficult to ascertain."

It would be. Everything that happened at St. Lawrence's was hushed up.

"I recently found out that she was brutally raped while there," he said. "The culprits, or so people believed, were Joseph Child and Gordon Riley. She never recovered. She'd been permanently damaged, thanks to life with a drug addict, being abandoned to St. Lawrence's, enduring a brutal rape—and, of course, never knowing a father."

"Molly Johnson," Dylan said softly.

"Yes. The daughter I never acknowledged. And never will now because she took her own life. In some small way, however, I do feel as if I've brought a little justice to her life. Too little and far too late, of course, but it's all I can do. As for the rest, I have to live with that."

"But didn't she—?" Dylan broke off. Belle had said Molly had a son that she named Zac, but whether that was true or not was difficult to know. Belle often went into a world of her own. There was no point mentioning it to Kennedy. "Any regrets? About Riley?"

"He would have been put away for a few years—although not enough years—at the British taxpayers' expense. I've saved them a great deal of money. On the other hand, there are the missing girls. I expect we can safely assume—"

"That they're dead." Given the state Anna—or Leah, to use her real name—had been in, it seemed likely.

Dylan longed to go home to his wife and kids. He

wanted to hug them to him and breathe in the knowledge that they were safe.

"Who knows you're Molly Johnson's father?" he asked.

There was no hesitation. "You. No one else. No one that I know of anyway. Whether the girl's mother told people, I don't know and I can't ask. It's over now." He rubbed his hands together, whether from cold or embarrassment, it was difficult to say. "We'll drive you home, Dylan."

He wasn't going to argue with that. He was so tired that his brain was mush. A hot bath, a stiff drink and bed. Bliss. "Thanks."

His mind refused to rest though. There were too many loose ends, too many unanswered questions. Nothing felt—finished. He'd failed to find Farrah and Caroline. Kennedy was right. It was unlikely that the girls were alive. But he hadn't found them and that hurt.

The car stopped for a red light and Dylan noticed a girl waiting to cross the road. In one hand she held an umbrella to ward off the rain, and in the other she carried a magazine. She was so engrossed in her magazine that the light changed to green and she missed the chance to cross.

She was seventeen or eighteen years old and blonde. Just like Farrah and Caroline. Thoughts flew into his mind, raced around and settled. The magazine—

Shit.

"Could you do me a favour and drop me off at Euston Station?"

"Of course."

Dylan felt in his pockets. "You don't happen to have

some cash I could borrow, do you? Davey Young was never exactly flush."

Kennedy—Sir Angus—opened a leather wallet, pulled out the paper contents and counted it. "There's a hundred and twenty. Is that enough?"

"Thanks. I appreciate it. I'll return it to you as soon as I can."

"Where are you going?"

"Back to Dawson's Clough."

Chapter Forty-Four

It was almost eight o'clock when Dylan tramped down the lane to Topham's farm. It was a bitterly cold night with a huge moon that provided light but promised more freezing temperatures.

Dylan was cold, exhausted and thoroughly bloody annoyed. He wasn't a man to be messed with right now.

He reached the farm's front door and banged his fist against it.

Lights were on so Topham was at home. He hammered on the door again.

A few seconds later, two bolts slid back and the door opened a fraction. It was enough for Dylan to jam his foot in the gap and barge his way inside.

"Where is she?" He grabbed Topham by his grubby sweater and pushed him back against the wall. "Tell me where she is or I won't be responsible for my actions."

"I—" Topham looked terrified. "I don't know what you're talking about."

A collie stood a yard from Dylan. It emitted a low growl. He tried to ignore it. "Yes, you do. Where is Farrah Brindle?"

"I don't—"

"Seriously, you would not believe the mood I'm in. If you don't tell me where she is, I'll break every bone in your sodding body. Now, where is she?"

The dog growled again. It sounded like a warning.

You break my master's bones and I'll tear the flesh from yours.

"I have no idea where she is. Who are you? What do you want with her?"

"I'm Dylan Scott, a private investigator. And you're lying."

"A private— But you—"

"I don't look like one? So I've been told." Dylan took a breath. On the train from London, he'd managed to convince himself that Farrah was alive. He could afford to take that breath. "I've been working undercover at Moorside Refuge, also known as the sodding funny farm, trying to discover the whereabouts of Caroline Aldridge and Farrah Brindle. Okay? Satisfied?" He gave the farmer a good shake. "I'll ask again. Where is Farrah Brindle?"

"What makes you think—?"

"The first time I called here, you needed a few seconds before you'd allow me through the door," Dylan said. "The second time, you'd been shopping. Remember? Call me a bluff old cynic, but you don't strike me as the sort of bloke to eat yoghurt or read glossy magazines."

Topham flushed with colour but he stood his ground. "I have no idea where she is."

"Anna Woodward went missing from the refuge," Dylan said. "So did Caroline Aldridge. But Farrah didn't, did she? Farrah had been living at home for a month." His voice rose with every syllable. "There was always something different about Farrah's disappearance. Now, tell me where she is or I promise I'll start by breaking your fingers."

He wouldn't. The bloody dog was beginning to unnerve him.

"I had nothing to do with it." Topham sounded indignant.

"In that case, you won't mind me taking a look around, will you?" He pushed Topham back against the wall and strode off to the stairs.

Another collie stood at the top of the stairs. The damn thing growled at Dylan. Dylan growled back. He very much doubted that Topham's dogs had been trained to attack, but right now he was so annoyed that it was a risk he was willing to take.

"It's okay, Penny," a voice said.

A pair of jean-clad legs came into view at the top of the staircase. Dylan looked up to see a blond-haired teenager wearing a thick sweater.

"Farrah," he said, and the shock of seeing her alive and in this place robbed him of further speech.

"Who are you?" She had no need to look so frightened. The dog looked more than happy to protect her.

As he explained who he was, he moved out of the way so that she could walk down the stairs. She did. The dog, with those bright intelligent eyes that didn't leave Dylan, walked in front of her.

She went to Topham and touched his arm. "It's okay, Walt."

Walt?

"How did you know I was here?" She faced Dylan defiantly, her arms folded in front of her.

"I didn't. Three girls vanished, two from the refuge and you. One girl, Anna, we found today—last night. She's in hospital."

"And Caroline?"

"Did you know her?" He was confused.

"No, but I can probably guess what happened to her." She walked into the kitchen—goose-free tonight—and they both followed. She filled an old black kettle and put it on the range to heat. It was as if she needed something to do with her hands. "There's a man, Gordon Riley—"

"You knew Riley?"

"Oh, yes." She sounded bitter. "He kept chatting me up. To tell the truth, I was flattered. He showered me in gifts that I refused to accept. He said he wanted us to go away together—for a night or a weekend. Of course, I couldn't go because of Penny." She fondled the dog's ears. "He said he understood and that we'd go out for a posh meal at some fancy restaurant instead."

The kettle began to hiss and she took three mugs from a cupboard, threw a teabag in each and poured boiling water over them.

"I thought it would be a nice evening," she said. "Except he kept driving. We'd been in the car for hours and the more angry I got with him, the more he yelled at me. I couldn't get out of the car because the doors were locked. He hit me. Anyway, he took me to this awful, awful place and he went—well, I can't describe it. Insane, I suppose. When I asked him what he planned to do with me, he said, 'Eventually, when I've had some fun, I'm going to kill you, you stuck-up little whore. In the end, you'll be begging me to kill you, just like that fucking Aldridge bitch was.'" She began to shiver. "I managed to run and get out of a window. There was a high wall all round this spooky old house, but he'd parked his car inside the grounds. He'd made sure it was hidden from view. I managed to jump onto the roof of his car and onto the wall. I buggered my ankle as I dropped down the other side and he was there. He'd got there fast because he was able to unlock the gate and get out that way. But I could outrun him, even with my dodgy ankle. He chased after me and, God, he was so angry. He was out of his mind. Literally. He was yelling at me as we ran. He said he'd kill me when he caught me. He'd kill me, kill my dog, kill my parents—"

"Bastard," Topham muttered, and Dylan assumed that was because Riley had threatened a dog's life.

"I was too terrified to think straight," Farrah said. "I had no money, nothing. I slept rough for a couple of months. I daren't let anyone know where I was because I knew he'd kill Penny. I just knew it." Again, she stroked the dog's ears. "I was permanently hungry and cold. I met a couple of nice people who stole burgers for me and took me under their wing, but I missed my home and my dog."

"Why didn't you call the police, for God's sake?" Dylan asked.

"Because it would have been his word against mine. When I left the refuge and went home, I didn't expect to see him again and I forgot all about him. But I ran into him at one of these dickie bow-tie functions. Oh, I wasn't there as a guest. I used to earn a few quid washing up, if they had a function on. He was on the top table with the mayor of all people. No one would have believed that the rich, successful businessman, the pal of the mayor, was totally freakin' insane, would they? In any case, he'd threatened to kill Penny. He'd have done it too." She suddenly stopped and looked at Dylan, panic in her eyes. "*You* believe me, don't you?"

"Oh, yes."

"Thank you." She nodded, satisfied. "I had no idea

what he'd do, but I thought my best bet was to stay hidden. No one knew about us so no one was likely to ask him about me. I hoped he'd think I'd been run down by a bus or something and forget about me. So that's what I did, stayed hidden. It was unbearable though. And then I thought about Walt. I hitched lifts back here, knowing Walt would give me a bed and keep me safe. More important, I knew he wouldn't put Penny's life in danger by making me go to the police."

"I did try," Topham said, shrugging his shoulders in a helpless gesture. "I said the police would sort it. She had her doubts though and—well, what do I know? I know about sheep and dogs, and that's all. If she'd gone to the police and anything had happened to the dog—" He left the sentence unfinished, then blurted out, "I said she could call her parents too, just to let them know she was safe, but she wouldn't do that either."

"I couldn't, Walt. You know as well as I do that they would have gone to the police, the news would have been on the TV or radio and he would have come after me."

Dylan had got it all wrong. On seeing that girl waiting to cross the road in London, her head bent over a magazine, looking so much like Farrah, he'd suddenly realised that the items in Topham's carrier bags that day had been for someone else. He'd guessed that someone else was Farrah. He'd thought Topham was holding her prisoner. He'd assumed that Topham, with the police looking for Caroline, had been happy to let them believe that Farrah and Caroline had met the same fate. He'd seen a cantankerous old man, one who kept photos of his dead daughter, one who appeared able to communicate only with dogs, and he'd thought the worst. That

Topham was doing what he thought was the best way to protect Farrah hadn't crossed his mind.

"It's safe enough to talk to the police now," he said, "because Gordon Riley is dead."

"Dead? Are you sure?"

At the light of hope in her eyes, he knew a moment's gratitude for Kennedy's rash action. "Yes. He's currently lying in a morgue in London."

"Oh, my God. He's dead, Walt." Forgetting Dylan, she hugged Topham. "It's over. It's finally over. He's dead." She grabbed the tall, leggy dog and scooped it into her arms. "We can go home, Penny!"

Then the girl who'd kept herself safe from the maniac that was Gordon Riley by sleeping on the dangerous streets of London began to cry like a baby.

Chapter Forty-Five

DR. KINCHIN SWEPT into the room, peering around the biggest bouquet of flowers Leah had ever seen.

"Happy birthday, favourite patient," he said as he handed them over.

She was so touched that she didn't know what to say. "Thank you. How did you know?"

"Easy. We have your date of birth on our records. Oh, and your parents happened to mention it."

"Thank you. They're beautiful."

"Just like you."

"You're a terrible flirt." She laughed and thought again how lucky she was to have such a lovely doctor.

"So how are you feeling this bright morning?"

"Good." She was surprised to realise she meant it. She'd spent the past fifteen days in this hospital bed and had felt fitter, stronger and less bruised—physically and mentally—as every hour passed. "How do you think I'm doing?"

"As much as I hate to say this, I think you'll be ready to go home in a couple of days."

"Really?"

"Yep." He sat on the edge of her bed. "How does that sound? Do you think you'll be ready?"

What he meant was, did she feel able to face the real world. She thought perhaps she did. It was going to be hard to leave this safe, secure room, but it had to be done.

"Julie will want to see you for a while," he said, "but that's okay, isn't it?"

She sagged with relief. Julie, a no-nonsense therapist, Yorkshire born and proud of it, had been her rock. Leah would miss her when the time came to say goodbye.

"It's better than okay," she said. "I like her."

"She likes you too." He held her hand between both of his. He had such strong, capable hands. "I'll be along to see you later and a nurse will bring you a vase for the flowers. Meanwhile, don't do anything I wouldn't. Okay?"

"Okay. And thanks again for the flowers. They're gorgeous."

When he'd gone, she put her flowers on the cabinet and took stock. She decided she was in reasonably good shape. She'd needed stitches to her mouth, so she'd probably always have the scar as a reminder, along with those from the cigarette burns. Dental work to replace her missing teeth was ongoing. One of her cracked ribs had been problematic, as had her broken jaw, but otherwise she was in fairly good shape.

Julie had said the nightmares would leave her. She wasn't to hide from what had happened but she must accept that she'd been the victim of a vicious man who hadn't been responsible for his actions. A man who was dead, she reminded herself. A man who could never touch her again.

The nightmares terrified her. They were so real, so vivid. Even the tablets they gave her to help her sleep didn't keep the dreams at bay.

The door opened and another enormous bouquet of flowers with three balloons leaping from it walked it into the room. Davey Young—she'd forgotten his real name—followed it.

"Happy birthday, you," he said, smiling. "Seventeen today, eh? I still say you look closer to fifteen or sixteen. And before you thump me, there will come a day when you'll take that as a compliment."

"I know. And I'm sorry I lied." She wished she'd listened to him from the start. She hadn't though. She'd thought him a boring nag, like her parents. "Are these for me?"

He looked around the room. "Unless you can see anyone else celebrating a birthday today—"

"No." She inhaled the scent and marvelled at the colours. Julie had told her to dress in bright colours, to go out and take the world by the throat. Maybe—just maybe—she could. "Are you going to eat me out of fruit again?"

"Sorry. You were a bit out of it when I last called so I didn't think you'd notice. Actually, I'm not a great fruit lover but I was starving."

"Between you and me, I'm not a great fruit lover either. Give me chocolate any day."

"Oh, no. Steak and chips beats chocolate every time."

"Rubbish!"

He dragged a chair over to sit beside the bed. "How are you doing, Anna—sorry, Leah?"

"It's funny but I always hated the name Leah. Now, it's like welcoming back an old friend. What's your name again?"

"Dylan. Dylan Scott."

"I'll remember it in future. I still can't get over the way you look. Didn't I tell you that you'd be a half-decent-looking bloke if you shaved off the beard and ditched those awful glasses?"

With the glasses and beard gone, and his hair dark, he looked totally different. Still trustworthy though. She'd thought that when she first met him. He'd fussed a bit, but she'd known deep down she could trust him.

"Yeah, well," he said. "I'm the same person—with or without the glasses. And I don't scratch so much with that beard gone."

She laughed. "I never noticed you scratching."

"I used to sneak off for an hour and have a good scratch in private. So how are you doing?"

"I'm doing good, thanks. I'm leaving here in a couple of days. Going home."

"That's great. I'm thrilled for you, Leah. And this time, stay at home, okay? You're loved, you're safe and you can do so much with your life. You could make your nan proud."

"I will."

She had no problem promising to stay at home, since there was nowhere she felt like going. Julie kept telling her she could make something of her life. She could go back to school, get some qualifications and go to university. She could study, maybe end up like Julie—

"How are *you* doing?" she asked. "You look kind of sad today."

"Do I?" He laughed, but she thought it took effort. "Sorry. It must be the dark, greying hair and the lack of glasses to hide behind. Maybe I'll adopt Davey Young's look after all."

"No, don't do that. Be yourself."

She should take her own advice. Trying to be someone else—the older, sophisticated woman of the world

Anna Woodward—had left her almost dead. She'd never lie about herself again. Some would say that she'd asked for everything she got. She'd flirted with Riley, just for fun, and when he showered her with expensive gifts and offered her a life of luxury, she'd lapped it up. Odd to think how charming he'd been and how, like a switch going on, he'd turned into a vicious maniac.

"Did I thank you for saving my life?" she asked Dylan.

"You did. Several times. No thanks needed. If I hadn't found you, someone else soon would have."

He sounded so sure of that. Leah wasn't. If he hadn't turned up, she would be dead now.

"They haven't found his killer yet, have they?"

"Not yet. Someone's done us a favour so I wouldn't worry too much about that."

Before she could comment on that, the door burst open and the room filled up with people. One of the nurses carried a huge cake but Leah lost sight of her when her mother came to hug the breath from her body.

"Happy birthday, darling."

"Thanks, Mum. Hey, don't start crying again."

Her mum bit her lip, shook her head and nodded at the same time, and Leah laughed.

"Happy birthday, sweetheart." Her dad looked different somehow. Less aloof, less distracted. He also looked a little smug. "We couldn't bring your present inside— against hospital rules. Health and safety and all that. You might be able to see it from the window though."

She didn't care about presents—being safe and surrounded by good people was more than enough—but she knew she must pretend to be excited for her parents' sake. She was helped out of bed, realised she felt much steadier on her feet this morning, and went to the window.

"Oh, my—" Sitting in the car park, with ribbons and birthday balloons tied to it, sat a brand new Mini. "Oh, my—"

People laughed, people hugged her.

"I haven't even had a driving lesson yet," she managed to say.

"They're booked," her father said.

"Thank you. I don't know what to say." That was an understatement.

She kept smiling, but she knew with a sudden clarity that she wasn't ready to face the world. She wasn't sure she ever would be. She'd never trust strangers again. How could she? Where would she want to go in a car? She wouldn't be able to go back to school, or to university—too many strangers. Driving lessons would mean sitting in the enclosed confines of a tiny car with a stranger.

Panic rose and sweat trickled down her spine. Her hands grew clammy. She kept smiling until she thought her face would crack.

"I'd better go, Leah." Dylan's voice seemed to be coming from a long way off. "Give me a call sometime, okay? Don't be a stranger."

"I will. And I won't. Thanks, Dylan." She hugged him tight, too tight, and then had to watch him walk out the room.

Don't be a stranger…

She wanted to scream but all she could do was smile inanely as everyone wished her well and told her what a great life she had ahead of her.

Chapter Forty-Six

DYLAN LAY ON his side, pretending to be asleep. He wanted to check the time on his phone, but he suspected that Bev was only feigning sleep too so he didn't want to move. His arm was numb. He tried to keep his breathing even and he tried to relax in the vain hope that he might drift off to blessed sleep.

"Dylan?" Bev's voice was a frightened whisper. "Are you awake?"

There was no longer any point pretending. Besides, he needed to move his arm.

"Yes." He rolled over and put his arm around her. "Can't you sleep?"

"No."

"Do you want something? A coffee? A glass of wine?"

"No. I just don't want to be on my own."

"You're not." He held her tight for a few minutes. "I'll get us a coffee."

Before she could argue, he was out of bed and padding barefoot down the stairs and to the kitchen.

While he waited for the kettle to boil, he paced the room. How the hell could he tell Bev to remain calm and positive when he was struggling to breathe at times?

If this were happening to anyone else, he'd be able to deal with it. He'd trot out facts and figures to prove that cancer could—and would—be beaten. It wasn't happening to someone else though. This was his wife. His kids. His life.

He made coffee, threw half of his down the sink and topped up the mug with whisky. He'd be an alcoholic before long but he'd worry about that later...

When he carried their drinks back to the bedroom, Bev was sitting up with the duvet pulled tight around her chin.

"Thanks." She smiled at him. "I don't really want a drink, but it'll be nice to chat for a couple of minutes. What time is it?"

"Twenty past three." It was the time of day when everything felt hopeless. Come the dawn, things would seem brighter. Daylight would bring hope.

He wished he could think of something to say, but there was nothing. Bev was about to start a gruelling course of chemotherapy and radiation therapy. There was no point talking about that and nothing else mattered a jot.

Her bedside table was stacked high with books about cancer. Sometimes he thought that reading up on the subject might help and other times he longed to burn the damn things. They had such long titles but the only word that leaped out at him was *cancer*. Everywhere he went, he saw that word.

"I'm hitting the shops with your mum tomorrow," she said, and amazingly she was smiling as she spoke. "I hope she realises that I'll probably need a nap after half an hour. I am so damn tired."

"Rather you than me. I can think of nothing worse."

"We'll have fun. Or we would if I wasn't so tired. What about you?"

"Meeting Frank for lunch and then I thought I'd call at the office and catch up on stuff there."

"Good idea. It'll be good to see Frank. Give him my love, won't you?"

"Of course."

Ex-DCI Frank Willoughby was making a flying visit to London, and they'd arranged to meet in a pub for lunch before Frank's train carried him north to Dawson's Clough. Half of Dylan wished he could get on that train with him.

"We should go out somewhere tomorrow night," he said. "If you feel up to it. Dinner or the cinema or something."

"That would be good," Bev said. "I'll see if your mum's willing to stay the night."

"She's practically moved in anyway."

"I know. And thank God she has. We're going to need her. I don't know how the treatment's going to affect me. Some people are fine and some are at death's door. I'm hoping I fall into the former category, but if not, it'll be good to have your mum around to help out."

He didn't want to talk about the treatment. Couldn't bear to even think about it.

"With me off work, and you needing to be around for the kids, I'm worried about the money, Dylan. What if we can't afford—?"

"We can afford whatever it takes." He was having no arguments on that score. They'd sell the house, sell his mother's place, rob a sodding bank if necessary. They'd do whatever it took. "Money is the very last thing we're going to think about. We'll have to take each day as it comes, Bev."

"I know. By the way, I forgot to tell you. When you

were out this afternoon, I had another of those phone calls.

"What? How many's that now?"

"Three."

"Tell me about them. Everything you can remember."

"That's just it. There's nothing to tell." She sipped her coffee. "When I answer the phone, no one says anything but I get the feeling someone's there, listening."

"How? What gives you that feeling? Can you hear breathing? Can you hear background noise? Think, Bev."

She shrugged a little apologetically. "I haven't heard anything. No breathing. No noise at all. I'm still convinced someone is on the other end though."

"In future, I'll answer it. Okay?"

"What if you're out? What if it's important?"

"People will leave a message and you can call them back."

"Okay," she said, but he guessed she'd answer the damn thing.

Dylan put his empty mug on the table and wished he hadn't ruined a decent whisky by adding coffee. He could quite happily empty the bottle.

Bev sipped at her coffee until it was gone.

"We'd better try to get some sleep, love," he said.

"Yes. Thanks for the coffee. I feel better now."

They lay in the darkness and Bev was soon asleep. Dylan just wished the daylight would hurry up and arrive.

Chapter Forty-Seven

ANGUS WAS CALLING himself all kinds of a fool. The shock of discovering he had a grandson had robbed him of coherent, logical thought. The years had passed, too many of them, because Zac was twenty-four, and not once had it crossed his mind that he might be a grandfather. Yet Zac was real enough. Angus had spoken to him on the phone, albeit very briefly, and foolishly had suggested meeting here at his club. Looking around him, Angus knew he'd made a huge mistake. The place was far too stuffy. Old men in suits sprawled on leather sofas, newspapers in their hands. The dining room was even more old-fashioned.

He didn't know if Zac even owned a suit. He did know that the boy had followed his father's footsteps into the building industry and was a bricklayer. Perhaps he would have preferred to eat at McDonald's. It would have made far more sense to suggest a pub meal. What the hell had he been thinking?

He knew what he'd been thinking. He had a grandson, and every time that thought flew to his mind, he was hit with a mix of excitement, panic and nausea. He couldn't believe the lad existed, he couldn't believe Dylan Scott had found him—

According to Dylan, it had been easy enough to trace Zac.

Angus had learned that Molly had committed suicide.

The investigator he'd hired had told him that much. What the investigator hadn't known was that Molly had married. The marriage ended badly, which, given that Molly was a heroin addict, wasn't surprising, but she'd had a child. Her husband, Tom, was a decent man by all accounts, a working man, but Molly had been beyond help.

On Molly's death, Tom and his parents had taken care of that child. Zac. His grandson.

Angus was no longer sure why he'd even suggested they have lunch. Nerves were performing somersaults in his stomach and he knew he wouldn't be able to eat. A chat in a coffee bar would have been a better idea.

It wasn't only the choice of venue that had him cursing his own stupidity though. It was a knowledge growing more certain by the second that this was a crazy idea. What could he tell Zac? How could he expect the young man to accept that Angus had thrown money at his grandmother for an abortion? Or that, on discovering she'd had a daughter, had thrown more money at her and hoped to God the problem would go away? Worse perhaps—how could he tell Zac that his grandfather had killed a man in cold blood?

Angus had been taught the difference between right and wrong from a very early age. He'd spent his working life wrapped up in the laws of the land. He shouldn't even have had that gun, never mind used it.

He'd known though, as soon as Dylan had suggested paying St. Lawrence's a visit, that they'd discover some kind of evil. He'd known it as sure as he knew that night followed day. He hadn't intended to kill anyone but he had been prepared to defend himself against that evil. Hearing Riley's laughter, hearing Riley talk about his daughter as if she were worthless—

The bile rose in Angus's throat as he acknowledged that he, too, had treated Molly as if she were worthless. He was no better than Riley.

And now, he was planning to meet his grandson in the hope that everything would be all right. Of course it wouldn't. How could it be? What had Zac done to deserve a grandfather who was a—

The door opened and Angus felt the air being sucked from his lungs. He couldn't breathe.

"Your guest, Sir Angus. Can I get you anything?"

Angus was on his feet. He heard the waiter but he couldn't take his eyes off the tall young man who smiled a little self-consciously. He was wearing a dark suit with a blue tie.

"Yes. Another whisky for me, please. What would you like, Zac?"

"Can I get a beer here?"

"Of course."

The waiter went away and Angus, not having a clue what to do, put out his hand, which was duly shaken. "It's good to meet you, Zac." The words sounded ridiculous. "That's an understatement. Sorry. It's amazing—all these years and I had no idea you existed."

"Likewise. It was a real shock when that private investigator phoned and asked if he could pass on my contact details."

According to Dylan, it had been easy enough to trace Tom, Molly's husband, and from there, Zac. He'd said he'd thought it best to speak to Zac before announcing the boy's existence to Angus.

"What do I call you?" Zac asked. "Sir—?"

"How about Angus?"

"Okay." Zac looked around him, and again, Angus knew he'd made a mistake.

"We can eat somewhere else if you like," he said.

"No way. This is great. Real posh. I bet the food's good."

Angus smiled with relief. Perhaps it hadn't been a mistake meeting here after all. "It's very good."

The waiter returned with their drinks and they sat on a long leather sofa, their glasses on the table in front of them.

"Mum said it would be—" Zac broke off, looking embarrassed. "Sorry, that's my mum, Joan. I don't mean your daughter. I'm afraid I don't really remember Molly."

"I don't suppose you do. How old were you when she died? Three?"

"Four. I sometimes think I remember her but then I wonder if all I remember is Dad talking about her."

"So your father married Joan when you were—what?"

"I was eleven. I'd just started secondary school. And Joan's lovely. You'd like her. Everyone likes her. And that reminds me, she's invited you to Sunday lunch."

"Really?" Angus was so touched that a lump of emotion wedged in his throat. He took a quick swig of whisky.

"Yes. Assuming you say yes, and assuming she doesn't have a nervous breakdown at the thought of entertaining a sir beforehand, you'll enjoy it. She's a lot of fun, and she's a good cook. None of your fancy stuff, mind."

"I'd be honoured. Really, I'm touched. Thank her for me and tell her I'd be delighted to accept."

"Yeah? I'll tell her. I expect it'll be roast beef with

all the trimmings followed by a choice of apple pie and custard or trifle."

"Sounds like heaven." After too long living on fish and chips and receiving a dozen eggs and a tenner as payment for his gardening skills, it truly did.

"Dad'll tell you about Molly," Zac said. "You never knew her, did you?"

"No. I never knew her. I—" This was so difficult. "Your grandmother and I—we weren't really a couple. It was just a—" He struggled for words.

"A one-night stand?"

"A little more than that, but not much." Angus sighed. "We both agreed that an abortion would be best all round. I come from a privileged background so money wasn't a problem. We decided she'd go to a top clinic, have an abortion and that, I thought, would be the end of it."

"Women often change their minds at the last minute." Zac spoke with the wisdom of someone twice his age. "These things happen, don't they? Mum says regrets are like umbrellas in the wind. A waste of time."

"She sounds like a sensible woman."

"She is. She also said you'd be a lot more nervous about this meeting than I was."

Angus chuckled. "She was right."

The waiter sidled over and put two menus on the table. Zac grabbed one and quickly ran a finger down the choices. "I'm starving. Are you?"

Nerves had robbed Angus of his appetite so that he'd hardly eaten anything yesterday and couldn't face breakfast this morning. Now, he was surprised to discover that he was hungry. "I am actually."

His appetite had returned and the exhaustion had left

him. Here he was, sitting down to have lunch with his grandson and daring to believe, finally, that the future was bright. Perhaps, after all, everything would be all right.

Ex-Detective Chief Inspector Frank Willoughby looked as smart as ever as he entered the pub. He walked tall, proud and erect. He smiled when he spotted Dylan, then signalled that he'd bring more drinks over.

It was odd to think back to the days when Frank had been his boss and they'd endured a mutual hatred for each other. Now, Dylan could think of no one else with whom he'd rather have lunch.

"Sorry I'm late." Frank put two pints of beer on the table and took off his coat. "Bloody underground system. I got on the wrong train and couldn't get back on track for ages."

"I forget you northerners don't have sophisticated means of travel."

"Ha. You can shove the underground where the sun don't shine." Frank grinned. "That reminds me of the best punch line ever."

"Go on."

"We don't have a back passage, doctor, so I shoved it in the bins instead."

Dylan sniggered. "Probably not the best ever, but not bad."

Frank took an appreciative swallow of his beer. "So how's it going? How's Bev?"

"Oh—'bearing up' is the best phrase, I suppose. There's not a lot else folk can do, is there? You have to get through it."

"It's a bugger. If you haven't got your health, you haven't got anything. Cancer—it's a bugger."

It was. A hateful, hateful disease.

"So what's happening, Frank?" He'd rather talk of easier things—like blackmail and murder. "Has anything else turned up?"

"Dribs and drabs are coming to light on an almost daily basis. Joe Child was one murdering—"

"You're telling me." Dylan was furious with Child. "I still can't believe he gave my name to Ben and Mark Fraser. They demand to know who's sending them death threats, that'll be Child, and who's killed their brother, that'll be Child again, and the bastard tosses *my* name into the bloody air."

Fortunately, Davey Young had been laid to rest before the Fraser boys could find him. Young's cover had finally been blown, thank God, and he'd never see the light of day again.

Frank was smiling at that. "As it is, he's the one pushing up daises. And not before time. He was worth millions, you know. According to Doll, who denies all knowledge of her late husband's wrongdoings, of course, they were planning to sell up and go abroad soon. She was hoping to be living beneath a hot foreign sun by Christmas. Naturally, she claims she had no idea how they were going to afford it. But yeah, he was worth millions. He had a different scam for every day of the week."

"You'd think Gordon Riley would have had more sense than to keep paying him, wouldn't you? Who the hell pays up for something that happened when they were a kid?"

"I suppose he thought he'd better hand over the cash

and keep Child quiet in case people found out that Molly Johnson was the first of many. Child slipped up there. As far as we know, he only put two and two together when Leah went astray. He must have thought he was made for life when he could pin a biggie like that on Riley."

"And instead, Riley walks into his office and puts a bullet through his head. Nice work." Dylan approved wholeheartedly.

"Part of me has to admire Child," Frank said with a grin. "You have to agree that sending death threats and then getting paid protection money is a great little earner. And there's proof he sent those notes to the Fraser boys. He got careless and left a partial print on one."

"What about Christian Fraser's murder?" Dylan asked.

"Child arrived at Tempo at around seven o'clock, as he did every week, and at first everyone thought he'd been there all night. He left around eight-thirty and managed to dodge all CCTV, except for a traffic camera on the Burnley Road. That captured him reasonably well."

"It doesn't prove—"

"It proves nothing," Frank agreed. "But you know and I know that he killed him."

"True."

In a way, Dylan wished it mattered. He'd have given a lot to see Child's face when he realised he was about to spend the rest of his days behind bars. On the other hand, the world was a far better place without him.

"As for being God's right-hand man," Frank said, "he loved it. Wielding such supposed knowledge, power and influence really appealed to him. I think he'd finally found his vocation. Of course, several people left him stacks of cash in their wills so that helped."

Dylan had still expected there to be more to it. "No drugs business? No sex-trade involvement?"

"Nothing that required so much brain power. Child preferred to bully his way through life."

"So what's the state of play at St. Lawrence's?" A month had passed since he found Riley and Leah at St. Lawrence's, and forensics teams had been busy ever since. It was a long, slow process. Every day, the old care home was the lead story on TV news bulletins.

"There's nothing you won't know. Four bodies have been found in the grounds to date. Caroline's been identified and one other girl. The other two, as yet, are unknown." Frank took a large slug of beer. "Leah would have been on the list if you hadn't got there in time."

"I know. Another twenty-four hours and who knows what we would have found?"

"Exactly what did lead you to that place?"

"Sheer bloody luck." An alcohol-fuelled hunch. Nothing more. "And something Bev said. I was convinced Child and Riley were involved in something together. And obviously, I knew they went way back—way back to St. Lawrence's. Bev was talking about how Luke had put a football through someone's window and was heading back there the following morning to apologise and offer to pay. She said he was returning to the scene of the crime." Dylan shrugged. "I knew—or suspected— that Child and Riley had raped young Molly at St. Lawrence's. I thought perhaps I should return to the scene of the crime."

"That's what I used to love best about police work. The way the inconsequential little details make all the difference."

"Lucky for Leah they do. The refuge was a great

hunting ground for Riley, wasn't it? Any young girls who ended up there were going to be troubled and vulnerable before he chose them. They wouldn't have stood a chance."

Dylan thought of his own kids and shivered. He prayed they'd both have more sense than to be taken in by anyone. Damn it, he'd make sure they did.

"Girls seem to go for the older man," Frank said. "Especially the rich older man. I suppose the experience, the sophistication and the charm dazzles them. Also, kids of that age are often getting grief from protective parents. Perhaps they saw Riley as a benevolent father figure."

"Probably. I know Leah said that young men seemed childish and immature once she'd met him. He fed her all the love-at-first-sight bollocks. She was expecting a night at the Savoy with a charming sophisticated man. She ended up being tied to a bed in a rat-infested hovel and used as an ashtray. Sick bastard."

But Riley was dead. No other young girls would have to suffer at his hands, thank God.

"What about Riley's business? Was that all it was cracked up to be?"

"Yes. Apart from the obvious, he was clean," Frank said. "Probably due to bad experiences with his mother as a child, he despised women. He charmed them, promised them the earth, and the fact that they fell for it infuriated him. He had to hurt them. Sexually, he couldn't manage anything unless he could see his victim in pain. The videos the sick bastard made were stored on a computer he used for nothing else."

Dylan shuddered. Riley would have ended up in a mental institution but it was better for all concerned that Kennedy—Sir Angus Holmes—had made that un-necessary.

"It's bloody frightening," Frank said, "how he could charm the girls so easily until they were ready to drop at his feet. One video shows him removing a huge dia-mond ring from Caroline Aldridge's finger."

Caroline would have been easy prey. The poor kid had been born to selfish parents who didn't give a damn about her. Her father had walked out when she was three, and there had been a succession of "uncles" until Tay-lor had married her mother. Riley, with his charm and his money, must have seemed like a fairy-tale hero to her. It was probably the first time she'd felt special and loved. *Bastard.* Caroline's future hadn't looked bright, but at least she'd had a future until Riley stole it from her.

"Years ago," Frank said, "a friend's young lad was asking me about my work as a copper. He'd have been about five or six years old at the time. He wanted to know how I'd fill my time when all the bad people had been caught. Christ, if only it were that simple. You think you've seen it all and then an evil bastard like Riley comes along." He toyed with a cardboard beer mat. "I suppose you have to look on the bright side and know that countless girls have been saved from going through what poor Caroline and others went through."

Frank was right. Nothing could make up for the cruel hand that fate had dealt Caroline, but others had been saved.

"I saw Leah last week," Dylan said. "She seemed to be doing okay, but it was her birthday and her parents had gone overboard. A brand-new Mini, and driving lessons booked. The poor kid looked terrified. She's got some therapist looking after her who, thankfully, suggested that the lessons be booked with a female instructor. Even so, it's going to be a long time before she gets over Riley."

"Bastard."

Total bastard.

"I saw the not-so-lovely Doll too," Dylan said. "I thought at the very least she'd been having an affair with John Taylor. Well, actually I thought she and him were involved in the girls' disappearances. But no. It seems that son Gary had big gambling debts. He lost ten grand to Taylor in a poker game, and knowing he didn't have the cash, and knowing his dad would kill him if he found out, he sent Doll to sort it out. Mind you, Doll probably offered payment in sexual favours."

Frank pulled a face. "What a horrible thought."

Dylan smiled. "Sorry. I'll get us another round of drinks in and then we'll order food, shall we?"

Frank glanced at his watch. "Good idea. I've got a couple of hours yet."

Whoever said men couldn't multitask was wrong. Dylan could order drinks and worry about what Bev had to face at the same time. He could wonder why the barmaid was smiling as if the world was her own personal playground and worry about Bev at the same time. He could carry drinks back to the table, ask Frank about the investigation and worry about Bev at the same time.

"Let's have some lunch, Frank. I'm starving."

AFTER WALKING TO the station with Frank and watching the train set off on its way to Dawson's Clough, Dylan went to his office. He'd spent precious little time in it lately, but he had to. They had no idea how long Bev's treatment would last or how her body would cope with it, and he needed to set aside some cash. He needed a few well-paying jobs.

He'd turned down two jobs in the past week. It had been easy to tell himself he'd been too busy finding Angus's grandson, but the reality was that both jobs had involved spying on suspected errant spouses and he simply hadn't been able to face it. Why couldn't couples talk to each other and, more important, be honest with each other? If they wanted to enjoy affairs, why couldn't they have the guts to admit to them?

He shuffled some papers around. He pinned a few receipts together. Given a little more enthusiasm, he could have put his accounts in some sort of order, but it was a job he hated. There would be plenty of time to panic when his accountant phoned to say it was time to submit a tax return.

He gazed out the window at the café on the opposite side of the road. Trade was brisk. People had little better to do than take a break from shopping to enjoy a coffee and a muffin.

His office phone trilled out and he snatched at it. *Please God let it be a well-paying job. An interesting job. Let it be something to take his mind off Bev and the future they faced.*

"Mr. Scott? Dylan Scott?"

"Yes. How can I help?"

"It's payback time."

He picked up a pen, ready to jot down pertinent details. "Sorry? Who is this?"

"You're going to die, Dylan Scott."

Before Dylan could say they were all going to die, the connection was cut.

There was no clue as to which particular idiot had made the call. The number had been withheld.

Bev had answered three strange phone calls. No one had said anything but she'd been convinced someone was on the other end. Coincidence?

"Sod it." Dylan grabbed his jacket from the back of his chair and shrugged it on.

He didn't have time to worry about crank calls. He was going home. Home to his wife and kids. Home to whatever the future was about to throw at them.

* * * * *